*Also by Rosie Goodwin*

# A Simple Wish

**Rosie Goodwin** is the million-copy bestselling author of more than thirty-five novels. She is the first author in the world to be allowed to follow three of Catherine Cookson's trilogies with her own sequels. Having worked in the social services sector for many years, then fostered a number of children, she is now a full-time novelist. She is one of the top 50 most borrowed authors from UK libraries. Rosie lives in Nuneaton, the setting for many of her books, with her husband and their beloved dogs.

# Rosie GOODWIN
# A Simple Wish

ZAFFRE

First published in the UK in 2021
This paperback edition published In the UK in 2022 by
ZAFFRE
An imprint of Bonnier Books UK
4th Floor, Victoria House, Bloomsbury Square, London, England, WC1B 4DA
Owned by Bonnier Books
Sveavägen 56, Stockholm, Sweden

A CIP catalogue record for this book is
available from the British Library.

ISBN: 978–1–83877–354–0

*Also available as an ebook and an audiobook*

1 3 5 7 9 10 8 6 4 2

Typeset by IDSUK (Data Connection) Ltd
Printed and bound in Great Britain by Clays Ltd, Elcograf S.p.A.

Zaffre is an imprint of Bonnier Books UK
www.bonnierbooks.co.uk

*This book is for the newest member of the family, our beautiful Jaiah-Rose Webb, born 2/2/2021 weighing in at 2lbs 1oz. You are a blessing and my little miracle and I love you to the moon!*
*Mamar xxxxx*

# Prologue

'There we are, luvvie, it's a little girl.' As the old woman straightened up from the bed with a newborn whimpering softly in her hands, the doctor glanced at her and solemnly shook his head. The child was tiny and weak and if he couldn't stop the flow of blood that was coming from the mother soon, it was doubtful either of them would survive.

'You should have sent for me sooner,' he scolded gently. 'Another *niece* of yours, is she?' The doctor was no fool and he had a good idea where the young women came from, but on the odd occasion Mrs Bradley had called him out to them, she always introduced them as her nieces.

She nodded and sniffed, avoiding his eyes. She'd only sent for him when she could see that the young mother was slipping away. Doctors cost money, which bit into her profits from dealing with these girls whose babies she delivered, and the madam at the whorehouse who sent them paid her little enough as it was. Even so, she was saddened to see the state of the young woman on the bed. She shook her head. She'd delivered dozens of babies in her time; how could things have gone so terribly wrong?

Almost four months this girl had been staying with her now and she seemed to be a cut above the girls who

1

had preceded her. They came with frightening regularity despite the birth control methods they practised, and as far as she was concerned most of them deserved no better. They would come to her once they became too big with child to earn their keep, then, once the birth was over, she would find homes for the babies – which meant yet more money for her – and continue to care for the mother until she was fit to return to work. Usually it wouldn't be long before the next one arrived and the cycle would start all over again.

But this girl had not come from the whorehouse and the old woman could only assume that she came from a good family who had turned their backs on her until she had got rid of the baby. Now, as she wrapped the infant in an old towel, she looked at the little face approvingly. She'd have no trouble at all placing this one – if she survived that was.

'I-is the baby all right?' the young mother asked weakly as she sagged limply back against the pillows.

Mrs Bradley smiled, displaying a mouthful of tobacco-stained and rotting teeth. 'She's better than all right; a right bonny little piece. Just look at this shock of red hair, an' she's got the bluest eyes I've ever seen. I reckon she'll grow into a little beauty.' Noting the tears that were slowly trickling down the girl's pale cheeks, she didn't tell her of her concerns about whether the child would survive.

'Can I . . . see her? J-just for a moment . . . *please?*'

Mrs Bradley frowned. She had explained to the girl that the babies were usually taken away as soon as they were born. It was easier that way because if the mothers didn't see them, they couldn't bond with them and it saved a lot of heartache. Yet how could she refuse the request if the girl was about to die?

Tentatively she approached the bed and pulling back the corner of the towel she leant towards the girl who lifted her hand and tenderly stroked the baby's cheek. 'I want her to be called Ruby,' she said softly. She was shocked at the feelings that were coursing through her. For months she had longed to just get the birth over with so she could get on with her life, and yet now she had glimpsed this beautiful little human being, she didn't know how she was going to be able to bear to part with her.

Mrs Bradley sighed. It was usually left to the adoptive parents to name the child but then, what harm could there be in going along with her wishes – for now at least – if it gave her some comfort? She nodded and as she left the room to bathe and feed the newborn, the girl on the bed turned her head to the wall and began to sob quietly, oblivious to the doctor as he battled to save her life.

Some hours later, looking haggard and weary, the doctor went downstairs. 'I've managed to stem the blood flow but there is nothing more I can do for her,' he told Mrs Bradley. 'It's all in God's hands now. I shall call back tomorrow.' He glanced at the baby, who was lying quietly in a drawer lined with a coarse blanket at the side of the fire.

'Is that really necessary?' Mrs Bradley looked disgruntled as she shuffled over to a tin on the mantelpiece to get his fee. Another visit meant yet another payment. 'I'm sure as I can see to 'er now if the bleedin's stopped. She'll just want peace an' quiet an' feedin' up to get 'er strength back. A few bowls o' my chicken broth will 'ave her back on 'er feet in no time.'

The doctor shrugged. Mrs Bradley could be a stubborn old devil when she had a mind to be. 'Very well, but if you have any concerns whatsoever you are to send for me immediately.' His steely blue eyes stared sternly into her faded grey ones and she nodded, setting her double chins wobbling.

'O' course I will, it goes wi'out sayin',' she spouted indignantly and following him to the door she saw him on his way before snuggling into the old wing chair at the side of the fire for a bit of a rest. It had been a long day and an even longer night.

Two days later, Mrs Bradley opened the door to Ruby's prospective parents. Despite her initial concerns, the baby seemed to be thriving, which was more than could be said for her mother, who was still hovering between life and death.

The Carters were a middle-aged couple and compared to most folk in the town were very comfortably off as Mr Carter owned his own thriving bakery in Queens Road in the centre of the bustling little market town of Nuneaton. They had approached Mrs Bradley some time before, expressing an interest in adopting a baby boy, but she had no doubt that Rita Carter would take little persuading to accept a girl, especially one as bonny as little Ruby. It was a well-known fact that Mrs Carter had suffered numerous miscarriages throughout the course of their married life and now she was desperate for a child.

'Come in,' Mrs Bradley encouraged. 'The baby I got word to you about is over there, fast asleep in the drawer.'

Rita Carter was a plump, kind-hearted soul and she hurried across the room to peep at the baby. The instant she saw her, tears sprung to her eyes and her face softened.

'Oh, Stan, come and look at him, he's just beautiful.'

'Ah . . . well, that's the only thing.' Mrs Bradley looked slightly uncomfortable as Bill Carter raised an eyebrow at her. 'It's a little girl. Her name is Ruby, although o' course, should yer decide to take 'er yer could always change it to a name o' yer own choice.'

'But I distinctly told you we wanted a boy to take over the business when I get older.' Stan looked less than pleased but it was already clear that his wife was quite smitten with the child, judging by the way she was looking at her.

'Oh, Stan, *please* just come and look at her!' his wife implored.

Looking less than happy, he crossed the room to do as she asked. 'She's bonny enough, admittedly. But what good will a girl be to us? I thought we'd agreed to wait for a boy who could carry on the family business.'

The old woman held her breath. Unlike his wife, who was a charitable soul, Stanley Carter was known to be a hard man and she suddenly saw the fee for Ruby disappearing out of the window. But she hadn't reckoned on Rita Carter's desperate need for a child.

'I *beg* you to let me take her.' Rita was openly crying. 'Just think of the help she could give in the bakery when she's a little older,' she went on cajolingly. 'We can teach her how to make the bread and see to the ovens and all sorts of things.'

Stan scowled. 'An' how much are yer askin' for her?' he snapped at Mrs Bradley.

She licked her lips, which were suddenly dry. 'I thought two guineas would be a fair price . . . it'd be three if she'd been a lad.'

'*Two guineas!*' He looked shocked, but then seeing the tender look on his wife's face as she gazed down at the infant, he knew he had lost. She would never forgive him if he didn't let her have the child.

'Very well.' Fumbling in his pocket he extracted some coins and flung them begrudgingly onto the old scrubbed table, then looking at his wife he snapped, 'Well, gather the child and her bits together then, woman. I haven't got time to stand about here all day. There's work waiting to be done.'

'Yes, of course, dear.' Rita gently lifted the child from the drawer and after wrapping her tightly in her blanket she scurried towards the door.

Once they had gone, Mrs Bradley snatched up the coins and smiled. But then as she glanced towards the ceiling the smile was replaced with a frown. She was sorry for the baby's mother, but the fact of it was that when the girl died, she would have to spend some of the money she had just made to pay for a funeral – and that consideration far outweighed any pity she felt for the girl who had shared her home for the last few months. Still, she told herself, she already had another girl lined up for a stay so she'd worry about that when she had to.

Humming happily to herself she went to put the kettle on, the coins jingling merrily in her pocket.

# Chapter One

*December 1885*

'Are them bleedin' ovens all lit?' Stan Carter asked shortly as he joined Ruby in the kitchen one cold, grey December morning.

'Yes, Dad. And the kettle's boiled for your tea. How is Mam this morning?'

'About the same,' he said grumpily. He seemed to have forgotten that it was Ruby's fifteenth birthday, and she had no intention of reminding him. She never did or said anything to put him in a bad mood if she could avoid it. She had learnt a long time ago that it didn't pay her to, especially during the last year when her mam had been ill and confined to her bed. She crossed to the enormous soot-blackened kettle and tipped some water onto the tea leaves she had placed ready in the big brown teapot before placing the tea cosy over it and leaving it to mash. Then she rushed over to the stove and flipped the bacon and eggs she had just cooked out onto a plate for him. Thankfully they were cooked just as he liked them. Woe betide her if they hadn't been. Her cheek was still bruised from a few days before when he had stormed that his egg yolks were too hard before slamming them up the wall, plate and all.

'I've made Mam some porridge. She might manage to keep that down,' she told him as she put his meal in front of him, but he merely grunted as he tucked in so she went to ladle some of the porridge into a dish and after sprinkling it generously with sugar she placed it on a tray and left the room. Once upstairs in the bedroom that her parents had shared until recently, she placed the tray down and swished the curtains open before saying cheerfully, 'Morning, Mam. It looks like we're in for some snow.'

The sight of her mother lying there looking so ill made her stomach turn over with fear, but she kept the smile in place as she hoisted her up onto the pillows and placed the tray across her lap. It wasn't hard. Her mother seemed to have shrunk in the last few weeks and she barely weighed more than a feather.

'So, how are you feeling today?' Ruby asked as she straightened the blankets. Her father had moved into the spare room so at least she knew her mother was allowed to get some rest now.

'I-I'm all right, pet.' As a fit of coughing shook Rita's frail frame she quickly covered her mouth with a piece of linen she had to hand. But not before Ruby had seen the scarlet blood on it, although she made no comment. Ruby moved towards the fire to stir it back into life before throwing some lumps of coal onto it and Rita managed a smile as she watched the girl she had always loved as her own. She patted the bed, and when Ruby came to sit beside her, she felt beneath her pillow and extracted a small paper-wrapped package and handed it to her. 'Happy birthday, pet. It's not much but I hope you'll like it.'

Ruby flushed with pleasure as she opened it to reveal a little silver locket suspended on a fine chain.

'Oh, Mammy, it's beautiful. But however did you manage to get this?' It had been months since Rita had been well enough to leave the house.

Rita smiled. 'My mother gave it to me on my twenty-first birthday but seeing as I won't be here when you're twenty-one I'd like you to have it now.'

The smile instantly vanished from Ruby's face and her eyes welled with tears as she flicked her long red plait across her shoulder. 'Don't talk like that, you know it upsets me. O' course, you'll be here!'

Rita shook her head sadly as she took Ruby's small hand in her own. No one would ever have believed she was now fifteen, for she was so small and dainty that she looked no older than ten or eleven at most. 'You know that isn't true,' Rita said softly. 'And when I'm gone, I want you to promise me something. I want you to leave here too. If you don't, him downstairs will work you to death.' *Just as he has me*, she thought, although she didn't say it.

Ruby was openly crying now as she wrapped her arms about the woman who had always shown her nothing but kindness.

'But I couldn't do that,' she answered. 'He's me dad for all his faults and he needs me to help him.'

Rita shook her head. It was time to share the secret she had hoped she would never have to tell. 'But he ain't your dad, sweetheart,' she whispered, her breath growing laboured. 'You see, I was never able to have children of me own so we adopted you when you was but a few days old. I rue the day now, 'cause he's almost worked you into the ground ever since you were knee-high to a grasshopper, and I want you to know I'm sorry.'

Ruby stared at her incredulously. It had never occurred to her that she wasn't their real daughter, although she had often wondered where her red hair, pale skin and freckles had come from. And then Stan's voice bellowed up the stairs and the moment was broken.

'Ruby, get your arse down 'ere right now else you'll feel the length o' me belt, girl!'

'Go,' her mother advised as panic gripped her. 'But promise me you'll do as I ask, and never doubt that I love you.'

With a little nod, Ruby left the room, her mind reeling at her mother's disclosure.

She had never had reason to doubt that the people who had brought her up were anything other than her birth parents but now she wondered where her real mother could be, and whether she would ever know.

Rita died late that night and Ruby felt as if her whole world had fallen apart. She was buried in Chilvers Coton churchyard the week before Christmas when the ground was covered in snow and so hard that it took two men almost a whole day to dig the grave. There was no wake because Stan said that it was a waste of money, and that night Ruby sat wrapped in misery at the side of the fire. Eventually she sank into a light doze only to jump awake as Bill's hand roughly shook her shoulder.

Blinking up at him she was surprised to see in the dim glow from the fire that he was clad in only his nightshirt and she frowned. He had been drinking steadily ever since they'd returned home and now his fetid breath fanned her cheek.

'Wh-what is it? What do yer want?' she muttered as she struggled to sit upright in the chair. Her heart was thudding uncomfortably and she felt uneasy. Why was he looking at her like that?

'Now then, me little beauty,' he slurred. 'Now yer mam 'ash gone I reckon it's time fer you to take her place. Come on up to bed wi' me, there'sh a good girl.'

Ruby shook her head vehemently. 'N-no. I have to be up at four to light the ovens so I'm stayin' in 'ere tonight,' she choked as sweat stood out on her brow.

'Oh no you ain't.' He chuckled. 'Tonight yer goin' to keep yer old dad warm in bed.' As his hand snaked out and roughly tweaked her tiny developing breasts, she shrank away from him. But before she could move, he took her arm in a vice-like grip and he was dragging her behind him up the stairs. Once inside the bedroom her mother had died in only days before, he flung her roughly onto the bed as she sobbed with terror. And then in a single movement he snatched his nightshirt off and stood before her naked, his manhood standing to attention. He was on top of her in seconds and although she fought for all she was worth, he soon prised her thin legs apart and thrust himself into her making her scream with pain.

'Dad . . . Dad, *stop*! Please,' she begged, but he was bucking away now making horrible grunting noises while she lay there feeling as if she was being torn in two. And then just when she was sure that she was going to die he suddenly gave a great shudder and dropped onto her pushing the air from her lungs and making her gasp. She was too terrified to try to move him in case he did it again, but thankfully soon he began to snore and she managed to roll from beneath him. Her most private parts felt as if they were on fire and she was sticky, but even so she crept from the room as quiet as a mouse and tiptoed back down to the kitchen where she sat and sobbed broken-heartedly. It was then that her mother's words came back to her, *I want you to leave here too.*

*Could it be*, she wondered, *that this was what her mother had feared would happen?*

After a time, she pulled herself together enough to pour some water into a bowl and scrub herself thoroughly from head to foot, but even though she scrubbed until she was sore, she still felt dirty. It was then that she knew what she had to do: somewhere out in the big wide world was her real mother and from this moment on she would not rest until she had found her.

Giving herself no time to change her mind she dressed quickly, then quietly crept back up the stairs to collect her few clothes and the locket her mother had given her for her birthday. Tying them into a bundle, she went back down to the kitchen and wrapped her shawl about her shoulders. From the hiding place behind a brick in the fireplace she collected the small amount of money her mother had slipped her over the years. Ruby had never questioned it before, but now it occurred to her that perhaps her mother had been trying to make sure she had something put by should she need to leave suddenly, and once again she wondered whether her mother had guessed this might happen one day. She would never know now, she reflected as she stared about the room for the last time. Then she turned decisively and hurried through the shop, where she snatched a loaf from the counter and thrust it into her bundle. Who knew when she might be able to eat again? Opening the door, she slipped through it and closed it quietly behind her and taking a deep breath she set off into the snowy night.

She had gone no further than Stratford Street when the full impact of what her father had done to her hit her like a blow, and sneaking into a shop doorway out of the snow she began to sob. She had led such a sheltered life – her dad had seen to that. He'd never let her out apart from to go to school, and even that had been restricted to two days a week for as long as she could remember. She didn't even have any friends to turn to because her father had always kept her too busy to make any. She had often wondered, as she lay in the bedroom that adjoined her parents', what the guttural noises coming from their room were. And now, after what he had done to her, she knew. The tears fell faster as she thought of what her mother must have suffered all these years. The noises had often been followed by the sound of her mother sobbing while her father snored.

'Oh, Mammy,' she whimpered to the dark night. 'I miss you so much!' At that moment a stray dog poked his nose into the doorway and she started. It was hard to see what colour he was in the darkness but as she tentatively put out a hand to stroke him, she could feel his ribs. 'You poor thing,' she whispered. 'Are you hungry?' The dog wagged his tail as if he understood what she was saying and sniffing back her tears she rummaged in her bundle and brought out the loaf. 'Here, boy, have some o' this.' She broke a chunk off and held it out to him and he gobbled it down so fast that he almost choked. In no time at all she had fed him the whole loaf and he licked her hand as she pulled herself to her feet. 'I can't stay any longer,' she told him. 'But you stay in 'ere, eh? At least you'll be out of the snow.'

The dog stood in the shop doorway as she set off into the night and she paused just once to look back at him before going on, with no idea whatsoever where she might be going. She only knew she needed to put some distance between herself and the man she had always believed to be her father.

A short time later she found herself outside the railway station and an idea occurred to her. There was a waiting room on the platform and there was usually a fire lit in there, and at least it would be some shelter from the cold. But first she would somehow have to sneak past the ticket office, if it was still open.

Cautiously she entered the building and there behind the counter was the booking clerk, snoring softly with his peaked cap pulled low on his forehead. With her heart in her mouth she crouched down and crept past him and soon she was on the freezing platform and on her way to the waiting room, praying that it hadn't been locked up for the night. She was in luck, the handle on the door turned easily and she hurried into the room.

The warmth wrapped itself around her like a blanket and after a few minutes her teeth stopped chattering as she held her hands out to the dying flames of the fire. She doubted there would be many more trains running that evening and hoped that if she was quiet enough she could stay there undetected until morning. Anywhere was better than being back at home or out in the cold. Crossing to the bench she lay down on it using her bundle as a pillow. But although she was worn out, sleep eluded her as she thought over the happenings of that night. She was still reeling with shock that her father could have done such a thing to her and she knew that she would never get over the shame of it.

She was sobbing softly when the door suddenly opened, letting in a blast of freezing-cold air, and a beautiful lady stepped into the room. She was expensively dressed with a thick fur stole over her dark-green costume, a matching feathered hat on her head and her hands hidden in a fur muff. Ruby could only assume the entire outfit must have cost a fortune.

The woman stopped abruptly as she caught sight of Ruby and for a moment she looked shocked before saying, 'My dear child! Are you all right? Whatever is a little one like you doing out all alone at this time of night?'

The woman's gentle voice was Ruby's undoing and the tears came again so fast now, that she feared they would choke her.

'Please, missus . . . I-I've run away from 'ome!' she sobbed. 'Yer won't tell the ticket man, will yer? Else he'll chuck me out an' I'll have nowhere to go.'

The woman looked perplexed. 'But won't your parents be worried about you?' she asked kindly.

Ruby shook her head. 'Me mam died some days ago.' She didn't bother to mention her father, she never wanted to think of him again after what he had done to her, and she could never tell anyone. She was too ashamed.

'I see. So are you saying that you have no one?'

Ruby nodded. It was only a white lie after all.

'Hm.' The woman stared at her thoughtfully for some minutes until they both heard the sound of the last train that night approaching. She seemed to make a decision and holding her hand out to Ruby she told her gently, 'Then you must come along with me, my dear. I shall look after you and you will be quite safe, I assure you.'

Ruby hesitated as the train roared into the station belching smoke and steam that rose into the air and floated around the rafters of the station. But then she looked into the woman's kindly eyes again and after wiping the tears from her cheeks she took her hand and allowed her to lead her to the train. After all, what could the woman possibly do to her that was worse than what her father had already done? she reasoned.

Minutes later, for the first time in her life, she found herself seated beside the fine lady in a railway carriage and as the train pulled away from Nuneaton, the place she had always known as home, she didn't look back, not once. For better or for worse this would be the start of a new life for her. But one day, she promised herself, she would come back and try to find her real mother.

# Chapter Two

'So where are we goin', missus?' Ruby asked tentatively as the train rocked along the tracks. For the first time she was wondering if she had done the right thing in coming with this stranger. Was her real mother somewhere back in Nuneaton? It seemed likely, but then for now she was just grateful not to be facing any more nights with nowhere to go. They were the only people in the carriage and beyond the window it was pitch black.

'We are going to my home in Birmingham,' the lady told her as she sat with her hands folded neatly in her lap. 'Once we are there my housekeeper, Mrs Petty, will look after you.'

'You 'ave a housekeeper?' Ruby's brilliant blue eyes stretched wide. 'Yer must be very rich then.'

The woman laughed, a soft tinkling laugh that was almost musical. Ruby was totally under her spell now and couldn't stop staring at her.

'I wouldn't say I was rich exactly, but I am very comfortable.'

'But why are yer helpin' me?'

Just for a second, she saw a look of sadness flit across the woman's face before she said, 'Let's just say that I can't bear to see anyone out in the cold. Now tell me, child, what is your name? And how old are you?'

17

'Me name is Ruby an' I'm just fifteen,' Ruby informed her solemnly.

'You're very small for your age,' the woman remarked. 'In fact you're so slight, you could be taken for nine or ten at the most.'

Ruby shrugged. 'I've always been small. Me mam says . . . or said, that I shouldn't be 'cause I eat like a horse.'

The woman smiled and Ruby asked, 'But what am I to call you?'

'My name is Mrs Bamber.'

'So you 'ave a husband then? Won't he mind yer bringin' me home?'

'No, I don't have a husband anymore,' the woman informed her, although Ruby didn't think she sounded very sad about the fact.

'Well, I could do some cleanin' for you,' Ruby offered quickly. 'An' I'm a very good cook.'

'Hm, we'll see. There are other things you can do to help me but we won't talk about that just now.' Mrs Bamber fell silent then so Ruby wisely settled back in the seat clutching her bundle as the train rattled on its way.

Eventually they drew into the station and Ruby hurriedly followed her saviour onto the platform. Once again there were very few people about but it was very late at night by then so Ruby supposed it was hardly surprising.

She followed Mrs Bamber out into the street where a hackney cab stood, the horse munching steadily on a nosebag and a thick blanket thrown across his back. It had started to snow again and Ruby felt sorry for the poor creature.

'Vittoria Street, if you please,' Mrs Bamber told the driver as she clambered up the steps into the carriage and he nodded before going to remove the horse's supper. The gas lamps cast pools of eerie yellow light onto the snow as the horse clip-clopped over the cobbles and Ruby stared from the window with interest. She had never been to Birmingham before and was surprised to see how big it was. There were rows and rows of houses with shops dotted in amongst them everywhere she looked but the harrowing experience she'd had with her father and the long day spent on her feet was catching up with her now and as she leant back against the grimy leather squabs she stifled a yawn.

'Don't worry. We haven't far to go now,' Mrs Bamber told her and Ruby managed a weak smile.

Eventually the horse drew to halt in front of a row of houses that seemed to stretch into the sky and as Mrs Bamber got out of the carriage and paid the driver, Ruby hastily followed her and glanced up and down the street. Further along she could see more rows of shops but it was so dark that she couldn't see what they sold.

'Here we are then, home sweet home,' the woman said as the carriage pulled away. Ruby eyed the frontage and wasn't overly impressed with what she saw. Mrs Bamber seemed so grand that Ruby had expected her to live in a mansion at least but this house was in a terrace of houses with little to distinguish one from another. The woman approached the door and taking a key from her bag she quickly unlocked it and ushered Ruby ahead of her. Ruby had taken no more than a few steps into the place when she stopped dead in her tracks and stared about her in amazement. If she had been somewhat disappointed with the outside of the house, the inside certainly made up for it. She found herself in a spacious hallway with highly polished black and white tiles on the floor and flocked velvet wallpaper in a rich crimson colour on the walls. There were heavy gilt-framed mirrors and beautiful paintings spaced along the walls and doors leading off either side of it. But she didn't have long to admire it for suddenly a door at the far end opened and a portly little woman with silver-grey hair bustled towards them.

'Eeh, me wench, I've been that worried about you, so I have. What took the ti—' Her voice trailed away as she caught sight of Ruby and for a moment she looked stunned but then, after looking her up and down, she stared at Mrs Bamber. 'An' who is this then?'

'This is Ruby, Petty dear, and she's going to be staying with us for a while. That's all right, isn't it?'

Ruby saw the older woman frown but she turned to her and said, 'Go an' wait in the kitchen for me, bab. I'll not be a minute. You can get warm by the fire.'

Ruby had never heard an accent like Mrs Petty's before and yet she had the strangest feeling that she had seen her before, but she nodded and went to do as she was told.

'Are you yampy or what bringing her 'ere?' she heard the woman ask as the kitchen door closed behind her, but then she forgot everything again as she stared around her. The kitchen was huge and so clean that Ruby was sure she could have eaten off the floor. There was a large inglenook fireplace with copper pans suspended the length of it that gleamed in the light from the fire, and to either side of it

20

were two leather wing chairs with pretty flowered cushions on them. A huge dresser stood against one wall on which was placed a large amount of fine china, and a big pine table surrounded by chairs stood in the centre of the room. A lump formed in Ruby's throat as she thought of how much her mother, as she still thought of her, would have loved this room. Their own kitchen back at home had been very austere – her father hadn't believed in knick-knacks or anything that wasn't completely essential.

She stood uncertainly feeling exhausted and upset and wondering if she had done the right thing in coming there with a complete stranger, but the door opened then and Mrs Petty appeared. 'Take yer coat off, bab. We don't stand on ceremony 'ere. I bet you're hungry, ain't yer? I'll get you some soup to keep you goin' till morning an' warm you up.'

Ruby quietly removed her coat and hung it across the back of a chair as Mrs Petty went to the range where a pot of soup was simmering, and started to spoon some into a dish, which she carried to the table for her. 'There, get that down you. You look like one good puff o' wind could blow you away. You need a bit o' fattenin' up.'

'Th-thank you.' Ruby sat down and had just lifted her spoon when the back door suddenly opened and a young woman walked in bringing with her a blast of icy air.

'Lord love us, whatever's happened to you?' Mrs Petty cried as she saw the state of her. The girl's lip was bleeding and the buttons on her coat were missing, leaving it to flap open. The woman nodded towards Ruby and gave the girl a warning glance as she said quickly, 'Fall over, did you?'

'Oh, er . . .' The girl frowned before answering, 'Oh, yes, yes, I did. I slipped in the snow and cracked my face on the floor.'

'We'd best get you cleaned up then. This here is Ruby. She's come to stay for a while. And, Ruby, this is Nell.'

The girl looked towards Ruby. 'How do.'

Ruby gave her a faltering smile. 'Hello.' The girl was quite plain and looked to be in her mid-teens with mousy-coloured hair that hung straight to her shoulders. She was stick thin and tall but her eyes were her saving grace; they were a deep-grey colour that reminded Ruby of stormy skies.

Ruby began to eat her food keeping one eye on Mrs Petty as she fetched a bowl of warm water and began to bathe the girl's face.

The girl winced once or twice and the older woman shook her head when she was done as she carried the bowl back to the sink. 'You'll have a right shiner on you tomorrer,' she warned. 'But you'd best get in to the missus now. She'll be waitin' for you.'

Without a word the girl rose and left the room as Ruby carried her empty bowl to the sink.

'All right for you was it, bab?'

Once again Ruby had the feeling that they had met before. 'Yes, thank you, it was lovely.' Suddenly she raised her hand to stifle a yawn and the woman gave her a sympathetic smile.

'You must be tired. Come along of me. I'll show you where you'll be sleeping. You can go in the room next to Nell.'

Ruby hurried across the room to collect her bundle before following Mrs Petty back out into the opulent hallway. As

22

they passed what she supposed was the sitting room she heard the murmur of voices before following Mrs Petty up the stairs and on to a long landing.

'That's where the missus sleeps up that end.' Mrs Petty gestured to the left. 'This side o' the landing is where we sleep.' She moved on and stopped at the last doorway. 'You'll be in 'ere, an' that door opposite is the bathroom.'

Ruby was impressed. An indoor bathroom, what luxury. Back at home she had bathed in front of the fire once a week in a tin bath that was kept on a nail in the wall in the yard.

When Mrs Petty threw the door open and ushered her inside, Ruby's eyes grew round. The room was quite small but very pretty. There was a single brass bed with a thick patchwork counterpane thrown across it and pretty flowered curtains framed the windows. There was also a wardrobe in a lovely rosewood with a matching chest of drawers, and a gilt-legged chair stood in front of the window where she could sit and watch the world go by.

'I'm sorry it's a bit cold in 'ere but I didn't know you were coming else I'd have lit the fire.' Mrs Petty nodded towards a small, tiled grate. 'But never mind, there's plenty o' blankets under the quilt an' you'll soon get warm once you cuddle down. I could bring a nice stone hot-water bottle up for you, if you like?'

'Oh no, really, this is lovely,' Ruby assured her quickly, not wanting to put her to any trouble. It was by far the prettiest room she had ever seen.

'In that case I'll leave you to it an' let you get some shut-eye.' The woman moved to the door where she suddenly paused and, turning, she asked, 'When is your birthday, bab?'

23

Ruby thought it was quite a strange question to ask but answered, 'I've just had it, I was fifteen on the fifteenth of December.'

The woman nodded and left without another word, and once she was alone Ruby sorted through her meagre bundle for her nightgown. She'd had it so long that it barely fitted her anymore. Her mother had made it for her some two years before and as Ruby thought back to her mother lovingly stitching it by the light of the oil lamp, a lump came to her throat again, but she pushed the thoughts away and hurriedly changed and clambered in between the cold linen sheets. Only then did she allow herself to recall the terrible thing her father had done to her and when she finally fell into a fitful sleep her cheeks were wet with tears. She had no idea what was going to happen to her now, but she knew that after what had happened that night she could never go back home again.

# Chapter Three

A tap at the door startled Ruby awake the next morning and for a moment she lay disorientated as she found herself in strange surroundings. But then the events of the previous night flooded back and she sat up just as Nell poked her head round the door.

'Mornin'.' She gave her a friendly smile. 'I didn't wake yer, did I? I've brought you a cup o' tea, look.' Crossing to the small table at the side of the bed she placed the cup and saucer down before going to the window and throwing the curtains back, allowing the cold grey light to creep into the room. 'Bloody snow's still comin' down thick an' fast,' she grumbled as Ruby watched her cautiously.

Just as Mrs Petty had forecast the poor girl had a black eye this morning and her lip was even more swollen now than it had been the night before.

'So, how did yer sleep then?'

Ruby gave her a weak smile. 'Very well, thank you, but I'm sorry if I've put yer to any trouble. Have I overlaid?'

Ruby grinned as she perched her backside on the edge of the bed. 'Not really. It's only just gone nine o'clock.'

'*Nine!*' Ruby was horrified. She was usually up at four lighting the ovens ready for her father to come down. 'I-I'm so sorry. I don't usually lie in this late.'

'Will you stop sayin' sorry! You ain't on the clock 'ere. Sometimes the missus don't get her arse out o' bed before dinner time.'

Nell glanced at Ruby's pathetic little bundle curiously before asking, 'So, got kicked out of 'ome, did yer?'

'N-not exactly.' Ruby felt her cheeks flame. How could she ever tell anyone why she had run away?

As if Nell could sense her unease, she shrugged. 'Ah well, wharrever yer 'ere for it's nice to 'ave someone closer to me own age to natter to. But I'll leave yer to drink yer tea in peace now, an' when yer ready come down to the kitchen. Mrs Petty's got some breakfast ready for yer. Make sure as yer try some of her porridge.' She grinned as she licked her swollen lip and rubbed her stomach. 'Ain't nobody makes porridge like Mrs Petty – she sprinkles sugar on it an' drips honey all over it, mm!'

She left then, and once Ruby had drunk her tea she quickly got dressed and tugged her hairbrush through her unruly red curls before making a visit to the bathroom, which was just as luxurious as she had expected. Once she had finished, and eager to get downstairs, she hurried back into her room and made the bed, intent on leaving everything just as she had found it. She took one last regretful glance about and sighed. It had been kind of Mrs Bamber to offer her shelter for the night but already she was wondering where she would be sleeping tonight. She had no idea how much a room somewhere would cost but she doubted the small amount of money she had would cover it. As she pictured herself shivering in some draughty shop doorway, she straightened her back and took a deep breath. She might not have much money but she did have pride aplenty so she would face whatever lay before her with as much courage as she could muster.

There was no sign of Nell when she entered the kitchen but Mrs Petty gave her a welcoming smile. 'So what can I tempt you with this morning, bab?' She pointed to a steaming saucepan on the range. 'There's some porridge or I could do you a nice rasher or two o' bacon an' an egg? An' how did you sleep? Yer certainly look a bit better this mornin' than yer did last night. Why yer looked like death warmed up, yer poor thing.'

'I slept very well, thank you.' Ruby gave her a grateful smile. 'And I'll just have some porridge, please. Nell told me that it's delicious.'

The woman's cheeks glowed at the compliment as she ladled a generous portion into a bowl and carried it over to her. 'There we are then; I've added some honey an' when you've done yer can go an' wait in the drawin' room till the missus decides to put in an appearance. I've lit the fire an' it's nice an' warm in there. Nell's already gone back to bed, bless 'er little cotton socks. That fall she 'ad last night has made her feel right dicky.'

Ruby looked confused. 'But why does Mrs Bamber want to see me? I was goin' to be on me way after thankin' you for your kindness an' havin' me breakfast.'

'You'll do no such thing!' She looked horrified. 'Why Maddie, that's Mrs Bamber, would 'ave me guts fer garters if you left now. So just get that down yer an' let's have no more talk of yer leavin', if yer please.'

Ruby obediently ate the porridge and just as Nell had told her it was delicious. She told Mrs Petty so when she carried her bowl to the sink and the woman smiled. 'Glad you liked it, bab. Now go an' wait for Maddie like I told yer. It's the second door along in the hall an' you'll find some magazines to read on the table . . . that's if yer can read?'

'Of course I can read.' Ruby was indignant. 'Me mam taught me an' I can do me numbers.'

'Good, then go an' relax a while an' think yerself lucky; I wish I had the time to lounge about. Ta-ra fer a bit, I'll see yer later.'

Ruby did as she was told and once inside what Mrs Petty had termed the drawing room, she wandered about admiring the fine paintings on the walls and delicate china in the fancy inlaid cabinets. Then she settled down to glance through the magazines Mrs Petty had told her about and before she knew it she found herself in another world as she examined the pictures of women in the latest fashions and others of rooms in houses that took her breath away.

'They're very entertaining, aren't they?'

The sound of Mrs Bamber's voice made Ruby start guiltily, but as she made to rise from the chair the woman gently placed her hand on her shoulder and pressed her back down. Today she smelled of lavender, which matched the shade of the beautiful day dress she was wearing. Her thick, dark, chestnut hair was piled into loose curls on top of her head and Ruby thought again how pretty she was, although she was quite old – thirty at least, Ruby reckoned.

Mrs Bamber took a seat close to Ruby and smiled. 'So how are you feeling today, my dear?'

Ruby almost felt as if she was in the presence of royalty. 'Better thanks, missus. And thank you for lettin' me stay last night an' all. I was goin' to be on me way earlier on but Mrs Petty said you wanted to see me afore I went.'

'On your way?' Mrs Bamber looked horrified. 'And on your way where, may I ask?'

Ruby opened her mouth to answer but then clamped it shut again. What answer could she give? She had no idea where she might be going.

'Hm, I thought as much.' Mrs Bamber smoothed the skirts of her gown. 'I think the best thing you could do is stay here for a while. At least until you decide what you want to do.'

'But I couldn't do that without earning me keep,' Ruby objected in a wobbly voice.

'But you would be earning your keep if you kept me company,' Mrs Bamber informed her. 'I can get quite lonely on my own. Petty is always so busy and Nell sleeps for most of the day because she works in the evenings so it would be nice to have someone to go out with.'

'Out where?' Ruby frowned.

Mrs Bamber shrugged her slim shoulders as she glanced towards the window through which she could see the snow still steadily falling. 'Well, there's shopping we could do together for a start. And in the spring, we could go for carriage rides and walks in the park. And of course, Christmas is only around the corner, so I shall need someone to help me carry all the bags when I do my Christmas shopping.

There's lots of things we could do together. But first, I think we'd need to get you some new clothes. I couldn't help but notice that those you are wearing only fit where they touch.'

Ruby's cheeks flamed as her hand dropped to her faded, patched skirt. For as long as she could remember her mother had had to buy all their clothes from the rag stall in the market because her father had always insisted that new clothes were a waste of money. It had never bothered her before. It was a case of what she had never had she never missed, but now in this beautiful house she suddenly felt very poor and very shabby indeed.

'We could go shopping today,' Mrs Bamber suggested with a radiant smile. 'We can get you a nice warm coat and some boots more suitable for the weather for a start off.'

'I . . . er, I ain't got no money fer new clothes,' Ruby mumbled, deeply embarrassed.

'You don't need money, I shall be paying,' Mrs Bamber told her with a smile.

Feeling vaguely uncomfortable, Ruby nodded, although it didn't feel right that this stranger should be showing her so much concern. But then she could hardly argue. What alternative did she have but to accept the kindness?

'Th-thanks, missus,' Ruby mumbled and Mrs Bamber laughed as she clapped her hands together.

'Excellent! There's nothing like a good shopping trip to get you in the mood for Christmas. And please call me Maddie. Missus sounds so formal. Now, run along and get ready and we'll set off in half an hour.'

Ruby quietly left the room, but as she approached the kitchen door, she heard raised voices and paused.

'So why ain't she goin' to do the same job as me?' she heard Nell ask heatedly.

'That's for Maddie to know, it's nowt to do with us,' Mrs Petty responded and taking a deep breath Ruby opened the door and entered the room. The talking stopped abruptly and she knew that they had been talking about her.

Nell was sitting at the table drinking a steaming cup of tea and she had the grace to blush as Ruby smiled at her tentatively.

'All right, nipper?'

Ruby nodded. 'Yes, thank you. Mrs Bam— Maddie is takin' me shoppin'.'

'That'll be nice.' Mrs Petty was just about to place a large leg of lamb in the oven. 'An' will yer both be back in time fer dinner, do yer know?'

Ruby shook her head as she fetched her down-at-heel shoes from the hearth where they had been left to dry. 'She didn't say.'

'Well, it's no matter. I can always keep it warm for you both.'

Ruby shrugged her arms into her old coat, painfully aware how small it was on her, then she sat down in the chair by the fire and waited silently for her new friend to fetch her.

It had been very dark when they had arrived the night before so when they set off down the street Ruby was surprised to see how many jewellers' shops there were dotted amongst the houses.

'Ah, that's because this is the Birmingham Jewellery Quarter,' Maddie explained when Ruby commented on it. 'There are some of the finest jewellers and silversmiths in the world working here and the pieces they make are sent all over the globe.'

She paused as Ruby stared into one of the shop windows, blinking with wonder at the sight. There were necklaces and rings set with sparkling stones all the colours of the rainbow, but one in particular caught her eye and she pointed to it.

'Look at that red one there,' she breathed. 'It's almost the same colour as my hair!'

'That's a ruby, one of the most precious stones in the world,' Maddie told her. 'And that's probably why your mother named you, because of your hair.'

'I-I never knew me real mother,' Ruby said suddenly as a lump formed in her throat. 'The person who I thought was me mam told me when she was dyin' that she an' me dad had adopted me when I was just a few days old. Me real mam must not have wanted me.'

'Oh, sweetheart, I'm sure that's not true,' Maddie said kindly as she placed an arm about her shoulders. 'There was probably a very good reason why your real mother couldn't keep you. But the one who brought you up was good to you, wasn't she?'

'Oh yes, she were the best.' Ruby's head bobbed. 'She were kind an' good but me dad . . .' When her voice trailed away, Maddie gave her a little hug.

'Let's not talk about that for now,' she urged. 'Today is going to be a good day, let's not spoil it.' She turned her attention back to the shop window, hoping to break Ruby's melancholy mood. 'That blue stone there is a sapphire and the green one is an emerald. But the clear white stones are the most expensive of all – they are diamonds and people will pay thousands of pounds for them.'

'Really?' Ruby was intrigued.

'Yes, but come along, we're getting covered in snow standing here.'

Ruby looked one last time at the sparkling display of jewels in the shop window then reluctantly followed Maddie. She could quite happily have stayed and looked at them for hours but Maddie was clearly keen to get to the clothes shops, wherever they might be.

# Chapter Four

'Good grief! Is there owt left in the shops?' Mrs Petty asked when Ruby and Maddie stepped into the kitchen loaded down with bags and boxes some hours later.

Maddie laughed as she dropped the ones she was carrying onto the floor and headed towards the warmth of the fire. 'I think we've got her everything she needs, for now at least,' she answered as she held her hands out to the welcoming glow. 'And we've had such a lovely time, haven't we, Ruby?'

'Oh yes.' Even Ruby seemed in a happier mood now, but then how could she not be after being so spoilt? She had never owned so many clothes in her whole life, let alone brand-new ones, although she had been a little disappointed with some of Maddie's choices. Being a teenager, she did find some of them a little young in style for her but she was hardly in a position to mention it and she could hardly wait to wear them.

'Take her up the Bull Ring, bab, did you?' Mrs Petty asked as she bustled about preparing a cup of tea for them.

It was Ruby who answered. 'We went to this huge market.' Her face was animated at all the things she had seen. 'And we looked in lots of jewellery shops and Maddie told

34

me the names of all the different stones.' She stared at Maddie with a look bordering on adoration. She had no idea why Maddie was being so kind; no one apart from her mother had ever been this nice to her. She began to open some of the parcels to show off her new clothes to Mrs Petty. There was everything she could have wished for. A beautiful navy-blue coat with a matching bonnet and little leather button-up boots, the sort she had only ever seen the nobs wear. Petticoats, underwear, nightclothes and two new dresses, one in a fine wool and the other in velvet that Maddie had said would be perfect for wearing at Christmas. Maddie had even bought her matching ribbons to wear with them, which Ruby secretly thought were rather childish, but all in all it had been a wonderful day. 'An' we went in a coffee house an' had tea an' fancy cakes,' Ruby rushed on. She had never been in such a place in her life before and had loved every minute of being waited on.

'I just hope you left room fer your dinner?' Mrs Petty grinned as the girl's head nodded vigorously.

At that moment Nell entered the room and stared at the numerous boxes, bags and clothes that were strewn about the place.

'Crikey, someone's been busy,' she remarked.

She herself was dressed now and seeing this, Maddie asked with concern, 'Are you quite sure you're up to working tonight, Nell? That lip and your eye are still very swollen. Perhaps you should stay in this evening?'

'I shall be fine.' Nell gave a nonchalant shrug. Crossing the room, she lifted Ruby's new velvet dress and stroked the fabric reverently. 'Looks like someone's been spoilt.'

Ruby nodded; like Nell she too wondered why Maddie was being so good to her, not that she was complaining.

'So, will you be entertainin' tonight?' Mrs Petty asked Maddie.

'Yes, yes I will, so I was hoping perhaps you could help to keep Ruby entertained?' Maddie suggested and Mrs Petty nodded. After glancing at the clock, Maddie took a gulp of her tea almost scalding her mouth before rising hastily. 'In that case I'm going to go up and have a bath before getting ready.' And with that she tripped away as Mrs Petty carried Ruby's dinner to the table.

'It might be a bit dried up 'cause I've been keepin' it warm in the oven,' she warned.

Nell had already had hers and she shook her head at Ruby. 'Don't take no notice o' that, Petty's dinners are always bostin'.'

'Bostin'?' Ruby really had no idea what some of the words that Nell, and Mrs Petty for that matter, used meant. It was like listening to a foreign language.

'Bostin' means good, excellent,' Nell explained.

Ruby shook her head. 'And why do you keep calling me bab?'

'It's a term of endearment used by us Brummies. Much as you'd say, love or dear, we say bab.'

Ruby was finding it all very confusing but no doubt she would get used to it in time. Meanwhile, the meal looked delicious and despite all the fancy cakes and pastries she'd eaten, she cleared her plate in minutes as Mrs Petty went about the room with a long spill lighting all the oil lamps.

'Right, now you'd best get all this new clobber up to your room and get it put away,' Mrs Petty advised, and Ruby was only too happy to oblige.

She was tempted to put one of her new dresses on but decided she would wait till morning when Maddie had told her they would be off on another shopping expedition. Mrs Petty had lit the fire in her room for her and crossing to the window, she watched the lighter in the street lighting the gas lamps. She stifled a yawn. It had been a busy old day one way or another so she decided she would just have a lie on the bed for a few moments. It looked so tempting and the room was so cosy that she was loathe to leave it just yet. She hopped beneath the pretty patchwork quilt and before she knew it, she was snoring softly.

The fire had burnt low when she awoke sometime later and she hurriedly tossed a few more nuggets of coal onto it before rushing downstairs. Whatever would Mrs Petty think of her doing a disappearing act like that?

She found the woman sitting at the side of the fire in the kitchen contentedly knitting and she smiled at Ruby as she entered. 'Had a little nap, did yer, bab?'

Ruby nodded as she looked around but there was no sign of Nell or Maddie.

'Maddie's entertainin' a friend in the drawin' room an' Nell's at work,' Mrs Petty informed her, almost as if she had been able to read her thoughts. 'An' if you look under that covered plate on the table, you'll find I've left you a bite o' supper to tide you over till mornin'.'

Earlier on, following the excellent dinner Mrs Petty had cooked for her, Ruby had been convinced that she wouldn't be able to eat another thing until morning, but as she saw the freshly baked bread and the slices of thick cheese Mrs Petty had left for her she suddenly realised she was hungry again and tucked in.

'So, does Nell work very far away?' she asked when she had eaten her fill and was washing the plate at the sink.

'Not too far,' Mrs Petty answered. 'But come an' sit down an' tell me all about where yer used to live.'

Ruby got the distinct impression that the old woman was keen to change the subject but she went to join her anyway.

'So why don't you tell me a bit about yourself now? Why you ran away from home, I mean.'

Ruby instantly closed up like a clam. What her father had done to her was still far too fresh in her mind and just remembering made her feel sick.

'I, er . . . never really got on with me dad,' she said in a small voice. 'So after me mam died I thought it was time to get out of there. Now, shall I make a cup of tea and take some into Maddie and her visitor?'

'Oh dear me, no!' Mrs Petty looked horrified at the suggestion. 'You must never *ever* disturb her when she's entertainin', do you understand?'

Ruby's eyes stretched wide and she felt confused. Surely it was good manners to offer visitors a cup of tea? Not according to Mrs Petty, though, and suddenly she was curious. 'So is the visitor a good friend of hers then?'

'Ask no questions an' I'll tell you no lies,' the woman responded shortly. 'And now ain't it time a young 'un like you were gettin' ready for bed?'

Somewhat subdued, Ruby nodded and after saying good-night she made her way up to her room. Already she was beginning to wonder at what a curious household she had moved into. There was Nell who was very evasive when Ruby asked about her work and her personal life, and then there was Maddie and Mrs Petty who had been arguing about her when they thought she was out of earshot, although she had no idea why. And how did Maddie manage to live in such an opulent house? She had no job from what Ruby could make of it, so perhaps she had rich parents who indulged her? She was certainly generous, going by what she had spent on her that day, and yet still something didn't quite feel right. Mrs Petty had almost jumped down her throat when she had suggested that she take tea into Maddie's visitor, but why?

With a shrug she slid out of her clothes and hopped into bed. The flickering flames in the fireplace cast dancing shadows on the walls and the ceiling and despite the questions about her new friends running through her mind, Ruby couldn't help but sigh with contentment. This was a far cry from the life she had led with her parents back in the bakery and she supposed she should just enjoy it while it lasted. In no time at all she was fast asleep.

The following morning a large Christmas tree was delivered and placed in a bucket of earth in the drawing room.

Maddie went away and returned moments later with a box full of the most beautiful glass baubles Ruby had ever seen, along with some tiny candles and holders.

Nell was still in bed following yet another late night and Mrs Petty was busy preparing the dinner in the kitchen so Maddie told Ruby, 'You may decorate it, if you like. I have to go out for a few hours and it will give you something to do.'

'Are you sure?' Ruby gazed dubiously at the pretty baubles. They looked so delicate that she was afraid she might break them. They had never had a Christmas tree back at home, her father had insisted they were a complete waste of money so she couldn't help but feel a little excited. 'I'm just a little afraid I might break 'em. They're so fragile.'

'I'm sure you won't and if you do we'll go out and buy some more.' Maddie gave her a kindly smile as she headed for the door. 'Have fun and I'll see you later.'

Ruby bit her lip as she began to lift the little ornaments from the box. Each had a tiny ribbon attached so that it could be hung on the tree and they were all the colours of the rainbow. Tongue in cheek she concentrated as she spread them across the tree and when she got to the top branches, she fetched a chair to stand on so she could reach them. Sometime later, she stood back to inspect it with satisfaction. The light from the fire was making the jewel-like colours of the baubles flash across the room and Ruby was sure she had never seen anything quite so beautiful in her life.

Next came the holders and the candles, which proved to be slightly more difficult to attach, but Ruby persevered and was so engrossed in what she was doing that she almost jumped out of her skin when Mrs Petty said, 'Your lunch is nearly ready, bab . . . Ooh! Now don't that look pretty, eh?'

Ruby giggled as she stepped away to look at the almost finished results. Thankfully nothing had been broken, and Mrs Petty was right. It did look very pretty indeed and she hoped that Maddie would approve of her efforts when she returned. Nell entered the room at that moment, knuckling the sleep from her eyes and yawning, and she too smiled when she saw the tree.

'That looks absolutely bostin'!' she said and Ruby couldn't have agreed more and felt quite proud.

'Maddie out, is she?' Nell asked.

Mrs Petty nodded. 'Yes, she is. She's gone to visit Serena. Now come along the pair o' yous! I've got a nice pan o' stew simmering on the range an' I don't want it burnt.'

As the two girls obediently followed her along the hallway, Nell glanced at the new wool dress that Ruby was wearing and Ruby felt herself blushing. The dress was calf length with a number of frilled petticoats and she was wearing thick woollen tights beneath it. To her mind the style was more suited to an eight- to ten-year-old, but even so it was the finest she had ever owned and she didn't wish to appear ungrateful. It was in a soft blue colour that matched her eyes and she had tied her riot of red hair back with a matching ribbon.

'Looks like Maddie's been treating you.' Ruby detected a note of jealousy in Nell's voice and flushed. Thankfully they entered the kitchen then and Mrs Petty ushered them both to the table so she was saved from having to respond.

'So how long will you be staying?' They had almost finished their meal before Nell spoke again and Ruby was unsure what to answer.

'I, er. . . ain't sure, to be honest.'

'That's none o' your business,' Mrs Petty scolded as she carried dishes of jam roly-poly covered in thick creamy custard to the table. Nell frowned as she lifted her spoon but didn't say any more.

Immediately after she had finished, Nell left the table and Mrs Petty told Ruby, 'Don't get takin' no notice o' Nell. She's harmless but I reckon she's feelin' a bit put out 'cause she ain't got Maddie all to herself now. But don't worry, she'll come round.'

'She did have a point, though. How long will I be stayin'? I can't expect Maddie to spend money on me an' rig me up for nothing. I should be earnin' me keep.'

'No doubt she'll have somethin' in mind for you.' Mrs Petty smiled as she carried the dirty dishes to the sink and plunged them into a bowl of hot water to let them soak. 'An' if yer so keen on helpin', yer can start by washin' these pots up while I put me feet up wi' a nice cup o' tea for half an hour.'

Ruby was only too willing to oblige but as she scoured the pots she frowned. Nell had made her think. How long *did* Maddie intend to keep her there and where was she to go when she was no longer welcome? It was a frightening thought.

# Chapter Five

'Merry Christmas, everyone!' Maddie said as they all sat down to their Christmas dinner. It was like nothing Ruby had ever seen before and she didn't quite know what to eat first. Her father had never believed in Christmas, saying that it was just an excuse for people to have time off work, so the ones she had known had been frugal. Now she looked in awe at the most enormous goose she had ever seen that took pride of place in the middle of the table, surrounded by all manner of treats. There was a steaming tray of Mrs Petty's home-made sage and onion stuffing, roast potatoes, mashed potatoes and a large selection of vegetables, as well as a jug of thick gravy.

'I'll carve, shall I?' Mrs Petty, who was looking very nice in her Sunday best dress, began to carve thick slices of goose onto their plates as they all helped themselves to everything else. The sight and the smell of such a feast made Ruby's stomach rumble in anticipation and yet when she lifted her knife and fork, she found that she could hardly eat anything, for a large lump had formed in her throat as she thought of her mother. It was her first Christmas without her and as wonderful as all this was, in that moment Ruby would have done anything to spend just one more Christmas with the woman who had never shown her anything but love.

As if Mrs Petty had guessed how she was feeling she smiled at her. 'Come on, bab, there's trifle or Christmas puddin' to follow an' we don't want it all goin' to waste now, do we?'

Ruby managed a weak smile and tucked in, and soon she was enjoying it. It would have been very hard for anyone not to as Mrs Petty really was a wonderful cook.

'I can't decide whether to 'ave the trifle or the Christmas puddin',' Nell mused when they'd finished their dinners.

Mrs Petty chuckled. 'So 'ave a bit o' both! It is Christmas after all.' And with that she began to load Nell's dish.

'Phew! I don't think I shall eat another thing fer at least a month,' Nell told them when she was done as she rubbed her full stomach.

'Hm, I've heard that before. What yer mean is yer won't eat another thing till teatime. I sometimes think you must have hollow legs.' Mrs Petty grinned. 'An' yet yer still as thin as a whistle, whereas I only have to look at food to put a pound on. But anyway, if everyone is finished, I reckon it's time to open us presents. I've been waitin' all mornin' fer this.'

Hurrying across to the Christmas tree she collected an armful of gaily wrapped presents that had been placed beneath it and started to hand them round. For Nell there was a pretty scarf and mittens that Mrs Petty had knitted herself, and for Ruby she had bought a selection of gaily coloured ribbons for her hair, which made Ruby blush uncomfortably.

'I'm afraid I didn't manage to get any presents for anyone.'

Mrs Petty waved her hand airily as Maddie opened her gift. 'Think nothin' of it, me little wench. We didn't expect you to.'

'Oh, Petty, this is beautiful,' Maddie exclaimed as she opened a fringed silk shawl in a beautiful shade of blue. 'You really shouldn't have. This must have been so expensive.'

'Well, it ain't as if I've got anyone else to spend me money on, is it?' Mrs Petty beamed as she watched Maddie wrap the shawl about her shoulders and stroke the fine fabric. It was Maddie's turn then and she too had bought each of them a gift, as had Nell, which made Ruby feel even worse.

'I shall buy you all something when I get a job,' she promised.

'We'll have no more talk of working today,' Maddie scolded gently. 'And, Petty, leave the pots, they can wait till later. I think we should all sit by the fire and put our feet up for an hour now while that delicious dinner goes down.'

Only too happy to oblige, Mrs Petty went and sat down in the fireside chair and in no time at all her gentle snores made them all smile.

'I'm going to clear the table and do the washing-up,' Ruby declared softly. 'I've got to do something to earn my keep.'

'Will you stop talking about work! As it happens, I do have a job in mind for you but we'll talk about it after the holidays,' Maddie said, exchanging a conspiratorial glance with Nell.

Ruby was intrigued as she wondered what Maddie was planning for her but she suppressed her curiosity and began to carry the dirty pots to the kitchen.

At teatime they dined on cold meat, cheeses and pickles, mince pies and Christmas cake and afterwards, Maddie and Mrs Petty settled down to a game of chess while Nell went to her room and Ruby started the new book that Maddie had bought for her. It was *Black Beauty* and within minutes she was lost in the story; so much so that she was shocked when Maddie said, 'I think it's time you were tucked up in bed, Ruby.'

Ruby scowled. 'Actually, I'm not a little girl. I'm fifteen.'

'Oh yes, of course you are.' Maddie smiled at her. 'Do forgive me, it's just that you're so small I forget your age.'

Ruby forgave her instantly. Maddie had been so kind to her that it would have been hard not to. Later, as she climbed the stairs, she wondered what job Maddie had in mind for her and she could hardly wait to find out.

The day after Boxing Day, Nell began to get ready to go out as darkness fell and feeling a little confined, Ruby suggested, 'I could walk with you, if you like, to keep you company. To work I mean.'

'Oh no . . . there's no need for that.' Nell looked horrified and Ruby wondered what she had said wrong. 'Look at the weather out there. It's fit for neither man nor beast. No, you stay 'ere in the warm.' And with that she lifted her hat and coat from the coat rack in the hallway and left without another word, just as Maddie appeared in the doorway of the drawing room.

'Ah, Ruby, there you are.'

Ruby noticed that she had on one of her best gowns, and was that rouge she was wearing on her cheeks?

'I'm entertaining this evening so would you mind staying in your room or in the kitchen with Petty?'

Ruby nodded and set off up the stairs to make herself scarce, wondering who the visitor could be. But then once in her cosy room she again lost herself in the pages of her book and didn't give the mysterious visitor another thought.

The following morning, Maddie joined Ruby in the drawing room and after sitting down on the elegant sofa she patted the seat at the side of her. 'Come and sit with me,' she invited. 'I have something I wish to talk to you about.'

Ruby did as she was asked without hesitation and gave Maddie a smile.

'The thing is . . .' Maddie paused as she chose her words carefully. 'As you can imagine a house like this takes a lot of money to run. I earn the money any way I can and I think you may be able to help me.'

Ruby nodded eagerly. Her father had worked her relentlessly for as long as she could remember and she was getting a little bored of having nothing to do.

Maddie looked relieved. 'Good, then we shall start this very day after lunch. We'll take a tram to the place I have in mind and then all you have to do is follow my instructions.'

A little worm of unease wriggled in Ruby's stomach. Whatever Maddie had in mind for her she was being very secretive about it but at least, she consoled herself, she wouldn't have too long to wait to find out what it was.

After lunch they wrapped up warmly and although Ruby felt a little ridiculous in the coat and hat that Maddie had bought for her, she was warm at least. They boarded a tram that took them right into Birmingham city centre and once they alighted Maddie walked briskly until they came to a jeweller's shop displaying very expensive items of jewellery in the window.

'Now, this is what I want you to do: I shall be looking at some rings but when I look at you and nod, I want you to pretend to feel faint and fall down. Distract the jeweller, in other words. Do you think you could do that?'

Totally confused, Ruby frowned. 'But why would you want me to do that?'

'Just do it.' There was a hard note that she had never heard in Maddie's voice before and Ruby chewed on her lip. Even so she followed her into the shop and stood silently as the jeweller fetched a selection of very expensive rings from the window for Maddie to look at.

'Hm, this sapphire is very pretty, but could I look at some emerald ones and perhaps a few diamond ones as well?'

The jeweller almost tripped up in his haste to please her as he smiled at Ruby. 'Of course, madam, and may I say what an enchanting little girl you have.'

'Thank you.' Maddie inclined her head setting the feathers on her very expensive bonnet bobbing as Ruby blushed. Little girl, indeed! She was fifteen years old, but then she supposed he could be forgiven for thinking she was younger in the clothes she was dressed in.

The man was back in seconds with yet more rings for Maddie to look at and as Ruby stared at them all sparkling in the light, she grew quite hot with nerves. What game was Maddie playing? she wondered, and why on earth would she want her to pretend to be ill? Eventually the counter was strewn with gems and still Maddie sighed uncertainly.

'Oh dear, it's so hard to make a choice,' she said and looking towards Ruby she gave a small nod.

Ruby knew this was her cue and said, 'I don't feel very well.' She began to sway before dropping to the floor.

'Oh, the poor child.' The jeweller was round the counter in a moment as he and Maddie bent over her. 'Perhaps a glass of water would help?'

'Oh yes, yes please,' Maddie answered, looking distressed, and he rushed away to get it. He was soon back and as Maddie held the glass to Ruby's lips, she blinked her eyes open.

'Oh, thank goodness, she's coming round.' Maddie made a great play of helping Ruby to her feet. 'I think I should get her home immediately. I'm so sorry for any inconvenience we've caused.'

The man almost ran to open the door for her. 'Don't worry about it, madam. Perhaps you can come back another day when the child is better?'

'Yes, of course. Goodbye for now.' Once out in the icy air Maddie kept her arm about Ruby's shoulders until she heard the door of the shop close behind the jeweller, then lifting her skirts, she told Ruby, 'Run!'

It was all Ruby could do to keep up with her and they didn't stop until the shop was far behind them. Maddie hailed a passing cab then and once they were inside and it was rattling on its way she waited until she had got her breath back and grinned. 'Well done. You were very convincing.'

Ruby looked at her dubiously. 'But why did you ask me to do that? I've never fainted in my life.'

Maddie stared at her for a moment before fumbling in her fur muff and pulling something out of it. 'This is why.' She held up a sparkling ring that glinted in the light coming in from the grimy windows and Ruby gasped. It had a large green, square-cut central stone surrounded by a halo of diamonds.

'B-but isn't that one of the rings the jeweller took from the window for you to look at?' she asked in a voice that came out as little more than a squeak.

Maddie grinned. 'It is indeed, and if I'm not very much mistaken it will fetch a pretty penny when I sell it on. The central emerald is quite magnificent.'

'But isn't that stealing?'

'I suppose it is, but that jeweller could easily afford to lose it.' Maddie tossed her head. 'Do you have any idea what the markup is on jewellery they sell to the public? The jewellers make at least three-quarters more than they are worth, so what does it matter to them if the odd item goes astray?'

She showed no remorse whatsoever for what she had done and Ruby realised in that instant that this was probably not the first time she had done it. 'But surely there was no need for us to come all this way when where you live is surrounded by jewellery shops?'

'My dear naive girl.' Maddie laughed. A harsh laugh that didn't reach her eyes as she studied the ring more closely. 'The first thing you have to learn in this trade is that you never work too close to home, I could be recognised. The second thing is that we all have to live, be it by fair means or foul. The food you eat, the coal that warms the house, *everything* has a price, and so I do whatever I have to to ensure that we all live well. Is that so very wrong?'

Maddie blinked as she chewed on her lip. Her parents, or at least the people she had believed were her parents, had brought her up to be honest, and this was taking some swallowing.

'Don't go getting all holier than thou on me,' Maddie warned as she watched Ruby's reaction. 'And just remember that in the eyes of the law you would be considered to be just as guilty as me if we were to get caught. All I asked you to do was swoon. It isn't as if I'm sending you out begging on the streets, is it? And surely that's nothing in return for a warm home to live in and plenty to eat.'

Until that moment Ruby had placed Maddie on a pedestal but now all her ideals crumbled and she had to blink back tears. Suddenly she understood why Maddie had bought her clothes that made her look much younger than she was. It was so people would look on her as a child when they were out together, and who would ever believe that such a well-dressed woman and child could be capable of such dishonesty? She bowed her head as she wondered what her mum would have thought of her stealing. They had never been rich but her mother had always been as honest as the day was long and she would have been so ashamed of her now.

'Do Nell and Mrs Petty know about this?' she asked in a strangled voice and Maddie laughed again as she tucked the precious jewel safely away.

'Why, of course they do. Nell was my accomplice till a short while ago but she got too big and while Petty doesn't approve of what I do she knows which side her bread is buttered so she chooses to turn a blind eye. But now I must ask you, are you prepared to help me when necessary in return for being well looked after?'

Ruby hesitated, knowing that if she didn't agree she would find herself back out on the streets. The thought of being homeless was terrifying, especially in such inclement weather, and returning to her father was completely out of the question. She would die rather than risk letting him touch her again, so what choice did she have? And yet what Maddie was asking was going against everything she had ever been taught. She stared down at her little black boots and the folds of her soft velvet dress peeping from the opening of her coat, and slowly she nodded. There was really no alternative.

# Chapter Six

Later that evening, after Ruby had retired to the drawing room to read her book, she heard raised voices coming from the kitchen, so creeping to the door she cautiously opened it a crack to listen. She knew that eavesdropping was wrong but after what had happened that day, she was beyond caring.

'I'm tellin' you sure as eggs is eggs this'll all end in tears, my girl!' This was Mrs Petty. 'That girl is little more than a babby an' she might not have been lucky enough to end up wi' the best parents in the world but I'd stake my life she's honest if nothin' else!'

Ruby realised that Mrs Petty must be speaking about her and her ears pricked up.

'So what do you expect me to do? Keep her in luxury from here on in?' Maddie sounded angry.

'Huh! An' here I was thinkin' you'd fetched her 'ere out o' the goodness of yer heart!' Mrs Petty sounded incensed. 'Have yer completely forgotten all the promises you made?'

'Of course I haven't but we have to live, don't we?' Maddie sounded as if she was crying now and Ruby was more confused than ever. What promises was Mrs Petty on about?

She heard the kitchen door bang open and someone stamp along the hallway so she hastily closed the door, hurried back to her seat and picked up her book. But she needn't have worried. Whoever had left the kitchen went straight upstairs, leaving Ruby to try and process her thoughts. She had thought herself to be very fortunate indeed the night Maddie had found her after she had run away, but now she was beginning to wonder. More than once she had thought there was something vaguely familiar about Mrs Petty's face and as she sat there it came to her. She had come into her father's shop on a few occasions – *that's* where she had seen her before. But why hadn't Mrs Petty told her that, and why would she have been shopping for bread in Nuneaton? Suddenly something else occurred to her and Ruby felt as if all the air had been sucked out of her lungs. Because she had only discovered that she had been adopted shortly before her mother's death she was still struggling to come to terms with it but could it be that Mrs Petty was keeping an eye on her for her *real* mother, the one who had given her up at birth? And if that was the case, who could it be? Her mind was racing now as the pieces of the jigsaw came together. *Maddie!* Could she be her real mother? The idea was preposterous and yet the more Ruby thought of it, the more it made sense. Admittedly their hair colour was completely different, but now that she came to think of it there were similarities between them – the pale skin and the sprinkling of freckles across their noses.

Quickly laying her book aside she pottered along the hallway to the kitchen to find Mrs Petty scrubbing away at the pots in the sink with a grim expression on her face. However, when she spotted Maddie her face softened and wiping her hands on her apron she asked, 'Want a nice mug o' cocoa before you go to bed, do you, bab?'

'Er . . . yes, please. That would be lovely.' Ruby sat down at the kitchen table watching as the woman fetched a jug of milk from the pantry and poured some into a saucepan. 'I've been racking my brains ever since I first met you,' she said innocently.

Mrs Petty scowled. 'Oh ar, an' why's that then?'

'Well, I just had the feeling I'd seen you before somewhere and this evening I realised where it was. Didn't you used to come into my dad's bread shop in Nuneaton sometimes?'

Mrs Petty's colour rose and she looked flustered, but after a moment she answered calmly, 'I have visited a bakery there from time to time. I had a friend who lived in Nuneaton, see, so I might well have popped in when I visited her.'

As she laid the mugs on the table Ruby noticed that her hands were shaking and she got the distinct impression that Mrs Petty was lying, although she didn't comment on it.

They were both seated at the table with steaming mugs in front of them before Mrs Petty spoke again. 'About what Maddie got you to do today . . . I just want yer to know that I don't approve of it.'

Now it was Ruby's turn to blush as shame washed over her. 'I-I've never stolen anything before,' she admitted in a shaky voice.

'Hm, well the way Maddie sees it, it ain't wrong if she only steals from them as can well afford it,' she said. 'But I want you to know she ain't all bad. She's had a hard life so now she just gets by any way she can.'

'Oh, what happened to her?' Ruby was intrigued to find out.

Mrs Petty glanced nervously towards the door to make sure they were alone before saying quietly, 'She came from a very well-to-do family who live not a million miles away from where we're sittin' right now – not that they ever acknowledge her. An' then somethin' happened an' they disowned her. She could have died for all they cared, poor ducks. So from then on, she had to make her way as best she could. Trouble was she'd been brought up as a lady an' her family expected her to make a good marriage so she wasn't trained to do anything. Luckily, she had a small inheritance that her grandmother left her and she moved in here. I've lived here with her ever since.' Mrs Petty suddenly sat up straighter and her expression hardened as if she regretted what she had just said, but Ruby was more curious than ever now.

'So what exactly *did* happen to her?' Ruby persisted.

'Nothin' that you need to know about.' Mrs Petty stood up and lifting the cups she carried them to the sink and began to wash them.

'So have you been with her for a long time?'

Mrs Petty shrugged. 'Oh, it must be for about fifteen or sixteen years or so now.'

Ruby bit her lip as her mind whirled. That would tie in with the time she had been born so could she have been right? Could it be possible that Maddie *was* her true mother? But somehow, she sensed that Mrs Petty was not going to tell her a lot more about Maddie this evening. It was obvious that she regretted telling her what she had.

'And what about Nell?' She carefully changed the subject. 'Has she lived here for long?'

Mrs Petty scowled at her. 'What's all these questions, eh? You're a right little nosy parker, but if you must know, Nell has been here for about five years or so now. Trouble is she'd got too big for . . .' She clamped her lips shut again as she realised that she had been about to confide yet more information. Ruby would find out what was expected of her when Maddie was good and ready to tell her herself, it wasn't her place to do so. 'Look, it's gettin' late. Why don't you get yerself off to bed?' she suggested and sensing that the conversation was now well and truly at an end Ruby did as she was told.

Maddie went out the next morning and when she came home, she found Nell waiting for her and they both disappeared into the drawing room, closing the door firmly behind them.

It was after lunch when Maddie told Ruby, 'I need to speak to you, dear. I have another little job I want you to do for me.'

Ruby panicked. Was Maddie going to take her to yet another jewellery shop and make her swoon again? There was only one way to find out, so she folded her hands primly in her lap and waited for Maddie to speak.

'The thing is . . .' Maddie had the grace to look slightly uncomfortable. 'Nell has had a very good tip-off.'

'A tip-off?'

'Yes.' Maddie nodded as she paced up and down. 'Nell has made friends with a great many of the young maids that live in Birmingham and one of them has told her of a golden opportunity that will happen this evening. But before I tell you what it is, I have to ask you . . . can I trust you, Ruby? And do you intend to stay here?'

Ruby nodded miserably. She had tossed and turned all night as she wrestled with her conscience but she could see no alternative. Had she been a little older she could possibly have found a position as a maid in one of the big houses but she was so small and young-looking that it was unlikely anyone would take her on at present.

'Good! Then tonight I want you to go out with Nell. There are some very big houses next to the Warstone Lane cemetery and some very wealthy people live there. I happen to know that the owners of one such house are going to the theatre this evening and as they have given their maid the night off the house will be empty for some hours.'

Ruby didn't like the way this conversation was going at all and she squirmed in her seat as her heart began to race.

Maddie went on, 'The lady of the house is known to have a substantial amount of very valuable jewellery and the young maid knows where she keeps it. They do have a safe, but the maid has told Nell that the woman rarely uses it and tends to tuck her jewels in the corner of her drawer in her bedroom. This evening you will go with Nell and climb through a back window that the maid will leave on the latch. You will then go upstairs and grab as much jewellery as you can find and bring it back to me.'

'But why would the maid tell Nell about it?' Ruby was horrified.

Maddie grinned. 'For money, my dear. It's what makes the world go round. I shall make the information very worth her while, never you fear.'

'B-but what if I get caught?' Ruby asked, her voice trembling with fear.

'There's very little chance of that happening,' Maddie assured her. 'And if the maid has given us the right information you can be in and out in no time. This could bring in ten to a dozen times what the ring I stole yesterday is worth when I pass it on to the fence I work with.'

'The fence?' Ruby had no idea what a fence was and wasn't sure that she wanted to know.

'A fence is someone who acts as the middleman between the thief and the person who will buy the stolen goods,' Maddie explained. If Ruby was to be working with her from now on, she needed to know. 'He takes whatever I can get my hands on for a fee and brings it to London to sell. There is much less chance of it being identified there, you see?'

A knot of fear formed in Ruby's stomach, but how could she refuse to do what Maddie asked. The woman was looking at her expectantly and so she nodded reluctantly.

'Excellent. Be ready to leave here at seven thirty. Nell has some dark clothes that don't fit her anymore. Wear those. We want you to be as inconspicuous as possible.'

Without a word Ruby went to her room where she sat with her arms wrapped around herself as she rocked to and fro with tears streaming down her face. If Maddie really *was* her mother how could she ask her to do such a thing? Surely mothers should be protective of their children, particularly after being parted from them for so long? But then she supposed that she had no proof that Maddie really *was* her mother as yet and suddenly she half hoped that she wasn't. Perhaps she had only been clutching at straws because Maddie had taken her in? It would be a huge disappointment to her if it turned out to be that Maddie was her real mother now.

Nell found her in her room sometime later and tossed a pile of shabby clothes onto the bed.

'Maddie said to give you these; they're too small for me now.' Her face softened as she saw the tears on Ruby's cheeks and settling next to her on the bed, she put her arm about her shoulders and gave her a gentle squeeze. 'Don't look so miserable, kid,' she encouraged. 'It ain't the end o' the bleedin' world, yer know. It ain't as if we're goin' to kill anyone. It's just a few trinkets after all, an' her as we're nickin' 'em from can easily afford to replace 'em.'

'But I . . . I don't know if I can do it,' Ruby whimpered. 'I'm so scared of being caught. What will they do to me if I am?'

'That ain't gonna happen.' Nell gave her a stern look. 'I shall be outside the whole time keepin' a look out, an' you'll be in an' out like a rat up a drainpipe. What I will say, though, is just *supposin'* we ever *did* get caught, yer must *swear* you would never lead 'em back 'ere. The coppers, I mean. Maddie looks after us in her own way an' the least we can do is protect her.'

'So have you done it before then?'

Nell snorted. 'O' course I bloody 'ave. They were the clothes I used to wear but they're too small for me now an' I'm too big to get in and out o' the winders easily. But I promise yer everythin' will go wi'out a hitch an' the more

60

you do it the easier it will get. I don't even think about it anymore.' She glanced through the window at the steadily falling snow. 'Try not to think about it an' we'll set off about half seven, so be ready.' And with that she left, leaving Ruby to watch the minutes tick away on the little clock on the mantelpiece.

Mrs Petty called her down for a meal at six, as she did every evening, but Ruby found that the food stuck in her throat and she couldn't eat a thing. Nell, on the other hand, tucked in as if she hadn't seen food for a month and Ruby wondered how she could be so calm. For the first time since being there she didn't offer to wash the pots when the meal was over but went back upstairs to change into the clothes Nell had given her. There were thick dark woollen stockings that had been heavily darned and a drab grey skirt that was patched in so many places it was hard to see what the original would have looked like. Over this she pulled on a shabby grey blouse and finally a woollen shawl that had been washed so many times the original colour was indistinguishable. She then brushed the ringlets from her hair and tied it tightly into the nape of her neck, and when she looked in the cheval mirror she hardly recognised herself. Even living back at home she had never looked as poor as she did now and anyone could easily have taken her for someone from the workhouse. Suddenly the bedroom door opened and Nell stood there dressed much as Ruby was.

'All right, kid. It's time to go.' She held her hand out and Ruby took it.

Mrs Petty and Maddie were waiting for them down in the hallway and Maddie looked at Nell. 'Now, are you quite sure you know exactly which house it is?'

Nell nodded, her face solemn while Mrs Petty wrung her hands together looking anxious.

'Right, off you go then, and be careful.' Maddie opened the front door letting a gust of icy wind in to lift the curtains. 'Luckily it's a shocking night so there won't be many about.'

The girls stepped through the door onto the lamp-lit pavement and once the door had closed behind them Ruby followed Nell along the street.

*I'm so sorry, Mam*, she said silently as she gazed up into the snowy night. Her mother would be so ashamed of her if she could see what she was doing, but what choice did she have?

# Chapter Seven

They walked along Vittoria Street in silence for a time and Ruby glanced at the jewellery school as they passed it. This, Maddie had told her, was where some of the greatest silver and goldsmiths in the country were trained. Eventually they turned into Frederick Street and it was there that Ruby asked, 'Are you scared, Nell?'

'Ner!' Nell shook her head sending a shower of snow into the air. 'You've just got to keep yer nerve an' everythin' will be fine.'

As they marched on, having to lift their feet high in the snow, Ruby wished she could feel as confident. Already her toes were so cold they were painful and she began to shiver with a combination of cold and fear. Soon they turned into Warstone Lane and Nell whispered, 'Not far to go now. The cemetery's just up 'ere. I just wish it weren't so bleedin' cold. I can 'ardly feel me 'ands an' feet!'

The street was almost deserted and those that were about didn't give the two girls a second glance, which Ruby was grateful for. Soon they passed the imposing wrought-iron gates leading to the cemetery and Ruby shuddered as she glanced through them at the rows and rows of headstones.

Then the moment she had dreaded came when Nell slowed her steps and hissed, 'This is it.'

Ruby glanced up at a large house that thankfully was in darkness and whispered through chattering teeth, 'S-so wh-what do we do now?'

After quickly glancing up and down the street to check that no one was about, Nell took her hand and dragged her through the gate and around the side of the house to the back. It was very dark round there with no street lights and Nell narrowed her eyes and peered at the windows to see which one had been left on the catch for them. It wasn't easy but after a short time she whispered, 'This is it. Come 'ere an' I'll give yer a leg-up.' She jiggled the catch on the sash cord window for a moment and when it eventually lifted a little, she beckoned to Ruby, who found her legs had suddenly turned to jelly.

'Now, into the hall, up the stairs an' the mistress's room is the third door on the right along the landin'. You'll find the jewellery in the top drawer of her dressin' table underneath her undies. 'Ave yer got that?' When Ruby nodded, Nell handed her a small cloth bag with a drawstring top and ordered, 'Put everythin' yer can find in there an' then come straight back down 'ere to me. I'm goin' to go an' stand by the front now an' if there's any sign of anybody comin' back I'll whistle an' yer get yer arse out o' there fast as yer know how – got it?'

Her eyes huge in her small face, Ruby nodded, as without another word Nell joined her hands together. Once Ruby had put her foot on them, she hoisted her up until Ruby could reach the sill where she drew her skirts to the side and somehow managed to wriggle through the gap. Once inside she sat for a moment catching her breath and letting her eyes adjust to the light, and discovered that she was in the kitchen. There was not a sound to be heard so she began to feel around with her foot, sending something crashing to the floor with a resounding bang.

'Bleedin' 'ell – watch what yer doin' will yer?' Nell's voice floated in to her. 'We're 'ere to rob the joint not wreck it.'

'Sorry, it was a tin bowl that was on the draining board,' Ruby hissed back as her heart slowed to a steadier rhythm. Taking a deep breath she scrambled down off the wooden draining board and felt her way across the room. After locating and passing through a green baize door she found herself in a huge hallway where an enormous grandfather clock was ticking away the minutes. The staircase loomed ahead of her and with her heart in her mouth she began to mount it. Every minute she expected a hand to clamp down on her shoulder, but at last she reached the top of the stairs and paused. What was it Nell had said . . . Ah, the third door on the right, that was it. She moved on and once she reached the door she tried the handle, sighing with relief when she found it unlocked. Cautiously she entered the bedroom, grateful to see that a cheery fire was burning in the grate giving her some light. It took her only moments to locate the dressing table and as she opened the top drawer and gazed down at the lady of the house's personal under-wear a wave of shame washed over her. Her mother would turn in her grave if she could see what she was doing, but she pushed the thought aside and began to rummage in the drawer.

Almost immediately her fingers closed around something and withdrawing it she gasped as she stared down at a glittering diamond necklace. But there was no time to stand and admire it, she was painfully aware that someone could come back to the house at any second so she delved again. The next find was a string of pearls that gleamed in the light from the fire, and after that a variety of rings. Working as fast as her shaking fingers would allow her, she crammed everything into the bag, not stopping for a second until she was quite sure that there was nothing she had missed. Only then did she tiptoe back to the door and scurry along the landing as fast as her legs would take her. She was going so fast that she slipped halfway down the stairs and painfully twisted her ankle as she grasped the bannister but she didn't pause in her flight. She was in a total panic now and all she wanted was to get as far away from the house as she possibly could.

At the bottom of the stairs she panicked again as she realised that she had forgotten the way back to the kitchen. The first route she took led her to a number of doors leading to various rooms and, almost sobbing with terror, she retraced her steps until she reached the grandfather clock. *It was this way*, she thought, but at that moment the clock struck the quarter hour and she dropped the bag she was clutching with fright. She dropped to her hands and knees, frantically feeling around the floor to retrieve the stolen goods. The jewels were scattered across the floor but at last she was certain that she had found everything and after stuffing them back into the bag she set off again, crying with relief when she once again entered the kitchen.

'I'm done,' she hissed as she struggled onto the draining board, trying to ignore the pain in her ankle.

'About bleedin' time an' all,' she heard Nell complain. 'It's freezin' standin' out 'ere.'

Ruby wiggled through the window backwards and once her feet were dangling below the sill, Nell caught her round the waist and lifted her down to the ground.

'Stand well back. We don't want the lady o' the 'ouse to think this were an inside job, we 'ave to make it look like it was a break-in,' Nell warned as she fished a good-sized rock from beneath the snow. She then closed the window and heaved the rock at the glass, shattering it into tiny shards that sparkled in the snow. Then she grabbed Ruby's hand and told her, 'Now run like the devil were after yer. We 'ave to get our arses as far away from 'ere as we can.' Hauling Ruby behind her she set off at a trot while Ruby valiantly tried to keep up with her, although the pain in her ankle was almost unbearable now. They had barely passed the gates to the cemetery when Ruby's ankle gave way and with a gasp of pain, she sprawled full length in the snow.

'Oh shit!' Nell swore as she leant over and tried to haul her to her feet. 'This is all we need.' Glancing quickly up and down the road to make sure that no one was coming she pulled Ruby unceremoniously to her feet and after pulling one of the huge gates open she dragged her inside the cemetery. Ruby was crying and in a total panic again.

'Calm down. You'll 'ave the rozzers after us at this rate,' Nell snapped.

With her arm about Ruby's waist she led her further into the churchyard and plonked her down behind a large tombstone where she wouldn't be seen from the road. With no street lights it was very dark and Ruby's heart began to thud painfully.

'What's best to do?' Nell scratched her head, seemingly oblivious to the snow that was falling thickly about them. 'You're too heavy fer me to carry you 'ome an' it's too cold to leave yer here; you'd freeze to death.'

Just at that moment she spotted someone walking past the gates and without a word she went sprinting off, leaving Ruby to shiver as she stared fearfully around her. The churchyard was surrounded by tall yew trees, their barren branches bending beneath the weight of the snow on them. For as far as her eyes could see were rows upon rows of gravestones, some of them leaning drunkenly to one side, and now her soft crying turned to sobbing as terror coursed through her. Where had Nell gone? *Surely* she didn't intend to leave her there all alone? She got her answer a moment later when Nell loomed towards her through the snow, but this time she wasn't alone. A tall lanky youth was walking beside her and he looked down at Ruby curiously.

'This 'ere is Bill Waters, he's a mate o' mine,' Nell introduced him. 'Lucky for us 'e happened by when he did 'cause he's goin' to 'elp us, ain't yer, Bill?'

The youth nodded. 'Can you manage to stand up?' he asked Ruby. 'If you can I'll give you a piggyback.'

Ruby nodded as she stared at him in the gloom. He was much taller than her and looked to be about seventeen or eighteen years old. He had a thick thatch of hair, although she couldn't distinguish what colour it was in the dark, and his clothes looked shabby. But when he smiled, she noticed that his eyes were kindly.

'Come on, shrimp, let's be havin' you.' With a grin he reached down and helped her to her feet then turning he said, 'Hop on me back and put your arms tight around me neck.'

Seconds later they set off and soon they had turned into Frederick Street where Nell breathed a sigh of relief.

'Phew, that were a close thing. We couldn't 'ave stayed there all night an' there were no way I could leave 'er. An' thank the Lord there's nobody about.'

Bill chuckled as he hoisted Ruby a little further up his back. 'I should think most folks would 'ave more sense than to be out on a night like this.'

'Hm, happen yer right.' They hurried on in silence as Ruby buried her face in Bill's shoulder. He was carrying her as if she weighed no more than a feather and although she had only just met him, she felt strangely safe with him. At last the house came into view and after hurrying round to the back, Nell threw the door open and they spilled into the kitchen, making Mrs Petty, who was knitting at the side of the fire, almost jump out of her skin.

'Good grief, yer give me a right gliff then . . . But what's happened?' Casting her knitting to one side she hurried across to help Ruby clamber off Bill's back.

'Ruby 'ad a slight accident an' hurt her ankle but luckily for us Bill came along, else I don't know what we'd have done.'

Mrs Petty helped Ruby into a chair just as Maddie entered the kitchen.

'What's happened?'

Nell quickly told her and Maddie shook her head before smiling at Bill. It appeared she knew him as she herself went to put the kettle on the range. 'Thanks, Bill. You must have a warm drink and something to eat before you go.' And then almost as an afterthought she asked, 'How is your mother?'

Bill shrugged. 'Oh, you know . . . as well as can be expected considerin' how cold it's been. But then we shouldn't complain. At least we still 'ave a roof over our 'eads, which beats sleepin' on a park bench, don't it?'

When he smiled his eyes twinkled with mischief and Ruby noticed that they were a lovely grey colour. His hair was dark and inclined to curl but he was painfully thin and only now did she see just how shabby his clothes were.

Now that she was seated, Mrs Petty was trying to remove her boot and all thoughts of the new friend she had just made flew out of the window as she gasped with pain.

'Well, would you just look at the state o' that!' Mrs Petty tutted as she stared down at her swollen foot. 'Yer don't do anything by halves, do yer, bab? Why, you'll be off this for days. Your ankle is already double the size it should be. Let's get it bound up tight. There ain't a lot more yer can do for sprains unfortunately. Nell run up an' fetch me one of the older sheets from the airing cupboard, would you?'

Nell hurried off to do as she was told as Mrs Petty gently bathed Ruby's foot in warm water. When she came back, Mrs Petty began to tear the sheet into strips warning Ruby, 'This is goin' to hurt like hell so try an' be brave, there's a good girl.'

Ruby gritted her teeth and closed her eyes as Mrs Petty tightly bound her ankle. When it was done, she went to fetch a stool, telling her, 'Now you need to keep your foot upright.'

Maddie meanwhile was pacing up and down the kitchen and unable to wait a second longer she asked, 'So how did the visit go?'

Fishing in her coat pocket Ruby handed her the bag and Maddie immediately spilled the contents onto the table, gasping with delight when the stolen jewels glistened in the light from the oil lamp.

'Oh, this is *beautiful* and worth a small fortune all on its own,' she said greedily as she lifted the diamond necklace and peered at it closely. 'And the quality of the diamonds is just *superb*.' Until then Ruby hadn't been aware that one diamond was any different from another but Maddie seemed to know what she was talking about. 'I must teach you what to look for,' Maddie said as she saw Ruby watching her. 'When it comes to diamonds you must look for cut, carat, clarity and colour.' She laid the necklace aside and began to look through the rest of the loot, again exclaiming at the colour of the stone in a sapphire ring. It reminded Ruby of the colour of the sea she had seen in picture books, although she had never seen the sea in real life. 'This is stunning too and quite rare to get an oval cut in such a good-sized stone.' One after the other she lifted and examined each piece before saying, 'Well, accident aside, you've done extremely well for your first time, Ruby. I can see you're going to be a great asset to us.'

Ruby's heart sank as she realised Maddie was intimating that this would be the first of many times, and again the hopelessness of her situation came home to her. Would she rather stay here and become a thief or return to her father? She shuddered at the thought as Mrs Petty pressed a steaming mug into her hand, glaring at Maddie disapprovingly all the time. Ruby didn't really have to think about it, for anything was preferable to going back to be abused again and so somehow, she was just going to have to try to get on with things, for now at least.

# Chapter Eight

The morning after the burglary, Maddie was up and out bright and early. As Mrs Petty served the two girls their breakfast, she clucked her tongue disapprovingly. 'She's no doubt gone to see her fence; she'll not want that stuff lyin' around here just in case we get a visit from the police. Not that that's likely,' she added hastily as she saw the look of panic on Ruby's face. 'Maddie ain't no fool; she always makes sure that there ain't no way of them findin' out she was involved in any wrongdoin's.'

Ruby breathed a sigh of relief. She had been awake most of the night suffering all manner of guilty feelings for what she'd done and the throbbing in her ankle hadn't helped matters either. Mrs Petty had already undone the binding on it early that morning and tutted to see that it was swollen like a balloon. 'I can't see you gettin' out an' about on that for a couple o' weeks at least,' she'd said, and although she was in pain, Ruby had felt relived. At least she wouldn't be asked to do another burglary until her ankle was healed.

After breakfast she and Nell went into the sitting room and Ruby picked up one of the books on gems that Maddie had given to her to look at. She was actually really enjoying learning where all the different gems came from and was fascinated to discover that such raw material could be turned into such sparkling jewels.

'I think I'd like to be a goldsmith when I'm older,' she told Nell thoughtfully.

The girl chuckled. 'It ain't as simple as that. It takes years to train a good goldsmith and there's a lot more to it than yer think.' She herself was poring over the morning paper to see if there was any report on the burglary. Thankfully there wasn't, not as yet, at least.

'So, how do you know Bill?' Ruby asked curiously.

'Me an' Bill come from the same neighbourhood an' we've known each other since we were nippers. His dad were a bleedin' nightmare an' used to knock the family about till he were knocked over an' killed by a dray cart a few years ago. That left him an' his mam an' a younger brother an' sister, but sadly the little 'uns died in the influenza epidemic a couple o' years back. An' now his mam's right poorly an all. Between you an' me I reckon she's got the consumption an' I don't think she'll last much longer. Bill bein' the oldest he sort o' took on the man's role when his dad were killed. He's always out scoutin' fer work – he'll do any sort o' work, but when he can't get none, he'll do the odd job fer Maddie just to keep a roof over his mam's head.'

'Poor Bill.' Ruby felt sad for him. It sounded like he was no keener on stealing than she was. 'And what about you, Nell? How did you come to be here?'

Nell looked distinctly uncomfortable and kept her eyes firmly fixed on the paper as she muttered, 'Ah, yer know, this an' that.'

She clearly didn't wish to speak about her past so Ruby turned her attention back to the book she was reading and soon she was lost in the world of gems.

Maddie arrived home mid-afternoon with a broad smile on her face and looking like the cat who'd got the cream.

'Looks like 'er fence gave 'er a good price for the latest lot,' Nell whispered to Ruby as Maddie made for the kitchen.

Ruby frowned. What they had done still didn't feel right but Nell seemed to accept that this was how Maddie made her living. 'Is this fence person the one that comes to see her of an evening sometimes?' she asked innocently.

Nell chuckled as she shook her head. 'No, that'd be her fancy man. She's been seein' him fer years. She met 'im when she were on stage, apparently.'

'On stage?' Ruby's eyes stretched wide. 'Was she an actress then?'

'No, a singer. An' accordin' to Mrs Petty, she were the darlin' o' the music halls at one time. That were when she took on the name Bamber. It ain't her real name but she thought Madeline Bamber had a ring to it. I've no idea what her real name is though.'

'So what made her give up singing?'

'Here yer go askin' questions again,' Nell groaned, then glancing at the clock she said, 'I'm off fer a lie-down fer an hour afore the evenin' meal is ready. I'm out tonight.'

Ruby would dearly have loved to ask where she was going but didn't dare. It was very frustrating: there was so much about these people she had come to live with that she didn't know and she wondered if she ever would. As Nell disappeared through the door she sighed and went back

to reading her book. There wasn't much else she could do,
with her ankle the way it was.

As it happened Maddie's gentleman friend called that very
night and Ruby found herself dispatched to the kitchen to
keep Mrs Petty company, but not before she had caught
sight of him through the hall window as he arrived in a
beautiful carriage pulled by four matching grey stallions.

'Maddie's friend must be very rich to own a carriage like
that,' she commented.

Mrs Petty glanced up from her knitting and nodded. 'Oh,
he's rich all right.'

'So, do you think he and Maddie might get married?'

'*Married!*' Mrs Petty snorted with a shake of her head.
'I should think there's very little chance o' that happenin'
when he already has a wife. I reckon she might have somethin' to say about it, don't you?'

'Maddie's friend is married?' Ruby looked shocked. 'So
why does he come to see Maddie then?'

'Eeh, bab, you 'ave a lot to learn, yer as green as grass.'
Mrs Petty shook her head again as she examined the
stitches on her knitting needles. 'Not all marriages are
made in 'eaven an' there's a lot o' chaps who keep a little
friend on the side. That one in there' – she nodded towards
the door – 'was born wi' a silver spoon in his mouth an'
I've no doubt his wife were chosen fer him. From what I
can make of it he an' his wife don't even *like* each other
let alone love each other, but that's the way the so called
upper classes carry on.'

'So why does Maddie stay with him if she knows he'll never marry her?'

'She loves 'im, that's why, an' love is a funny thing. Deep down I reckon she lives in hope that he'll leave his missus one day an' they'll be together.'

Ruby shuddered as she suddenly thought of what her father had done to her. 'Well, I shall *never* get married!' she stated firmly.

Mrs Petty smiled as she started a new row of stitches. 'Never is a long time,' she said wisely. 'An' I've no doubt you'll feel differently when you're older an' you meet the right chap.'

'I won't!' Ruby's head wagged determinedly from side to side and glancing towards the hall door she suddenly felt sorry for Maddie. How awful it must be to know that the man she loved would never be hers. Grown-ups were strange beings, there was no doubt about it.

It was much later that night when Ruby was tucked up in bed that she heard Maddie's gentleman friend leave and then the sound of voices from the hallway.

'When are yer goin' to see the light an' get yerself a chap that's worthy of you?' This was Mrs Petty's voice.

'Oh, please *don't* start on that again, Petty. You know Jethro's position.'

'Hm, well I certainly know yours an' from where I'm standin' yer wastin' yer life as his bit on the side. Surely you realise by now that he'll never leave her? You're still a good-lookin' woman, Maddie, an' young enough to get someone who loves you enough to make an honest woman o' you.' The voices faded as the women made their way into the kitchen and Ruby lay staring up into the darkness, but then she gave a large yawn and was soon fast asleep.

By the end of January, the snow had finally stopped falling, only to be replaced by sleeting rain that turned the pavements into slushy skating rinks. Ruby's ankle had now healed and she began to wonder how long it would be before Maddie expected her to start earning her keep again. She didn't have to wait long to find out, for as she sat in the kitchen with Mrs Petty one evening, the rain lashing against the windows, Maddie joined them. 'I thought we might have a little trip out the day after tomorrow, Ruby,' she said.

Ruby had been in the process of winding some wool for Mrs Petty but now her hands became still as she looked at Maddie with fear in her eyes.

'Wh-where to?' Her voice came out as a squeak and Mrs Petty looked up sharply with a frown on her face.

'I thought we'd take the train to Leicester. You'd like another train ride, wouldn't you?'

When Ruby remained silent, Maddie frowned and lifting her skirts swished out of the room, clearly not happy with the girl's reaction.

'I can't do it, Mrs Petty!' Tears gathered in Ruby's eyes and began to spill down her suddenly pale cheeks as her head wagged from side to side. 'I can't do it. It's not that I'm ungrateful. I'm happy to work but I can't go stealing again. Me mam would be so ashamed if she knew what I'd done.'

The tears erupted into sobs and rising from her seat the kindly woman hurried over to Ruby and wrapped her arms around her.

'Couldn't I earn me keep some other way? Cleanin' in one of the big houses or somethin'?'

Seeing how distraught she was, Mrs Petty's lips pursed into a straight, grim line. 'Look, get yerself off to bed now an' let me see what I can do,' she said gently and Ruby rose from her seat and left the room with her chin on her chest as Mrs Petty chewed thoughtfully on her lip. What was happening wasn't right. Ruby had clearly been brought up to be honest and was not cut out for the life Maddie had lined up for her. Making a decision, she hastily removed her apron and after shrugging into her warm coat she pulled her outdoor boots on and set off into the bitterly cold night. She knew that Maddie wouldn't be at all happy with what she was about to do but it couldn't be helped. Ruby was an innocent, not streetwise as Nell had been when she first came to them, and she deserved better.

Ruby started when someone gently shook her arm early the next morning.

'Come on, bab.' She recognised Mrs Petty's voice as she leant up on her elbow and knuckled the sleep from her eyes. 'I want you to get up an' pack yer things as fast as yer know how. I've put a bag here for yer but don't make a sound, mind! Just come down to the kitchen soon as yer dressed an' ready.' With that she crept from the room, leaving Ruby to wonder what was going on as she fell out of bed and did as she was told.

Minutes later she was down in the kitchen where she looked at Mrs Petty with a question in her eyes.

'I've found you a job, a proper job, an' somewhere to stay,' the kindly woman informed her as she paced nervously up and down.

'Oh!' Ruby looked shocked. 'What sort of job?'

'I'll tell you on the way, but come along, it's in Erdington, so we've got a long walk ahead of us and I want you gone before Maddie knows what I've done. Get your coat on, there's a good girl.'

Still half asleep Ruby quickly obeyed her then followed her out into the cold early morning. The streets were busy with men and women making their way to work and Ruby wondered where they were going.

'Is it much further?' she asked after some time and Mrs Petty shook her head.

'Not too much further now,' she said breathlessly. They seemed to have been walking for hours but at last they turned into a long road lined with large detached houses, each standing well back from the main thoroughfare. As they trooped along Ruby stared at them in awe. She could only imagine that the people who lived in them must be very rich indeed. She had thought that Maddie's house was nice but these were even grander.

'Here we are then,' Mrs Petty panted after some time. 'This is it.'

Ruby stared down a long, tree-lined drive to the house beyond and the breath caught in her throat. It was like something out of one of the magazines Maddie was so fond of and she couldn't imagine what it must be like to live there.

'Is this where I'm going to be working?' she dared to ask.

'It is indeed. Come along, let's get out o' this drizzle. I'm soaked through.'

They set off again and once they came to the end of the drive, Mrs Petty led her around to the back of the house where they found themselves in a huge cobbled yard with stables on one side and a number of small outhouses and the kitchen on the other. The yard was walled with a large gate over which Ruby could see the tops of trees.

Approaching the kitchen door, Mrs Petty knocked and it was answered almost instantly by a young maid in a starched white apron and mop cap.

'Ah, come in,' the girl said in a friendly fashion. 'Miss Wood is expecting you, Mrs Petty.'

Mrs Petty ushered Ruby ahead of her into the most enormous kitchen she had ever seen. She had thought the one at Maddie's was big but that was small by comparison.

A woman with a ruddy complexion and a kindly face approached them and smiled at Mrs Petty. From the way she greeted her Ruby guessed they must know each other.

'Hello, Ethel, you're looking well.' She glanced towards Ruby and winked before gesturing to the table. 'Sit yourselves down, there's tea in the pot and I've no doubt you could do with one after being out in the cold. Miss Wood shouldn't be long. And this is Ruby, is it?'

'It is,' Mrs Petty confirmed. 'And thank you, Ada, a cup o' tea would go down a treat. It's enough to cut you in two out there.'

Ruby sidled onto a chair and sat down as the woman bustled away, returning a moment later with two large, steaming mugs. 'Help yourselves to sugar.' She pointed to the pressed glass bowl on the table, then turned her attention back to Ruby. 'Have you been in service before, bab?'

Ruby shook her head as she warmed her hands on the mug. 'N-no, I haven't, but I used to work hard in me dad's baker's shop.'

'That's good. Oh, and I'm Mrs Baxter, but everyone just calls me Cook.'

At that moment the green baize door at the end of the room opened and a woman with fair hair wound into plaits about her head and blue eyes appeared. She was slim and straight-backed and dressed in a plain bombazine gown with a chatelaine about her waist. The keys that were attached to it jingled when she walked but her eyes were kindly as she approached Mrs Petty with her hand held out.

They shook hands and only then did Miss Wood turn to look at Ruby. 'Hm, she's quite slight, isn't she?' she commented worriedly. 'I just hope she is able to stand up for herself. As you know, Miss Miranda can be quite, er . . .' She paused as though searching for the right word and ended, 'Challenging, shall we say?'

Ruby frowned. Who the hell was Miss Miranda and what did it matter to her how big she was?

'Ah well, the thing is, I ain't actually had a chance to explain to Ruby what her job is to be,' Mrs Petty explained with a worried glance at Ruby. 'But all the same I feel she'll be up to it.'

'Time will tell,' Miss Wood answered. 'But we shall have to think about getting Ruby some new clothes. She can hardly be seen wearing those if she's going to be catering to Miss Miranda's needs.'

Humiliated, Ruby stared down at her shabby skirt. She had left everything Maddie had bought for her behind – it had seemed wrong to take it – and so she was once again dressed in the clothes she had arrived in before Christmas.

Lately, it seemed that everyone was keen to dress her. She just hoped that Miss Wood would choose her something a little more grown-up than Maddie had.

'Not to worry,' Miss Wood said softly as if she sensed that she had embarrassed her. 'We're sure to have a maid's dress somewhere that you can wear till we can get you some new things.'

Suddenly Ruby was aware of the tantalising smell of frying bacon. Cook was busily preparing the breakfast and she realised that she was hungry. She hadn't been able to eat a thing the night before after Maddie had told her what she had planned.

'Right, it's time I was off.' Mrs Petty drained her cup and stood up. 'You be good now and I'll be back to see you soon, eh?'

Ruby was touched to see that there were tears in her eyes and rising quickly she gave her an impulsive hug, realising how much she was going to miss her. There had been so many goodbyes in her life recently.

Mrs Petty bustled away without another word as Miss Wood gently pressed her back into her seat. 'You just sit there and have some breakfast and when you're done, we'll see about finding some clothes that fit you and I'll explain what your job entails.' She gave Ruby a gentle smile and left the room. Once she was alone, Ruby wondered what this next stage of her life would entail. One thing was for sure, nothing could be as bad as having to return to the man she had always called her father, and somehow, she would make the best of it, especially if it meant she didn't have to steal jewellery for a living.

# Chapter Nine

As soon as breakfast had been served to the family, the staff sat down to eat and Ruby was shocked at the number of people seated around the table; she could only assume that the family must be large to warrant so many servants. She had no idea what their names were as yet, although she had no doubt she would get to know them all in time, so she sat quietly listening to them chatter. She was just finishing her meal when the door slammed open and the young maid who had admitted them earlier came in, her crisp white apron stained with tea and her mop cap all askew.

'I wonder why that little bloody tyrant always picks on me,' she ranted, clearly upset.

'Calm down, Betty,' Cook urged. 'What's she done now?'

'I was serving her breakfast when she knocked her cup over. It went all over me an' the tablecloth an' when I bent down to pick the cup up, she pulled me hair and yanked at me cap.'

Cook tutted. 'Well, you ought to be used to it by now,' she said gravely. 'Did her mother not say anything?'

'Huh! As usual she stuck up for her and said she'd knocked the cup over accidentally but I know she didn't!'

'Never mind. Sit yourself down and get some food inside you and then you can go and get changed before you go back in to clear the table.'

Scowling, Betty removed her sodden apron and plonked down at the table. For the rest of the meal the incident wasn't mentioned, although Ruby was longing to know who had been the cause of all the trouble.

As soon as the meal was over Miss Wood, who had her meals in her own rooms, appeared and beckoned to Ruby.

Cook gave her an encouraging smile as she lifted her bundle and followed the woman along a passageway that led off from the kitchen until they reached what she discovered were Miss Wood's private rooms. There appeared to be two, one of which was a very cosy little sitting room with a door leading off it and one that Ruby assumed was her bedroom.

There were a number of dresses laid across the back of the chair and Miss Wood told her, 'I'm going to take you to your room now. Do take these with you and try them on, then keep the two that fit you best until I can get you some new ones ordered.'

'Thank you, missus.'

The woman smiled. 'Miss Wood will do nicely when you address me, Ruby. But before we go, I'd like to explain what your duties will be. You are going to be . . . shall we say a maid-cum-companion to the young mistress of the house. I believe she is about your age but I should warn you she can be quite . . .' She frowned as she searched for the right word. 'Challenging, I suppose.' She sighed and lowered her voice as she went on cautiously, 'You will be the fourth maid she has had in as many months. I'm afraid Miss Miranda has been rather spoilt, by her mother mainly, and she can be quite spiteful. But who knows, it might be that you two will get along famously. We can always live in hope.'

Ruby lifted the dresses as her stomach churned. This Miranda sounded like hard work, but then she was used to that and she needed the job. Miss Wood showed her to a room in the servants' quarters up in the attics. It was spotlessly clean and looked comfortable enough. There were two metal-framed beds with a chest of drawers at the side of each of them and some nails knocked into the back of the door where she could hang some clothes. Against another wall was a marble-topped washstand with a large jug and bowl standing on it and above that was a slightly cracked mirror where she could do her hair. It was nowhere near as pretty as the room she'd had at Maddie's, but she thought it would do nicely. After all, if this Miranda was half as bad as she was expecting it wasn't as if she'd be in there for long anyway.

'You'll be sharing with Betty, the parlour maid,' Miss Wood told her. 'I believe you've already met her, and I'm sure you'll get along. But now I'll leave you to put your things away and try those dresses on and when you're ready, go back down to the kitchen and I'll take you through to meet Miss Miranda, if she's finished her lessons with her tutor that is.'

'Thank you missu— Miss Wood.'

Once the woman had gone, Ruby quickly folded her few clothes into the drawers and began to sort through the dresses. They were all a soft-grey colour made of a fine wool fabric and although they were somewhat plain, they were much more grown-up than the ones Maddie had bought for her. Eventually she tried on two that fitted quite well and she turned to study her reflection in the mirror. The one she was wearing had tiny pearl buttons up the front of it from the waist to the high neck and a nice full skirt that reached to the floor, which made Ruby feel very grown-up indeed. It was fractionally long but she knew that she could alter that herself when she had some time off. She scowled as she stared at the ringlets floating around her shoulders. Maddie had insisted she should wear her hair that way but it was a very babyish style so she yanked out the ribbon and brushed it thoroughly before tying it back neatly into the nape of her neck.

*That's better*, she thought as she stared back at her reflection, and after lifting the rest of the dresses she set off for the kitchen, hoping that she would remember the way. She had barely reached the end of the long landing when the door at the end opened and Betty barged through it, almost knocking Ruby flying.

'Sorry!' She smiled at her before flapping her hand at the tea-stained apron she was holding. 'I was just comin' up to get a clean one. I tell you, that Miss Miranda is a little she-devil. It's about time somebody put her over their knee an' gave her arse a good old-fashioned spankin'!' Her hand flew to her mouth then. 'Ooh, sorry again! I just realised you're going to be working for her, ain't you? But just take a bit o' well-intended advice and be on your guard.'

'I will,' Ruby promised and then with Betty still cursing beneath her breath as she hurried on to the room they were to share, Ruby went downstairs.

She found Miss Wood having a tea break with Cook and as she entered the room the woman looked at her admiringly. 'Why, Ruby, you look quite smart now. Well done.'

She took the dresses that were not required and told her, 'We may as well take you to meet Miss Miranda. She should be finished her morning lessons by now, although I think she has a piano lesson booked for this afternoon. We'll go and see, shall we?' With a friendly nod towards Cook, Miss Wood led Ruby from the room and once in the main part of the house Ruby stared about her in awe. Her feet sank into one of the thick pile rugs that were scattered about the floor, and the black and white tiles beneath them gleamed like mirrors. However, Ruby didn't have long to admire them before a door further along was suddenly flung open and a girl who appeared to be about her age emerged looking red-faced.

'I *shan't* do any stupid homework!' she stormed to whoever was still in the room she was leaving. 'And you can tell my mother for all I care. She won't make me.' Spotting Miss Wood and Ruby, she stopped screeching abruptly and frowned. 'And who is this, then?' She approached them and began to circle Ruby, staring at her up and down, much as Ruby had seen the farmers back at home do to the cattle on market day.

Ruby felt her cheeks grow hot but she remained where she was, keeping her eyes trained firmly ahead.

'This is Ruby, Miss Miranda. She's come to be your new maid,' Miss Wood informed her. 'And I *do* hope you'll be a little nicer to her than you were to the last girl.'

Miranda stopped abruptly and glared at her, hands on hips. 'Don't you try and tell me what to do, Wood,' she said rudely. 'Otherwise I shall tell Mother you've been horrible to me.'

'And she will know that that isn't true.' Miss Wood stood her ground and stared coldly back at the girl. She was clearly used to her rudeness and her tantrums. Ruby meanwhile had the chance to get a good look at her and was struck by the fact that the girl's hair was a similar colour to her own, not such a deep shade but definitely auburn. But there any similarities ended for the girl was at least a head taller than her and while Ruby's hair was curly Miranda's was as straight as a poker. She was also quite plump, whereas Ruby was small and dainty, but her clothes, Ruby noted, were top quality and very fashionable.

'You'd better come with me then. Mother doesn't pay you to stand about, and my room needs tidying,' the girl told Ruby rudely.

Miss Wood caught her breath but didn't comment as Ruby obediently followed the girl up the stairs. On the first floor Miranda led her into a bedroom that was so grand it almost took Ruby's breath away. It was huge and Ruby had never seen a prettier room. An enormous four-poster bed draped with thick velvet curtains in a lovely pale green, matching the ones that hung at the window, stood against one wall and Ruby was sure it was big enough for a whole family to sleep in. A darker green carpet covered the floor and a cheery fire was burning in a pretty marble fireplace. There was a large French-style armoire with matching drawers against another wall and a fancy escritoire and chair stood in the deep bay window. But there were clothes scattered everywhere and as Miranda saw Ruby looking at them, she barked, 'Get on with it, then!'

Without a word Ruby began to gather the clothes and when she had collected them all she laid them on the bed, which was covered in a pretty floral, lace-trimmed counterpane.

'You'll have to show me where they all go,' Ruby said politely.

The girl turned on her. 'Why, haven't you got eyes in your head? Open the drawers and look where they go yourself,' she spat, eyeing her scornfully. 'How old are you anyway?'

'I'm fifteen.'

'Fifteen! You only look about ten or eleven.' Miranda curled her lip. 'And when you address me you say *miss*!'

Ruby's temper was bubbling to the surface now, but she gritted her teeth and began to open the cupboards and drawers as she worked out where all the discarded clothes should go. It was hard to believe that one person could own so many, especially one as rude as Miranda who clearly didn't value them at all.

'And where are you from?'

'I was brought up in Nuneaton . . . miss!'

'Why have you ended up here, then?'

Ruby remained tight-lipped as she continued to fold the clothes and place them neatly away in what she hoped were the right places. She might be working for this rude creature, but the way she saw it, it didn't give her the right to delve into her past.

'Cat got your tongue, has it?' Miranda mocked. 'Or have you run away from someone or something?'

Ruby's heart did a little lurch but still she didn't answer and eventually the room was tidy again.

'That's everything put away, is there anything else you'd like me to do, miss?'

Having watched her work, Miranda now stood up abruptly and crossing the room she began to drag everything back out again, flinging clothes about the room. 'It isn't done to my satisfaction,' she said haughtily. 'Do it all again and make a better job of it this time, otherwise I shall tell my mother.' With that she swept from the room with a smirk on her face as Ruby's hands clenched with rage; Miss Wood hadn't been joking when she had told her that her new mistress could be challenging. Suddenly despair washed through her and her shoulders sagged. She had thought anything would be better than being made to steal but could she put up with the girl's spiteful behaviour? Only time would tell.

'So how has your first day gone?' Miss Wood asked when the staff assembled in the kitchen for supper that evening.

'It, er . . . wasn't too bad.'

One look at Ruby's glum face told its own story and Miss Wood smiled at her sympathetically. 'I did warn you that she could be difficult,' she said and leaning towards her she whispered, 'What she needs is someone to stand up to her and give her as good as she gets. That's the only way to handle a bully in my experience but sadly all the other maids she has had have been too afraid of her to do it.'

Their conversation was interrupted as a maid began to lay the cutlery on the table and soon after Miss Wood left to return to her own rooms.

Within no time the staff were all seated and Cook began to dish out helpings of a delicious, piping-hot cottage pie.

'Help yourself to vegetables,' she encouraged Ruby. 'And don't look so worried. No one is going to eat you. Soon as the meal is over, I'll introduce you to everyone.'

Ruby gave her a grateful smile, suddenly wishing she were back in the kitchen at Maddie's house with Nell and Mrs Petty. At least there she had felt welcome. Here, Miranda had made her feel anything but and had done nothing but taunt her all day. But all she could do was pray that things would improve.

# Chapter Ten

As promised, Cook had introduced Ruby to the rest of the staff after dinner but there were so many of them that Ruby had forgotten half of their names already and now as she lay in bed watching the shadows dance on the ceiling, tears started to roll down her cheeks. *I wonder what Maddie said when she knew I was gone? Did she care?* Once again, she wondered if it was possible that the woman was her birth mother. Perhaps she had only imagined the similarities between them because her dearest wish was to know who her real mother was? Because if she was, wouldn't she have told her? And surely, she wouldn't have wanted her to steal for her. It was all so confusing and Ruby half wished that her mam had never told her that she'd been adopted. Already she was finding it hard to remember every line on her beloved face, which made her feel worse because she had been the only one who had ever shown her true love and without her Ruby felt bereft. But somehow, she knew she was going to have to find the strength to go on and build some sort of life for herself. When she finally slept her cheeks were still wet with tears and her dreams were troubled.

'Wakey, wakey, rise and shine.'

Betty's cheerful voice brought Ruby starting awake early the next morning and she quickly sat up in bed feeling disorientated as she looked around at the unfamiliar room.

'Come on, bab, it's time for a cuppa before we start work.' Betty was getting dressed and she flashed her a bright smile, wondering how long the poor girl would last with Miss Miranda to contend with. Ruby was so inoffensive and naive and everyone who had felt Miranda's wrath knew how difficult she could be. Ruby, meanwhile, was dragging herself out of bed and snatching up her clothes, which she had folded neatly over the back of the chair the night before.

'See you downstairs.' Betty hurried out of the room, leaving Ruby to have a hasty wash and tug a brush through her unruly curls.

Minutes later she arrived in the kitchen to find a cheery fire blazing and Cook, Betty and Nancy, the little kitchen maid, sitting at the table with steaming mugs in front of them.

'Help yourself.' Cook pushed a mug towards Ruby and nodded at a sturdy brown teapot in the middle of the table.

Ruby quietly did as she was told before joining them. 'So what's the name of the family who live here?' she asked hesitantly after a time as her curiosity got the better of her.

Cook snorted. 'Lord love us, do you not even know that? It's Pembroke. There's the master an' mistress, not that we see a lot of her 'cause she's an invalid and spends most of her time in bed. There's Miss Miranda, who you've met. An' then there's old Master Pembroke, the young master's

95

father. He's retired now an' the young master has taken over his business.'

'Oh, and what's that?' Ruby was interested.

'Why, old Walter Pembroke was one o' the best gold-smiths in Birmingham,' Cook informed her. 'He's made jewellery for royalty in his time, so he has, and he's got jewellery shops all over the country. The young master manages them now and he's a good jeweller himself, to be fair. The old man still has a workshop here but none of the servants are allowed in there even to clean it. He still likes to come up with original designs, although he leaves it to his son to have them made up these days.'

'I see.' Ruby was thoughtful; this new family she had come to work for sounded like a talented bunch and she was curious to meet them, especially considering they made jewellery, which ever since she'd read those books at Maddie's house, she'd decided she would love to do herself. Of course, it was out of reach for a girl like her, but still, it would be exciting just to get a look at the workshop. But her thoughts were interrupted when Cook told her, 'You'd best get Miss Miranda's tray of tea ready for her. She likes to have it in bed then she'll probably come down to have breakfast with her father before he leaves for work. And don't forget, don't take no nonsense off her. That's been the trouble with all the other maids she's had. She bullied them somethin' rotten but not one of 'em was brave enough to stand up to her.'

Ruby nodded and as she prepared the tray she thought on what Cook had said. The trouble was the advice she had given was more easily said than done. She had only just started here so she could hardly cause trouble just yet when she had nowhere else to go. Once the tray was ready, she carefully carried it up the stairs and tapped on Miranda's door. There was no answer so she tapped again a little louder but still there was only silence so she tentatively inched the door open. She could see Miranda's shape beneath the bed covers and after placing the tray down she crossed to the window and swished the curtains aside, allowing light to flood into the room.

'What the *hell* do you think you're doing?' an angry voice growled from beneath the blankets.

'I've brought you your tea up, miss.' Refusing to be intimidated, Ruby crossed to the fire and threw some coal onto the dying flames.

Miranda's head appeared bleary-eyed with her hair tousled. 'Pass it over then. I can't reach it from here, can I?'

Ruby obediently laid the tray across the girl's lap and plumped up the pillows behind her before asking politely, 'Will there be anything else, miss?'

'Well, of course there will, *you idiot.*' Miranda scowled at her as she took a sip of her tea. 'You can sort out what I'm going to wear today and then fetch me some hot water to wash in. You should know what needs to be done without being told!'

'Sorry, but as I explained I've never worked as a maid before, but I'm sure I shall soon pick it up. So what would you like to wear?' Crossing to the elaborate armoire Ruby opened the doors and was again shocked to see the many lovely gowns hanging there.

'I think the dark-blue brocade. It's nice and thick and warm.' Miranda took another very unladylike slurp of her tea. 'And I shall need the petticoats to go beneath it and some clean underwear laid out as well.'

Ruby efficiently did as she was asked before shooting off to the kitchen to fetch a jug of hot water. She found Cook expertly flipping bacon in a huge frying pan on the range and the moment Ruby entered the room she asked, 'So what mood is the little madam in today, then?'

Ruby smiled as she filled the jug from the kettle. 'Oh, not too bad. Not yet at least.'

The kitchen was a hive of activity as servants rushed about laying the table in the dining room and helping prepare the breakfast for the family. The huge table in the centre of the room was already covered in a variety of dishes that made Ruby's stomach rumble with anticipation.

'How many will be down to breakfast?' she asked, thinking that perhaps the family had visitors.

'Oh, just the two men an' the young miss,' Cook informed her.

Ruby was shocked. There was so much food. How could three people possibly even eat a fraction of it? she wondered.

As if she could read her mind Cook chuckled. 'Don't worry. None of it goes to waste. Miss Wood will take a tray up to the mistress and the staff finish what's left.'

Ruby smiled and shot off back up the stairs with Miranda's hot water. The girl was out of bed by then and she frowned at her as she entered. 'About time too,' she muttered ungratefully, but again Ruby kept the smile plastered to her face.

'You can go now,' Miranda ordered when Ruby had poured the water into the bowl. 'And while I'm down at breakfast you can come back up and tidy my room.'

'Yes, miss.' With clenched teeth but her smile still firmly in place Ruby left the room thinking what a spoilt little pig Miranda was. Her manners were appalling.

By the time she got back downstairs the maids had carried the food through to the sideboard in the dining room ready for the family to help themselves, and now that the rush was over Cook was seated at the table again with another cup of tea in front of her before she got breakfast ready for the staff.

Ruby joined her. 'How old is Miranda?' she asked.

'She'll be sixteen in March.'

Ruby was surprised to hear that she was older than her, she certainly didn't act it, but she didn't comment. The woman stood up then with a sigh, 'No peace for the wicked.' She smiled at Ruby. 'I'd best get you lot fed now.'

Ruby rose too. 'That will be lovely but I'd better pop up and tidy Miss Miranda's room as she told me to.' She hurried upstairs again, hopeful that the tidying would only take a few minutes after all the work she had done the day before, because she was very hungry now. The minute she opened the bedroom door, though, she sighed with dismay and frustration. Almost every drawer was hanging open and the contents were scattered across the room. She'd obviously decided she didn't want to wear the outfit that Ruby had got out for her after all!

*Spiteful little bitch*, Ruby thought resentfully as she once again set about putting everything away. Miranda had clearly done it on purpose but all Ruby could do was grin and bear it.

It took some time and she was just finishing when Miranda breezed in with a nasty smile on her face. 'I changed my mind about what to wear and didn't know where you'd put everything so I had to get it all out again,' she said with a smirk. 'I *do* hope I haven't made you miss breakfast.'

'Don't worry about it, miss, I'm sure Cook will rustle something up for me,' Ruby forced herself to say calmly, and without another word she left the room closing the door quietly behind her.

'Ah, here you are.' Cook raised an eyebrow as Ruby stormed into the kitchen. 'What kept you? Everyone else has eaten, but don't worry I kept some food warm for you.' She hurried to the oven and returned with a plateful of fried black pudding, bacon, sausage and eggs.

Ruby gave her a grateful smile as she took a seat at the table and told her what Miranda had done.

'Hm, it don't surprise me a bit.' Cook wiped her hands down her apron. 'She'd have done that just to rile you, but don't rise to her bait.'

'I'm trying not to but I feel like slapping her,' Ruby admitted as she speared a tasty forkful of bacon into her mouth. She was not normally a vindictive girl, she had never had cause to be, but it was obvious that Miranda was doing everything she could to annoy her and it seemed so pointless.

As soon as she had eaten, she made her way back upstairs to see if Miranda wanted anything else doing and she had just entered the hallway when a tall gentleman with grey hair who looked to be in his early forties came out of the drawing room. He stopped abruptly when he caught sight of her, but then forcing a smile he said, 'Ah, you must be Ruby. Miranda said she had a new maid. I hope she is treating you well? I am Miranda's father.'

'Hello, sir.' Ruby bobbed her knee blushing under his close scrutiny.

'Miranda informs me that you are from Nuneaton?'

Ruby nodded. 'Yes, sir.'

'So, what brings you to Birmingham?'

'Er . . . my mother died.' Ruby didn't wish to tell him more than that but he seemed to accept it.

'I see, I'm very sorry to hear it.'

She squirmed as he continued to stare at her for a time before asking, 'And how old are you, Ruby?'

'I was fifteen in December, sir.'

He nodded. 'Very well, do go on with what you were doing. Oh, and try not to mind Miranda's bossy ways, my dear. I'm afraid her mother rather spoils her.'

Ruby didn't quite know how to respond to this so she merely smiled and scuttled away up the stairs like a cat with its tail on fire. There was something about the way Mr Pembroke had looked at her that she found quite unnerving.

She didn't have long to think about it, though, because as soon as she reached Miranda's room the girl snapped at her, 'Go and get your coat on. I want to go for a stroll around the park and get some fresh air but I'm not allowed to go alone so you'll have to come with me.'

'Yes, miss.' Ruby's heart sank as she thought of the old coat she had arrived in. She had left the one that Maddie had bought for her behind and she could just imagine how Miranda would mock her when she saw it. But it was the only one she owned so she went and put it on.

Just as she had thought Miranda's eyebrows rose into her hairline when she arrived back at her room. 'Is that the best coat you have?' she sneered.

'I'm afraid so, miss.' Ruby stared back at her.

'Ah well.' Miranda sniggered as she tugged her warm kid gloves on. 'At least everyone will know you're my maid dressed like that. Just make sure you walk a few steps behind me.' She herself was wearing a beautiful dark-green coat trimmed with black braid and a matching hat that Ruby guessed must have cost a small fortune.

They set off, although as yet Ruby had no idea where they were heading, and eventually turned into some gates that led into a large park with an enormous duck pond in the centre of it. Miranda headed for the water and Ruby was careful to walk well behind her but suddenly the girl stopped and snapped, 'Can't you keep up with me or something?'

'But you told me to walk behind you!'

'I've changed my mind. Come and walk beside me. And it's "miss" remember!'

Ruby felt vaguely uncomfortable. She didn't trust Miranda as far as she could throw her, although she didn't yet know her very well, but she did as she was told and for some time they walked on in silence, admiring a family of ducks that were swimming serenely on the surface of the lake. Then suddenly Miranda stuck her foot out and before she could stop herself Ruby tripped over it and sprawled into the water. She clambered out, wet and bedraggled, as Miranda laughed helplessly.

'You did that on *purpose*,' Ruby muttered as tears of humiliation stung her eyes and she tried to wring the water from her sodden, muddy skirt.

'Of *course* I didn't, you're just clumsy,' Miranda responded and turning she set off for home with a spiteful smile on her face. For a moment Ruby stood there watching her go with her hands clenched. Miranda was a spoilt, selfish brat and for two pins she could have turned and walked in the opposite direction. But then the little voice of reason kicked in and asked, '*But where would you go?*' And the answer came back, '*You have nowhere!*' So, with a heavy sigh, she set off behind her new mistress, her boots squelching with every step she took.

When she entered the kitchen, dripping mud all over Cook's clean floor, the woman stared at her in horror. 'What the hell has happened to you?' she gasped.

Shamefaced, Ruby stared at the floor as she muttered, 'I, er . . . tripped by the side of the lake and fell in.'

'Hm, and a purple pig just flew past the window,' Cook retorted angrily. 'It were that little madam that pushed you weren't it?'

'Well . . . she didn't exactly *push* me,' Ruby said in a small voice. 'But she stuck her foot out and I tripped over it. I'm sorry about the mess.'

Cook clucked her tongue in annoyance. 'This ain't the first time she's done this,' she confided angrily. 'She did exactly the same to the last little maid she had. The poor girl only stuck it for two weeks. You should have pushed her back. It's about time somebody gave her some comeuppance and I'd love to be the one to do it an' all!' Then seeing how distressed Ruby was her face gentled. 'Why don't you go and get cleaned up and change your gown, then come down and I'll make you a nice cup of tea. I

103

suppose we should just be grateful that she didn't hurt you, the little minx. But I shall be having a word with Miss Wood about this, never you fear.'

Half an hour later Ruby was back downstairs with her sodden boots in her hand and her filthy dress over her arm.

'I shall have to let these dry by the fire,' she told Cook. 'And I'm afraid I shall have to go barefoot till they dry. I only have the one pair.'

'Don't worry about that, I'm sure we can find you something to wear,' the woman told her kindly. 'Take that dress along to the laundry room outside then come and have this hot drink. Let's just hope you haven't caught your death of cold!'

When Ruby returned, she found Cook telling Miss Wood what had happened and the housekeeper looked none too pleased. 'I'm so sorry about this, Ruby,' she apologised. 'You can be sure I shall tell Mrs Pembroke what she did.'

'Huh! An' a fat lot o' good that'll do,' Cook snorted in disgust. 'That girl gets away wi' blue murder, so she does. All the mistress will do is ask her not to do it again and send her on her way. Seems to me the young miss can do as she likes as long as she keeps out of her mother's way.'

'Yes, well, I can but try,' Miss Wood answered with an apologetic smile at Ruby. Thankfully the subject was dropped when the bell from the mistress's room tinkled.

Betty, who had just sat down for a well-earned tea break, gave an exasperated sigh. 'Crikey! What does she want *now*,' she groaned. 'She's had me runnin' up an' down them bleedin' stairs all day!'

'Language, young lady,' Miss Wood scolded and looking suitably chastened, Betty hurried upstairs again.

When Miss Wood followed her soon after, Ruby asked, 'So what's wrong with the mistress, Cook? You said she's an invalid?'

'Huh! If you can call her that.' Cook shook her head as she rolled the pastry for an apple pie she was making. 'Between you an' me, I imagine young Mr Pembroke rues the day he ever met her. Women like her should never get married. She comes from a very wealthy family and was spoilt rotten by her parents. It was clear from the day they wed that she didn't like . . . shall we say, certain aspects of married life? Which was why we were all shocked when the young master told us they were expecting a child. Admittedly she had a difficult birth with Miss Miranda, but after that she insisted the young master move out of her room. She told him that if she were to have another child, she feared it would kill her, and as far as we can gather, she's never lain with him since. Poor man. She took to her bed soon after Miranda was born and she's had the whole household running around after her like headless chickens ever since. I don't know how the young master puts up with it; he certainly isn't happy.'

She flushed, realising that she might have said too much, so Ruby took her mug to the sink, rinsed it and went upstairs to see if Miranda needed anything. *One thing's for certain,* she thought, *this isn't a happy household but for now I'll just have to put up with things and hope they improve.*

# Chapter Eleven

Two days later when Ruby went into the kitchen early in the afternoon she found Mrs Petty sitting at the table with Cook, and her face lit up at the sight of her.

'Mrs Petty!' She flung herself into the woman's arms, almost making her drop the cup of tea she was holding.

Mrs Petty laughed as she placed it down on the table and hugged her. 'Hello, bab. I thought I'd call in an' see how you were settlin' in and Cook here tells me you're doin' just fine.'

Ruby was so pleased to see her that she had to blink to hold back tears as she asked, 'Is Maddie all right? And Nell?'

'They're both fine,' Mrs Petty assured her as she brushed a stray tear from her cheek with her thumb. 'But how are you? Standin' up to that spoilt little madam, are you?'

Ruby shrugged. Miranda was getting no easier. But she was presently having a piano lesson so at least she had a little respite from her for a time. 'I'm fine.' Her voice held no conviction and Mrs Petty frowned. She wasn't at all happy with having to bring her here but it had been the best she could do at short notice so poor Ruby was going to have to stick it out for now.

'I'll leave you two to have a bit of a chat,' Cook said obligingly as she pottered off to start peeling the potatoes for the evening meal and Ruby took a seat.

'Was Maddie very angry at you for slipping me away as you did?' she asked worriedly.

Mrs Petty grinned. 'Well, let's just say she were none too pleased but she'll get over it.' She could hardly admit that Maddie had ranted and raved at her for a solid hour when she discovered that Ruby was gone, could she? Even so, she had no regrets. She adored Maddie as if she were her own daughter but she had recognised very quickly that Ruby was not the sort of girl for the life Maddie had in mind for her, and so to her way of thinking she had been left with no choice.

'Does she know where I am?' Ruby sounded fearful.

Mrs Petty was quick to reassure her. 'She ain't got a clue where you've gone, so stop worrying and tell me what you've been up to.'

'Just running around after Miss Miranda mainly. But I do get a break when her tutor comes for three hours each morning. Then twice a week she has piano lessons in the afternoons – she's quite good actually – and then she has a singing lesson on another afternoon.' She gave Mrs Petty a cheeky grin. 'She's not so good at that, to be honest. In fact, she's awful, although I wouldn't dare to tell her that.'

Mrs Petty chuckled as she lifted her cup of tea again. The next half-hour passed quickly until Mrs Petty glanced at the clock and quickly stood up, saying, 'Right, I must be off. I've a good walk ahead o' me an' the dinner to organise when I get back. Oh, an' before I forget, Nell wants to know if she may come and see you, perhaps on Sunday afternoon when you've got free time?'

'Oh, yes please.' Ruby's eyes shone at the thought of seeing her friend again. Minutes later, after giving Ruby a quick peck on the cheek, Mrs Petty was gone.

With mixed emotions Ruby began to make her way upstairs to tidy Miranda's room again. She was finding that she sometimes had to do it at least three or four times a day. She knew that Miranda simply threw her clothes about to annoy her but as yet she'd managed not to say anything, although there had been times when she had come dangerously close to it. The fact that Miranda had started to give her spiteful little pinches as she passed her didn't help, but again she'd been able to control her temper, although she didn't know how much longer she'd be able to. She was passing the door to the day room where Miranda was having her piano lesson when it was suddenly flung open and Miranda appeared, red in the face with rage.

'I did *not* get the notes wrong!' she raged across her shoulder to the poor music teacher she had left sitting beside the piano. 'And that's it for today. I've had enough!' She barged past Ruby so quickly that the poor girl was sent flying just as Miranda's father appeared in the doorway of his study with a frown on his face.

'Whatever is going on here?' One glance at Ruby sprawled across the hall floor and Miranda stamping towards the stairs told him all he needed to know and his lips set in a grim line as he ordered, 'Miranda! Come here this *instant*!'

Unused to being told off, the older girl scowled and reluctantly turned back to him. '*What?*'

'Don't talk to me like that, young lady. Just what do you think you are doing?'

Miranda stared back at him defiantly so he turned his attention to Ruby, asking, 'Did my daughter just knock you over, my dear?'

'I, er . . .' Ruby felt her cheeks flame as she scrambled up from the floor.

'It's all right, you don't need to say anything. I saw enough to know what went on. Ruby, go about your business. And you, Miranda, get in here immediately! I will not have such behaviour in my house, do you hear me?'

With a glare at Ruby, Miranda stormed past her father and when the door had closed behind them, Ruby let out a deep breath. Mr Pembroke might think he was doing her a kindness in correcting his daughter but Ruby knew that it would be her that paid for it eventually.

Betty appeared in the drawing room doorway then, and cocking her head over her shoulder she told Ruby, 'The mistress would like to see you.' Her eyes seemed to be flashing a warning and Ruby's stomach turned over. Even so she straightened her dress and with what dignity she could muster followed Betty into the room. At a glance she saw that, like the rest of the house, this room was beautiful but she had no time to admire it for her eyes were drawn to the woman who reclined on a chaise longue by the fire beneath layers of blankets, and she blinked with surprise. If this was Miranda's mother, she was nothing at all as she had expected her to be. She was grotesquely overweight and her fat fingers were so weighed down with rings containing stones all the colours of the rainbow that Ruby was surprised she could lift them. A box of sweetmeats was open beside her and her cheeks were heavily rouged, making her appear much older than she surely was. Her hair was fair and intricately curled and her gown was quite beautiful, although it was straining across her ample chest.

'So, you are Miranda's new maid,' she said, eyeing Ruby up and down with an expression that suggested there was a dirty smell beneath her nose. 'And what was all that noise in the hall just now? I heard Miranda shouting. Have you upset her?'

Ruby gulped. 'No, ma'am. I think she was shouting at her music teacher.'

Mrs Pembroke raised a delicately plucked eyebrow. 'Very well, send her in to me immediately. If he has upset her, I shall see that he is dismissed.'

'She is in with her father at present.'

'What? Whatever for? Go and tell them both that I wish to see them in here straightaway.'

Ruby bobbed her knee and shot away and seconds later she was tapping on the study door to pass on Mrs Pembroke's message.

Mr Pembroke nodded and ushered Miranda, who was clearly in a sulk, in front of him as Ruby scuttled back to the kitchen. The next minute the master and the mistress's voices could be heard all over the house.

In the drawing room Mr Pembroke faced his wife, his eyes blazing as Miranda stood pouting. Unused to seeing him that way, his wife's eyes filled with tears. 'Why, darling, whatever is the matter?' she simpered.

'Our *daughter* is the matter!' He glared at Miranda who glared back at him. 'I think perhaps it's time you taught her a few manners!'

'But whatever do you mean, Oscar? If you're talking about the little altercation that just took place in the hallway, I did hear it, but I'm sure it wasn't Miranda's fault.'

'*Huh!*' He was struggling to contain his temper. 'And what would you know about it? I saw what occurred and she pushed the young maid over with no provocation from the girl whatsoever. It seems to me that as long as you don't have to spend any time with Miranda, you're happy to let her do as she pleases. She only has to say what she wants and she gets it, and it has to stop. It's time she learnt some social skills, and she certainly isn't learning any from you.'

His wife began to whimper as she struggled to get her obese frame into a sitting position. As he watched he felt a wave of revulsion; there was a time when he had worshipped the very ground she walked on and he would have moved heaven and earth for her. She had been quite exquisitely beautiful when he had first met her and he had thought he was the luckiest man on earth when she had agreed to be his wife. Admittedly he had known that she had been spoilt and pampered by her parents, but then she had been the only child of a very wealthy family so he supposed that was to be expected. He had been only too happy to indulge her every whim and for a time they had been happy. Until she found that she was to have a child, and everything had changed. Looking back, he realised that she had never been keen on the physical side of their marriage, but immediately she found out she was pregnant she had barred him from her

111

bed saying that intimacies would be dangerous for the baby. He had been so naive back then that he had believed her, but after Miranda's birth things had got no better.

'You surely don't want to put me through all that again?' she had wailed each time he visited her room. 'Don't you realise I could have died having Miranda?'

Eventually guilt had kept him away. She had even refused to see the child for the first few weeks after she was born. And so it had continued. Miranda could have anything she wanted as long as she didn't bother her mother. Miss Wood had been more of a parent to her than his wife had been and now he had had enough.

'I think it's time we thought of sending her away to a finishing school,' he said coldly.

Miranda's eyes almost popped out of her head. 'But I don't want to go!' she protested, horrified, as her pudgy hands clamped into fists. It wasn't the first time her father had suggested it but this time he seemed set on the idea.

'Oh, darling, surely not.' Lydia's hand flew to her mouth. 'I-I couldn't bear it if you did that. *Please* give her one more chance. I'm sure she won't upset anyone again!'

Oscar Pembroke felt himself weakening, just as he always did. Even now Lydia could always make him feel guilty, as if somehow the reclusive state she had resorted to was his fault.

'Very well.' His shoulders sagged and his temper subsided as quickly as it had come. 'But only one more chance, mind you,' he warned. 'Enough is enough. One more incident and I shall have no option but to send her away. Do you both understand?'

Their two heads nodded quickly in unison as he turned to leave the room. Suddenly the sight of them both sickened him and he just wanted to find sanctuary in his workshop.

In the kitchen they heard the door slam as he left the drawing room and Cook let out a sigh. 'Crikey, sounds like he really lost his temper,' she said. 'An' it sounds like that little madam is goin' to get her comeuppance if she don't start behavin' herself.'

Ruby chewed on her lip as she stared fearfully towards the door. She had no doubt that Mr Pembroke might have unwittingly made things worse for her. Miranda was sure to be out for revenge now and the thought made her stomach churn. She quietly stood up from her chair and made for the door; there was a pile of Miranda's clean washing that had just been ironed and needed putting away, and it wouldn't do itself.

She had just reached the door with it in her arms when Cook's voice stayed her. 'Don't you go puttin' up wi' any more nonsense from her now. Do you hear me? If she starts bein' spiteful again come an' tell me or Miss Wood straightaway an' we'll have a word wi' the master.'

Ruby realised Cook meant well but knowing Miranda as she did, she knew that things were probably set to get worse now, rather than better, and she went on her way with a heavy heart.

# Chapter Twelve

Although Miranda ignored Ruby completely for the next two days, she at least left her alone and Ruby was pleasantly surprised. And then at last it was Sunday and Ruby was looking forward to seeing Nell again and having a whole afternoon and evening to herself. She hurried through tidying Miranda's bedroom in the morning while Miranda was at church with her father, then after brushing her hair into a neat plait and fetching her shawl, she sat anxiously watching the clock in the kitchen as she waited for Nell to arrive after lunch.

'You're like a cat on hot bricks.' Cook chuckled as she glanced towards her after lunch. Now that the family's meal was over, she was relaxing by the fire with a glass of stout in her hand and her tabby cat curled on her lap. Betty had told Ruby that when Cook had first adopted the cat as a kitten the mistress had strongly objected to having it in the house, saying that she was allergic to animals. But Cook had gone to the master saying that she needed the animal to keep down the risk of rodents in the kitchen, and promising to restrict him to that room, and so he had given his permission to keep it. The staff all knew that Cook secretly adored the cat and they also knew that it was far too fat and spoilt to catch rodents, but even so he had become a favourite with everyone.

At last there was a tap at the door and there she was. Ruby hurried out to greet her with a broad smile on her face and Nell gave her a hug, asking, 'So how are things, kid?'

Ruby's face clouded as she shrugged. 'Not too bad, although Miranda can be rather spiteful. But tell me all about how things are back at the house.' She tucked her arm into Nell's but before the girl could answer, they turned the corner of the house and Ruby's face lit up as she saw Bill waiting there.

Nell chuckled. 'We thought we'd come together an' surprise you,' she told her.

Bill self-consciously ruffled Ruby's hair. 'It's nice to see you again, kid,' he told her. 'But where can we go to get outta this wind? It's enough to slice you in two.'

'There's a park not far away with a bandstand, we could go there,' Ruby suggested, leading the way.

The park was deserted and soon they were settled on the floor of the bandstand and although it was still bitterly cold at least they were sheltered from the wind.

'How is your mum?' Ruby asked Bill.

He shook his head. 'Not good, to be honest. She's got a hacking cough and she really needs to see a doctor but she won't hear of it; says they're too expensive.'

'Well, I've got a little bit of money tucked away from when I left home, you're welcome to that,' Ruby offered kindly.

Bill shook his head again. 'Thanks, but we'll manage.' He was fiercely independent and it went against the grain to take money from a girl, especially one as young as Ruby. 'As long as I can keep Mom warm an' fed an' make enough to pay the rent we'll be fine.'

Ruby couldn't help but smile. She was still getting used to the way the Brummies always referred to their mothers as mom, rather than mum or mam as they did back in her hometown, but then they had a lot of sayings that she was having to get used to. 'And how is Maddie?' she asked. 'When Mrs Petty called to see me the other day, she said that she was very angry when I left.'

'Angry don't come close to it,' Nell admitted with a wry grin. 'She near on blew her bleedin' top when she got up to find you gone, but she's calmed down now. Mrs Petty only did what she did 'cause she knew you weren't cut out for the life Maddie had in mind for you.'

Ruby felt a pang of disappointment. She had hoped that Maddie would be angry because she missed her. Surely if she was her mother, she would have done? But she had to stop thinking of that now and so she went on to tell them about some of the spiteful tricks Miranda had played on her.

'You need to give as good as you get an' she'll soon bloody stop,' Bill chided. He hated to think of her being bullied.

Ruby sighed. 'That's what Cook said, but it's easier said than done.' She wrapped her arms about herself as she shook her head. 'She's so much bigger than me for a start off.'

Bill wagged a finger at her. 'That don't matter. You know what they say: "The bigger they are the harder they fall." And bullies don't like a taste o' their own medicine, so next time she starts, give her a good old kick in the shins.'

Ruby grinned at the thought. 'I think she might behave after the episode a couple of days ago when she sent me flying. Her father saw her do it an' he told her that if she did anything again, he'd send her away to a finishin' school.'

'Huh! Best place for her an' all,' Nell said grumpily.

They went on to talk of what they'd each been up to and all too soon the afternoon began to darken and a slow drizzle started to fall. Glancing at the sky, Nell said, 'We ought to be goin'. We've got a good old walk ahead of us an' we're goin' to get soaked judgin' by that sky.'

So they hauled themselves back to their feet, feeling stiff after sitting on the cold boards of the bandstand for so long. At the gates of the park Nell gave Ruby a quick peck on the cheek. 'You look after yourself now, bab, an' we'll come an' see you again soon as ever we can, won't we, Bill?'

'Aye, we will.' He grinned as he again ruffled Ruby's red curls and then they were off, leaving Ruby to make her way back to the house feeling suddenly very lonely. So very much had happened in such a short space of time. She had lost the woman she had always thought of as her mother, her father had raped her, she had run away from home to be befriended by Maddie, who Ruby still secretly hoped was her real mother, but seeing as the woman didn't even seem to miss her, she was beginning to have her doubts, and now here she was working as a maid in a big house. It was all so much to take in.

'Ooh, you look perished,' Cook said when she stepped into the kitchen a short time later, letting in a blast of icy, damp air. 'Get over here by the fire an' get warm else you'll catch your death o' cold.'

Ruby willingly did as she was told as she unwound the damp shawl from her shoulders and placed her sodden boots in front of the fire to dry, then she sat watching the staff rushing about as they prepared the family's evening meal. Sunday was the only night of the week when they had a light meal having had a cooked meal at lunchtime, and tonight Cook had prepared them a large bowl of salad, cold cuts of meat left over from lunch and a selection of pickles along with a pork pie, hard-boiled eggs, a large crusty loaf and a fancy plate full of dainty cakes she had baked that afternoon.

'That should keep 'em happy for a while,' she said with satisfaction as Betty rushed the last of the meal through to the dining room. 'I'll just have a nice cup o' tea an' then I'll see about gettin' us lot fed.'

Cook made them all tasty sandwiches for tea but Ruby found that she couldn't eat a thing and wondered if perhaps she had caught a chill. With this in mind she excused herself as soon as the meal was over and decided on an early night, and within minutes of snuggling down beneath the cold sheets, she was fast asleep.

She woke early the next morning feeling ill and for the first time since she had been there, she hooked the chamber pot from beneath the bed and was violently sick into it, waking Betty.

'Crikey, looks like you've eaten somethin' that disagreed with you,' Betty commented as she swiped the sleep from her eyes. Then glancing at the dark window and realising that it was still very early, she turned over and went back to sleep again.

118

'You look a bit peaky, are you feelin' unwell?' Cook asked kindly when Ruby went downstairs sometime later to prepare a breakfast tray for Miranda who had come down with a cold and had decided to have breakfast in bed.

'I was sick when I woke up,' Ruby answered innocently. 'But I feel all right now. I think I must have got Miss Miranda's cold.'

Cook was stirring a large pan of porridge on the stove and gave her a funny look but then shook her head before going back to what she had been doing. Morning sickness usually meant one thing, but then she told herself, Ruby was as innocent as they came and not much more than a child herself so it couldn't be that, and she pushed the thought to the back of her mind.

However, when the same thing happened the following morning, her fears were raised again and she asked softly, 'Have you started your monthly courses yet, bab?'

Ruby nodded and pulled a face. 'Yes, I started them a few months ago just before my mam . . .' She bit her lip and blinked back tears as she thought of the woman she had loved. 'They're horrible but me mam told me all girls have them.'

'She was quite right.' Cook nodded. 'And do you have them regular like?'

Ruby paused in the act of loading Miranda's tray. She was staying in bed for breakfast again, which Ruby guessed would probably mean another day of her running up and down the stairs to wait on her. 'I, er, don't think I have had one for a while, now I come to think of it,' she said thoughtfully. 'Is that normal?'

119

'Oh, I'm sure it is if you've not long started,' Cook assured her, but she was gravely concerned. Could it be that this girl wasn't as innocent as she had thought? Only time would tell.

At the mistress's insistence, the doctor called to see Miranda later that morning and Ruby stood outside the bedroom door while he examined her. 'Not much wrong with her,' he told Miss Wood and Ruby. 'She's just got a chill. Keep her warm and make sure she drinks plenty of liquids and she should be right as rain in a day or two.'

Miss Wood followed him downstairs to show him out as Ruby went into the bedroom to see if there was anything that Miranda wanted. The second she stepped through the door, the girl snapped peevishly, 'Go and get me a jug of lemonade *immediately*, and make sure it's cold. The doctor told me I'm *very* ill and must drink plenty of liquids.'

Ruby knew she was exaggerating but she whisked off to do as she was told just the same. The rest of the day followed much the same pattern with Ruby rushing here and there collecting books, magazines and anything else Miranda demanded to keep her occupied and by evening Ruby was exhausted.

'Hm, I notice the mistress were worried enough to call the doctor in to her but not worried enough to get off her fat arse an' go an' see her,' Cook commented as she lifted a large leg of pork out of the oven. 'She ain't no better; she's had poor Susie runnin' up an' down the stairs for her all day. I tell yer, there ain't a lot wrong wi' neither of 'em.'

Ruby grinned. Poor Mr Pembroke would be dining alone this evening but then she supposed he was used to it by now;

in fact, he probably preferred it. At least he wouldn't have to listen to his wife and daughter moaning about something or another, poor chap.

After the master had been served, the staff sat down to eat a rather delicious fish pie that Cook had made, but as soon as Ruby smelled it she clapped her hand across her mouth and rushed outside to the lavatory.

'Looks like she's comin' down with the bug an' all,' Betty said innocently as she tucked into her meal – Cook made the best fish pie she had ever tasted.

'Aye, you could be right,' Cook answered but she was growing seriously concerned now. So much so that she decided she'd have a word on the quiet with Miss Wood when she got the chance.

It finally came much later that evening when the rest of the staff had retired to bed and Miss Wood came into the kitchen to fill her stone hot-water bottle. She was clad in her dressing robe with her hair in a long plait over one shoulder and she looked surprised to see Cook was still up.

'Why, I thought you'd be all tucked into bed by now,' she said pleasantly as she picked up the kettle, which was softly singing on the hob, to fill her bottle.

'I would have been.' Cook crossed the room to peer into the hallway to make sure they were alone and closed the door firmly before telling Miss Wood of her concerns. The woman's eyes stretched wide and she lifted her hand to finger the lace about her throat.

'Surely not, Cook!' She looked horrified. 'Why, Ruby is only a child herself and she certainly doesn't seem to be the sort to be fast and loose with her favours. In fact, if asked

I'd have said she probably doesn't even know about . . . you know, the birds and the bees yet.'

'I would have said the same,' Cook agreed. 'But I've seen the symptoms wi' me own eyes. The question is, what do we do about it? I don't want to lose her, she's a good little worker an' nice to have about the place.'

Miss Wood stared thoughtfully into space for a while, tapping her lip with her forefinger, before finally saying, 'Let's do nothing for now, eh? Let's just watch and see what happens and hope you're mistaken.'

Cook nodded reluctantly. She didn't think she was mistaken and she couldn't help worrying about what was to come, but for now she would do as Miss Wood suggested, although she would be keeping a close eye on little Ruby.

# Chapter Thirteen

Early in March, much to everyone's relief, the weather began to improve and suddenly the trees were showing tiny, tender green shoots, and daffodils and primroses began to peep from beneath the hedges.

Miranda had now made a full recovery from her cold, although it hadn't improved her temper and she continued to be spiteful. Ruby was quite proud of the fact that as yet she had been able to put up with her sulks and tantrums, especially as she wasn't feeling well herself. Admittedly the awful sickness she had been experiencing each morning had eased but now her breasts were sore and tender and she felt tired all the time. Even so she still did all that was asked of her and one morning while Miranda was in with her tutor, Cook asked her, 'You couldn't take this tray o' coffee through to the master's workshop for me, could you, bab?' Betty would usually do this, but she had gone to do some shopping for Cook, so Ruby was the only person she could ask.

'The workshop?' Ruby frowned. 'But I thought no one but the master himself was allowed in there.' The thought of taking coffee to Mr Pembroke made her nervous, but she was also a little excited at the prospect of seeing the workshop.

'They ain't when he's not there,' Cook admitted with a smile. 'But I reckon he'll be glad to let you in wi' a tray o' coffee an' biscuits. So go on, get off with you.'

Ruby obediently lifted the tray and carefully carried it along the long hallway to a door at the far end. Balancing it in one hand she knocked on the door. 'Come in,' a voice said, and when she entered the room her eyes grew wide. There were all sorts of pieces of machinery everywhere and the master was leaning across a worktop scattered with partially completed pieces of jewellery set with gems that glistened in the weak March sunshine that shone through the window and cast rainbows across the ceilings and the walls. Ruby was so taken with the kaleidoscope of colours that she just stood there with her mouth open.

'Good morning, Ruby.'

Mr Pembroke's voice broke the spell and she started, almost dropping the tray before she said nervously, 'I, er . . . I brought you your coffee, sir.'

'And very welcome it will be.' He gave her a cheerful smile. 'Just pop it down on that little table there, would you?'

'Yes, sir.' She quickly did as she was told but instead of immediately leaving, she crossed to the worktop and stared down at the jewellery in awe.

The master removed his eye glass and ordered, 'Open your hand.'

Ruby did as she was told and he dropped a glittering stone into it.

'That,' he told her, 'is one of the finest Brazilian emeralds I have ever seen. Just look at that colour. What does it remind you of?'

'Grass, sir, when it's been raining and it's all shiny and clean.'

He laughed as he took it back and reverently placed it back on the worktop. 'And very soon that will be set into a filigree gold mount. A very wealthy customer of mine has commissioned me to make her an emerald pendant and this stone was the finest I could find.'

'It's really beautiful,' Ruby breathed, and she meant it. She leant over to study a deep-blue stone. 'That is a sapphire, isn't it?'

He nodded approvingly. 'It certainly is. A Ceylon sapphire to be exact and very soon that will be set into a ring for another customer. Look, I have the mount almost ready for it.'

He lifted a fine gold band and Ruby smiled as she pictured the gem sparkling away in it. She had learnt a lot about jewels from the books she had read while staying with Maddie and she couldn't help but imagine Maddie's eyes greedily looking at the beautiful stones he was showing her.

He watched her face for a moment and then asked, 'Do you find this interesting?'

'Oh yes.' Ruby's face lit up. 'When I were younger workin' in me dad's baker's shop I never gave a thought to what I might want to do when I grew up but now I can't think of anything nicer than to work with beautiful gems making beautiful things that will give people pleasure.' She remembered who she was talking to then and blushing furiously she backed towards the door. 'I, er . . . I'd better go now. Miss Miranda will be finished her lessons and she'll wonder where I am.'

125

'Very well.' He gave her a smile and long after the door had shut behind her, he stood there with a thoughtful expression on his face.

Miranda had finished her lessons and unfortunately she was in a bad mood. She was in the drawing room with her mother and as Ruby passed the open door on the way back to the kitchen, she heard Miranda saying, 'But *why* do I have to have my piano lesson on such a nice day? I'd much sooner go out!'

'I know you would, darling, but you know what your father said. You've cancelled so many times lately and he is tired of having to pay for lessons you haven't had. We don't want to upset him again, do we?'

Miranda was so used to having her own way that she stamped her foot in temper before storming from the room and almost colliding with Ruby. 'Earwigging, were you?' she spat.

'N-no, I was just on my way to the kitchen,' Ruby mumbled.

'I have some jobs for you to do so you can come with me!' And with that Miranda flounced up the stairs.

Knowing that she had no choice, Ruby reluctantly followed her and found Miranda standing at her bedroom window staring down at the garden.

'Tidy up, then!' Miranda glared at her as Ruby stared around at the already tidy room.

'But I already tidied it this morning.'

'Really, then you didn't do a very good job of it. Do it again!' Miranda hurried to the drawer that contained all her pretty undergarments and before Ruby could say a word, she pulled it out and tossed the contents all over the floor, throwing the drawer after them.

Ruby stared at her for a moment, her hands clenched, but then without a word she replaced the drawer and began to lift the clothes and refold them as Miranda smirked. Inside, Ruby was crying. She had hoped that when Mrs Petty found her a position in this house, she would finally find peace but she didn't know how much longer she could cope with her young mistress's spiteful ways. She continued with what she was doing until Miranda's next words made her head jerk up to stare at her in horror.

'And would you have any idea where my amethyst ring has gone by any chance?' Miranda had seen the gentle way her father addressed Ruby and that, added to the fact that Ruby was so little and dainty while she herself was plump and plain, made her hate the girl all the more.

'No, I wouldn't!' Ruby stared at her, her face flushed with indignation. Miranda's jewellery box stood on her dressing table but Ruby had never once even opened the lid.

'Well, it's strange that you are the only one who has access to my room, isn't it?' Miranda's pale-blue eyes flashed with spite. 'Who else could have taken it?'

'Perhaps you've just mislaid it?'

'Hm, then you won't mind if I ask my father to let one of the maids search your room, will you? I'm sure he wouldn't want a thief living under our roof.'

Ruby opened her mouth to protest but immediately clamped it shut again as shame burnt through her. After what Maddie had made her do, she *was* a thief, albeit a reluctant one. Tears pricked at the back of her eyes and, humiliated, she nodded. 'Go ahead if you want. I've nothing to hide.'

Miranda snorted with satisfaction as she headed for the door and once on the landing, she shouted down the stairs, 'Betty! Come here immediately.'

There were footsteps on the stairs and Betty, who had just arrived back at the house, appeared looking flummoxed. 'Yes, miss?'

'I want you to go and thoroughly search Ruby's room,' Miranda ordered. 'An item of my jewellery has gone missing and I believe that she has taken it.'

Betty looked shocked. After sharing a room with Ruby since her arrival she had grown fond of her. The girl wouldn't say boo to a goose and certainly didn't seem the sort to steal, but she was in no position to tell Miranda that so she merely nodded.

'Very well, miss. And may I ask what's missin'?'

'No, you may not. If it's there you'll find it, now go and get on with it this instant.'

Miss Wood appeared in the doorway and glancing at the clothes strewn about the floor, she asked, 'Whatever is going on in here? I can hear the shouting from downstairs and your father is in his workshop trying to work, Miss Miranda.'

With a smug expression on her face, Miranda pointed at Ruby. 'I believe she has stolen an item of jewellery from me and I've ordered Betty to go and search her room.'

'I see.' Miss Wood joined her hands and pressed them into her waist as she stared at Miranda coldly, then with a nod to Betty, she told her, 'Go ahead and do as she asks, please.'

Clearly reluctant, Betty scuttled away, but as Miranda made to follow her, Miss Wood held her hand up. 'I'm sure she can manage quite well on her own, Miss Miranda. We'll just wait here, shall we?'

As the minutes ticked away, Ruby's heart began to thud but at last they heard Betty returning and soon she appeared in the doorway. 'It's not in our room, miss. You must have mislaid it.'

Miranda's face was a picture as colour flooded into her cheeks. 'B-but it must be there! Who else could have taken it? Have you looked beneath her mattress and her pillow?'

Betty inclined her head. 'Yes, miss, and everywhere else I could think of.'

'I didn't take *anything* from her,' Ruby told them with a wobble in her voice. 'I *swear* it.'

'Then let's just wait until it turns up, shall we? You have clearly misplaced it.' Miss Wood held her hand out to Ruby but Miranda wasn't finished yet.

'I shall go and look *myself*,' she declared and barged past Miss Wood with a thunderous expression on her face.

As soon as she had gone, Betty opened her hand to expose the ring in her palm. 'I saw the little madam sneakin' into our room this mornin' before she went down to breakfast,' she confided. 'I wondered at the time what she was doin', an' then when she asked if I'd looked under the mattress or the pillow, I knew she'd planted it there to get Ruby into

129

trouble. It's not the first time she's got a maid dismissed by pullin' this trick.' Crossing to Miranda's jewellery box she dropped the ring into it just as they heard Miranda stamping back along the landing.

'Why don't we check your jewellery box?' Miss Wood said calmly. 'You have so many lovely pieces you might just have overlooked it.'

'I have not,' Miranda spat. 'She's taken it, I tell you.'

Ignoring her, Miss Wood crossed to the ornate box and, opening it, she pretended to look closely inside before lifting the amethyst ring out. 'Is this the one you thought was missing, miss?'

Miranda's mouth gaped slackly open with shock but then her face twisted with rage. 'It *wasn't* there, I tell you!'

Miss Wood and Betty stared back at her.

'Well, all is well that ends well,' Miss Wood told her. 'It's very easy to overlook one piece when you have so many. Now, I suggest we all get back to work.' And with that she turned and left the room with Betty close behind her.

Once they had gone, Ruby cringed as Miranda rounded on her. She was almost beside herself with rage knowing that her little trick had backfired and for a moment Ruby feared that she was going to hit her, but then she turned on her heel and stormed out of the room, slamming the door so resoundingly behind her that it danced on its hinges.

Once alone, Ruby began to cry. She had no idea why Miranda appeared to hate her so much. She had always done everything that was asked of her but now she realised that her days there might well be numbered. And then where would she go? She could never go back to the man she had thought was her father, nor to Maddie's – she hadn't even been to see her once since she'd been there, so clearly she didn't miss her or care about how she was – so once again her future was uncertain and it was a terrifying thought.

# Chapter Fourteen

Downstairs in the workshop, Miss Wood briefly told Mr Pembroke what had happened upstairs, although she didn't enlighten him to the fact that Miranda had planted the ring in Ruby's room, merely that she had accused her of stealing it when it had been in her jewellery box all along.

He frowned. 'I see. It appears that my daughter is too quick to jump to conclusions. Would you like me to have a word with her?'

Miss Wood shook her head. 'No, I think that may only make matters worse. For some reason, Miss Miranda seems to have taken a dislike to Ruby, although I have found her to be a very willing little worker. I am only telling you what occurred in case you should hear it from someone else.'

'You did quite right, thank you, Serena.' Miss Wood had worked for him and his wife since soon after they were married and had proved herself to be invaluable. She ran the house like clockwork and nothing was ever too much trouble for her, so over the years they had grown to be familiar with each other when out of earshot of the other staff. 'I appreciate you keeping me informed but it might be as well if you don't mention this to Lydia. You know what she's like, she'll only blame Ruby, even though the ring is safe.'

'Of course.' Miss Wood inclined her head and left the room, but once in the corridor her hand rose to her throat. Once, a long time ago, she had been engaged to be married but sadly her fiancé had met with an accident and been killed, so soon after she had taken on the job of housekeeper to the newly-wed couple. Oscar and Lydia had seemed so happy at the start but things had changed drastically when Lydia had discovered she was to have a child and their marriage seemed to have spiralled downhill ever since. Looking back, Serena couldn't remember when it was that she had first started to develop feelings for him, yet now it seemed as if she had loved him forever, although she knew that nothing could ever come of it. Oscar was loyal and even though his marriage was now a farce, Serena Wood knew that he would never leave his wife. Even so, it was enough just to be near him and to try and make his life as comfortable as she possibly could. After taking a deep breath to compose herself she hurried along to the kitchen to discuss the day's menus with Cook, but she had an awful feeling that things weren't over with Miranda and Ruby yet, not by a long shot. Miranda was a vindictive little madam and one way or another Miss Wood was sure she would find a way to make Ruby suffer.

'So what's this I hear about that little maid stealing Miranda's ring?' Lydia Pembroke asked her husband later that day when she finally decided to come down to the drawing room for an hour or two.

Oscar Pembroke was reading a newspaper and he scowled. 'Ruby never stole the ring. It was in Miranda's jewellery box all along if she'd only cared to look properly for it!'

Lydia sniffed as she plonked onto the chaise longue. This wasn't the first time her husband had been short with her lately and it was all over that little chit of a girl again.

'I don't know why you have to be so protective of a common little maid,' Lydia whined as she helped herself to a sweetmeat and popped it into her mouth. As she chewed her double chins wobbled and Oscar frowned.

'Miranda really hasn't taken to the girl. Perhaps we should think of dismissing her and getting her a new maid?'

'*Another* one!' He gave her a cold stare. 'And how many will that be? She finds fault with every one that comes. No, this time she'll have to get used to the girl. I've spoken to Miss Wood about the situation and from what she tells me Ruby has done nothing to warrant Miranda's dislike. To be honest, I don't think we will ever find anyone that suits her!'

'Oh, Oscar . . . don't be cross with me.' Lydia's eyes filled with tears as she pouted. 'I can't understand why you are so defensive of the girl. She's only a *maid* after all.'

'Even maids have feelings,' he pointed out shortly. 'And I'm growing tired of Miranda's tantrums. I still think it would do her the world of good to attend a finishing school.'

Just as before, Lydia looked horrified at the mention of such a place, and yet he found it hard to understand why. It wasn't as if she ever spent any time with the girl. In fairness to himself, he had tried to. He'd hoped that Miranda might develop the same fascination for precious stones as he had and that she would join him in the family business, but as he had soon discovered, Miranda wasn't remotely interested in anything that involved work. Like her mother, she thought it was her right to be waited on hand and foot and to be spoilt rotten. He supposed he was partly to blame there. He should have put his foot down with Lydia years ago but she was too set in her ways to change now.

'Well, I don't like her!' Lydia declared. 'I think she has a sly look about her.'

Screwing the newspaper up he flung it aside and bounced out of the chair. 'Ruby is little more than a child,' he said angrily. 'And from what I've been told she's recently lost her mother so perhaps you should try to be a little more compassionate. But now I'm going out. I shan't be dining here this evening; I'll have dinner at my club.' And with that he strode away leaving Lydia with a frown on her face.

So now there would be just Miranda and herself for dinner because her father-in-law was ill in bed, but then it did have its compensations: there would be all the more for her. She so hated the way Oscar looked at her every time she took a second helping. Picking up a magazine, she popped another sweetmeat into her mouth and settled down amongst the cushions.

'Don't look so glum, bab,' Cook said to Ruby later that evening. The chores for the day were done and the staff were having a well-earned cup of cocoa before retiring to bed. The elderly Mr Pembroke was quite poorly at present and confined to bed and they were all having to work extra hard to meet the demands of the mistress, Miranda, and now him; not that the old man could help it. Ruby hadn't met him yet but she'd heard the rest of the staff say that he was a kindly soul.

'I just wish I knew what I'd done to make her dislike me so much,' Ruby said with a sigh as she sat staring miserably into the fire.

'Just take a look in the mirror and that should give you your answer.' Cook took a sip of her cocoa then wiped the froth from her lip with the back of her hand. 'You're a pretty, dainty little thing whereas she . . . well, let's just say she's going the same way as her mother. It's unbelievable the amount o' food that miss can put away in one sittin'. She eats more than a grown man so it's no wonder she's runnin' to fat and gettin' spots.'

Betty chuckled; she loved it when Cook got on her high horse.

'I haven't thanked you yet for what you did earlier,' Ruby told Betty then. 'If it hadn't been for you and that ring had been found in our room, I would have got the sack, that's for sure.'

'Don't give it another thought. I guessed straightaway what the little madam were up to; she tried it before wi' one of her other maids. But what I will say is, you need to be on your guard now. She's a spiteful bitch an' I wouldn't put anythin' past her. Just make sure you come an' tell us or Miss Wood if she tries to hurt you.'

When Ruby flushed and looked down Betty frowned. 'She has been hurting you, hasn't she?' she said sharply.

'Not too much,' Ruby replied in a small voice and without a word she drew her sleeve up her arm.

Both Betty and Cook gasped with horror when they saw all the little bruises on Ruby's skin. The other arm when she revealed it was no better and neither were her lower legs when she showed them where Miranda had kicked out at her.

'She loses her temper very quickly and at the least little thing,' Ruby admitted miserably. 'If I don't do a job quickly enough, or even if she catches me looking at her, she lashes out.'

Cook's chest swelled to almost twice its already ample size as she drew in a deep breath. 'Why! This is absolutely bloody disgustin' an' you can bet I shall be havin' words wi' Miss Wood about it the first chance I get. That little minx has got to be stopped in her tracks afore she does you serious harm. But why have you been puttin' up with it? Why didn't you say somethin' afore?'

Ruby shrugged. 'I have nowhere else to go so I don't want to lose my job.' She rose from her seat and after raising a smile for them both she slowly headed off to bed. At least there she was safe from Miranda's spite.

Two days later, Ruby was carrying a load of Miranda's dirty washing along the hallway on her way to the laundry room when she met the elderly Mr Pembroke for the first time. Susie, Mrs Pembroke's lady's maid, was helping him downstairs so he could spend a little time in the drawing room as he was feeling slightly better and Ruby hastily stood to one side to allow them to pass. He stopped abruptly to peer at her through the steel-framed spectacles that were perched on the end of his nose, and Ruby felt as if she was looking at an older version of the younger master. They were very alike.

'And who are you then, m'dear?'

'I'm Ruby, sir . . . Miss Miranda's maid.'

'Are you now.' He stared at her for a few moments more then continued on his way, leaning heavily on his walking stick.

Ruby fled. There was something about the way he had stared at her that had unnerved her slightly, but there was no time to dwell on it. Miranda had ordered her to go straight upstairs to help her dress and she knew better than to disobey.

When she appeared in the room some minutes later, Miranda was sitting on the stool in front of her dressing table. 'Where the hell have you been?' she snapped. 'I thought you were just nipping to the laundry. You could have washed and ironed everything in the time you've taken!'

Ruby didn't bother to answer. She knew there would be no point, so she merely went to the bed and got Miranda's clothes ready for her.

It was at lunchtime when she heard Miss Wood talking to Cook in the kitchen and her ears pricked up.

'We have to find a new gardener-cum-handyman-cum-groom and quickly. Robert left yesterday without giving any notice and now that everything is growing again the gardens will be in a state in no time if we don't find someone quickly. The horses won't look after themselves neither. Mr Pembroke is seein' to them for the time bein'.'

'I think I know someone who might be able to help,' Ruby piped up before she could stop herself. 'My friend

Bill is looking for regular work and I'm sure he'd do a good job.'

'Really?' Miss Wood stared at her thoughtfully. 'And where does this friend of yours live?'

'I'm not sure exactly but Mrs Petty is coming to see me tomorrow and she could get word to him.'

'Very well, ask her to tell him to call and see me and we'll see if he's suitable.'

Ruby's heart gave a little flutter of excitement. She knew how hard Bill had been trying to find any sort of job that would enable him to look after his mother, and she was sure he'd jump at the chance of a permanent position. Suddenly she could hardly wait to see Mrs Petty the next day.

When Mrs Petty and Nell arrived the following afternoon, they both thought Ruby's idea was a brilliant one.

'Not that I think he'll have his mother to worry about fer much longer, she's in a right bad way,' Mrs Petty said sadly. 'But anyway, we'll make sure he gets the message, won't we, Nell?'

After that, all Ruby could do was keep her fingers crossed, excited at the thought that she might be able to get to know Bill a bit better. Though she'd only met him on a few occasions, whenever she saw him, life always seemed that little bit brighter.

It was almost a week later when Bill presented himself at the back door for his interview with Miss Wood, and as she stepped out into the yard to greet him, one look at his face told Ruby that something was wrong.

'Me mom passed away late last Sunday night,' he told her solemnly, his eyes bright with unshed tears. 'An' I buried her yesterday so I've nothin' to go backwards an' forwards for now, an' I was wonderin' if I got the position here if Miss Wood would let me live in.'

'I don't see why not. Robert had a room above the stables. But I'm so sorry about your mum, Bill.'

He shrugged. 'Well, it weren't entirely unexpected. She'd been ill for a long time, as you know. The trouble is, I used up what money we had to pay for the funeral so I won't be able to pay the rent on the rooms an' I'll be on the streets.'

'It doesn't matter if it was expected or not, she was still your mum,' Ruby said sympathetically. At least on that subject she could talk knowledgeably, having so recently lost her own mother, and although she didn't know Bill that well, she found him surprisingly easy to talk to. 'Come in and I'll let Miss Wood know that you're here. I think she was beginning to think you didn't want the post but I'm sure she'll understand why you didn't come before when you tell her what's happened. Oh, and it will be so nice to have you here if you do get the job!'

The minute they entered the kitchen and Ruby introduced Bill, the kindly woman ushered him to the table and served him with a large slab of fruit cake and a mug of steaming tea while Ruby hurried off to find Miss Wood.

An hour later, after Miss Wood had spoken to Bill privately in her room, they both came back into the kitchen and Ruby could tell it was good news by the look on Bill's face.

'Bill will be moving into Robert's old room above the stables this evening,' she told them. 'He has agreed to a month's trial starting tomorrow, so he's going to go now and fetch his things back here. You'd better allow a bit extra for a new member of staff at this evening's meal, Mrs Baxter.'

'I certainly will,' Cook said, smiling broadly. The poor lad looked like he could do with feeding up. He wasn't as far through as a clothes prop, bless him, and she'd taken an instant liking to him.

'Why don't you go with him to help, Ruby?' Miss Wood suggested and Ruby was instantly worried.

'B-but what about Miss Miranda? She's having a piano lesson at the moment but if I'm not there when it's finished she'll—'

Miss Wood held her hand up to stop her flow of words. 'Don't you get worrying about the miss. Leave that with me.'

And so Ruby and Bill set off with Bill looking considerably happier and more than a little relieved.

'Thanks for thinkin' o' me, Ruby,' he said as they marched along the pavements in the March sunshine.

She grinned. 'It was my pleasure and I'm sure you'll like working there. Most of them are really nice.'

'Most of them?' he gave her a quizzical look.

She smiled ruefully. 'Miranda, the daughter of the house who I work for, can be a bit of a tyrant,' she confided. 'She's a bit older than me, but don't worry, you'll be outside so it's unlikely you'll see much of her.'

Soon after they came to the two tiny rooms Bill and his mother had called home. They were in a tall tenement block, the door to the house opening directly onto the pavement and as they entered Ruby almost gagged at the vile smell of stale cabbage, urine and a number of different smells that she couldn't recognise that met them – not that Bill seemed to notice, but then Ruby supposed he was used to it. Children with runny noses and matted hair running with lice were playing with marbles on the hall floor and from upstairs the sound of someone arguing and a baby wailing floated to them. Bill led her along the gloomy passage and into a room that was very scantily furnished but surprisingly clean.

'This is it,' he told her sadly. 'I slept on that old sofa over there an' me mom slept in there, that's the bedroom.'

She perched on the edge of a rickety wooden chair while Bill went through to the other room to fetch an old pillow slip into which he began to throw his meagre possessions.

'That's it,' he said minutes later as he stood looking around. 'But before I go, I just want to have a quick word with Mrs Platt, the lady next door, if you don't mind. She was always good to me an' Mom so I want her to come in an' have first pick of anythin' she might be able to use afore the rest of 'em get to it. Soon as ever they know I've gone they'll come an' empty the place, believe me. The folks round here are like a plague o' locusts.'

Ruby sat patiently waiting and soon he was back again. He lifted a thin gold band from a little table at the side of the fireplace. 'Mustn't go wi'out this. It were me mom's weddin' ring.' He threaded it onto a piece of string and tied it about his neck. 'All ready, then,' he said sombrely.

Ruby's kind heart went out to him as she watched him look around, almost as if he were committing every inch of the place to memory. The two rooms weren't up to much, but they had been his home for as long as he could remember and she guessed it would hurt him to leave them.

Crossing quickly to him she linked her arm through his and said cheerfully, 'Right then, we'll be off and hopefully this will be the start of better times for you.'

He nodded and after one final glance around he allowed her to lead him away.

# Chapter Fifteen

Within days of him starting work everyone was singing Bill's praises.

'Have you taken a peek at the orchard?' Cook asked Miss Wood as they sat in the kitchen over morning coffee. 'Why, he's scythed all the grass down an' done all the prunin' in there already. I've never seen it look so tidy an' I wouldn't mind bettin' we'll have a bumper crop of apples an' pears this year. An' he's plantin' in the kitchen garden now. He's a good lad, I tell you.'

'Yes, he is proving to be a pleasant young man,' Miss Wood agreed approvingly. 'And he's so obliging and polite. I had to tell him to finish work at seven o' clock last night or I'm sure he would have gone on.'

Ruby entered the kitchen to fetch a cold drink for Miranda, and hearing them saying how well Bill was doing she smiled. They still didn't know each other well, but she had taken to Bill from the first moment they'd met and it was nice to have him working here.

When she'd left the room, Miss Wood lowered her voice to ask, 'And has there been any change in Ruby's, er . . . condition? I've noticed she's been looking very peaky this last few weeks.'

The smile slid from Cook's face as she shook her head. 'Not that I know of. She's stopped bein' sick of a mornin' but have you noticed how tight her dress is gettin' across her chest? If she is expectin' a baby we can't ignore it much longer.'

'No, I know.' Miss Wood tapped her fingers thoughtfully on the table. 'I suppose I should speak to her and get the doctor to have a look at her. But I hate the thought of what might happen to her if she is having a child. The mistress would have her out on the street straightaway but I can't help but think that if she is, it isn't her fault. She's little more than a child herself and not that sort of girl at all. Do you think someone could have forced themselves on her?'

Cook sighed. 'I've no idea. I only know that time is goin' on an' it needs to be addressed.'

'Very well, leave it with me,' Miss Wood said reluctantly, standing up and heading for the door.

Later that morning, Miranda met Bill for the first time and she was instantly smitten with him. She had gone out to get some fresh air and the minute she saw him digging in the kitchen garden she stopped abruptly in her tracks. He had rolled his shirt sleeves up, showing his muscular arms and his thick dark hair was flopping across his forehead, and she had a sudden urge to stroke it back for him.

She approached him boldly and gave him what she hoped was her most winning smile. 'Good morning. You must be the new gardener-cum-groom.'

He glanced up at her pudgy, plain face and guessed instantly that this must be Miranda, the daughter of the house.

He nodded. 'I am, miss.'

She waited for him to say more but when he continued with his digging she rushed on, 'I'm Miranda . . . this is my parents' house.'

He nodded again but continued working and she began to feel annoyed. Surely he should be pleased that she was bothering to speak to him? He was only a servant, after all. Even so she was experiencing a strange feeling in her stomach, like a million little butterflies fluttering about, and she found she was unable to drag her eyes away from the muscles in his arms. She had never felt like this before so she went on, 'It's a lovely day, isn't it?'

'Yes, miss, but I have work to do so if you don't mind, I'd best get on.' He would have liked to tell her to clear off after hearing how she treated Ruby but he was no fool and guessed that it would likely cost him his new job.

'Er . . . yes, yes of course. I've no doubt we'll meet again.' She could feel the colour burning into her cheeks as she turned away and for the rest of the day she could think of little else but the new employee.

As Ruby was helping her to get changed for dinner that evening, Miranda said casually, 'I understand you know the new gardener, Ruby?'

Ruby was taken aback. It was one of the very rare occasions when Miranda had spoken to her civilly. 'Yes, miss, I do, but not well.'

'Just *how* well?'

146

Ruby was aware that Miranda was watching her closely and she shrugged. 'We met a short time ago. He knew the people I last stayed with.'

There followed a string of questions about him, many of which Ruby could not answer, and she wondered why Miranda was showing such an interest in him. She usually treated all the servants as menials and had no interest in them. At last the bell sounded for dinner and Miranda left her to tidy her room while she went down to dine with her father. Mrs Pembroke had taken to her bed again, but Ruby was getting used to that now.

Once the family had been served the staff sat down to eat and Bill joined them, his mouth watering at the sight of the large steak and kidney pie and the dishes of steaming vegetables Cook had made for them. He had never eaten so well in his life and was thoroughly enjoying living and working there.

'I met the young mistress earlier on,' he said conversationally as he speared a carrot on his fork. 'Not the prettiest of girls, is she?' Then realising that he was probably being cruel he rushed on, 'Although she seemed friendly enough.'

'That'll be a first, then,' Cook chortled. 'She normally speaks to the staff like they're dirt on her shoes. You should think yourself lucky – or perhaps she's taken with you?' she teased.

Bill blushed a dull brick red. 'I wouldn't think so,' he said, clearly embarrassed.

Cook looked highly amused. 'Whyever not? You're a good-lookin' lad, Bill. An' you'll be better still when I've fattened you up a bit.'

Ruby giggled. Oh, she did like the staff here and it was even better now that Bill had joined them. The only dark spot on the horizon was her young mistress, but there wasn't much she could do about that.

As if thoughts of her had conjured her up from thin air, Miranda suddenly breezed into the kitchen and the staff immediately all fell silent and laid their knives and forks down.

'Ah, Cook.' She gazed straight at Bill while speaking to Mrs Baxter. 'My father and I were wondering if we might have a little more gravy?'

'Well, o' course you can, miss. But you only had to ring the bell.' Cook was flabbergasted. She could never remember Miranda doing this before but it seemed that she'd hit the nail on the head when she'd teased Bill about her fancying him, because the girl couldn't take her eyes off him.

'Why don't you go back through to the dinin' room and I'll get Betty to bring some through straightaway?'

'Oh, it's quite all right. I can wait,' Miranda responded with a simpering smile aimed at Bill.

Cook quickly heaved herself up, hurried to the range, filled another gravy boat and handed it to Miranda saying, 'Now, mind you don't spill it down you, miss.'

'Thank you.' Miranda breezed back out the way she had come and for a moment silence reigned before they all began to chuckle.

'Well, I suppose there's a first time for everythin',' Betty said. 'I've never heard that little miss be so reasonable.'

Over the next few days, Miranda seemed to be constantly strolling around the gardens or coming into the kitchen unannounced whenever she thought Bill might be there, much to the amusement of the staff.

'It's a wonder she don't wear a sign round her neck sayin' "I fancy you",' Cook teased Bill but he took it all good-naturedly and kept out of her way as much as he could.

On Sunday, Ruby was looking forward to her afternoon off. Nell was coming to see her and intended to go for a walk with her and Bill, but first she had to help Miranda get ready to go to church with her father and then pander to her when she got back until after lunch when she would be free for the rest of the day.

Finally, Nell arrived and the three chattered non-stop as they walked to the park. Bill told her how much he was enjoying his new job. When they got there, they found it was full of families out to enjoy the sunny afternoon. Children rolled around the grass or played ball and the sound of laughter floated on the air.

They were strolling around the lake when Nell suddenly told Ruby, 'I think Maddie is really missin' you, you know. An' I think she regrets tryin' to make you . . . well, you know what I mean. She asks about you all the time, though neither me nor Mrs Petty have told her where you are as yet.'

'Really?' Ruby's face became solemn as she paused to stare down into the water. Could it be that Maddie was missing her because she really *was* her real mother? Still, the suspicion lurked in the back of Ruby's mind and she just couldn't let go of the idea. She'd tried telling herself that if Maddie *was* her real mother, then surely she'd have made more effort to see her, but if Maddie hadn't known where she was, then she wouldn't have been able to.

'Let's not get all solemn,' Bill urged. 'Look, there's a cart over there selling lemonade. I'll treat you both to a glass an' we can sit on the grass under that tree an' drink it. How would that suit you both?'

The girls nodded and with a grin he went off to fetch it while they settled themselves under the spreading branches of a weeping willow. The afternoon passed all too quickly but this time when Nell said she needed to leave, Ruby wasn't as downhearted as usual. Now that she had Bill living close, she didn't feel quite so lonely. They said their good-byes outside the park gates and once Nell had gone Ruby and Bill strolled leisurely back to the house.

'I wonder what Cook has made us for tea this evenin'?' Bill said when the house came into sight.

Ruby giggled, Bill always seemed to be thinking of his belly, and if she wasn't very much mistaken he had already put a few pounds on. Mind you, so had she, and no doubt it was all due to Cook's excellent cooking. It suited him because now his face had lost its gaunt look.

At the house, they found some of the staff sitting outside in the yard enjoying the last of the afternoon sunshine and while Bill stopped to chat to them, Ruby went inside to see if there was anything she could do to help Cook, and soon she was calling everyone inside for the evening meal.

They had barely finished their food when Ruby started yawning. 'I reckon all that fresh air has made me tired. I might go up and get an early night.'

'You do that, bab.' Cook watched her go with a worried frown on her face. Miss Wood hadn't managed to have a word with Ruby about her condition as yet but she couldn't put it off for much longer, because if she wasn't very much mistaken Ruby's dress had looked uncomfortably tight about the waistband this evening. With a sigh she began to carry the dirty pots to the sink.

Early the next morning Ruby went into the kitchen and collected a jug of hot water for Miranda to wash with and when she tapped on the bedroom door and entered, she was surprised to find Miranda sitting up in bed waiting for her.

'So, where did you go yesterday afternoon?' she spat before Ruby had even had time to set the water down.

'Why . . . I-I went for a walk in the park,' Ruby stammered, not that she could see what it had to do with Miranda on her day off.

'*Who with?*' The words were fired at her like shots from a gun.

'I went with my friend Nell and Bill came along.'

'Oh *did* he now?' Miranda's lips curled back from her teeth in a feral snarl. 'And don't you know that my parents do not allow any hanky-panky between the servants under this roof? This is a respectable household!'

Ruby looked astounded. 'But there wasn't any hanky-panky! We simply went for a walk around the lake.'

'*Don't* give me that!' Miranda shot out of bed and stood so close that Ruby could feel her breath on her cheek as she jabbed her sharply in the shoulder with her finger.

'Ouch!' Water spilled over the floor as Ruby hastily slapped the jug down and rubbed at her shoulder. 'What

151

did you do that for? I haven't done anything wrong. Bill is my friend.'

'Oh *yes*? Do you think I'm a fool! I've seen the way you look at him and make up to him, you little slut!' Miranda was so angry that spittle was gathering at the corners of her mouth, and realising that she needed to be left alone to calm down, Ruby turned and made for the door.

'*Wh-where* do you think you're going when I'm speaking to you? Get back here *now*!' Miranda roared.

But Ruby ignored her and kept on going. She'd had enough of her young mistress's temper tantrums and just wanted to get to the sanctuary of the kitchen until Miranda had calmed down. She was almost at the top of the stairs when she became aware of the girl charging up behind her.

'How *dare* you ignore me!' Miranda's face was purple with rage as she grabbed Ruby's shoulder and swung her about to face her. At the same moment Ruby saw Miss Wood hurrying along the landing towards them but she had no time to call for help for Miranda suddenly brought her fist back and thumped Ruby on the nose.

Ruby felt a sharp pain then became aware of something warm and sticky running down into her mouth and dripping off her chin. Her hand rose to wipe it away and she saw with shock that it was blood, but then Miranda suddenly swung her fist again and this time it hit her hard on the shoulder and she felt herself falling backwards. The stairs were right behind her and seconds later she had the sensation of flying through the air before she began to fall head over heels down the steep staircase, landing with a

152

loud thud at the bottom with her leg twisted at an unnatural angle beneath her. She could hear someone screaming but the pain was so intense that she could do nothing but gasp for air, and then a warm darkness began to settle over her and she welcomed it.

# Chapter Sixteen

'Oh, dear God, Miranda, what have you *done*?' Miss Wood screamed as she lifted her skirts and raced down the stairs to the prone figure lying at the bottom. And then all hell broke loose as Mr Pembroke appeared from his workroom and the servants came running.

Taking in the situation at a glance, Mr Pembroke barked, 'Betty, go outside and find Bill and tell him to run for the doctor. Tell him there's been an accident and to come straightaway, would you?'

'Yes, sir.' White-faced, Betty shot off.

Cook ran over and bent over Ruby, but when she went to move her, Mr Pembroke told her sharply, 'No, Mrs Baxter. We mustn't move her until the doctor gets here. Go and fetch some pillows and blankets.' At this point he had no idea if Ruby was even alive and he felt sick with fear. She looked so tiny and vulnerable.

Miss Wood dropped to her knees beside the girl and felt for a pulse and when she nodded, he let out a sigh of relief before asking, 'But what happened? Did she trip or something?'

Miss Wood raised her head and stared up the stairs to where Miranda was standing as if she had been turned to stone, and never taking her eyes from the girl's face, she told him, 'No, she didn't trip. Miss Miranda pushed her. I saw what happened.'

'*What?*' Oscar Pembroke gulped deep in his throat and when he had managed to compose himself, he stared up at Miranda before saying, '*Get* to your room immediately and don't come out until I send for you! You've gone too far this time, miss!'

Miranda opened her mouth as if she was about to defend herself but his eyes snapped as he said coldly, '*Now!*'

Mrs Pembroke appeared at the top of the stairs then, leaning heavily on her maid's arm. She was dressed in a ridiculous peignoir trimmed with lace and feathers that did nothing whatsoever to enhance her grotesquely obese figure. 'What's going on out here? I'm not feeling at all well, Oscar. How am I supposed to sleep with all this noise going on?' she said moodily.

He glared up at her as he gently lifted Ruby's head to lay it on a pillow, and as his wife saw the small motionless figure she gasped.

'Why don't you ask your daughter what's happened?' he said through gritted teeth. 'She has just pushed Ruby down the stairs and the girl is in a bad way.'

'Oh no, there must be some mistake. Miranda would never—'

'*Shut up,*' he growled. 'And if you can't do anything to help, get out of my sight.'

'Well *really*!' Lydia said indignantly, and turning about she lumbered away, muttering under her breath.

Cook meantime had fetched a blanket and now she tucked it gently around Ruby's twisted body saying tearfully, 'Do you think she's going to be all right, sir?'

'I honestly can't say, Cook.' Sitting back on his heels he ran a hand across his eyes. He had been warning his wife for years that Miranda was getting out of hand but would she listen? Would she hell. In fairness he was painfully aware that he couldn't lay all the blame at her door. He should have stepped in and introduced some discipline long ago, but he had followed the rules of his parents. Mothers disciplined the girls and fathers disciplined the boys. It had worked in their household, *but it certainly hasn't worked in mine*, he thought ruefully.

Betty had gone to peer down the drive for a sign of Bill and the doctor returning and now all they could do was wait, which was a lot easier said than done when every minute of staring at Ruby's chalk-white face felt like an hour.

At last the doctor appeared, looking flushed and breathless, and without a word he knelt down and began to examine Ruby as they all stood back.

'Well, her leg is broken, that's for sure,' he told them. 'It's going to need to be set and the best time to do it is while she's still unconscious. Could you find me something that will serve as splints? And I'll need bandages, as many as you can lay your hands on. Or rip up a sheet into strips for me, but first let's get her into bed.'

Bill went to find something that would be suitable as splints while Betty rushed off to tear a sheet up. Meanwhile the doctor very gently lifted Ruby and carried her to a room Miss Wood directed him to on the first floor.

Once Bill and Betty came back with what he needed he soaked a pad of cloth with some foul-smelling liquid. 'I'm going to have to twist her leg back into the right position and it'll be agony if she's awake so if she shows any sign of coming round put this across her nose and keep it there until I tell you,' he instructed Miss Wood. 'Once that's done, we'll look at her other injuries.'

Twenty minutes later the leg was splinted and heavily bandaged and as Miss Wood and the doctor gently undressed the girl they both gasped as they saw the state of her arms and legs. They were covered in bruises, some fresh, some fading.

'What the hell?' The doctor was appalled. 'How did she come by all these?'

Miss Wood frowned. 'I wouldn't mind betting Miranda did them. She's very fond of lashing out if things aren't done the way she likes it.'

'Disgusting! It's about time her parents took a belt to her and taught her how to behave,' he snorted. 'You can be sure I shall be having words with them before I leave.' He continued his examination and after a few minutes he glanced at Miss Wood and asked solemnly, 'Were you aware that this girl is about three months pregnant?'

Miss Wood wrung her hands together. 'Cook did have her suspicions,' she admitted. 'But we hoped she was wrong. I can't understand it. Ruby is such a good girl.'

At last he straightened. 'There don't appear to be any other serious injuries but she's going to need careful nursing and she's going to be in a lot of pain when she wakes up so when it gets too bad give her a few drops of this in water.' He handed her a small glass jar full of a dark-brown liquid.

After showing him to the door, she asked tentatively, 'And what about the baby? Ruby is only a child herself.'

He shook his head. 'There's a good chance that after today's fall she could lose it,' he told her honestly. 'And if she doesn't . . . well, as you said, she's little more than a child herself so it's not a good situation for her to be in, but we'll just have to wait and see. I shall call back tomorrow, but if you need me before then don't hesitate to send for me.'

'Of course. Thank you, doctor.'

He paused with his hand on the door handle. 'Oh, and perhaps before I go I should have a word with Mr and Mrs Pembroke about . . . Ruby's condition?' It was wasn't something he was relishing telling them so he was somewhat relieved when Miss Wood shook her head.

'Oh, don't worry. It might be better coming from me,' she told him quickly and once he had left the room, she stared down at Ruby's inert form worriedly, wondering what would happen to the poor girl now. She wasn't looking forward to telling her mistress and had no doubt that once Mrs Pembroke knew Ruby was with child she would order her from the house immediately; the woman didn't have an ounce of compassion in her. Thankfully, as it turned out she didn't have to tell them for as the doctor descended the stairs, he found Oscar Pembroke waiting in the hall for him.

Dr Markham had attended Oscar since he was a child and thought highly of him, although he couldn't say the same for his wife. She frequently sent for him for the least little thing and he couldn't recall having ever met a more self-centred, neurotic person. Their daughter, the cause of this upset, wasn't much better. Putting that from his mind he told Oscar gently, 'As I thought, the leg is broken. I have set it and apart from cuts and bruises there seem to be no other serious injuries. I have given her something to make her sleep for a while. I'm afraid she's going to be in a lot of pain when she wakes up. But I also ought to inform you that my examination also showed that, er . . .' He squirmed uncomfortably for a second before rushing on, 'My examination also confirmed that the girl is about three months pregnant.'

'*What?*' Oscar had thought things couldn't get much worse but they just had, and the colour drained from his face like water from a dam. 'Are you quite certain?'

'Oh yes, there can be no doubt.' The doctor patted his arm. 'Although whether she will miscarry after the fall she just took is anybody's guess. All we can do is wait and see. Meantime, you know where I am if you need me, Oscar.' And with that he lifted his hat from the hall table, plonked it on his thick thatch of silver-white hair and walked off, leaving Oscar to stare after him in shock.

After a few moments he became aware of Miss Wood coming down the stairs and he said shakily, 'I can't believe what the doctor has just told me, Serena. That little Ruby is having a child!'

As always at the sight of him her heart skipped a beat. She had loved him for so long and yet she had never given him a sign and she was confident that he had no idea of her feelings for him. He was a married man, albeit in name only, and it was enough for her just to be able to see him each day and be near him.

'I'm afraid there can be no doubt,' she told him sadly.

He sat down heavily on the little gilt chair in the hallway and dropped his face into his hands. 'What a mess,' he groaned. 'Lydia is going to go mad when she knows.'

159

But then after taking a deep breath he rose. 'Putting that aside, what Miranda has done is quite unforgivable and now she must realise that there are consequences to her actions. Excuse me.'

He took the steps two at a time as he went to summon his daughter to her mother's room and Serena Wood sighed. After seeing the look on Oscar's face, she wouldn't like to be in Miranda's shoes, that was for sure, although to her mind the girl deserved everything she had coming to her.

Once Oscar had entered his wife's room, he sent her maid to fetch Miranda and soon the girl appeared with her arms crossed across her chest and a scared expression on her face. He dismissed the maid and after closing the door he looked at Miranda and asked pointedly, 'Well? Would you like to explain what happened to elicit such appalling behaviour?'

Miranda gave a defiant shrug as she looked at her mother for support but for once Lydia stayed silent.

'She . . . she annoyed me,' she said eventually and to her dismay she saw her father's hands clench into fists.

'She *annoyed* you! Is that the best excuse you can come up with?'

When she gave another shrug, he took a step towards her and for an awful moment Miranda thought he was going to strike her. But then thankfully he managed to control himself, although his voice shook with rage when he told her, 'I'm afraid you have gone too far this time. I told you a short time ago that should there be any more incidents I would send you away and this time that is *exactly* what I intend to do. I have already made tentative enquiries to a finishing school a colleague of mine told me about in France, and the headmistress there wrote back to me to say that should I ever wish to send you, there is a place available.'

'No, Oscar . . . you *can't*!' Lydia cried.

Her glared at her. 'Don't you realise that she could have killed the girl?' His voice was as cold as ice.

His wife covered her mouth with her plump hand and began to cry. 'But *surely* you are overreacting, darling? She is only a *servant*, after all!'

'Believe it or not, servants are human beings too,' he spat with disgust, wondering again what he had ever seen in her. 'And there will be no more discussion on the subject. My mind is made up. I shall be writing to Madame Babineaux this very day to secure Miranda a place at the school and I shall expect her to be there within the month. Please ask your maid to help with her packing.'

Miranda was crying too now and in a panic, she pleaded, 'But I *don't* want to go, Father—'

'Perhaps you should have thought of that before you pushed the girl down the stairs. Furthermore, you should start to pray that she survives because if she doesn't the police could become involved and then it won't be a school you'll be going to but a prison.'

Miranda's mouth gaped with shock but he couldn't bear to be in her company a second longer and he slammed out of the room leaving her to throw herself at her mother and sob. Even that failed to move him. He knew the tears were not out of remorse for what she had done to Ruby but out of fear of what might happen to herself, and in that moment he rued the day she had been born.

It was decided that Betty and Miss Wood would care for Ruby and during the rest of that day they took it in turns to sit in a chair beside her bed, willing her to wake up. Bill was furious about what had happened and it was all Cook could do to stop him seeking Miranda out, throwing her across his lap and giving her backside a good old tanning.

'That's what my mom would have done to me,' he stated stoically.

Cook patted his shoulder. They were all fond of Ruby and she could well understand how he felt. 'I've no doubt she would have, lad,' she told him regretfully. 'But unfortunately, that ain't how the toffs work, more's the pity. Still, at least the mister is sayin' he'll send her away.' Neither she, nor Miss Wood had told him about the baby as yet. They had decided to face each problem as it arose and the first thing they needed was for Ruby to wake up.

# Chapter Seventeen

It was nine o'clock in the evening and Miss Wood was sitting in a chair close to Ruby's bed reading *The Moonstone* by Wilkie Collins, when a slight groan from the bed made her drop the book and quickly spring up. Outside, the March wind was hammering on the window as if it was trying to gain entry, but inside the fire was glowing brightly in the grate and the oil lamp on the bedside table made the room look warm and cosy.

'Ruby, Ruby, dear . . . can you hear me?'

Ruby's head was moving from side to side and beads of sweat stood out on her forehead and Miss Wood hoped that at last she was coming around. Taking a cool cloth from a bowl on the bedside table, she gently wiped Ruby's face. 'Ruby, try to open your eyes, dear,' she urged. 'You are quite safe.'

Ruby blinked and then very slowly her right eye blearily opened. The other was black and swollen from the fall down the stairs. Disorientated, she tried to sit up, crying out with pain. She ached everywhere but the pain in her leg was excruciating and she began to whimper.

'Wh-what happened?' Her lips felt dry and sore and there was a sharp pain throbbing behind her eyes.

'You had a fall,' Miss Wood said gently. 'But you're going to be all right, I promise.' Her heart ached for the girl; she looked so small and frail, and in that moment, she could willingly have strangled Miranda for what she'd done.

Picking up a glass of water, she gently lifted Ruby's head and held it to her lips. When Ruby tried to gulp at it she shook her head. 'Just little sips now,' she told her and Ruby did as she was told before flopping back onto the pillows like a broken rag doll.

'M-me leg hurts,' she said miserably, and then as everything suddenly came rushing back to her she gasped. 'It was Miranda . . . she *pushed* me!'

'Yes, she did, and I'm afraid you've broken your leg. But the doctor has set it for you so it will mend in a few weeks' time. Meantime, we're going to look after you.' She didn't mention the baby, feeling it was more important to face one problem at a time. The door opened then and Betty appeared with a cup of cocoa for Miss Wood. When she saw that Ruby was awake, she let out a deep sigh of relief.

'Crikey, kid. You had us worried for a while back there,' she told Ruby gently as she smiled down at her. 'How are you feelin'?'

'Like I've been run over by a tram,' Ruby told her as she tried to raise a smile. 'But Miranda . . .'

'Oh, you've no need to get worryin' about her anymore. Her dad is shippin' her off to France to a posh school for the foreseeable future. An' good riddance, that's what I say. What she's done to you is unforgivable. I'm just thankful you didn't break your neck. But why don't you try an' get some rest now? Me granny allus reckoned sleep were the best cure for all ills. An' don't fret, you won't be on your own. Me an' Miss Wood are goin' to take it in turns to stay with you till you're on the mend.'

'First I want you to have some of this that the doctor left for you, it will help with the pain,' Miss Wood told her kindly as she added some drops of medicine to the glass of water. Ruby dutifully sipped at it and soon her eyelids drooped and she was fast asleep again.

'Thank goodness she came round. I was starting to get a little frightened,' Miss Wood confided as she and Betty stood looking down at the patient.

'Yes, and bein' in here you've missed ructions.' Betty shook her head. 'The master an' mistress have been goin' at it hammer an' tongs. We could hear 'em all over the house. She threatened to leave him an' go back to her parents if he sent Miranda away an' he actually stood up to her for once an' told her to go ahead.'

'Really?' Miss Wood was surprised. Oscar usually gave in to his wife's every whim but perhaps he had finally had enough of her selfish behaviour and the way she ruled the roost. 'And do you think she'll follow her threat through?'

Betty shrugged. 'Who knows? But off the record I wish she would piss off! Ooh, beggin' your pardon,' she said with a guilty grin.

'And what is Miranda doing?'

Betty frowned. No one in the entire house was feeling very kindly inclined towards the girl at the moment after what she'd done. 'Mr Pembroke has confined her to her room an' she's sulkin'.' She grinned. 'Serves her right an' all, although I don't think she really believes her dad will carry out his threat of sendin' her away. But why don't you go an' rest for a bit. I'll stay here an' keep me eye on Ruby.'

'Well . . . only if you're sure,' Miss Wood answered doubtfully, glancing at Ruby. She was feeling rather stiff after sitting there for most of the day. 'In that case I'll stretch my legs but I'll be in the kitchen if you need me and we'll take it in turns through the night.'

'I'll be right as ninepence an' I won't take me eyes off her, I promise.'

And so Miss Wood left Betty to it and carried her mug down to the kitchen. It looked set to be a long night if they took it in turns but she was just grateful Ruby was still alive.

Ruby had a restless night and she was in a lot of pain, but when Miss Wood carried a breakfast tray up to her early the next morning at least she was properly awake, which was a good sign.

'So how are you feeling today, dear?' she asked gently.

'I hurt everywhere.' Ruby's face was as pale as lint and the spattering of freckles across her nose stood out in stark contrast. 'It's my leg and my back mainly.'

'I'll give you some more drops of the medicine,' Miss Wood told her. 'That should ease it a little.' She sighed as she prepared it. At some point she was going to have to speak to Ruby about the child she was carrying and there seemed no point in delaying so after helping Ruby to sip at the drink she sat down at the side of the bed. 'Why did Miranda attack you?'

'I think it was because she saw me an' Bill go for a walk on Sunday.' Ruby frowned. 'I think she was jealous because she likes him, at least I think she does. Bill says she's always hanging around him when he's working outside.'

'I see.' Miss Wood nodded choosing her words carefully. 'And do you like Bill too, Ruby?'

'Of course I do, he's me friend,' Ruby stated in surprise. 'So is Nell. We all went for a walk together.'

This was proving harder than she had expected and Miss Wood licked her lips. 'And have you and Bill ever, er . . . gone for a walk alone?'

Ruby looked puzzled. 'I don't think so. Why?'

'Well, I just wondered . . . what I mean is . . .' She took a deep breath. 'While the doctor was examining you yesterday, he discovered something quite shocking, Ruby . . . He discovered that you are going to have a baby.'

Colour flooded into Ruby's cheeks as she stared at her in disbelief and for the moment, she was struck dumb with shock.

'What I'm trying to ask is, have you and Bill ever . . .' Miss Wood gulped deep in her throat. 'Have you ever slept together?'

'Of *course not*, I've always slept alone,' Ruby said indignantly. 'An' I can't be having a baby 'cause I'm not married. I've never even kissed Bill and anyway, me mam told me you have to be married to make babies!'

'Oh dear.' Miss Wood wrung her hands together as Cook entered the room and she stared at her helplessly.

'I've just explained to Ruby about the baby,' Miss Wood told Cook with a quiver in her voice. 'And she insists that she's never slept with anyone.'

'Hm.' Cook sighed. 'In that case what I have to ask is: Ruby, has anyone ever, er . . . done bad things to you. You know? Down there?' As she pointed to her private parts, Ruby suddenly flinched as she thought back to the night she had run away. The night her father had forced himself on her.

'Yes . . . just once. It hurt an' as soon as it was over, I ran away.'

The two women stared at each other in horror. They had no cause to doubt the girl.

'Then you were raped and this is the result,' Cook told her sadly.

Ruby began to panic. 'But I don't *want* a baby,' she said tearfully. 'What will happen to me? Where will I go?'

She was getting so distressed that Miss Wood patted her hand and changed the subject quickly. 'Let's not worry about it for now, dear. Let's just concentrate on getting you well again and then we'll decide what's to be done about the baby. For now I want you to rest. The doctor will be calling to see you shortly and we don't want you all upset when he arrives, do we?' She tenderly tucked the blankets beneath Ruby's chin and after a nod at Cook they went out of the room, leaving Ruby to come to terms with what they had told her.

'Poor little bugger,' Cook said angrily when they were out on the landing. 'I guessed it would be somethin' like that. Who do you think it was?'

'I've no doubt she'll tell us when she's good and ready,' Miss Wood responded. 'But now I suppose I should tell the mistress.'

'Phew, rather you than me!' Cook looked horrified. 'I'd leave it to the master to tell her if I were you.' And with that she turned and went about her duties, her heart aching for Ruby.

Could Cook have known it, at that very minute, Mr Pembroke was standing outside his wife's bedroom door plucking up the courage to do just that. He had no doubt she would hit the roof but it had to be done, so after taking a deep breath he tapped on the door and strode into the room.

He found Lydia still in her peignoir having just eaten every single thing on her breakfast tray. He stifled a smirk. It seemed that no matter the upset, nothing made his wife lose her appetite – unlike himself who had been unable to even face a cup of tea this morning.

'Oh, Oscar!' She gave him a simpering smile. 'Are you in a happier mood this morning, darling?'

'Not particularly,' he informed her shortly as he crossed to the window to stare down into the street below with his arms folded behind his back.

'Why? Is the girl worse?'

'No, she isn't, and she has a name. It's Ruby.'

Lydia twisted her pudgy fingers together, the gemstones on them sending rainbows of colour about the room as the early morning sunshine peeped through the curtains and reflected in them.

He turned back to face her. 'But unfortunately, another problem has been highlighted.'

When she raised a finely plucked eyebrow, he went on, 'While the doctor was examining her, he discovered that Ruby is . . . is going to have a baby.'

'*What!*' Lydia's eyes were bulging out of her head and angry colour seeped into her cheeks. 'Why, the *dirty* little slut! Didn't I try to tell you she was trouble? And you are prepared to send our daughter away for chastising a little trollop like that! I want her out! Do you hear me? I won't have her bring shame on our home.'

'Oh *shut* up, Lydia,' he snapped, his patience stretched to the limit, and she was so shocked at being spoken to in such a way that for now she did as she was told.

'I'm fairly sure that there's more to this than meets the eye,' Oscar went on. 'The staff all assure me that Ruby is an innocent. Let's face it, she's little more than a child herself.'

'Even so, think of the gossip it will cause if it gets out,' she answered, finding her voice again. 'Why, I couldn't bear the shame of it.'

'I'm afraid you have no choice till her leg is mended, at least,' he told her, his eyes flashing. 'Think of the gossip if it gets out what our daughter has done to her!'

Lydia looked distraught. She hadn't thought of that; she had high hopes for Miranda making a good marriage one day and this could affect it if word got out. 'But you're *surely* not meaning to go through with your threat to send Miranda away?' She was standing now and walking up and down like a caged animal.

'I have every intention of doing just that. In fact, I've already written to Madame Babineaux, so you had better get used to the idea.'

Lydia stared at him boldly. 'I thought you would be in the mood to be more reasonable this morning but it appears I was wrong, so I will repeat what I said last night. If you *do* go ahead with this, I shall have no choice but to leave you and return to my parents' home.'

'And *I* shall repeat what I said,' he countered. 'Go ahead. Let's face it, Lydia, ours has been a marriage in name only for many years now. We should have parted long ago.'

Temper stained her cheeks an unflattering red as she glared at him. 'But you *know* why I couldn't sleep with you anymore, and why I insisted on us having our own rooms! Should I have fallen for another child it might have *killed* me!'

'I know you were never cut out to be a wife, or a mother for that matter, so go with my blessing and I hope one day you will meet someone who will make you happy. Goodbye, Lydia!' He turned and left the room, closing the door firmly on his farce of a marriage without once looking back.

# Chapter Eighteen

The doctor arrived mid-morning along with Maddie, Mrs Petty and Nell. Bill had taken it upon himself to go and tell them what had happened and now that Maddie had discovered where Ruby was she had wasted no time in rushing to see her. The doctor had just gone in to Ruby when Maddie burst in and he stared at her, 'And who are you, may I ask?'

'My name is Madeline Bamber and I am Ruby's friend.' Maddie approached the bed and despite everything that had happened Ruby was pleased to see her and clung to her hand as if it was a lifeline. 'How are you?' Maddie asked.

Ruby started to cry. 'Miranda pushed me down the stairs and I've broken me leg an' now the doctor says I'm goin' to have a baby and I've got terrible pains in me stomach.'

'I see.' Maddie looked shocked.

'It were me dad,' Ruby said between sobs. 'He forced himself on me. That was why I was running away the night you found me.'

In the doorway, Mrs Petty gasped and rushed towards her, smoothing her hair away from her face. 'Oh, me poor little lamb,' she said gently, while Nell stood at the end of the bed feeling helpless in the face of her friend's pain and anguish.

'Try not to worry, Ruby,' Maddie said. 'We are all here to help now.'

Ruby barely heard her as the pain in her stomach intensified and she bit her lip as she tried not to scream.

The doctor sighed sadly. 'That explains it then. Poor little devil. It looks as if she's going to lose the child anyway,' he said quietly to Maddie. 'I can't see how she could keep it after the fall she had yesterday and all things considered it might be for the best. But it's not going to be easy for her . . . she's so small and so young . . . '

'Then we must do what we can for her,' Maddie told him calmly.

'I think me courses have started again,' Ruby whimpered, and when the doctor pulled the bedclothes back, he frowned as he saw the blood in the bed.

'I'm afraid it is as I thought,' he told the women present. 'Ruby is losing the baby. Perhaps you would all like to wait downstairs and I'll do what I can. Please ask Miss Wood if she will come to help.'

As the morning wore on the bleeding increased and the doctor became concerned. 'I don't like the amount of blood she is losing,' he whispered to Miss Wood. The girl's head was tossing from side to side and she was almost incoherent with pain.

'Is there nothing you can do to help her?' Miss Wood was frantic with worry and felt helpless as she bathed Ruby's burning forehead and whispered soothing words to the poor girl.

The doctor shook his head. 'I'm afraid not. It's all in God's hands now.'

At last, almost an hour later, Ruby let out an unearthly scream and after bending to examine her the doctor nodded.

'It's all over,' he told Miss Wood regretfully. 'Now if we can only staunch the bleeding, she just might come through this. Fetch me more towels, if you would, and more clean water.'

The woman sped away to do as she was asked, wishing she could do more to ease Ruby's pain.

It was after lunch by the time the doctor returned to the kitchen. 'I have managed to stop the flow and she's sleeping,' he informed the waiting women wearily. 'There is nothing more I can do, but God willing, she will survive.'

Cook quickly made the sign of the cross on her chest as they all breathed a sigh of relief.

The doctor snapped his bag shut. 'If she does come through this, I fear it's going to be a slow recovery for her, what with her other injuries to contend with as well. I hope that she will make a full recovery eventually however . . .' He paused. 'I cannot say what her chances of having any more babies will be later in life after this happening at such an early age.'

'Poor little soul.' Mrs Petty started to cry. 'I'd like to get me hands on that father of hers, I don't mind telling you! He should be shot.'

The doctor inclined his head and once he had left, Mrs Petty hurried upstairs to check on Miss Wood who was still sitting beside Ruby's bed.

'You'd best go an' tell the master what's happened,' she suggested.

Miss Wood went to do as she was told and when she found Oscar in his office, she was shocked to see that he seemed to have aged overnight and his face was grey.

'Ah, Serena.' He wearily ran his hand through his hair. 'How is she?'

'She's lost the baby,' she told him. 'It transpires that the child was her adopted father's. He raped her.'

He momentarily closed his eyes and shuddered. 'Then perhaps it's for the best,' he said quietly. 'She's so very young . . . it's so sad. Oh, and I should tell you, Lydia wants you to go and help her pack. She is returning to her parents' home later today. For good . . .'

'I'm so sorry, sir.'

He smiled ruefully. 'Don't be. I'm sure I have no need to tell you that we have lived separate lives for a very long time. I think Lydia will be happier back with her parents.'

'And Miss Miranda?'

'She will be staying here until I can escort her to France where she will be schooled until she is eighteen,' he informed her. 'You may as well tell the staff what's happening. They'll find out soon enough anyway. But tell them not to worry. Their positions are secure and everything will go on as before.'

'But what will happen to Ruby when she recovers?' she questioned. 'She will no longer have a job to do if Miranda isn't here.'

'We'll cross that bridge when we come to it, shall we? Let's just concentrate on getting her well again first.'

Seeing that the poor man looked at the end of his tether, she quickly left the room, closing the door softly behind her. It had certainly been a very eventful couple of days one way or another, she thought as she hurried towards her mistress's room.

Pushing open the door, she found Mrs Pembroke pacing the room. The woman glanced up hopefully as she entered and then promptly burst into tears. She had clearly expected it to be her husband coming to apologise.

'Oh . . . it's you, Miss Wood. Have you seen my husband?'

'Yes, ma'am. I believe he is in his study. He asked me to come and assist Susie with your packing.'

Mrs Pembroke dabbed ineffectively at the tears on her plump cheeks with a scrap of a lace handkerchief. 'Really! Why it's almost as if he can hardly wait to get rid of me,' she said angrily. 'But I've had a change of heart. This is my home and I've decided I shan't leave it. At least I shan't if he decides he won't send Miranda away. I can hardly believe that Oscar would take the part of a mere servant rather than his own daughter.'

Miss Wood clamped her lips shut. There was so much she would like to say but it wasn't her place. Lydia was her mistress after all.

'How is the girl anyway?' Lydia asked then.

'Not good, I'm afraid.' At least Serena could be honest about that. 'She has lost the baby and that coupled with her injuries and her broken leg have made her very poorly indeed.'

Lydia tossed her head and sneered. 'Huh, I'm sure she'll recover in time. And as for the baby . . . well, she'll probably be expecting another one in no time. These street girls tend to breed like rabbits!'

'I really don't think Ruby could be described as a street girl, Mrs Pembroke.' Serena had lost all patience and could not keep the scorn from her voice. 'From what I can gather she has led a very sheltered life and it transpires that the baby was the result of rape. Now, if you don't need my help I must be about my business.' And she swept from the room leaving Lydia to stare after her with her mouth agape.

Over the next few days, Ruby slowly began to improve but the doctor informed them that it would still be some weeks before she was properly well again. And then the letter Mr Pembroke had been expecting arrived and he summoned both his daughter and his wife to his study.

'I have received a reply from Madame Babineaux in France,' he told them shortly. 'She says there is a place available for Miranda in her school as soon as we like and so I shall arrange for us to leave the day after tomorrow. Make sure you have packed what you wish to take with you, Miranda. I shall, of course, accompany you.'

Lydia's face crumpled. She had really believed that he would change his mind and had gone out of her way to be nice to him over the last few days, not that he seemed to have noticed. If anything, she felt he had been avoiding her.

'You *can't really* be serious about this, Oscar,' she whined as she made to place her hand on his arm, but he stepped away from her, a look of revulsion on his face. 'I was sure you would see sense once things had calmed down. There is no need for Miranda to go away now. The servant girl is getting better, isn't she? And Miranda has assured me that she will never do such a thing again.'

'Of course, she won't, until the next time,' he said sarcastically.

Lydia's expression changed and she stamped her foot petulantly as she saw that he would not be swayed. He had always been so pliable and she had been able to wrap him around her little finger but suddenly he was treating her as if she were a stranger.

'I *won't* let you do this!' she declared, but again he simply stared coldly back at her and after inclining his head to them, he strode out of the room without giving either of them a backwards glance.

It was late on Thursday evening after everyone had retired to bed, when Ruby's bedroom door inched open. She had convinced them all that she was quite well enough to sleep alone again and she thought it was just Miss Wood or Betty come to check on her so she was surprised to see Miranda standing there, her face twisted with malice.

'I suppose you know I'm being sent away to France tomorrow?' Miranda spat as she approached her.

Ruby cowered beneath the covers. Her leg was still tightly splinted and she knew she would stand no chance if Miranda started on her again.

'And it's all because of *you*! *You bitch!* But don't feel too pleased about it because I've come to tell you that one day I shall be back and when I *do* come back you are going to pay!'

'B-but I haven't done anything,' Ruby protested feebly.

Miranda's teeth showed in a feral snarl as she leant down so that their faces were dangerously close. 'Oh, so you haven't been making sheep's eyes at Bill when you knew I liked him? I shall *never* forgive you for causing this and just remember, I'll be back and it will be God help you when I am!' She turned abruptly and left the room as quietly as she had come as Ruby lay there feeling as if her heart was about to jump out of her chest.

Bill drove a very sulky Miranda and her father to the railway station in the carriage the following morning. The carriage was piled with trunks, hat boxes and all manner of things that Miranda had insisted she simply must take with her. Back at the house, Lydia was charging from room to room like a woman possessed, despite Miss Wood's best efforts to calm her down.

'Let me fetch you a tray of tea,' she suggested. 'You could perhaps put a drop of brandy in it to soothe your nerves.'

Lydia stared at her scornfully. 'Forget the tea but I will have the brandy. Fetch me the decanter and the glass *now*!'

Within an hour it was apparent that Mrs Pembroke was very drunk indeed and in the kitchen Cook shook her head. 'It's disgraceful behaviour,' she said in disgust. 'And she calls herself a lady. Huh!'

The rest of the staff nodded in agreement as they tried to carry on with their chores but it was very hard with the mistress raging about the place. Every now and again they heard a crash and they would glance at each other. It sounded as if she was smashing the house up, not that they much cared. Everything in the house was hers to smash after all, although they did feel sorry for the master.

'There'll be nowt left worth havin' by the time he gets back if she carries on at this rate,' Cook commented as she kneaded the dough on the table. But after an hour or so everything went quiet and they guessed that she had probably drunk herself into a stupor.

The following morning, Lydia summoned Bill to the drawing room. She was stone-cold sober by then and her eyes were as hard as marbles as he removed his cap and asked, 'What can I do for you, ma'am?'

'You can go up into the attics and bring me some trunks down,' she told him coldly. 'And you can tell Miss Wood to come and help Susie pack. I have decided to return to my parents after all. You can drive me and what luggage I am taking to the train station. My father will send for the rest of my things at a later date.' She secretly very much doubted there would ever be any need for that. Oscar was sure to see sense when he got home and found her gone. He'd no doubt be on the first train to fetch her back with his tail between his legs for treating her so abominably, but it would serve him right as far as she was concerned.

'Very well, ma'am.' Bill left the room and soon returned with the first of the trunks and Miss Wood.

'Just one more should do for now,' Lydia told him, and when he had gone she pointed to the pile of gowns she had tossed carelessly onto the bed. 'And you can start to pack those and any underwear and footwear you think I shall need. You can get out my green travelling suit too.'

'As you wish,' Miss Wood said calmly, as she started to help Susie do as she'd asked.

As she swept out of the room, Lydia was a little peeved that the woman didn't plead with her to stay.

In the drawing room, Betty was clearing up the mess her mistress had made the day before. Two crystal decanters had been smashed across the floor along with a number of very valuable ornaments. The port and the sherry that the decanters had contained was splashed up the furniture and all across the expensive Turkish carpets and Betty doubted she would ever be able to get the stains out of them, although she knew better than to voice her thoughts. As far as she was concerned, it was high time someone put the mistress across their lap and gave her arse a good whippin' an' all – that was if anyone could fit her across their lap. She stifled a smile at the thought, but even so she was appalled at such disrespect for such beautiful things. She was sure some of the lovely figurines and items of cut glass that the woman had wantonly smashed would have cost a king's ransom. It just went to show how little regard the mistress had for anything and had she been asked, Betty would have admitted that she wouldn't miss her in the slightest!

# Chapter Nineteen

'She got off all right, then?' Cook asked as Bill entered the kitchen later that day after delivering the mistress to the train station.

Bill nodded. 'Yes, she did and I can't say I'm sorry to see the back of her,' he confessed. Although he hadn't worked there long, he had quickly reached the conclusion that the mistress had been spoilt rotten.

'Good!' It seemed that none of them were going to miss her although they were all wondering how the master would react when he got home to find her gone.

'How is Ruby today?' he asked as Cook popped a rich fruit cake into the oven.

She smiled. 'Getting better by the day, although it'll take some time for the leg to set.' She placed a scone fresh from the oven in front of him and he took it gratefully. He had never eaten so well as he had since coming to work here and it was all thanks to Ruby for putting in a good word for him.

'So how long do you think it will be before she's well enough to come downstairs for a while? She must get lonely stuck up there on her own.'

'I dare say the doctor will tell us, although you'll probably have to carry her down for a while,' Cook warned him.

'And as for bein' lonely, I've told her to make the best of the rest. Lord knows what will happen to her when she's fully recovered. Now Miranda an' the missus have gone I can't see the master keepin' her on.'

Bill hadn't thought of that and he frowned with concern. What would Ruby do? She was only a kid and nowhere near ready to fend for herself out in the big bad world. But then, he had found Mr Pembroke to be a reasonable man so he'd probably sort something out for her. If he didn't, he was sure Maddie would have her back, but that wasn't the sort of life Ruby would be happy with. She might be only a kid but she had principles and he admired her for that. Meanwhile all the staff were looking forward to a few easy days with all the family being gone, apart from the old master, who was still ill and confined to his room, and they intended to make the best of it.

Mr Pembroke returned home nine days later looking stressed. Miranda had been a nightmare on the journey to the school, which was no more than he had expected, and he had been relieved when he was able to leave her in Madame Babineaux's care.

The house was strangely quiet when he entered through the front door but he assumed that Lydia would be in her room being waited on hand and foot as usual, until Miss Wood approached him to say, 'Welcome home, sir. I hope the journey wasn't too tiring?'

He gave a rueful grin as he handed her his hat and coat. 'Actually, it was more stressful than tiring, Serena,' he admitted and noting that she looked quite tense he asked, 'Is everything all right here?'

'Well . . .' She was trying to find the kindest way to tell him, but eventually gave up and said quietly, 'I'm afraid not. Mrs Pembroke returned to her parents' home the day after you left. She asked me give you this letter.'

She picked up an envelope from the hall stand and handed it to him, then turned to go. 'I'll leave you to read it in peace while I fetch you a tray of tea and something to eat to keep you going till lunchtime. You must be tired and hungry after your long journey.'

As he watched her slim figure disappearing down the hallway, he shook his head. In most households it would be the lady of the house coming to greet their husband but not in this one! With a sigh he took the letter into the drawing room and after settling on the chaise longue that Lydia had favoured he split it open with his thumb and began to read.

*My Dear Oscar,*

*It is with great sadness that I write this letter, but I fear you have left me with no choice. I am still finding it hard to believe that you would have taken such drastic measures as to send our daughter away over a silly altercation with a servant girl. Until the very second you both left the house, I was praying that you would come to your senses but it seems I misjudged you. And so, I feel I have no choice but to return home for the foreseeable future, to Mama and Papa who I know will be as appalled with the situation, and with you, as I*

184

*am. Should you see reason and return our daughter
home you know where I will be. Until then I remain,*
  *Your devoted wife,*
  *Lydia x*


With a snort Oscar tossed the letter aside as he rubbed his
tired eyes. He had endured a very rough passage on the ferry
home and was quite worn out, but he didn't at all regret
what he had done. If anything, he realised he should have
done it some time ago. Miranda might have turned out differently then but now he held little hope for her. She was
just as spoilt as her mother and he doubted he would miss
either of them. Furthermore, he had no intention of rushing
off to speak to Lydia, so she would just have to stew in her
own juice for a while.

There was a tap at the door and Miss Wood appeared
bearing a tray with a selection of sandwiches, some fancy
cakes and a pot of tea.

She didn't ask about the content of the letter and he
hadn't expected her to. Over the years she had proved herself to be the soul of discretion and he had often secretly
wished that his wife could be more like her. Serena Wood
was still a very attractive woman, but more importantly she
had a kind heart, which was more than could be said for
Lydia, who only ever thought of herself. 'Why don't you go
and fetch another cup and saucer and join me, Serena?' he
said wearily.

Somewhat surprised, Serena went to do as he asked,
sensing that he needed someone to confide in right now,
poor man.

'I suppose you've realised that Lydia has left me?' he said shortly after as they sat sipping their drinks.

'Yes, I had.' She gave him a tentative smile. 'But I'm sure she'll come back when she's had time to consider things.'

He shook his head and surprised her when he answered sadly, 'I don't *want* her to come back, Serena. You must have observed our marriage was over a very long time ago, and I think we will be better apart. I dare say when Miranda finishes her schooling in a couple of years' time she will join her mother at her grandparents' home, so it looks like it's just me and my father left here from now on, but I'm sure we'll survive.'

Serena had to rapidly blink back tears as she looked at him. He didn't deserve this; he was such a good man and she so wanted to put her arms about him and comfort him, but of course she couldn't.

'Anyway, how are my father and Ruby?' he asked and she was glad to change the subject.

'Your father is quite well and asking to see you when you get back, and Ruby is improving by the day,' she was pleased to be able to tell him.

'Excellent, I shall go and see my father straightaway.' Ignoring the food on the tray, he drained his cup and with a nod towards Serena he left the room.

'Ah, you're back then, lad.' His father stared at him as Oscar entered his room.

'Yes, Father, I'm back. I trust they've been looking after you while I've been gone?' His father seemed to have shrunk in the short time he'd been away, or was it that he had never noticed before? he mused. Despite this, though, his brain seemed as sharp as ever.

'Miss Wood allus looks after me, she's a good woman,' the old man responded as he patted the bed beside him. 'And did you get Miranda settled in that school all right?'

Oscar sat down wearily and nodded. 'I wouldn't say I left her settled, but I got her there,' he answered, wondering why he felt so guilty.

'Good thing an' all. You should have done it years ago. Happen she wouldn't have turned out so much like her mother,' the old man said sharply. Although Miranda was his granddaughter, they had never been close. 'An' I suppose you know by now that Lydia is gone an' all?'

When Oscar nodded, he sighed and his old wrinkled hand rested on his son's. 'Try not to be too upset,' he urged. 'She ain't never been much of a wife to you. I tried to warn you before you married her but at the end of the day you have to let your children learn by their mistakes. You're not thinkin' o' goin' to fetch her back, are you?'

'No, Father. There would be no point,' Oscar admitted despondently.

His father nodded. 'Happen you're right. Sometimes you just have to know when to call it a day, but things will get better, you'll see. We've got a thriving business that needs your attention an' when I'm gone, it'll be all yours and Hermione's.'

Oscar scowled. 'Don't talk like that. You've got years left in you yet.'

His father shook his head. 'We both know that ain't true,' he said quietly. 'The doctor told me this old ticker o' mine

187

could pack up any day now, but I ain't complainin'. I've had a good life. An' I had a good wife an' all. Why, when I met your mom I hadn't got a pot to piss in an' we built the business up wi' blood, sweat an' tears. Not once did she ever complain, even though for years we had to live hand to mouth – not like that one you chose. But then we're all allowed one mistake. Learn by it, son, an' next time you get close to a woman make sure it's one that's worthy of you.'

Oscar stared at him as if he'd taken leave of his senses. 'That's not likely to happen while I'm still married to Lydia, is it? And anyway, I *never* want another relationship.'

'Who knows what the future holds?' his father said wisely. 'You're still a relatively young man and you shouldn't have to live as you have been any longer. Especially when there's a woman not a million miles away from here who would walk through fire for you.'

Oscar looked shocked. 'Oh yes, and who would that be then?'

His father chuckled. 'Just take them blinkers off and you'll soon find out. But now if you don't mind, I reckon I'll have a little kip. Miss Wood will be bringin' me lunch up soon. But just think on what I said, eh?' With that he turned over and pulled the blankets up to his chin as Oscar quietly left the room.

Later that day, after having a short rest, Oscar went to see Ruby and he was pleased to see how much better she looked.

'Miss Wood informs me that you are finally on the mend now, my dear.'

She smiled at him nervously. 'Yes, I am, sir, and I'm sorry about what happened with—'

He held his hand up. 'If you were going to say "with Miranda", don't trouble yourself about it. She was totally out of order picking on you like that. And if truth be told she'll benefit greatly from her time at the finishing school. No, you just concentrate on getting well again for now. Meanwhile, if there is anything we can do for you, just tell Miss Wood.' He stared at her for a time then, making her feel quite uncomfortable, before he turned and quietly left the room.

When the doctor called later that day, he pronounced that Ruby was well enough to get out of bed and sit in a chair for a while, provided she rested her splinted leg on a stool. And so soon after Betty and Miss Wood positioned a chair by the window and Ruby was able to sit and watch the world go by for a time.

Her thoughts were all over the place, for she was still struggling to come to terms with the undeniable fact that she had been going to have a baby. How could she not have known? she asked herself. But then, her mother had never really talked to her about what she had termed 'the birds and the bees', apart from to tell her that a girl should always be married before she had a child. And Ruby had led such a sheltered life after leaving school that she had never had any friends her own age to talk to about such things. The thought of giving birth to a child that her adopted father had sired made her feel sick to her stomach and yet she couldn't help but feel sad for the baby. Worse still was the fact that the doctor has said he didn't know whether losing the child at such an early age could affect her chances of having any more babies when she was older. She had always dreamed of having her own family one day, but she supposed if what her father had done to her was what married women had to suffer then she would never want to be wed anyway. And then she began to think of what was to become of her when her leg was healed. She wouldn't be needed now that Miranda was gone and she constantly worried about it. Would she find herself out on the streets again with nowhere to go? All she could do was wait and see.

Could she have known it at that moment Mr Pembroke was discussing that very situation with his father in the old man's room.

'She's a good girl,' the elderly Mr Pembroke told Oscar, and he nodded in agreement.

'That's why I've been thinkin' about what she might do when she's recovered,' the old man went on. 'I was thinking she might make a good companion for Hermione. She's always enjoyed the company of young people, never having had any children of her own.'

'Hm, you could be right there,' Oscar answered thoughtfully. Hermione was his father's sister. When she was younger, she had been heavily involved in the business but she had retired and now lived in Bedworth, a small town just outside Nuneaton, although she still spent her time, or some of it, making designs for the jewellery they made. Her designs were highly praised and she had even been commissioned by royalty to make special pieces for them. 'Maybe I'll go to see her and put the idea to her.'

Once he had left his father to rest, he decided that there was no time like the present. He was long overdue for a visit to her so if he went that afternoon, he could kill two birds with one stone.

Ruby was gazing out of the window deep in thought when her door opened and to her delight, Nell and Maddie appeared.

'Oh, you look *so* much better,' Maddie said with relief, coming over to her and resting a hand on her shoulder. 'You really scared us for a while.'

Ruby grinned. 'Oh, I'm so happy to see you! I don't remember your other visit at all, though Miss Wood told me you'd been here.'

Maddie took her hand. 'I'm just sorry I couldn't come back sooner. The three of us have been beside ourselves with worry, haven't we, Nell? But what with one thing and another . . .' She waved her hand airily, as though this explained everything, and looking at Nell's flushed face, Ruby decided she'd rather not know what had been keeping them away from her.

'Still,' Maddie went on brightly, 'Bill's been keeping us informed, so we know you've been in good hands.'

'Yes, they've all been looking after me very well, so there was no need to worry because I'm fine,' Ruby assured her. 'Or I will be when I can get this splint off.' She patted the offending splint.

'Hm, well don't get trying to rush things,' Maddie advised. 'Nell, could you go and organise us a nice tray of tea? Oh, and some of Cook's fancy cakes wouldn't go amiss if there are any going begging.' She pulled the pin from her hat and placed it on the chair then settling into her seat, she gazed at Ruby earnestly. Finally, she drew a breath. 'I want you to know that I'm sorry,' she said, looking away. 'Petty and Nell have told me off enough times, but they don't need to. I should never have tried to force you to work for me like that.'

Ruby felt tears come to her eyes. 'I'm sorry too,' she said quietly. 'You were so kind to me, taking me in like that when I was in such a bad situation . . . You can't even know how desperate I was . . .'

Maddie put a gentle finger to Ruby's lips. 'Shh. Don't say any more. I know very well what you were running from, and it just makes me feel more guilty. Can you forgive me?'

Ruby smiled through her tears. 'Of course I can. I would have died if it wasn't for you.'

Maddie shook her head. 'Oh, I think you'd have managed. You're stronger than you think, you know. But enough of that, let's talk about something else.'

Maddie began to tell her a funny story about an argument Mrs Petty and Nell had had the night before, and soon they were chatting like old friends and when Nell joined them, carrying a tray loaded with tea and treats from Cook, it almost felt to Ruby as though they were having a tea party.

Later that evening, there was a tap on her door and Miss Wood entered the room with Mr Pembroke beside her.

He smiled. 'I think I may have some good news for you, my dear. Now that Miranda is no longer here, I think I've managed to find you another position with my aunt. She's retired and gets quite lonely so she's agreed to take you on as her companion. I'm sure you'll get along. If you want the position, that is?'

'I, er . . .' Ruby didn't know what to say. There had been so many changes in her life recently but then she supposed that at least this would give her somewhere to go. Secretly she'd been hoping that Maddie would ask her to come back and live with her. But as she hadn't, it seemed she had no choice but to go along with Mr Pembroke's suggestion. 'Th-thank you, sir.' It sounded rather inadequate but what else could she say? She had known there would be nothing here for her to do and at least by accepting this post she would have a job and a roof over her head. And anything was better than having to go back to her father. She shuddered at the thought.

'Excellent!' Mr Pembroke looked pleased. 'It won't be for some time, of course. We need to get you properly well first,' he reassured her.

'Thank you,' she said again and once they had gone, she wondered what life had in store for her now. So much had happened since the terrible night her father had raped her that sometimes she couldn't quite take it all in. And now she was about to enter yet another household! She just hoped that Mr Pembroke's aunt would be a kinder mistress than Miranda, especially as it sounded like she'd be living with her

# Chapter Twenty

'I made a rather good job of that even if I do say so myself,' the doctor declared with a smile as he examined Ruby's leg. It was now mid-May and finally the splints were being removed from her leg.

'My leg looks sort of thin,' she commentated.

He laughed. 'It will do for a while, m'dear. Your muscles haven't been working for some time but as soon as you start to move about it will be back to normal again in no time. Now, just do a little walk across the room for me, would you, and tell me how it feels.'

Ruby dutifully did a little lap of the room. It felt strange to be walking again, but she didn't feel any pain.

Doctor Markham smiled, well satisfied with his efforts. 'Very good. That's my job here done, I believe. But just don't go overtiring it too soon. Good day, Ruby.'

Once he had gone Ruby quickly got dressed in her day clothes for the first time in weeks and made her way slowly downstairs.

Cook and Betty were delighted to see her up and about again, although Cook wouldn't hear of her doing anything to help them. They had been told that she would shortly be going to work for the master's aunt and although they would miss her, they felt it was an excellent idea.

'You'll like Hermione,' Cook told her as Ruby watched her rolling pastry. 'She's a bit crusty on the outside but soft as butter inside.'

'And where does she live?' Ruby hadn't thought to ask before.

'In Bedworth, a small town just outside of Nuneaton.'

Ruby knew it; she had gone to the market there once with her mother for material for a dress.

'So when do you think you'll be goin'?' Cook asked, adding hastily, 'Not that we want to get rid of you, of course. We'll miss you, won't we, Betty?'

'We will that.' Betty blinked tearfully. 'But then you can allus hop on the train an' come an' see us when you get time off. We'll all want to know how you're getting along.'

Miss Wood entered the room at that moment and she too was pleased to see Ruby up and about again. Since the mistress had left, things in the house had relaxed drastically and now all the staff called each other by their Christian names.

'I was just sayin', Serena, that Ruby will have to come an' see us when she moves on,' Betty said.

Serena nodded in agreement. 'She certainly will.' She had grown very close to Ruby while she'd been ill and she would be sorry to see her go. 'I was talking to the doctor before he left and he suggested sometime next week might be suitable, when your leg has had time to strengthen up a little. Would that suit you, Ruby?'

Ruby nodded, thinking how kind they had all been to her, especially since she'd broken her leg. She thought wistfully of the few occasions when Bill had carried her down to the kitchen; she'd felt so safe in his strong arms, and though she'd miss them all, she couldn't deny that perhaps she'd miss Bill most of all.

The week seemed to pass by in the blink of an eye and suddenly it was time for Ruby to begin her new job. Bill would be driving Ruby, Miss Wood and Mr Pembroke to the train station in the carriage, but first she had to say her goodbyes.

'You look after yourself now, do you hear me?' Cook told her as she folded her in her ample arms. 'An' don't forget we're always here if you need us, bab.'

One by one Ruby said goodbye to the rest of the staff ending with Betty and then she followed Miss Wood and Mr Pembroke outside to where Bill had the carriage waiting for her. She had said goodbye to Maddie and Nell the day before and now she was feeling tearful.

'It'll be all right.' Miss Wood squeezed her hand as they settled back against the leather squabs and the carriage set off.

The train station was buzzing with people as Bill hopped down from the driver's seat to say his goodbyes before they caught the train. 'You just take good care o' yourself now, little 'un, do you hear me?'

She nodded numbly as she swallowed the large lump that had formed in her throat and, conscious that the elders were watching them, she resisted the urge to throw her arms around him. Oblivious to her thoughts, Bill climbed back onto the carriage and urged the horses on. In no time at all they were on the train. Ruby watched from the window and the bustling streets of Birmingham were soon left far behind them.

When they arrived in Bedworth, Mr Pembroke hailed a hackney cab and after giving them his aunt's address they were off again.

'She lives in Marston Lane, quite close to the canal,' he told Ruby. 'You'll be able to walk along the towpath and watch the barges in your time off, if you wish.'

Ruby knew that he was trying to put her at ease. He and Miss Wood had kept up a steady stream of chatter ever since they had left the house but her stomach was in knots and she was so nervous she felt a little sick. What if she didn't like his aunt? Worse still, what if his aunt didn't like her? There were so many questions she wanted to ask but didn't dare. Soon the hackney drew to a halt and as Ruby peered anxiously out of the window she found herself outside a modest-looking detached house surrounded by a picket fence. There was a path leading from the gate to the front door and the garden either side of it was a profusion of flowers – chrysanthemums of all shapes, colours and sizes, hollyhocks, geraniums and foxgloves, to name but a few – and as they stepped down from the carriage the scent was heady.

'I forgot to tell you,' Mr Pembroke said with a smile after he'd paid the driver and sent him on his way, 'Aunt Hermione is a keen gardener as you've probably noticed.' He opened the gate and before they reached the brightly painted green door it opened and a plump, motherly looking woman wearing a voluminous white apron over a grey serge dress stood there beaming at them. Ruby thought she must be quite old as she had snow-white hair piled into an untidy bun on the back of her head and her blue eyes were faded but kindly.

'Why, Oscar, how lovely to see you,' she exclaimed in a very familiar fashion and Ruby wondered if this was his aunt. If she was, she was certainly nothing like Ruby had expected her to be. 'Come on in now. I've got the kettle on an' your aunt's been waiting for you. She's in the sitting room, so go on through and I'll bring you some tea in.' She smiled at Ruby then, a welcoming smile and Ruby decided that she liked her. 'And you must be Ruby, luvvie. I'm Mrs Bablake, Hermione's cook-cum-cleaner-cum bottle washer, but everybody calls me Mrs B. Welcome, we've been lookin' forward to meetin' you.'

Ruby returned the smile as she was ushered through the doorway and then Mrs B bustled off to the kitchen to prepare the tea.

The house was nowhere near as large or as grand as Mr Pembroke's but it was very comfortably furnished and everywhere was spotlessly clean. As they entered what she presumed was the sitting room she glanced about. There were comfortable leather wing chairs and a large chenille sofa covered with cushions, and a highly polished mahogany sideboard stood against one wall. Dark-green velvet curtains framed the large window room which had a warm comfortable feel to it and wasn't at all ostentatious.

'Ah, so you've arrived!' A strong voice came from the depths of one of the wing chairs and looking over Ruby saw a woman sitting there. She hadn't noticed her straightaway, which was hardly surprising because she was tiny and extremely thin – the complete antithesis of Mrs B.

Oscar hurried over to her and gently kissed each cheek as Ruby stood nervously next to Miss Wood.

'So, you've brought the girl then?' She was wearing metal-framed spectacles on the end of her nose and was dressed in a very plain black bombazine gown with a high neck. But it was the jewels she was wearing that Ruby could hardly tear her eyes away from. On a gold chain about her neck was the most beautiful sapphire pendant framed with diamonds that Ruby had ever seen, and on each of her tiny fingers were rings set with different gemstones that sparkled with every slight movement she made. Her grey hair was plaited and coiled about her head and her face was heavily wrinkled, making it hard for Ruby to judge how old she might be. But even so, the regal way she held herself and her bright-blue eyes told her that she must have been a beauty in her day and Ruby wondered why she had never married. 'Well, come here then, girl, an' let's have a look at you,' the woman said sharply and Ruby hastily stepped forward.

The woman gazed at her closely for a long time before exchanging a glance with Oscar who lowered his eyes. Finally she said, 'You are most welcome. Ruby, isn't it? And when Miss Wood and my nephew have gone, I shall explain your duties to you. I am sure we shall get along very well. Oscar tells me you like gemstones.'

'Yes, ma'am. Though I don't know much about 'em.' Ruby flushed under the close scrutiny, but thankfully the woman turned her attention to Miss Wood then, asking, 'And you, Serena, how are you? Better, I should imagine, now you haven't got that flibbertigibbet wife of his to run after all the time.'

It certainly seemed that, tiny as she was, the woman wasn't afraid to speak her mind.

'I'm very well, thank you, Miss Pembroke,' Miss Wood answered tactfully.

The door nudged open then and Mrs B appeared wheeling a tea trolley laden with wafer-thin cucumber sandwiches, an assortment of tiny tarts and fancies, a large sponge cake and a pot of tea.

'There we are then, me lovelies,' she said cheerfully. 'That should fill you all up fer the time bein'. I'll show you to your room when you've eaten, Ruby. I've got it all ready fer you an' I think you'll like it. It's got a lovely view across the back garden. It's lookin' grand at the minute. Like gardenin', do yer?'

Ruby had never had a garden and she didn't quite know what to say. 'I, erm . . . I'm sure I shall,' she said eventually.

Mrs B nodded. 'Good, well get that lot down you then.' And with that she swept away, humming merrily to herself.

While Ruby and Miss Wood sat quietly, Ruby nervously nibbling at a cucumber sandwich, Mr Pembroke and his aunt discussed work. Eventually Mrs B came back and with a smile at Ruby asked, 'Do yer want to come an' see yer room, luvvie?'

'I'll come with you,' Miss Wood volunteered and so the three of them followed the portly woman up the stairs.

As Mrs B had told her, the bedroom had a splendid view of the garden, which was much larger than Ruby had expected it to be and was divided into different sections. At the top of the garden were a selection of fruit trees and to the left a large vegetable plot. There was a lawned area surrounded by borders that were ablaze with roses and flowers all the colours of the rainbow and Ruby thought how beautiful it was. It was certainly a world away from the plain slabbed yard that had been her only playground when she was a child. The bedroom was pretty too, with a brass bed covered with a brightly coloured patchwork quilt and pretty chintz curtains hanging at the window.

'So, do you think you'll be comfortable in here?' Mrs B asked.

Ruby nodded enthusiastically. 'Oh yes, thank you, it's very comfortable.'

'Right, well I'll leave you to put your things away then.' Mrs B gave her an approving smile; she was looking forward to having someone young in the house. 'Just come down when you're ready.'

Once she had gone, Ruby began to unpack her few possessions from the small valise that Miss Wood had given her, but tears were threatening and she didn't trust herself to speak.

Sensing that she was upset Miss Wood placed her arms about her slight shoulders and gave her a squeeze. 'You'll be fine,' she said softly. 'I've known Mr Pembroke's aunt for many years and I promise you she is nowhere near as frosty as she appears.'

Ruby nodded and gulped. Right until the last minute they had left Mr Pembroke's house, she had hoped and prayed that Maddie would appear and beg her to go home with her, especially as she'd felt closer to her after the chat they had had after she'd been injured. Ruby had imagined Maddie confessing that she was her birth mother and them living happily ever after together, but that obviously wasn't going to happen now. If Maddie really was her mother it was clear she wanted her no more now than she had when she had been born.

'You must come and see us often. It takes no time at all on the train,' Miss Wood urged. 'We're all going to miss you so much.'

Ruby managed a watery smile and continued placing her things into the chest of drawers, and once it was done, they made their way back downstairs.

'Ah.' Mr Pembroke rose from his seat. 'We really ought to be going, Serena. I believe we shall be just in time for the next train back to Birmingham if we leave now.'

Hermione Pembroke's eyebrow rose at her nephew's familiarity in using his housekeeper's name but she said not a word as Miss Wood nodded. Much like her brother, she had long ago realised that Serena Wood had feelings for Oscar and she wondered now if they were being reciprocated. She hoped so, he was overdue a bit of happiness. He had certainly never known any with that horrid little strumpet of a wife of his! Admittedly, Serena was only a housekeeper, but she was a genteel, kind woman and Hermione secretly thought her nephew could do a lot worse. The trouble was he was still tied to Lydia, for now at least.

'I shall be back to see you all very soon,' Oscar promised as he took Miss Wood's elbow and led her towards the door. 'And I hope you will be very happy here, Ruby. You know where we are if you need anything.'

'Yes – thank you, sir.'

# Chapter Twenty-One

'Come and sit down here and tell me all about yourself, girl,' Hermione said when they were finally alone.

Ruby obediently perched on the edge of one of the leather chairs and mumbled, 'There's not much to tell really, Miss Pembroke.'

'You must call me Hermione. I can't be doing with standing on ceremony. And as regards to my question, that isn't what my nephew told me,' Aunt Hermione answered in her no-nonsense voice. 'He informs me that you've had quite a difficult time of it lately.'

Ruby wondered where she was to begin. She had no idea how much Mr Pembroke had already told the woman so there would be no point in lying.

'I . . . I suppose it started just before last Christmas when my mother died,' Ruby began in a faltering voice. 'And just before she passed away, she informed me that she and my father had actually adopted me when I was just a few days old and they weren't my natural parents as I had always believed. And then on the day of her funeral my father came to my room . . .' Slowly she recounted what had happened to her over the last few months, omitting nothing, and the old woman listened without interruption.

'Hm, it seems you have had a rough time of it,' she said when Ruby had finished. 'And from what I can make of it none of it was your fault. The question now, though, is what do you intend to do about it?'

Ruby frowned as she stared at her in confusion. 'I'm sorry . . . I don't understand what you mean.'

'What I mean is, you've had it hard but so have a lot of others. Let me tell you me and my brother Walter came from nothing! We lived in a two-up two-down in the slums of Birmingham with our parents, an army o' siblings and rats for company. When we left school, our Walter worked every hour God sent to save enough to enter the jewellery school an' become an apprentice goldsmith, an' look at him now! He, or should I say *we*, the family, have a string o' jewellery shops all over the country an' I'm proud of it. We earned 'em through blood sweat an' tears. Luckily our Walter married a good woman who backed him all the way, she was Oscar's mother an' we all got involved in the business in one way or another. There's a lot to learn, you see. So basically, what I'm saying to you is, there's two ways you can go now. You can wallow in self-pity an' let what's happened to you ruin the rest o' your life, or you can make somethin' of yourself. Which is it to be?'

Ruby was taken aback. Hermione certainly wasn't afraid to say what she thought. 'But I-I don't know what I *could* do,' she admitted. 'All I'm really good at is cleaning and baking.'

'And didn't Oscar tell me that you were interested in gemstones?'

'Well, yes, I do like them, but I don't know anythin' about them.'

'And neither did me and Walter when we first got into the business, so that's where I can come in. I do most of the designs for our jewellery collections and I'd be happy to pass on what I know to you as well as teach you everything else that's involved in gold- and silversmithing. If you want to learn, that is?' Hermione searched Ruby's face for a reaction. Suddenly the girl's eyes lit up, quite transforming her small face, and in that moment, Hermione saw that here was a beauty in the making.

'Oh, yes . . . I'd love that,' Ruby breathed hardly daring to believe her luck.

'Right, then you'd best be prepared to work,' Hermione warned. 'I'm a hard taskmaster an' I don't suffer fools gladly so you can have today to settle in an' tomorrow we'll begin your lessons.' With that she swept from the room leaving Ruby to stare after her. And in that moment Ruby decided to put her childhood and all that happened behind her as best she could.

That evening Ruby dined with Hermione in the small dining room. The meal Mrs B had cooked for them was simple – lamb chops, mashed potatoes and vegetables from Hermione's own garden – but it was very tasty. It was followed by a bread and butter pudding and custard that reminded Ruby of the ones her mother used to make, but she wouldn't allow herself to be sad. A new life was about to open up for her and she intended to make the best of it.

As they were sitting over coffee, Hermione asked, 'So, this woman who took you to her home the night you ran away, her name wouldn't happen to be Madeleine Bamber of Vittoria Street by any chance, would it?'

Ruby looked mildly surprised that Hermione knew her. 'Why, yes, it would actually. Do you know of her?' Ruby had told Hermione how Maddie had tried to set her on a life of crime and that she hadn't liked it.

'I know of her.' Hermione dabbed at her lips with her napkin. 'And don't think you are the only girl, or boy for that matter, that she has set on the path to crime. She's well known in the neighbourhood and has many people, young ones usually, that will steal for her.'

'Really? B-but she was so kind to me,' Ruby said waveringly. 'She took me in when I had nowhere to go. I would have been on the streets if it wasn't for her.'

'Hm, and what price would you have paid for that home eventually if her housekeeper hadn't got you out of there, eh?' Hermione sniffed disapprovingly. 'The police are well aware of how she makes a living but she's clever and they've never managed to catch her with any stolen jewellery as yet. She has a fence who she passes the pieces to and he sells most of it for her. I'm surprised she took you in, though. From what I've heard of her she usually just lets them come to her when they have something for her.'

Ruby was surprised. While she'd stayed with her, there hadn't been any young visitors, other than Bill. But then, she'd only been there a few weeks, and maybe they'd come once she'd gone to bed. Hermione didn't strike her as the sort to make up lies about people, so she realised she was probably telling the truth. But why had she taken her in, unless of course Maddie really was her mother and her conscience was troubling her for abandoning her at birth?

She decided to try not to think of it, and when the meal was over, she volunteered to help Mrs B with the dinner pots, an offer that was gratefully accepted. When that was done, she rejoined Hermione in the sitting room and read to her from the newspaper. Her schooling had been limited but her reading had vastly improved while she was staying with Maddie, so although she stumbled slightly over a few of the longer words she managed it.

'You will improve the more you read,' Hermione assured her. 'And I'm also going to give you a few elocution lessons. You've adopted a lot of local slang and that won't do if you ever have to work with our customers in any of the shops.'

'Work in the shops?' Ruby looked slightly worried but Hermione merely smiled.

'Why, of course. There's a lot more to the business than learning how to make the jewellery, it also has to be sold. Not that you'll be expected to attempt everything. But there's so much more to producing it than people think. For instance, do you know what the term annealing means?'

When Ruby stared at her blankly, Hermione went on, 'Annealing is the process of heating valuable metal like silver and gold to make it more workable. Then we have the chasing and the repouseé. And there's damascening – this is a way of making a decoration by cutting incisions into the metal before introducing threads of gold or silver wire which is then beaten into the cut for embellishment. And, of course, enamelling is very popular at the moment. This is where colourful powdered glass substances are introduced on to metal and fused with heat. And that is only a part of it – there is so much more.'

Seeing that Ruby was looking concerned she smiled. 'Don't worry. You won't be expected to learn everything overnight, or even attempt all of it. We tend to find that each person in the jewellery school has something that they excel at and they usually stick to that, so making one piece of jewellery can involve many different people. I myself enjoy designing the pieces and deciding which gems would be most suited to the style. Brooches are highly sought after at the moment, so I've been designing quite a lot of those. Tomorrow I shall take you into my workshop and you can look at what I do.'

Ruby nodded, feeling a little apprehensive. She had always imagined that a jeweller just sat down and made a piece and had never imagined that there were so many different processes involved.

'I think we shall also need to get you some new clothes if you are to accompany me when I go to the shops,' Hermione said as she stared at her thoughtfully. 'The dress you are wearing is very dull. I prefer to see young people in bright colours so I shall take you to my dressmaker to look at fabric and patterns as soon as possible. Perhaps we'll go into Coventry one day this week for anything else you may need as well.'

Ruby perked up considerably at the thought of that. The dress she was wearing was quite drab, although it was better than the ones Maddie had made her wear, but she was trying to put Maddie from her mind, so she said, 'Thank you, that'd be lovely. I ain't never really had anything bright before.'

'That *would* be lovely,' Hermione corrected. 'And it's "I haven't", not "I ain't".' And so began the first of Ruby's many elocution lessons.

Despite the fact she was in yet another strange bed, Ruby slept well that night and when she went down to breakfast the next morning, she found Mrs B with a pan of porridge bubbling away on the stove.

'Is Hermione not up yet?' Ruby enquired as she took a seat at the table.

Mrs B chuckled. 'Hermione is up wi' the lark every mornin',' she informed her. 'She said to let you sleep in just this once but she's already at work in her workshop. You're to go through to her once you've had breakfast.'

Feeling slightly guilty, Ruby rushed her meal and then Mrs B showed her to the room Hermione used as a workshop. It was tucked away behind a door at the far end of the corridor, which turned out to be steps leading down to a cellar. Once she reached the bottom of the steps, Ruby looked around and her eyes stretched wide with amazement. A multitude of gas lights made the vaulted room as bright as day, illuminating the long trestle workbenches along the walls, each covered in strands of gold and silver that glinted in the light. Hermione was sitting at one of them with a glass eyepiece in her eye working on something, and as Ruby drew closer she saw that it was a ring.

'Ah, here you are.' Hermione looked up as Ruby stopped beside her. 'I was just choosing a jewel for this mount. Which one do you think suits it best?' She gestured at three different-coloured jewels gleaming on the table. 'Do you know what these jewels are?'

Ruby licked her lips. 'That one is an emerald.' She pointed to the green one. 'That one is a diamond, and that one' – she pointed at the final stone – 'is a sapphire.'

'Very good. And which one do you think has the most value?'

Ruby's brow furrowed as she tried to remember what Maddie had told her. 'It's the diamond, I think.'

'That's correct. But did you know that not all diamonds are worth the same?'

When Ruby shook her head, Hermione said, 'You grade a diamond by its cut, clarity, colour and carat.'

Ruby nodded, remembering now that Maddie had told her this.

'A good diamond should be white with no tint of colour, and it should have no carbon inclusions,' Hermione went on. 'And the facets, or the cut, must be exceptional, which is where the master craftsmen come into play. Of course, it is rare to come across an internally flawless diamond so minor inclusions are acceptable provided they don't detract from the stone's beauty. Also, you will always find that one perfect diamond of a good size will be worth much more than a number of smaller stones. Diamonds are measured in carat weights and the larger the diamond the more it will be worth. People will pay thousands of pounds for such a stone.'

Ruby was finding the talk fascinating: there was so much more to it than she had realised, but then her eyes settled on some drawings and she was instantly distracted from what Hermione was saying.

'Did *you* do these?' she asked in awe.

Hermione nodded. 'Yes, every year we try to introduce new designs into our shops and these are some of my ideas for the next season. Hopefully they will be transformed into brooches.'

There was one of a bird with its tiny wings in flight, another of a leaf and yet another of a flower bud just opening.

'They're beautiful,' she breathed.

Hermione smiled with satisfaction. She was proud to know that many of the shops' bestsellers came from her designs. 'Some of these will be fashioned in silver, others in gold,' she explained. 'And many of them will be set with precious stones. This one, for instance' – she pointed to the bird – 'I should like that to have a tiny sapphire for the eye, and this one' – now she pointed to the leaf – 'will be crafted in gold and will have minute diamonds that will resemble dewdrops on it. The silver brooches will be set with semi-precious stones like topaz, amethyst and slightly less expensive gems.'

She turned her attention back to the ring she was holding then. 'These tiny prongs that you see are called tines and once the stone has been chosen to suit the mount, they will hold it in place. And yes, I think you are right, a diamond would suit it nicely. This diamond is approximately one carat in weight so a goodly size, although the real money comes in when you go over two carats.'

'It's much more complicated than I thought,' Ruby confessed, wondering how she was ever going to remember it all. But it was the designs that really captured her imagination. She had always loved to draw and without thinking she blurted out, 'Have you ever thought of making animal designs for the brooches?' And then promptly blushed for being so forward.

Hermione, however, didn't seem to mind at all. 'What sort of animals did you have in mind?'

'Well . . .' Ruby spread her hands. 'Most people like animals so you could do many different sorts – cats and dogs and even wild animals like panthers an' things.'

'Hm, you could have something there.' Hermione looked thoughtful. 'Why don't you try your hand at doing a few now?'

And so, feeling very self-conscious, Ruby sat down next to her and after taking up some coloured pens and paper she began to think. Within minutes she had her first idea and soon she had forgotten that Hermione was even there until the woman said, 'I think we will stop for a tea break now. It's gone eleven o'clock. Mrs B will have it ready for us.'

'Oh!' Ruby had been so engrossed in what she was doing that she had lost all track of time, but she couldn't remember a morning when she had enjoyed herself so much.

Hermione came to stand behind her and after placing her spectacles on the end of her nose she smiled. 'Some of these are actually very good,' she praised. 'Although they are rather out of proportion. But that is nothing to worry about. In future, though, I suggest you scale them to the size of the jewellery you imagine them becoming.'

Ruby flushed at the praise, and side by side they climbed the stairs to go and join Mrs B for their break.

The rest of the first week passed in a pleasant blur for Ruby. She and Hermione visited the dressmaker who eyed Ruby up and down before making suggestions as to what styles she thought might suit her, and they then spent a pleasant half an hour choosing the fabrics for two new gowns. The following day they boarded the train to Coventry and came home loaded with bags of things that Hermione insisted Ruby would need, although Ruby was a little concerned at how much the woman had spent on her.

'Oh, don't get worrying about that.' Hermione waved her hand breezily when Ruby broached it. 'Eventually you will be spending time with clients and in the shops so it's in my interest that you look the part.' She went on to tell Ruby what her wages would be. 'And you may have each evening after eight o'clock and every Sunday afternoon to do as you please.'

Ruby was more than happy with the arrangement, and realised how lucky she was to have been given this chance. But despite this, she still missed the friends she had made and thought of them all often. So when someone rapped on the front door late in the afternoon the following week and Hermione told her to answer it, she was delighted to find Miss Wood and Betty standing there.

'Hello, my dear,' Miss Wood said. 'We thought we would come and see how you are settling in. Mr Pembroke would have come too but he had an appointment with a client this afternoon who has commissioned him to make some jewellery for them.'

Ruby ushered them inside with a broad smile on her face and once she had shown them in to Hermione, who was in the sitting room, she hurried off to make a tray of tea for them all. She didn't like to ask Mrs B to do it as she was busily preparing the evening meal.

'How nice that they've come to see you,' Mrs B commented when Ruby told her who the guests were. 'They must have thought quite highly of you.'

Minutes later, Ruby carried the tray, laden with scones fresh from the oven and a pot of tea, to the sitting room.

'She seems to be settling in nicely,' she heard Hermione tell the visitors as she entered the room, and while they chatted on, she strained the tea into Hermione's highly prized china cups and saucers. Hermione had told her that they had once belonged to her mother. They had been the only decent thing the poor woman had ever owned, by all accounts, so Ruby was always terrified of breaking them.

'How are things back at the house?' Ruby asked when everyone had been served, hoping that she didn't sound too forward.

When Miss Wood hesitated before answering, Hermione snapped, 'Tell us, then! You might as well, because if you don't Oscar will when he next calls.'

'Erm, we had a visit the other day from Mrs Pembroke,' Miss Wood confided uneasily. 'And she and Mr Pembroke had a terrible row. We could hear them all over the house, couldn't we, Betty?'

Betty's head bobbed in agreement – she loved a bit of a gossip. 'Not 'alf. They were goin' at it hammer an' tongs, but the master gave as good as he got. We couldn't hear what they were sayin', but she were in a right temper when she left.'

'And have you heard anythin'– sorry, *anything* from Miranda?'

Miss Wood shook her head. 'Not us personally but I believe she has written to her father.'

Shortly after, the two younger women went outside to look at the garden, leaving Miss Wood and Hermione to chat and once outside Betty asked, 'So, how are you? *Really*, I mean?'

Ruby's smile was genuine. 'I'm fine, honestly. I really like Hermione; she's taught me so much already and she thinks I might get to be a jewellery designer eventually. She's taught me a lot about gardenin' an' all – I mean, *gardening as well*.' She gave a guilty smile. 'Hermione is teaching me to speak correctly for when I have to meet clients or work in any of the shops, but I still tend to say things wrong.'

'Hm.' Betty smiled at her. 'I don't mind tellin' you, we miss you, all of us, though we don't miss Miss Miranda, or her mother for that matter.'

'Do you still think there's no chance of her and Mr Pembroke getting back together?' Ruby asked as they stopped to admire a cluster of delphiniums.

Betty shook her head. 'I doubt it very much; I think he's got used to bein' on his own now, an' long may it last. The house is so much more peaceful without them.'

They continued their tour of the garden until eventually Mrs B came outside to tell them, 'Sorry to break this up, dears, but Miss Wood is ready to leave now. You don't want to go missin' your train.'

And so the two girls went back inside and after saying goodbye, the visitors hurried away, leaving Ruby feeling quite sad. She was happy enough where she was but she still missed them.

# Chapter Twenty-Two

At the beginning of July a letter arrived for Hermione and when Ruby collected it from the doormat, she noticed that it had a French postmark. She suspected it was from Miranda, and when Hermione opened it, she was proved to be right.

'Huh! The little madam wants to know if she can come and live with me.' Hermione snorted. 'She says she hates the school and the teachers and can't stay there another minute!'

Ruby's heart started to beat a little faster at the possibility of having to live under the same roof with her again but her fears were unfounded when Hermione declared, 'There is absolutely *no* chance of that happening! Why, we'd be at each other's throats in no time because I wouldn't put up with her tantrums. She's obviously already tried her father and he's stood firm, which is to his credit, but I wonder if she's tried her mother? If she has and Lydia has told her she won't have her, then I'm surprised.' She tapped her lip thoughtfully for a moment but then she threw the letter onto the table and stood up. 'Come along. I think we'll do a bit of work in the garden this morning. It's far too nice to be locked away in the workshop, then this afternoon

Mrs Besom is bringing your new gowns and not before time, eh? But then she has apologised for being a bit late. Apparently, she's been very busy.'

Ruby had been for her final fitting the week before and now she could hardly wait to see the finished gowns and when they arrived later that day, she was delighted with them and thought they had been well worth waiting for. Mrs Besom had recommended she try the latest fashion, which was a tight-fitting top with a straight skirt at the front and a small bustle at the back. They were easily the most fashionable gowns that Ruby had ever owned and they made her feel very grown-up. Since losing the baby she had noticed that her breasts were developing and although she realised she would always be petite, at least she was beginning to feel more womanly now.

She thanked Hermione profusely for them when Mrs Besom had gone but the woman waved her thanks aside. She was not one for shows of affection as Ruby had discovered.

'Just go and put one on and let's see you looking a bit more colourful,' the woman told her, and Ruby was only too happy to oblige.

'You look lovely, luvvie,' Mrs B told her when she entered the kitchen a short time later wearing a pretty lemon linen gown covered in tiny sprigs of lavender. 'But . . .' She tapped her lip thoughtfully with her forefinger for a moment before suggesting, 'Perhaps it's time we did something a little bit more grown-up with your hair too. Not that your plait doesn't look nice but . . .'

Ruby grinned. 'And what would you suggest?'

'Well, most o' the young girls I'm seein' out an' about have their hair taken up at the back with little ringlets hangin' down either side. Yours should work a treat seein' as you have naturally curly hair. Go an' get some grips off Hermione an' we'll have a little practice, eh?'

The next hour was one of the nicest Ruby could remember as she and Mrs B played with her hair and finally between them they managed to get it into some sort of style. When Mrs B nudged her in front of the mirror hanging above the fireplace, Ruby was shocked to see a young woman staring back at her. So shocked that she barely recognised herself.

'I . . . I feel so different,' she whispered.

Mrs B grinned. 'You're growin' up,' she said stoically.

Ruby said nothing. She could have told her that she'd been forced to grow up on the day her father had raped her, but she didn't want to spoil the mood and so instead she donned a huge apron to protect her lovely new dress and went outside to find Hermione, who was once again working in the garden.

Back in the house in Erdington, Mr Pembroke was in his workshop when Betty tapped on the door and went inside. 'I'm sorry to disturb you, sir, but the mistress is here to see you.'

Oscar looked surprised and stood up. 'Thank you, Betty, I'll be right out.'

He wondered what Lydia could want. The last time she'd called they'd ended up having a blazing row after she had insisted that he should raise her monthly allowance. When he had refused, she'd had a tantrum and he hoped it wasn't going to be the same today.

However, when he joined her in the sitting room she looked remarkably composed and even managed a smile when he entered the room.

'Ah, Oscar,' she greeted him. 'I have come to ask a little favour.'

'Oh yes.' He remained standing as he eyed her warily.

'The thing is, Miranda has written to inform me that she will be having a three-week holiday from school the week after next and I wondered if she might stay here with you? I am going away myself, you see? I thought a little break would do me good and she'll be bored staying with Mama and Papa.'

'Of course she can,' he said instantly, although he was mildly surprised. Lydia had never ventured anywhere alone before. 'And are you going anywhere nice?'

'I'm going to Spain,' she told him as she rose from her seat. 'But now that is settled, I really must be going. I shall write back to Miranda and ask her to let you know when to expect her.'

As she pulled on her gloves, he fancied that she had lost a little weight, and was that a new gown she was wearing? He couldn't remember seeing it before but it looked very expensive. He stifled a sigh. She would no doubt have charged it to his account but at least she was being civil, in fact, she looked better than she had for a long time. Their being apart clearly suited her.

'I shall be off then, things to do, you know!' And with that Lydia left, the feathers on her hat dancing.

The reason for her good mood became clear a few nights later when, after a visit to one of his shops, Oscar called in to the gentleman's club that he occasionally frequented. He was aware that news of his and Lydia's separation would have spread like wildfire by now but he was ready to face the gossips.

'Ah, Oscar, old chap. Come and join me,' a middle-aged man with a large moustache invited as he strode towards the bar. Oscar wasn't at all keen on Victor Fellows; his wife was a close friend of Lydia's and he had no doubt that Victor would be fishing for more news on the break-up. But not wishing to appear rude he took a seat, thinking it was best to get it over with.

'Over here, Charles.' Victor summoned a waiter and once he had ordered a drink for Oscar he puffed on his cigar for a while before saying, 'Well, this is a fine kettle of fish, is it not, old chap? Lydia finding a new love so quickly, I mean. You could have knocked me down with a feather when Belle told me.'

Oscar narrowed his eyes. 'What do you mean?'

'Oh dear, don't tell me that you didn't know? According to my wife she's been seen out and about with a certain gentleman – a lord no less. But then he'd have to be to afford her, wouldn't he? He's an old friend of her parents, by all accounts. Much older than her but rich as they come, which is probably the attraction. You *did* know, didn't you?'

The waiter appeared with his drink on a tray at that moment and once he had placed it in front of him, Oscar answered truthfully, 'I didn't know, but all I can say is, I hope he makes her happy. She's certainly not been happy with me for many years.'

Victor puffed on his cigar contemplatively. 'So, what will happen now? Have you spoken of divorce?'

Oscar took a sip of his drink and shook his head. 'Not as yet, but I dare say that will come in time. There's no chance of a reconciliation. On reflection I realise now that we were never really suited to each other, but these things happen and you just have to get on with life, don't you?'

'And is there no one new on the horizon for you yet?' Victor pressed.

Oscar had to stifle a grin. He knew that everything he said would be fed back to Belle the instant Victor arrived home. 'No, you know what they say, Victor – once bitten twice shy.'

'Rubbish!' Victor scoffed. 'Why, you're still a young man in your prime – and good-looking. The women will be queuing up for you once they know you're available again.'

'I doubt that very much.' Oscar was highly amused. 'And even if they did, I wouldn't be interested.'

Victor stared at him reflectively. 'That's what you say now but time is a great healer.'

Keen to change the subject, Oscar quickly moved on to talk of other things. He stayed for only the one drink and once at home again, Miss Wood hurried into the hall to greet him and take his hat and coat.

'Cook has kept your dinner warm for you,' she told him with a smile. 'Shall I serve it in the dining room?'

'Not at all, I'll come into the kitchen and have it in there.' It was funny, he thought as he followed her along the hallway, he would never have dared do that while Lydia was there. She had always frowned on him becoming too friendly with the servants but he was finding that he enjoyed their company more than he had hers. And it was so nice to come home to Serena's smiling face rather than a grilling from Lydia about where he had been.

'Has Father eaten?' he asked when they stepped through the green baize door.

Miss Wood nodded as she hurried to fetch his meal from the oven. She had given Cook and the rest of the staff the night off and now they found themselves alone, so he told her what Victor had told him at the club.

'I see, and how do you feel about that?' she asked softly as he lifted his knife and fork.

He shrugged. 'Surprised, I have to admit. I never dreamed she would find someone else so quickly, and shocked, I suppose, that it didn't hurt me to hear it. But I wish her well. Perhaps with this elderly lord she will find the happiness she never found with me.'

Serena's heart ached for him. She had loved him for so long but even now she was painfully aware that nothing could ever come of it. He was the master of the house while she was just the housekeeper. With a sigh she bustled away to put the kettle on and left him to eat his meal in peace.

He recounted what he had heard at the gentleman's club once again that evening when he visited his father in his room before retiring to bed.

'And how do you feel about it?' the old man asked, much as Serena had done, as he eyed him keenly.

'Funnily enough, very little,' Oscar admitted sadly. 'So I suppose it just goes to show that our marriage was over long before we parted.' They talked of the business then for a time and eventually Oscar retired to bed alone, much as he had done for many years.

When Miranda arrived, Oscar realised immediately that she wasn't at all happy in France. Her face was sullen when he went to greet her and her first words were, 'So how much longer are you going to keep me at that *stupid* school? It's like being in prison and Madame Babineaux is like a gaoler! All the girls there are snobs and their fathers are all lords or such like and they all look down on me.'

Oscar tried to keep his patience. 'I'm sure it can't be as bad as you say, darling, and you really haven't given yourself time to settle properly, have you?'

'All this because of a *stupid* little servant girl,' she spat as she removed her gloves and flung them at Serena.

Oscar gave her an apologetic glance. He had hoped that a little time away would make his daughter appreciate what she had but that didn't seem to be the case at all.

'And the food . . . ugh!' Miranda went on. 'I have never liked French food but you don't get a choice there. I shall be as thin as a rake by the time I leave there.'

At this Oscar had to stifle a smile. Miranda had her mother's build and was robust to put it very politely, so he thought that was very unlikely.

'Well, never mind. I'm sure you'll enjoy your dinner today. Cook has made you one of your favourites: roast beef and roast potatoes with all the trimmings with apple pie and custard to follow,' Serena informed her, but Miranda merely glared at her and stamped off to her room.

'Hm, welcome home,' Oscar murmured.

Serena just smiled – she was more than used to Miranda's moods – and set about helping Bill take Miranda's luggage up to her room.

Miranda had been home for two days before she asked her father casually one evening over dinner, 'So how is she – Ruby – settling in at Aunt Hermione's?'

'Very well as far as I know,' her father answered.

Miranda sat seething. *Not for much longer if I have anything to do with it*, she thought to herself but she said nothing and quietly got on with her meal.

It was Miss Wood's afternoon off the following day, and she had informed Miranda that she would be going into town to do some shopping. She had even asked if Miranda would like to accompany her but the girl politely refused.

As soon as Miss Wood had set off, Miranda crept along the landing to the housekeeper's room. She always kept her door locked but it had been easy for Miranda to take the spare key from the set in the kitchen that were kept for emergencies.

Miss Wood's room was just as Miranda had expected it to be: neat and tidy and very cosy. She stood looking around for a few moments then stealthily began to peep in the drawers. She wasn't even sure what she was looking for but her hatred of Ruby was so strong and her resentment at Miss

Wood for standing by the girl so fresh that she was determined to find something that would punish her for causing her to be sent away. Most of the drawers she opened revealed nothing other than neatly folded articles of clothing but then suddenly her heart began to race as she spotted something. It was a diary. Lifting it quickly Miranda opened it and found that it went back many years. There was far too much to read in one afternoon so she began to skim through it and as the minutes ticked away, her heart began to race and she smiled maliciously. It was only when she dared stay no longer for fear of Miss Wood returning that she placed the diary back exactly as she had found it and crept from the room with an exultant smile on her face.

# Chapter Twenty-Three

'I was thinking I might go and see Aunt Hermione this afternoon,' Miranda told her father casually the following day at breakfast.

Oscar glanced at her in surprise. Miranda had never been that keen on visiting her great-aunt before, but he supposed she was bored.

'That's quite a good idea actually,' he answered. 'In fact, I might come with you. I've got nothing urgent on today and it would be nice for us to spend some time together before you have to return to school. Oh, and I noticed you had a letter delivered this morning. Was it from your mother? And if it was, is she well?'

'Yes, it was from her actually,' Miranda answered cautiously. 'And yes, she's having a splendid time by the sound of it.' She still felt quite resentful that her mother had decided to travel abroad without her but she supposed that was because of her new beau. She knew all about her mother's new boyfriend but wasn't sure if her father did. 'I, er . . . suppose you know that Mother has a new . . . friend?' she said innocently and was surprised when her father smiled and nodded.

'Yes, I do know and I wish them both all the best.'

Miranda was shocked, but then wondered why she should be. Both he and her mother seemed so much happier apart.

'Right, so what time shall we set off for Aunt Hermione's then?'

'We could go this morning, if you like?' her father suggested. He was aware that he hadn't spent nearly enough time with her in the past and was feeling guilty, although looking back, whenever he *had* suggested they do something she had always made an excuse not to. *Still*, he thought, *better late than never.*

And so, just after ten thirty, they set off. It was an awkward journey as despite Oscar's best efforts to begin a conversation she would merely give a short reply and stare back out of the train window. He was also feeling decidedly uncomfortable now and was wondering if this had been such a good idea. After all, this would be the first time Miranda and Ruby had seen each other for some time and he knew how spiteful Miranda could be.

Even so, Aunt Hermione seemed pleased to see him when they arrived, although she said little to Miranda, who she had never grown close to. 'You're just in time for lunch, I'm sure we can rustle something up for you,' she invited as she pecked her nephew on the cheek. 'Mrs B has made a panful of her delicious beef broth and some wonderful crusty bread to go with it so there's more than enough to go round.' She narrowed her eyes and peered at Miranda. 'And how are you settling down at your new school?'

'Very well thank you, Aunt Hermione,' Miranda simpered. 'I'm still a little homesick but then as Father said that's to be expected, so I'm sure I shall be fine.'

230

'Hm!' Hermione was surprised to say the least. Miranda was usually such a surly girl, but then she supposed she shouldn't complain. At least she was making an attempt at being civil. Could it be that the French school was doing some good already? She decided to reserve her judgement as she led them into the sitting room, then bustled off to ask Mrs B if she would get them all some tea.

'And how is young Ruby settling in?' Oscar asked when she returned.

'Very well. In fact, I have some good news for you,' Hermione beamed. 'Within a very short time of her being here she expressed an interest in goldsmithing so I began to explain to her some of the techniques involved. But it soon became clear that her real flair lay in design so I allowed her to do a few sketches. Some of them are remarkably good so I showed them to Mr Clamp, the goldsmith at the school in the jewellery quarter. He was so impressed that he's having a few of them made up even as we speak. Ruby has a great eye for detail and I have a feeling that her designs are going to sell really well. She seems to have a natural talent for it. She's in my workshop right now, and she can't get enough of it.'

Miranda felt bile rise in her throat as she listened to her great-aunt praising the girl who had been the cause of her having to leave home, but she managed to keep the smile in place as she sipped daintily from the bone china cup. The door opened, then, and speak of the devil, there she was, and looking so different to how Miranda remembered her that she barely recognised her. Ruby seemed older some-how, no doubt owing to the more grown-up hairstyle and

231

the dress she was wearing. Whatever it was, Miranda felt a pang of jealousy as she was forced to acknowledge how attractive she looked.

The first person Ruby saw when she entered the room was her former employer and she smiled broadly, but when she noticed Miranda, the smile slid from her face and she faltered to a stop.

'Ah, Ruby, look who is here. We have guests for lunch,' Hermione said.

Remembering her manners, Ruby smiled an acknowledgment. 'Good afternoon, Mr Pembroke, Miss Miranda.' Ruby inclined her head politely.

'How are you, my dear?' Mr Pembroke's voice was kindly.

'I'm very well, thank you, sir.' She looked hesitantly towards Miranda then and was surprised when the older girl gave her a radiant smile.

'And Aunt Hermione tells us that you are trying your hand at designing,' Miranda said. 'How lovely. You must show me some of your drawings before we go.'

'Yes . . . of course.' Ruby wasn't sure whether she should dip her knee or not so decided to just stand there, reeling with shock at the change in Miranda's attitude towards her. She could never remember her speaking civilly to her before and didn't quite know what to make of it.

Thankfully, Hermione broke the awkward silence. 'Sit down then, girl. You're making the place look untidy. There's some tea left in the pot. Help yourself to a cup.'

Only too glad to have something to do, Ruby did as she was told, aware that Miranda was watching her all the time. Eventually they went in to lunch, which proved to be as tasty as Hermione had promised, and once it was over Miranda suggested, 'How about showing me some of these designs, Ruby? Aunt Hermione spoke very highly of them.'

Ruby glanced towards Hermione who inclined her head. 'Of course, would you like to come this way?' Ruby said reluctantly.

The two girls crossed the hallway and Miranda followed Ruby down the stairs to the workshop where a number of semi-precious gems glittered in the lights from the oil lamps, and sketches were spread across the workbench.

'These are some of mine,' Ruby said, pointing to the ones she had been working on. 'Hermione asked me to try what stones I think they should be set with. For instance, this one.' She pointed to a drawing of a peacock with its tail feathers spread. 'I'm thinking of a mixture of gemstones for that one. Amethyst, garnet, topaz, the more variety of colour the better really, but of course they will have to be tiny stones to get the effect. And this one.' She lifted a design of a rosebud. 'I think this should be worked in gold with a single ruby set in the bud.'

Miranda was forced to admit to herself that the designs were very good indeed, although she wouldn't say it out loud, of course. Instead she said, 'Hm, I can see that some of them have promise and I'm sure you'll get better as you go along. But is this what you really want to do? I thought you had come to be a companion to my aunt?'

'I had . . . what I mean is, I am her companion; we work side by side on these designs and we also spend a lot of time in the garden,' Ruby told her, unable to keep the enthusiasm from her voice.

When Miranda didn't respond, Ruby shuffled the papers on the table, unsure what she should say next. After everything that had happened and the way Miranda had treated her, she felt uncomfortable being alone with her. But nothing could have prepared her for what the girl said next.

'I suppose I owe you an apology for the way I behaved on the day you fell.' Miranda sounded so contrite that Ruby was shocked.

'It's all in the past now, let's just forget about it, shall we?' she answered good-naturedly. Ruby had never been one to bear a grudge.

Miranda nodded. 'Yes, let's. We'll make a fresh start and who knows, we might even end up being friends, although I'm afraid I'm going to be away for most of the next two years. Still, I shall visit when I come home and you are always welcome to pop back to our house to see me when I'm there. Bill wishes to be remembered to you by the way.' She smiled sweetly. 'He's getting so handsome, isn't he?'

Ruby blushed, mainly because she had thought exactly the same thing the last time she had visited just a few weeks before. It had quite shaken her because she had never looked at a boy that way before and didn't quite understand herself.

'Anyway, getting back to this.' Miranda waved her hand across the expensive gems. 'Isn't it quite dangerous to leave all these precious stones lying about? They must be worth hundreds of pounds.'

'Oh, we don't,' Ruby assured her. 'As soon as we've finished with them for the day, they are all safely locked away in the safe back there.' She waved her hand towards the huge old metal safe that stood in one corner of the cellar. 'And then Hermione locks the door to the workshop as well so they are doubly protected.'

The two girls returned to the sitting room soon after this and another pleasant hour passed before Mr Pembroke said reluctantly, 'We really should be thinking of going now, Miranda, if we are to catch the next train back to New Street.'

'Yes, Father.' Miranda rose from her seat and after kissing her aunt and nodding goodbye to Ruby, they departed.

'What did you make of that?' Hermione asked when the door had closed behind them. 'I've never known Miranda be so amicable. I must admit that although she's my great-niece there have been times over the years when I've wanted to throw her across my lap and give her a good whacking.'

There was a twinkle of amusement in Ruby's eyes as she looked back at her but she said not a word. As far as she was concerned, she didn't really care what had brought about the change, she just hoped it lasted.

Over the next few months Ruby continued to visit the Pembrokes' house frequently on her afternoon off, and before she knew it, it was December and she was facing her first Christmas with Hermione. Her confidence had grown during the time she had been in Hermione's care, especially when some of her designs had proved to be very popular indeed in the shops. So much so that Hermione had given her a rise in wages, so one afternoon she dared to ask, 'Would you mind very much if I changed my Sunday afternoon off to a day in the week next week? I'd like to do a little Christmas shopping and the shops are shut on Sunday.'

'No, you can't change your day off,' Hermione answered shortly and when Ruby's face fell, she went on, 'but you can have a week day afternoon off as well. You've earned it. Where were you thinking of going to do your shopping?'

Ruby lowered her head. 'I . . . I'd like to go into Nuneaton but . . .'

'But you're afraid you might bump into your adoptive father?'

Ruby nodded miserably. She hadn't been near the town since the night she had run away.

'Well, you know what they say' – Hermione looked at her sternly – 'face your demons! You can't run away from them all your life. And just remember, it was *he* that was in the wrong, not you. You go into Nuneaton, girl, and hold your head high.'

The more Ruby thought on what she had said, the more she realised that Hermione was right, and so one cold and frosty afternoon she set off. Her heart was hammering as she stepped off the omnibus and looked around at the familiar streets. It was a year since she had been there but so much had happened in that time. She was now almost sixteen years old and no longer the frightened little girl she had been back then but a young woman on the brink of becoming an adult, so with a deep breath she set her shoulders and marched into the market place. She was wearing a new coat and bonnet that she had recently bought from her wages and she received more than a few admiring glances as she strode along, which gave her confidence. It was market day and as she wandered among the stalls that sported almost everything anyone could need, from various foods to pots and pans and second-hand clothes, she made a few purchases and tucked them away into her bag. She was studying some brightly coloured buttons on one such stall when someone tapped her gently on the shoulder and wheeling about she found herself face to face with one of the regular customers who used to come into the bakery.

'Why, bless me soul. I thought it was you, young Ruby.' The woman who spoke was plump and middle-aged and Ruby smiled at her.

'Hello, Mrs Green, how are you?'

'I'm very well, luvvie. And so are you by the look o' yer!' The woman eyed her up and down approvingly. 'Why you've grown up, an' a right pretty young lady you're makin' an' all. I missed yer smilin' face in the shop when yer first went but yer dad wouldn't say where you'd gone.'

Ruby squirmed uncomfortably. Mrs Green was lovely but she also liked a good gossip so there was no way she could tell her. Instead she simply said, 'I decided after Mam died that I'd try my hand at something else.'

'Can't say as I blame yer, bein' left alone wi' that old sod.' Mrs Green swiped her runny nose on the sleeve of her shabby coat. 'Yer mam were a lovely woman but I pitied yer bein' left alone wi' that tight old bugger.' She grinned then, revealing a row of tobacco-stained teeth. 'Yer dad were run-nin' around like a headless chicken fer a time after yer went. Served him right an' all. Happen then he realised just how much work yer did fer him. The shop ain't never been the same wi'out you an' yer mam. An' now Lil Best 'as got 'er feet under the table an' the business is goin' down by the day. Serves him right, that's what I say.'

'Lil Best?' Ruby was shocked. Lil was well known in the town for being loose with her favours where gentleman were concerned, but then after what her father had done to her she decided he deserved no better.

Mrs Green nodded. 'Yes, it's as true as I'm standin' 'ere. She's as different from yer mam were as chalk from cheese. But anyway, I'd best get on. My Bert'll be 'ome fer his dinner in a couple of hours and he can be right funny if it ain't on the table. Bye, luvvie, it was lovely to see yer.' And with that she hitched up her wicker basket and strode away, leaving Ruby to stare thoughtfully after her.

After a short while, Ruby moved on and soon she found herself standing over the road from the bakery staring into it through the stalls. The first thing she noticed was that the windows were filthy. That had always been one of her first jobs of the day to clean them and sweep the floor inside and out, but now they looked as if they hadn't been touched for months. She could see Lil standing behind the counter in a dirty apron with a pipe dangling from the corner of her mouth, and as she watched she saw her father enter from behind her with a basket of fresh bread, which he plonked down on the counter. From what she could see, they appeared to be rowing as her father started to wave his hands about, and although she had never been a spiteful person, she found that she was smiling. Perhaps he was finally getting what he deserved. Suddenly plucking up her courage she crossed the road, and as she marched into the shop the bell above the door tinkled and her father looked towards it. Shock registered on his face as he saw who it was and he was momentarily struck dumb.

'Hello, Dad, you're letting your standards slip a little, aren't you?' She wiped her finger along the edge of the counter and grimaced as she held it up to show the dirt it had collected.

'Why you . . . you cheeky little bitch! I don't know how you dare show your face in 'ere after yer left me in the lurch as yer did!' he spluttered.

Her face hardened. 'And why did I leave you in the lurch, eh? Perhaps you would like me to tell Lil?'

The colour drained from his face as he waved towards the door. 'Get out – go on! We don't want no trouble here!'

'With the greatest of pleasure,' she answered calmly and glancing towards Lil she smiled. 'I hope you'll be very happy together.' And with that she turned about, her elegant skirts swishing, and marched from the shop with her head held high, wondering why she had ever feared him so much.

# Chapter Twenty-Four

'Oh . . . hello, Miranda.' Ruby looked mildly surprised when she answered the door the following week. She had visited the Pembroke household the week before and Miss Wood had told her that they were expecting Miranda home from school for Christmas, but Ruby hadn't anticipated seeing her at her Aunt Hermione's quite so soon.

'How are you, Ruby? I'm sure you've grown again,' Miranda said as she hurried in out of the cold. 'Father tells me your designs are proving to be really popular now and that you've been spending some time at the school and in the shop.'

Ruby took Miranda's coat and hung it up for her as she removed her hat. 'Yes, Hermione is keen for me to know the whole process of jewellery-making and I'm really enjoying it. Your aunt is in the sitting room. She's got a bit of a chill, unfortunately, so she isn't working today. Can I fetch you some tea?'

'That would be lovely.' As Miranda made for the sitting room Ruby bit her lip and headed for the kitchen. Miranda was still being nice to her and yet for some reason Ruby still didn't completely trust her.

She found Mrs B rolling pastry for a steak and kidney pie and when she told her that Miranda had arrived the woman frowned.

'I've never known her visit so much; I wonder what she's after?' Mrs B said thoughtfully. It seemed that Ruby wasn't the only one who had doubts about her.

Ruby loaded a tray and carried it through to the sitting room. But when she made to leave, Miranda said, 'Oh, aren't you going to join us, Ruby? I haven't seen you since the summer. It's so hard being away from home.' She pouted. 'Although I don't really know where home is at present. I'm neither living at my grandparents nor at my father's full-time.'

'I would have thought you'd stay with your mother when you aren't at school,' Hermione said bluntly as Ruby reluctantly took a seat and began to pour the tea.

'Oh, I would to, but Mother is hardly ever there.' Miranda frowned. 'She's always off out with Lord Chumley somewhere and never seems to have any time for me. But then she never did. And Grandmama and Grandpapa are always so busy . . .'

If she had expected sympathy, she was sorely disappointed when Hermione ignored the remarks and asked, 'And how is your schooling going?'

Miranda shrugged her plump shoulders. 'Much the same. It's quite boring actually. The chateau is so far out in the hills that it's almost impossible to get to the nearest town so it's like being in a prison for most of the time, and I still have almost another year to do there . . . unless . . . Well actually, I was wondering if perhaps I couldn't come and stay here with you, Aunt Hermione?'

Ruby held her breath. Despite the fact that Miranda was being nice to her now she still didn't fancy having to live under the same roof as her again. But she needn't have worried, for Hermione raised an eyebrow and snorted, 'There's no chance of that happening, m'dear. Mrs B has enough to do looking after me, although I must admit Ruby is a great help to her. No, there's more than enough bodies in this house as it is.'

Ruby thought she detected a hint of resentment flare in Miranda's eyes but it was gone so quickly that she decided she must have imagined it when Miranda smiled and said cheerily, 'Aw well, another year isn't such a long time. It was just a thought.'

Soon after, Ruby excused herself and went back to the workroom where she was working on some designs for a new Christmas selection. The ones she had designed this year had already been made in the workshop in Birmingham and one in particular was selling very well – a small robin fashioned from gold with tiny rubies studded on its chest. Brooches had proved to be very popular in the lead-up to Christmas and so Ruby was creating new designs for the next festive season to give the workshops plenty of time to produce enough stock to satisfy demand.

Soon she was so engrossed in what she was doing that she was startled when a voice at her elbow suddenly said, 'That's nice. Is it a snowman?'

Ruby nodded. 'Yes, this one is being aimed at the younger customers. It will be made in silver and have tiny semi-precious gems for eyes.'

Miranda stared down at the sketches and had to admit that Ruby did indeed have a flair for design, as her father never tired of telling her. Personally, she couldn't think of anything more boring than having to sit doing sketches all day, but she supposed it was each to his own.

'So, will you be staying at your father's for Christmas?' Ruby asked after a time, feeling that she at least ought to make some attempt at conversation.

Miranda shook her head. 'No, I shall be going to my grandparents the day before Christmas Eve to spend it with them and my mother, if Lord Chumley doesn't whisk her off somewhere, that is,' she added glumly. 'But what about you? What will you be doing and what would you like for Christmas?'

'I shall be spending it here but ... Well, what I'd like more than anything in the world you can't buy,' Ruby said sadly.

'Oh!' Miranda was all ears now. 'And what would that be then?'

Ruby hesitated, wondering if she could trust Miranda.

'Oh, do tell me,' Miranda urged. 'I know you have no reason to trust me, but I honestly have changed. And it might be something I could help you with.'

Ruby couldn't deny that this seemed to be the case. And anyway, what harm could there be in sharing her dream? 'When my mother died she told me that I had been adopted at birth,' she explained. 'And what I'd like more than anything in the world is to find my birth mother.'

'I can understand that,' Miranda said sympathetically. 'It must be awful not knowing who she was. Perhaps I could help you trace her?'

'That's doubtful when you're living in France,' Ruby pointed out.

243

'Ah, but I won't be there forever, will I?'

Miranda sounded so kind that Ruby felt a stab of guilt. Perhaps she had misjudged the girl and she really had changed for the better? They chattered on about the designs for a while and when Miranda finally left shortly after lunch, Ruby saw her to the door.

'Don't forget, when I come home from school, we'll start to look for your mother in earnest,' Miranda told her and Ruby smiled. 'Meantime, I'll see you when you come next week. You did say you were coming to Father's house, didn't you?'

'I'll be there; I have to deliver some presents,' Ruby told her and once Miranda had gone, she found that she was smiling.

'Miranda was in a good mood again, wasn't she?' Hermione commented when Ruby returned to the sitting room.

'Yes she was, I'm beginning to think she's really changed.'

'Hm, we'll see,' Hermione answered doubtfully, before turning her attention back to the newspaper she'd been reading.

The following week Ruby spent a morning in Mr Pembroke's shop in the jewellery quarter and was surprised to see how busy they were. Many wealthy people were coming in looking for gifts for their loved ones for Christmas, and Ruby was shocked at the amount of money they spent.

'We have a very elite selection of clients,' Mr Cushing, the manager of the shop, told her after a gentleman with an enormous moustache bought a diamond ring that cost far more than Ruby could have earned in years. He grinned and went on, 'And the gentleman who just left is a regular customer, although I doubt very much that the ring he bought was for his wife, if you know what I mean?'

Ruby stared at him blankly for a moment then realising what he meant she blushed prettily. Mr Cushing laughed. Ruby was a pleasure; she was so naive and pleasant and was proving to be a great favourite with the customers, as were her designs.

When the shop eventually closed, Ruby hopped into a horse-drawn cab and took the opportunity to visit Mr Pembroke's house in Erdington to deliver the small gifts she had bought. She had also bought gifts for Maddie, Mrs Petty and Nell, which she would leave with Miss Wood who had promised to make sure they were delivered to them.

She entered the house through the back way as she always did and Cook's face lit up at the sight of her. 'Why, I swear you look a bit more grown-up every time I see you,' she declared as Ruby placed the gifts she had bought for them on the table. Ruby was wearing a very smart costume that she had recently bought in a lovely shade of forest green that complemented her figure, and over it she was wearing a warm, fur-lined cloak.

Cook hurried over to the stove to lift the kettle that was singing gently on the range and make some tea. At that moment Bill strode into the kitchen and stopped short at the sight of Ruby, suddenly seeing her as a young woman for the first time. He had always thought of her as a child and it was a shock to see her looking so grand.

'You, er . . . look nice,' he said quietly, aware that he was dressed in his oldest clothes as he had been cleaning the stables out.

'Thank you. There's a little gift for you here,' Ruby told him and he noticed that she even sounded different now. Hermione's elocution lessons were paying off. 'But you mustn't open it till Christmas morning.'

He felt even more confused at that as he stuttered, 'That's really kind of you . . . but I'm afraid I haven't bought you anything. I haven't got around to doing any shopping yet.'

Ruby giggled. 'That doesn't matter. I didn't expect you to,' she assured him. 'And it isn't anything much really.'

Betty came in then and gave Ruby a hug. It was always lovely to see her, especially looking so well.

'So tell me all you've been up to,' she urged as they settled at the table with steaming cups of tea in front of them, and Ruby happily told them about the designs she'd been working on. All too soon it was time for her to leave, but as she put her cloak on, she asked, 'Has Miranda left to go back to her grandparents yet?'

'Huh! Unfortunately not,' Betty said with a shake of her head. 'But between you an' me, I can't wait to see the back of her, the stroppy little madam.'

Ruby frowned. 'But she's been really nice to me on the odd occasions I've seen her.'

The girl shrugged. 'Well, she ain't been nice to me, or anybody else 'ere for that matter, so just watch your back; I wouldn't trust her as far as I could throw her.'

Once they had said their goodbyes, Ruby set off for the train station in a thoughtful mood as she mused on what

Betty had said. However, the windows of the shops she passed were glittering with Christmas decorations and the frosty streets had taken on a magical air, so soon she was so busy admiring them that she forgot all about it.

When she arrived back at Hermione's house in Bedworth, she found the woman waiting for her, eager to hear all about how her day had gone. She was really enjoying having someone young in the house.

'It was wonderful,' Ruby told her, her eyes animated. 'And while I was there, Mr Cushing sold at least two of the brooches I designed. He says one design in particular is proving to be very popular. So popular, in fact, that he's ordered some to be made in silver for next year for those customers who can't afford the gold version.'

'I'm not surprised,' the old woman told her. 'And now I have some news for you. A letter arrived from Oscar today asking me – and you, of course – to spend Christmas with him. How do you feel about that?'

Ruby was surprised. 'But what about Mrs B?'

Hermione waved her hand. 'Oh, she's more than happy with the idea; she's going to spend it with her sister in Bulkington. The poor woman was recently widowed so she'll be glad of the company.'

Ruby realised she didn't have much say in the matter, although she was secretly pleased to think of spending time with Cook and Betty – and Bill, of course.

Two days before Christmas, Hermione and Ruby caught the train to Oscar's house. 'You will dine with me, Oscar and Walter – if he's well enough – over Christmas,' Hermione informed her as they rattled through the countryside.

Ruby shook her head. Sometimes she wasn't really sure where she fitted in anymore, for although she was supposed to be Hermione's companion, she still considered herself to be a servant, and she knew she would feel more comfortable dining in the kitchen with the rest of the staff, especially Bill. The thought of him brought a flush to her cheeks and she quickly gazed out of the window so Hermione wouldn't see it as she replied, 'That's really kind of you but I think it might be best if I ate in the kitchen. I'm not family, after all.'

Hermione sniffed as she clutched the bag on her lap. She didn't usually venture far from home these days and wasn't enjoying the train ride at all, nor the cold weather, if it came to that. 'As you wish,' she said shortly and thankfully the subject was dropped.

They arrived at the house to find a number of Miranda's trunks packed ready in the hall, although she wouldn't be leaving until the next morning.

Hermione went to take tea with her nephew in the drawing room while Miranda commandeered Ruby immediately. 'Oh, it's *so* nice that I got to see you before I go,' she gushed, appearing to be genuinely pleased to see her. 'I didn't know you were spending Christmas here or I would have asked my father if I could stay too. It's going to be so *boring* at my grandparents'.'

'I'm sure you'll have a lovely time,' Ruby answered as she went to carry her own small bag to the room she had once shared with Betty; she was looking forward to them having a good old catch-up.

Miranda pouted, but then perked up again as she said, 'Aw well, at least we can have a good chat this evening.'

Ruby gave her a faltering smile. She'd hoped that she could spend the evening in the kitchen with the rest of the staff, but she didn't want to hurt Miranda's feelings so she nodded. 'Very well, perhaps after dinner. But I'd best go and put my things away. I'll see you later.'

Miranda watched her mount the stairs and once she was out of sight she turned and made for the drawing room with a sly smile on her face.

# Chapter Twenty-Five

Once the family and staff had eaten, Ruby helped with the clearing up and headed for her room. After she'd gone, Cook smiled. 'It's good to see Ruby lookin' so well, ain't it?' she said. 'She seems to 'ave settled well at Hermione's place an' the old woman speaks highly of her from what I've heard.'

'So I believe.' Serena nodded.

'She's a good girl,' Cook went on. 'For all the fancy gowns she has now, she still ain't scared of lendin' a helpin' hand about the place. An' who'd have thought she'd turn her hand to designin' jewellery, eh? It's just a pity Miss Miranda can't be a bit more like her. That little madam still expects to be waited on hand and foot!'

Serena sighed, but said nothing.

Meanwhile, Ruby was hoping to get upstairs before Miranda sought her out, but in that she was unlucky when she found the very person she was trying to avoid waiting at the top of the stairs for her.

'Ah, here you are.' Miranda grinned. 'Father and Aunt Hermione are just settling down for a game of chess and Grandfather's still not well enough to come downstairs, so I thought I'd find you.'

'Oh, I was just going to hang your aunt's clothes up,' Ruby answered, hoping that Miranda would take the hint and find something else to do.

'Fine, I'll help you,' Miranda volunteered, and knowing when she was beaten Ruby trudged along the landing with Miranda close behind.

Miss Wood had put Hermione in Miranda's mother's old room and when they entered it Miranda looked momentarily so sad that Ruby couldn't help but feel a little sorry for her.

'I can't believe that Mother will never come back here,' Miranda said glumly. 'I'm sure she would have if she hadn't met that loathsome Lord Chumley!' She grimaced. 'He's completely besotted with her, you know. In fact, I heard him ask Mother when she was going to ask Father for a divorce,' she confided.

'A divorce!' Ruby was shocked.

Miranda nodded, her face miserable. 'Yes, I overheard them when he came calling at Grandmama's. I suppose they'll get married if she does get one, which will mean that Mother will go to live with him in his house. He has a stately home somewhere, I believe.'

'Really? Then you might enjoy living there,' Ruby answered.

Miranda tossed her head and snorted. 'Me? Huh! There's little chance of that happening. Mother didn't have time for me when she lived here so I suppose I'll get left behind with my grandparents. Unless I come back here to live with Father, of course. But that wouldn't be for a while anyway. I believe it can take years for a divorce to go through and I still have almost another year to do at that dreadful school in France with the dreaded Madame Babineaux!'

Ruby didn't quite know what to say as she hung one of Hermione's gowns onto a hanger and placed it neatly in the armoire. But she needn't have worried, Miranda had enough to say for both of them.

'So, was Bill at supper this evening?' Miranda asked casually.

Despite herself, Ruby felt a little colour creep into her cheeks. 'Er, yes, I believe he was.'

'Hm, I think he likes me, you know,' Miranda said with a sly glance at her.

'Really?' Ruby hastily lifted another of Hermione's gowns from the trunk and hung it away. She was remembering what had happened the last time Miranda had spoken of Bill and was keen to change the subject. 'So what are you hoping to get for Christmas?' she asked casually.

Miranda grimaced. 'I *know* what I shall get,' she said ungratefully. 'It will be a piece of expensive jewellery from Father and clothes from Mother. Then I shall get embroidered handkerchiefs from Aunt Hermione. It's the same every year.'

Ruby thought how wonderful it must be to get such lovely gifts, although she didn't say so.

'And what do you want?' Miranda asked then. 'Apart from to find your birth mother, I mean.'

Ruby frowned, wondering whether she should tell Miranda about her suspicions of Maddie being her mother but then decided against it. Deep down she hoped that if it were true, Maddie would one day confess it, but for now, she decided it might be wise to keep her suspicions to herself, especially as over the past few months she hadn't seen that much of Maddie, and she couldn't help feeling a little hurt. If Maddie was her mother, surely she'd make more effort to see her?

'I've never really expected or asked for anything,' Ruby answered instead. 'Although, your great-aunt has hinted that she's bought me some gifts which is really kind of her.'

'But what about when you lived at home with your adopted parents?'

Ruby shrugged. 'The man I thought was my father was never keen on Christmas,' she admitted. 'He was very hard-working, for all his faults, and he begrudged having to close the shop. I'm sure if it hadn't been for my mother, we wouldn't even have had a Christmas dinner.'

'That's awful.' Miranda narrowed her eyes before saying quietly, 'And is it true what they said about you when you first came here . . . that you had run away after he raped you and got you with child?'

Ruby felt hot colour burn into her cheeks. It was a subject she tried not to think about anymore. 'Yes, it's true,' she said in a small voice. 'But there, that's everything put away now. Shall we go back downstairs?' She was keen to speak of other things, so without waiting for an answer she hurried from the room leaving Miranda to stare thoughtfully after her for a moment before following her down the stairs.

'The young madam seems keen to be your friend all of a sudden, don't she?' Betty said that night as she and Ruby got ready for bed.

Ruby nodded. 'Yes, she does, which is quite surprising really seeing as not so long ago she couldn't stand me.'

'Hm, well just take care,' Betty said as she tugged her nightgown over her head. 'I still don't trust her.'

Ruby didn't answer, but deep down she felt exactly the same.

Lord Chumley's fine carriage came to collect Miranda the following morning and Ruby felt a little easier once she had left. She spent the morning in the drawing room helping Betty decorate the Christmas tree that had been delivered, while Hermione looked on. She was feeling happy as she'd had word that Maddie, Nell and Mrs Petty were calling to see her that afternoon, and as the morning wore on a little bubble of excitement began to grow in her stomach. Christmas Eve was a special day, after all, so if Maddie *was* her mother, perhaps today would be the day she chose to reveal the truth.

On that point she was doomed to be disappointed, for although the guests arrived as planned, Maddie made no effort to get her on her own. Now that Miranda had gone the atmosphere in the house was relaxed and the mood in the kitchen was light. Betty made a large pot of tea and they all sat together at the table drinking it and eating some of Cook's delicious mince pies while Cook sat plucking the most enormous turkey that Ruby had ever seen, sending feathers flying everywhere.

'Crikey, I reckon you'll 'ave a battle on yer hands to get that in the oven,' Betty joked, and they all laughed. Even the elderly Mr Pembroke had felt well enough to get up that day and was presently sitting in the drawing room with his son discussing the latest designs that Ruby had done with Hermione.

By four o'clock it was pitch dark and Maddie, Nell and Mrs Petty took their leave, making Ruby promise to visit them before she returned to Hermione's house in Bedworth.

'Oh dear, I shouldn't 'ave eaten so many o' them mince pies,' Betty groaned as she rubbed her stomach. 'I shall never make room fer me dinner.'

'Well, that'll be a first then.' Cook chuckled. 'I've never known you refuse food afore!' She often joked that she thought Betty had hollow legs because she could usually eat more than Bill.

Once the family were served their meal in the dining room that evening the staff sat down to eat theirs in the kitchen and Ruby found herself seated next to Bill.

He had washed and changed and with his hair gleaming in the light from the oil lamp that stood in the centre of the table, Ruby thought how handsome he looked and instantly blushed.

'Well I have to say I wasn't sorry to see Miranda go this morning,' he admitted as he tucked into his dinner.

'I'm not surprised, the way she were followin' you about,' Cook snorted. 'She makes no secret of the fact she's got her eye on you.'

'I can assure you it'll do her no good, even if she has,' Bill answered with a frown. 'I wouldn't look the side she's on if she were the last girl on earth.'

'Oh yes, an' why's that then?' Cook said teasingly. 'Got your eye fixed on someone else, 'ave you?'

Bill glanced at Ruby and they both blushed the colour of rhubarb. This wasn't lost on Cook who looked at Betty with a knowing smile. The talk went on to other things then, although Ruby felt so uncomfortable, she could hardly swallow her food.

Later that evening she was summoned to the drawing room where she found Mr Pembroke and Hermione waiting for her and her stomach immediately did a somersault as she wondered if she had done something wrong.

'Don't look so worried, there's nothing amiss, my dear,' Mr Pembroke assured her as he beckoned her into the room. 'In fact, I have some very nice news for you. As your designs have been selling so well, one of our best clients, Mrs Lavender-Hughes, has asked me to commission you to design a ring for her. She's very wealthy indeed so money is no object. She would like a diamond ring, a cluster consisting of different cuts. Do you think you could manage that?'

'I, er . . . yes, of course. I'll try,' Ruby said, delighted.

'Then when we get home, I shall sort a selection of diamonds out of the safe for you to study,' Hermione told her. It would be the first time that Ruby had been trusted to work with diamonds, the most expensive of all the stones, and she felt honoured.

She almost skipped up to her room that night but she knew deep down that the happy feeling wasn't purely down to the commission. It was partly due to Bill too, for suddenly she couldn't look at him without getting butterflies in her tummy and if the way he had been watching her that evening was anything to go by, she suspected and hoped that he might feel the same about her.

'Betty . . . what does it feel like when you fall in love?' she asked innocently as they prepared for bed.

Betty laughed. 'This question wouldn't 'ave anythin' to do wi' young Bill, would it?' When Ruby quickly looked away her question was answered. 'To be honest I probably ain't the right one to ask,' she confessed. 'I'm more the love 'em an' leave 'em type meself and I don't reckon I've ever been in love.'

Ruby clambered into bed feeling utterly confused. After what her adopted father had done to her, she had thought she would never want anything to do with a man again, yet she wondered if with Bill it might be different. He was kind and good and when she was with him, she felt happy. Was that love? she wondered. And she was still wondering when she fell asleep.

For Ruby the following day was magical. She attended church with Mr Pembroke and Hermione in the morning, and once they were home, she helped with the preparations for dinner. Hermione had said again that she would like Ruby to dine with her and the two Mr Pembrokes, but Ruby politely told her that while she was very grateful for the invite she really would prefer to eat with the staff in the kitchen. But first was the ritual of the present-opening and she and the Pembrokes assembled in the drawing room.

Ruby gave out the gifts she had bought them first. There were crisp white linen handkerchiefs for the two Mr Pembrokes with their initials embroidered on them, which they were delighted with, and scented soap and bath salts for Hermione.

Eventually it came to Ruby's turn to open her gifts and she flushed as she unwrapped a delicate gold locket set with a ruby on a slender gold chain from Mr Pembroke.

'Oh!' She was so taken aback she hardly knew what to say. It was clearly a very expensive piece of jewellery and suddenly she was embarrassed. 'I-i-it's beautiful, thank you . . . but you really shouldn't have.'

'Nonsense,' he said, clearly thrilled to see how much she loved it. Then it was Hermione's turn to give her a gift.

Once again it was in a tiny velvet box and when Ruby opened the lid she gasped. Inside, nestling in a bed of silk, was a ring set with the most beautiful ruby she had ever seen. 'B-but isn't this the stone you had in your safe?' she stammered. 'The one I admired some time ago?'

Hermione nodded. 'It certainly is, do you like it?'

'*Like* it!' Ruby could only shake her head, for words failed her. The oval stone had been set into a rose-gold mount with no adornment whatsoever and yet it was the sheer simplicity of the style that made it so stunning. Eventually she said chokily, 'It's just beautiful. Thank you so much. I shall never take it off.' And with that she put it on her finger, turning her hand this way and that as she admired the way the light played on the stone.

Hermione looked pleased at her reaction. 'Good! I thought it was quite apt. A rare ruby for Ruby, and it'll go well with the pendant Oscar gave you.'

Ruby nodded in agreement as she fastened the pendant about her neck.

Miss Wood, who had been asked to join them, handed Ruby her gift then, saying, 'I'm afraid my present isn't quite as grand as theirs, but I hope you'll like it, dear. I had it made for you.'

It was in a large box and Ruby felt her hands shaking as she untied the string and lifted the lid. Once again she gasped as she took out a lovely gown made of sea-green satin trimmed with lace. It was the sort of gown she had only ever dreamed of owning, although her practical mind was wondering when she might ever get the chance to wear it.

'I . . . I really don't know what to say,' she said in a wobbly voice. 'You've all been so kind to me . . . thank you.'

'No more than you deserve,' Hermione said shortly. She was never comfortable around shows of affection. 'Now ring that bell and get Betty to bring us some coffee, would you? My mouth is as dry as a bone.'

Ruby grinned as she rose to do as she was told, thinking how very lucky she was that these wonderful people had taken her under their wings.

# Chapter Twenty-Six

Christmas dinner in the large kitchen with the rest of the staff was a merry affair and they all drooled over Ruby's new necklace and ring as she proudly showed them off.

'They must be worth a fortune,' Betty said as she admired them.

Ruby chuckled. 'They may well be but I'd starve rather than ever part with them. They're priceless to me.'

'Hm, I can understand that. They certainly seem to think very highly of you,' she commented thoughtfully.

The family had given generous gifts to all of the staff but nothing like the value of the gifts they had given Ruby. Not that she begrudged her them for a minute. Every one of them had taken Ruby to their hearts, although looking at her now it was hard to remember the shy, haunted little soul she had been when she had first joined them. Her figure had filled out, she was taller, and working for Hermione had built her confidence to the point that Betty thought young Ruby could be taken for a lady of class now.

The meal Cook had made for them was delicious. The turkey had been served to the family and Betty had struggled when she carried it through to the dining room because of the size of it, but for the staff, she had cooked a goose that was so moist and tasty it fell apart in their mouths. To go with it was a selection of vegetables – Brussels sprouts, carrots and peas – all cooked to perfection. There was also a big dish of Cook's home-made sage and onion stuffing, roast potatoes and buttered potatoes, a large jug of gravy and a jar of home-made apple sauce. To follow was a pudding, which had been soaking in brandy for months, and hot mince pies served with thick cream or creamy custard.

There was a lot of laughter around the table, and once they had eaten, they were so full it took them a while to move.

'Leave the washing-up for now,' Cook told them. 'It'll keep for an hour. I'm goin' to put me feet up by the fire for a while wi' a nice drop o' sherry. It is Christmas Day, after all.'

The others were only too happy to oblige and when Ruby sat down on the settle at the side of the fire Bill came to join her.

'I, er . . . got you a little something,' he said awkwardly. When she frowned, he hurried on, 'It ain't much, really, but I know you like reading so I hope you'll enjoy it.'

The gift was crudely wrapped in brown paper and once Ruby had undone it, she found a small book of Shakespeare's sonnets inside.

'It's not brand new,' he told her apologetically. 'I got it from that little bookshop down by the market. I hope you like it.'

'I love it,' she assured him.

He grinned. 'That's all right then, and thanks for me scarf. It'll be just the ticket these cold mornings.'

'Come on, you pair,' Betty's voice interrupted them. 'Get yourselves to the table. We're goin' to have a game o' cards afore we start the clearing away.'

And so with a happy smile the two went to do as they were told.

'Hasn't it been a wonderful day?' Ruby said happily as she and Betty got undressed for bed later that night. The snow had started to fall and outside it looked like a sparkling winter wonderland.

'It certainly has! An' all that food has made me tired.' Betty gave a big yawn as she hopped into bed and within minutes her gentle snores were echoing around the room as Ruby lay in the darkness thinking about Bill, a thoughtful expression on her face.

At that moment in the rooms he had made his own above the stables, Bill was also thinking of her. Just like Ruby, the feelings he had for her were making him feel confused. Each time he had seen her lately he had noticed how much she had changed. Gone was the shy little girl he had first known and in her place was a very attractive young lady, who looked to be hovering on the brink of becoming a very beautiful woman. But at the moment she was just sixteen years old, although no one who didn't know her would ever guess it. Ruby had been forced to prematurely leave her childhood behind her long ago. Bill sighed as he tried to put his feelings into some sort of order. When he was with her, he felt happy and when they were apart, he missed her. He had never felt like this about any girl before but he was sensible enough to realise that they were still far too young to think of entering a relationship – a romantic one at least. He was now nineteen years old, considerably older than her. But then, he consoled himself, she wouldn't be sixteen forever and they had all the time in the world. Perhaps next year when she was seventeen, he would declare his feelings for her and ask her if she would be his girl. In the meantime, he would spend as much time as he could with her so they could really get to know one another. On that happy thought he finally slept.

The holidays passed quickly and before Ruby knew it, it was almost time to return to Hermione's.

'I just wish the weather had been a bit better so I could have gone to see Maddie,' she confided to Miss Wood as they sat enjoying a hot drink in the kitchen together as Cook prepared the lunch. The snow was still falling and now lay thick on the ground, which would have made the long walk to Maddie's very difficult.

'Why don't I ask Mr Pembroke if Bill could drive you there in the carriage?' Miss Wood offered kindly.

Ruby instantly looked flustered. 'Oh no . . . thank you for the offer but it would seem very cheeky.'

'Why would it?' Serena grinned as she rose from her seat. 'Just leave it with me.' And she left before Ruby could say another word. She was back within minutes to tell her, 'Mr Pembroke has no objections at all. He wasn't going anywhere today anyway so if Bill is happy to take you, there's no problem. Will you ask him, or shall I?'

'Ask me what?' Bill entered the kitchen carrying a large scuttle full of coal, which he placed on the hearth next to the roaring fire.

'We were wondering if you would mind driving Ruby to visit Maddie in Vittoria Street this afternoon?'

'Of course I wouldn't.' He gave Ruby a warm smile. 'What time would you like to leave?'

'Not afore she's had some lunch!' Cook piped up, her face rosy from leaning over the vegetables that were bubbling on the range. 'Make it about two o'clock.'

Bill nodded, only too happy to oblige.

They set off promptly after lunch and as Bill helped her up into the carriage and placed a warm rug about her knees, Ruby felt quite the lady. She just wished that he could have travelled in the carriage with her rather than having to drive.

The journey took slightly longer than usual because of the conditions on the road, but thankfully the main roads were clear, although still treacherously slippery so they went slowly as Bill was concerned about the horses damaging their legs.

'We can't stay too long,' he warned Ruby when they eventually arrived. He threw two warm blankets across the horses' backs and attached their nosebags. 'I don't want the horses getting a chill.'

Ruby willingly agreed and together they entered the house. Nell and Mrs Petty were in the kitchen and she greeted them effusively. 'Eeh, I never thought you'd make it in this weather, bab.' Mrs Petty quickly helped them off with their coats and ushered them towards the chairs by the fire. 'You must be perished through,' she said kindly. 'I'll make you both a nice hot drink.'

Ruby removed her hat and placed it on the table before asking, 'Where is Maddie?'

'She's in the drawing room reading the newspaper the last I saw of her,' Mrs Petty informed her. 'Why don't you go through?'

'Thank you, I will.' Ruby hurried along the hallway.

Maddie was sitting by the fire when Ruby entered the drawing room, and she looked up and beamed when she saw who was there. Patting the seat beside her, she said, 'Come and sit down. What have you got there?' she asked eyeing the package in Ruby's hand.

'It's just another small gift,' Ruby told her as she handed it over.

Maddie opened it to reveal a beautiful fringed shawl in autumn colours. 'Why, it's beautiful! But the gloves you gave me were quite enough. I also have a little something for you as it happens.' She rose from the sofa to fetch a prettily wrapped package from the sideboard and gave it to Ruby.

Ruby's face lit up when she opened it to find a lovely fur stole inside.

'I thought it would go nicely with that pretty coat you treated yourself to a while ago,' Maddie told her and Ruby impulsively leant across to peck her cheek. She was surprised to find that her heart was hammering so loudly she was worried Maddie might hear it. It always did when they met and Ruby suspected that it was because each time she saw her, she wondered whether this might be the time that Maddie would admit to being her real mother. On that score, however, she was to be sadly disappointed yet again and they simply spoke of what they had each been doing over the holidays.

'And how is that appalling daughter of Oscar's behaving now?' Maddie asked just as Ruby was preparing to leave.

'I haven't seen much of her,' Ruby admitted. 'She left to spend Christmas with her mother the day after we arrived, but I'm really beginning to think she's changed for the better.'

'Oh yes, and what makes you think that?' Maddie raised an eyebrow.

'Well . . . she's offered to help me find my mother – my real mother, I mean,' Ruby said quickly as she felt colour flooding into her cheeks.

Maddie's smile faded, and just for a moment Ruby could have sworn she saw a look of unease flit across her face. 'It's up to you, of course,' Maddie said primly. 'But you are well settled in a good home with an interesting career ahead of you, so my advice would be to leave well alone. Let sleeping dogs lie.'

Disappointment made tears burn at the back of Ruby's eyes and she furiously blinked them away. If Maddie really was her mother, then once again she had chosen not to confess it.

Still, she told herself, the truth was bound to come out in the end and although it was frustrating, she could wait.

Maddie kissed her warmly when she left, and by the time they arrived back at Mr Pembroke's, it was dark.

'The days seem to be passin' in the blink of an eye,' Cook complained as she bustled about putting the last-minute touches to the evening meal. She had made a large

266

pan of turkey stew with leftovers and fluffy dumplings, which smelled absolutely delicious. Waste not want not, was Cook's motto and Ruby was continually surprised that she seemed able to make a tasty meal from almost nothing. She and Hermione would be setting off back to Bedworth in the morning and although Ruby had enjoyed her stay immensely, she thought of Hermione's house as home now and would be happy to go back to it.

'Don't leave it too long,' Cook told her the next morning as Ruby kissed her goodbye. Ruby nodded as she tripped out to the carriage where Hermione was already waiting for her. Bill helped her inside and then climbing up onto the driver's box he steered the horse towards the railway station. He was half hoping that the trains would be cancelled because of the snow but to his disappointment, although the trains were slightly delayed, they were all still running.

'Right . . . well take care of yourself and I'll hopefully see you again soon,' he told Ruby self-consciously as he helped her down from the coach. The cold air had made her cheeks glow and he thought he had never seen a more beautiful girl. Hermione meanwhile was looking on with an indulgent smile. If she wasn't very much mistaken that young man was greatly taken with young Ruby. But then Ruby was turning into a very pretty young woman and Hermione had no doubt there would be a lot of young men who would feel the same before very much longer.

Ruby was suspiciously quiet on the train home and eventually Hermione asked, 'Is everything all right, Ruby?'

'What . . . ? Oh, er, yes thank you.' Her mind had been miles away and now she stared at Hermione thoughtfully for a moment before confiding, 'I was just wondering about who my real mother was again . . . although I think I might know.'

'*Really?*' Hermione looked shocked. 'And who might that be then?'

'I . . . I have an idea that it might be Maddie . . . Mrs Bamber from Vittoria Street. Why else would she have taken me in as she did?'

Hermione looked almost relieved as she shook her head. 'I think you're barking up the wrong tree good and properly there,' she said. 'And if I were you, I would drop this silly idea of finding your birth mother. I know you've had it hard in the past but you're comfortable now with a wonderful career ahead of you. Why can't you let that be enough?'

'Because . . .' Ruby shrugged. 'Because there's this ache in here.' She touched her chest. 'I just want to know who she is and why she didn't want me.'

'Hm, well happen I have something to tell you that might take your mind off things,' Hermione said. 'I was going to tell you before but thought I'd keep the surprise until after Christmas.'

'Oh?' Ruby was intrigued.

Hermione chuckled. 'The thing is, your designs aren't just selling well in the Birmingham shop. Oscar sent some of the pieces you had designed to the London shop in Oxford Street and they've sold very well there too, so he asked me if you might like to visit there with him.'

'*What?* Me ... go to London!' Ruby was stunned and thrilled at the same time. She had always longed to see the capital and now it looked as if she was about to. 'Why, I'd *love* to go!'

'Good.' Hermione nodded setting the feathers on her hat dancing. 'We will let Oscar know and he can decide when it's to be.' And with that she turned her attention back to the scenery passing the window, leaving Ruby with a happy feeling in the pit of her stomach as she thought of the adventure ahead of her.

# Chapter Twenty-Seven

'Oscar was thinking the beginning of February for the visit to London. Does that suit?' Hermione asked one morning at breakfast.

'Oh yes, I can hardly wait.' Ruby's eyes shone with excitement at the thought of it. She had always wanted to visit London, although while she had lived with her adopted parents, she had never dreamed there would be a chance of it happening. But now thanks to Hermione and Mr Pembroke she felt as if a whole new chapter of her life was opening up and she was loving it. Throughout the month Hermione had bought her more clothes that she insisted she would need for the forthcoming trip and now Ruby could scarcely wait to wear them.

'Where will we be staying?' she asked as Hermione dabbed at her mouth with a snow-white linen napkin.

'With Mr Chatsworth, I believe, the manager of the shop in London. He and his wife are great friends of Oscar's.'

'And . . . are they very grand?' Ruby asked hesitantly.

'I don't know about grand, but he's an excellent goldsmith. And even if they are grand, what does it matter? Just remember you are as good as them and hold your head up and do me proud, girl.'

'I'll do my very best.'

Hermione nodded approvingly. 'Good, one can ask for no more. Now if you've finished your meal, I think we should get back to work. The design for the diamond ring is almost done, isn't it?'

Ruby nodded. 'Yes, I just need to measure the diamonds for it and then it can go off to be made.' Recently Hermione had allowed her to handle the more expensive jewels – the diamonds, sapphires and rubies – and though Ruby loved them, she was always nervous of losing one because she knew that each stone was probably worth more than she could dream of earning in a couple of years. She was now trusted to lock them securely away in the safe each night when she finished work and she was forever checking that they were all accounted for – not that Hermione seemed concerned.

When they got to the workshop, Hermione took the diamonds from the safe and tipped them out onto the table. They gleamed and sparkled in the light as Ruby began to move the ones she thought would work for her new design to one side.

'I thought this larger rose-cut one for the centre,' she said thoughtfully. 'The flat bottom and domed top will make an ideal centrepiece for the design and with this cut only having the twenty-four larger facets it catches the light more and makes it stand out. Then I thought these two slightly smaller ones in the same cut on either side of it, and then two old mined round-cut on either end for a contrast. It makes a boat shape, do you see, and makes it a little different to the more traditional round cluster. What do you think?'

Hermione studied the design and the stones and nodded in agreement. 'It is actually very unusual,' she admitted. 'And I'm pleased to hear that you've been doing your homework on the different cuts. Tell me what you like about the old mine cut?'

'Well, they usually have a slight tint to them and aren't quite as white as the round brilliant cut, but they do sparkle beautifully in candlelight or sunlight,' Ruby answered without hesitation. 'Although . . .' She hesitated. 'I do understand that the stones I've chosen for this ring are worth a great deal of money so I think they are worthy of being set in platinum, but then it will make this piece extremely expensive. Do you think the person who has commissioned it will be able to afford it?'

Hermione chuckled as she examined the stones in the light. 'Oh, don't worry on that score. I know the client in question and believe me money will be no object if she likes it, which I'm sure she will. Well done. Now put the stones safely in that small box there and when Oscar calls later this afternoon, he can take them and the design back to the workshop to be started.'

Ruby flushed with pride and did as she was told.

'And what are you working on now?' Hermione asked.

'Well, I thought I'd try a few designs for hat pins. Not ordinary run-of-the-mill ones but some set with semi-precious stones, like this.' She nudged a drawing towards her employer.

Hermione studied it for a moment then nodded.

'Knowing how fashionable hats are I thought ladies might like to match the colours with gems like topaz, citrine and garnets, etc. And I've also been designing some cufflinks for gentlemen.'

Hermione was more than pleased with her protégée's designs and felt sure that Oscar would be too, but never one for overpraising she simply nodded and left Ruby to continue with her work.

As Hermione had anticipated, Oscar was delighted with the designs, which she showed him when he visited later that day. 'I wouldn't have thought of putting those two different cuts into one ring,' he said thoughtfully. 'Or of that shape, for that matter, but it certainly does make for a very unusual piece. I fail to see how my client could be anything but thrilled with it so I'm more than pleased.'

Hermione then told him of Ruby's ideas for hat pins and once again he was impressed. 'We'll take some of the designs to London for William to look at when we go,' he told her.

As he was about to leave, he told her, 'I had a letter from Lydia yesterday. She's asked me for a divorce. It wasn't entirely unexpected. I think she's hoping to marry her lord.'

'Hm.' Hermione frowned. 'And how do you feel about that?'

He chewed on his lip for a moment before confessing, 'To tell the truth, I'm almost relieved, which makes me feel rather guilty. She is the mother of my child, after all, and this will be so final . . . the end to our marriage.'

'I don't see why you should feel guilty,' Hermione said shortly. 'That woman has led you a merry dance for many a year, so I would expect you to feel relieved. At least then you will be free to get on with the rest of your life. Just make sure you choose more wisely next time.'

Oscar chuckled. 'I'm not planning on jumping out of the frying pan and into the fire just yet,' he assured her.

But Hermione didn't share his amusement. 'Then you're a bigger fool than I took you for,' she said caustically. 'You have a woman who adores the very ground you walk on and who would walk through fire for you – and I think you know who I am speaking of! Serena Wood is twice the lady Lydia will ever be.'

Twin spots of colour appeared in Oscar's cheeks. 'She is also my housekeeper,' he pointed out.

'Why, Oscar, I never took you to be a snob,' she admonished him, much as his father had done. 'You might do well to remember that your father built this business up through blood, sweat and toil. Had he not you would not be where you are now. Just remember that and don't get above your station!'

It was not until he was seated on the train back to Birmingham that Oscar thought on her words. A lot of what his aunt had said was true. Serena was a truly lovely woman, who had stood by him throughout all the difficult years of his marriage. He flushed as he thought back to the time after Miranda had been born when Lydia had banished him from their room and told him in no uncertain terms that she never intended to lie with him again. He had been distraught and it was Serena who had given him comfort in more ways than one. On more than one occasion he had crept along the landing from his lonely room and found her willing and able to love him as he longed to be loved without asking for anything in return. But after a time common sense had kicked in and he had apologised to her for the way he had behaved and had kept his distance ever since. But even then, there had been no word of reproach from her and she had continued to ensure that his house ran like clockwork and that all his needs were catered for. Now as he thought of her he felt a warm feeling spring to life in his stomach. Serena was still a fine-looking woman and he was shocked that some man hadn't come along and snapped her up years ago. Could what his father and his aunt thought be true – that she really did have feelings for him?

He decided he would watch her closely to see if she gave any sign of having feelings for him. And if she did . . . who knew what might become of it once his divorce was finalised? And then an idea occurred to him: he could ask her to accompany him and Ruby to London. It would be perfectly acceptable; he would tell her that he needed a chaperone for Ruby. Thinking about it, it would not be the done thing to take a young lady of Ruby's age away without one – he didn't want to set tongues wagging. And so he decided he would ask her the moment he arrived home.

As it happened, she was in the hall when he rushed through the front door, kicking the snow from his boots. She hurried forward to take his hat and coat, saying cheerfully, 'Oh dear, you look very cold. I've just made up the fire in the drawing room, so go through and I'll bring you a tray of tea.'

'Lovely.' He smiled at her, making her heart race. 'And could you bring an extra cup for yourself while you're at it. I have something I'd like to ask you.'

All of a fluster she set off wondering what it could be.

She returned soon after and as she poured the tea, he told her about the letter he had received from Lydia asking for a divorce.

'I see . . . I'm sorry,' she said, outwardly calm as she handed him his cup. But when she lifted her own cup her hands were shaking slightly.

'Don't be. It was inevitable and I shall be writing back today to tell her that I agree to it on any grounds she likes. It won't happen overnight, though. It could take a few years before the divorce is final.'

When she nodded but made no further comment he went on, 'But that isn't what I asked you in here for actually. You see, I wondered if you would care to accompany myself and Ruby to London in a couple of weeks' time?'

She was so taken aback and thrilled at the request that it was a moment before she found her voice. 'I would love to.'

He rubbed his hands together. 'Excellent. It will make things appear more formal – compared to me travelling with a young woman on my own, I mean. I don't want to start tongues wagging. There'll be enough gossip when word of the divorce gets out.'

'It's nice that you've been so kind to the girl,' Serena said quietly.

He smiled. 'It would be hard not to be. She's such a lovely girl, isn't she? And so keen to learn the trade. I always hoped that Miranda would want to be a part of the family business but it doesn't look like that's going to happen. I like to encourage young people, and another one I'm considering setting on at the jewellery school is young Bill. He's expressed an interest in the trade and I thought I might offer him a part-time apprenticeship. That way he could still live and work here and I could hire another young chap to help him. What do you think?'

'I think it's a wonderful idea.' When she smiled, he noticed how attractive the dimples in her cheeks were, and he quickly averted his eyes.

'Of course, if there are any clothes or anything you need for the trip do please charge it to me,' he said, hurriedly.

Serena shook her head. 'Thank you but I'm sure I have everything I shall need, and anyway, surely I shall be dining with the servants once we get there?'

'You most certainly will not,' he told her firmly. 'You are my companion for this trip and you will be dining with myself and the Chatsworths. Do you have an evening dress?' he queried. 'I'm sure William and his wife will be throwing dinner parties while we're there and I want you to feel comfortable.'

'Oh!' She hadn't thought of that and realised he was probably right. She had all the clothes she needed but nothing grand enough for a formal occasion.

'Here.' He dipped into his pocket and withdrew a number of notes, which he passed across the table to her.

Deeply embarrassed she gulped. 'B-but that's far too much,' she said in a weak voice.

'No, it isn't.' His smile was kindly. 'I don't want you feeling out of place. Please take some time off and go shopping. Get a nice gown and a new bonnet or whatever you need to go with it. I insist.'

'Then perhaps I could pay you back out of my wages?' Serena had her pride.

He wouldn't hear of it, though. 'Absolutely not! Don't forget, you're doing me a favour by accompanying me so let's hear no more about it.'

The conversation turned to other things after that, and if anyone had passed by and glanced through the window they would have taken them for a happily married couple.

# Chapter Twenty-Eight

It was the day of their departure and in Hermione's house in Bedworth all was hustle and bustle as Ruby put the last of her luggage into a smart new valise that Hermione had insisted she should have.

'Are you quite sure you have everything you need?' Hermione asked.

Ruby giggled. 'You've already asked me that at least ten times,' she pointed out. 'And if I try and cram anything else into either of these two valises, I shan't be able to carry them.'

'Hm, well better to take too much than not enough. And I don't want my nephew to think I haven't ensured you have all you need. Now, let me have a look at you.'

Ruby straightened and as Hermione looked her up and down, she nodded with approval. Ruby was dressed in a smart two-piece costume in a lovely shade of dark green that showed off her eyes and her shape to perfection. The skirt was straight at the front with a fashionable bustle on the back and the jacket was fitted tight into the waist with a tiny peplum. She had also treated Ruby to a snazzy little hat to go with it, although she would have to wear a cloak because it was so cold, which Hermione felt was a shame.

'You'll do,' she said, straight-faced. 'But come and eat something before you go. Oscar and Miss Wood will be here to pick you up at any minute and I know you haven't eaten a thing. Betty told me you didn't touch a bite at breakfast.'

'I'm too excited to eat,' Ruby confessed as she checked that she had her sketches safely packed yet again and her face suddenly clouded with worry. 'What if Mr Chatsworth doesn't like my designs?'

Hermione tutted. 'Of course he'll like them. If Oscar didn't think they were good enough to take to the London shop he wouldn't be taking you on this trip, would he?'

The words had barely left her lips when the doorbell sounded and when Ruby hurried to open it, she found Bill on the step smiling broadly. He had travelled over on the train with Mr Pembroke and Miss Wood to help with the luggage.

Whipping his cap off he respectfully nodded towards Hermione before turning his attention to Ruby, who looked absolutely stunning.

'Mr Pembroke and Miss Wood are waiting in the carriage when you're ready, Ruby,' he said, forcing himself to look away from her. Slipping his cap back on he lifted both of the valises as if they weighed no more than a feather as Ruby hurriedly put on her bonnet and draped her warm cloak about her shoulders. It had stopped snowing the week before but it was still bitterly cold outside.

'Right, off you go and enjoy yourself,' Hermione told her. 'And don't forget what I told you. Hold your head high and be confident.'

'I will . . : and thank you . . . for everything.' Ruby leant over and impulsively pecked Hermione on the cheek.

'Oh, get off with you,' Hermione scolded, but Ruby saw her blink rapidly as she turned to hurry out to the carriage.

Hermione watched from the doorway as Ruby clambered in, helped by Bill, and after she had waved them off and closed the door there was a satisfied smile on her face. If she wasn't very much mistaken, Ruby was about to embark on a very successful career. The girl had talent and Hermione was proud that she had been able to help her develop it.

In the carriage, Ruby admired Miss Wood's travelling costume and thought how different she looked. She tended to wear rather plain, darker colours in her role as housekeeper at Mr Pembroke's, but the burgundy velvet she was wearing with a pert little hat to match made her look entirely different. In fact, if Ruby hadn't known who she was she would have taken her for a lady of class.

'You look very lovely,' she told her shyly.

Miss Wood flushed with pleasure. 'Why, thank you, dear. I must say you look very smart yourself.' Could Ruby have known it, Miss Wood was looking forward to the trip almost as much as she was.

Once they were at the station, Bill carried the cases to the luggage van and after a hasty goodbye he went to catch the train back to Birmingham while they climbed into the London train. They found a carriage that was almost empty, apart from an elderly gentleman with the hugest handlebar moustache Ruby had ever seen. He seemed pleasant though, and once the train had puffed out of the station, he smiled at them.

'Holiday or work, is it?' he enquired in a friendly fashion.

'It's a bit of both actually,' Oscar told him.

The man nodded as he leant on his ebony-topped cane. 'Good show. I like to see families working together.'

'Oh, but we're no—' Oscar clamped his mouth shut and grinned at Ruby and Serena. The old fellow had clearly thought they were a family unit and who was he to disabuse him of the idea?

Later, Oscar led them to the dining car where he bought them lunch and Ruby felt as if she had entered another world. It was nice to be waited on and addressed as miss, and Mr Pembroke and Miss Wood were such good company and so easy to talk to that she found she was enjoying herself.

It was late afternoon and already dark when the train pulled into Euston and Ruby was shocked at the number of people milling about. She had found Birmingham busy compared to the small market town she had come from when she had first arrived there with Maddie, but that didn't compare to this and she was suddenly nervous. What would she do if they were to become separated and she got lost? She needn't have worried, though. While Mr Pembroke summoned a porter to collect their luggage, Miss Wood watched over her like a mother hen.

'Grip tight to your bag,' she whispered in Ruby's ear. 'I'm afraid the pickpockets are rife in London and they are so good at what they do that you don't even feel them steal anything.'

Ruby stiffened and cautiously stared around for suspects. The porter soon arrived with their luggage on a trolley and led them out of the station to where a number of hackney cabs were waiting for fares. Ruby's eyes almost popped out of her head as she stared at the scene in front of her. There was traffic everywhere and more people than she had ever seen in one place in her life. Smartly dressed women in elaborate gowns and bonnets, and gentlemen in expensive overcoats and top hats jostled with others who were dressed in little more than rags and held their hands out to them for coins as they passed. If Ruby had been asked, she would have been forced to say that her first glimpse of London was rather disappointing. From the pictures she had seen she had always imagined it to be a glamorous city where the streets were paved with gold, but from what she could see of it, it looked dirty and overcrowded. To make matters worse, a thick smog was settling across the streets, and in the dim glow of the street lights it bathed everything in an unhealthy yellow glow.

She didn't have long to ponder on it, however, because Mr Pembroke was already ushering them into a cab and once their luggage had been loaded, he gave the porter a healthy tip and the driver an address in Belgravia. As the driver steered the horse into the fast-moving traffic, Ruby peered from the cab window with interest. There were a number of stalls and barrows dotted about on the edge of the streets selling everything from jellied eels, which she thought looked quite revolting, to women selling tiny bunches of dried heather. They were all shouting their wares and that, added to the noise of the many wheels rattling on the cobbled road, was so loud that Ruby felt a headache beginning to form behind her eyes.

'Is it far to Mr Chatsworth's house?' she asked as they passed through Marylebone.

Mr Pembroke shook his head. 'Only a couple of miles or so,' he told her with a smile.

Nodding, she settled back against the grubby leather squabs and continued to stare out of the window. Eventually they began to travel through Mayfair and the grubby streets gave way to grander residences. They then passed through Westminster and she blinked with delight as they passed Westminster Cathedral – it was even bigger and grander than she had imagined. Finally they arrived in Belgravia where the cab pulled up in front of a large town house that was shrouded in the late-afternoon smog. It had steps leading up to an imposing oak front door that boasted an enormous brass knocker, and a picket fence ran all along the front of it with steps leading down to what Ruby rightly guessed must be the kitchen.

The cabbie carried their bags up the steps for them and once they had all alighted the carriage Mr Pembroke rang the bell. It was answered almost instantly by a young maid in a starched white apron and a mob cap trimmed with broderie anglaise, who gave them a welcoming smile.

'We are expected,' Mr Pembroke told her.

She nodded. 'Yes, sir, the master and mistress are in the drawing room. Would you like me to take your hats and coats before you go through?'

As they were handing her their outdoor clothes, a door further along the hallway opened and a man who looked to be about the same age as Mr Pembroke appeared, beaming broadly.

'Oscar, it's so good to see you!' He hurried forward with his hand outstretched and once he and Mr Pembroke had shaken hands, he inclined his head with a smile towards the ladies. He was nowhere near as tall as Mr Pembroke and was slightly tubby with dark hair that was greying at the temples but his smile was kindly and Ruby liked him immediately.

'Come on through,' he urged, ushering them ahead of him. 'Esther has been so looking forward to your arrival. But you must all be tired after your journey? Never mind, there's plenty of time for a nice cup of tea and to freshen up and get changed before dinner.' He turned his attention to the young maid, asking, 'Hattie, would you have our visitors' luggage taken up, please? And make sure there is hot water in their rooms for them to wash with.'

'Yes, sir.' The maid bobbed her knee and scuttled away along the black and white tiled hallway.

Their host opened the door to the room he had just come out of and urged them ahead of him. It was a beautiful room with a fire roaring up the chimney and thick red velvet curtains hanging at the windows. Comfortable sofas with brightly coloured cushions scattered on them were dotted here and there and the atmosphere was one of warmth and comfort. It was clearly a family home, although nowhere near as grand as Mr Pembroke's house.

'Oscar!' A woman who had been sitting in a deep leather wing chair to one side of the fireplace rose and hurried forward to kiss Oscar warmly on the cheek before giving a welcoming smile to Miss Wood and Ruby. 'You are all very welcome,' she told them and turning her attention to Ruby she smiled. 'In fact, William has been very much looking forward to meeting this promising new young designer that Oscar has told him so much about.' The woman's fair hair was piled on top of her head in curls and her slight figure was dressed in a dark-blue velvet gown. She was the antithesis to her husband, but just as friendly, and although approaching middle-age she was still a very attractive woman.

'Thank you, ma'am. And thank you for having me.' Remembering what Hermione had taught her, Ruby bobbed her knee.

The woman waved her hand. 'Oh, my dear, you don't have to stand on ceremony when you are with us,' she told her. 'You are our guest and most welcome. And, Serena, how are you? It's been some time since I last saw you.' The two women had met on a number of occasions when she and her husband had visited Oscar in Birmingham, although that had been some time ago now.

'I'm very well, thank you.' Serena extended her hand, but before they could say another word the door opened and the most beautiful young woman Ruby had ever seen burst in like a ray of sunshine, closely followed by an extremely attractive young man.

'Caroline, please remember your manners,' Mrs Chatsworth scolded, although her eyes were twinkling with amusement. 'I'm so sorry. You must excuse my daughter's rather hasty entrance. She's been so looking forward to you coming,' she told the visitors.

Caroline made a beeline for Ruby and thrust her hand out saying, 'Hello, you must be Ruby. Papa has told us all about you and how clever you are. I'm Caroline.'

'I'm pleased to meet you.' Ruby was smiling as she looked back at her. Caroline's hair was straight and platinum blonde, almost silver, and fell down her back like a silken cloak. Her eyes were a lovely lavender colour and she was tall and slim. Ruby judged she must be about the same age as herself but she didn't have time to take in any more before Caroline unceremoniously grabbed the young man's hand and yanked him forward. 'This is George, my brother. He's older than me and very studious. In fact, he's no fun at all.' She pouted but her eyes were laughing as he grinned and made to clip her ear.

He too held his hand out to Ruby and as their hands connected, could she have known it, his heart did a funny little flip. She was a complete contrast to his sister. Whereas Caroline was tall, Ruby was small and petite and with her shock of curly red hair he thought she was quite beautiful.

'George is at medical school training to be a doctor, but he's on holiday this week,' Mrs Chatsworth explained with a note of pride in her voice as the door opened once more and the maid rolled a tea trolley in.

Once the tea had been served, Caroline drew Ruby to one side and soon they were deep in conversation as the elders discussed the shop and business.

'It's so nice to have someone close to my own age to stay,' Caroline chirped happily. 'How old are you Ruby?'

'I'm seventeen.'

'Oh, then you are a little younger than me. I'm eighteen,' Caroline informed her. 'And George here is twenty-one. Very old indeed.'

Again, he playfully cuffed her ear and Ruby could see that despite the banter they were actually very close. His fair hair was slightly darker than his sister's but his eyes were the same lovely colour as hers and he was tall and remarkably handsome.

'How much longer will you be training for?' Ruby asked him.

'Oh, I've got another month to go,' he answered. 'Although I haven't yet decided what line of medicine I want to go in to yet. I could continue training to become a surgeon, or when I've completed this next term, I may decide to become a general practitioner.'

'And what do you do?' Ruby asked Caroline.

'I help out in the shop,' Caroline told her. 'At busy times, that is. I'm afraid I haven't trained for anything else. I think Mama and Papa want to marry me off to a rich husband.'

'Huh! That's if they can find one that would put up with you,' George teased.

Just for a moment, Ruby felt sad. The two clearly doted on each other and she realised how much she had missed by not having any siblings.

They chatted on for a time until Mrs Chatsworth said, 'I'm very sorry to disturb you young people, but perhaps our visitors would like to freshen up before dinner is served. Would you show Ruby up to her room please, Caroline?'

'Of course.' Caroline took Ruby's hand and trotted her away, talking non-stop all the way up the stairs. 'I've had you put in the room next to mine,' she told her. 'How long are you going to be staying?'

'About a week, I think.'

'Oh, wonderful! In that case we'll have time for me to take you on a few sightseeing trips. We could go shopping too. And of course, we must take you to a show. You simply can't visit London without seeing a show.'

'Well ... I'm not sure I'll have time,' Ruby answered uncertainly. She had come here to work after all, but Caroline didn't seem the sort to take no for an answer when she had made her mind up about something.

'Rubbish!' she snorted. 'Of course, you will. I shall ask Papa to make sure of it. You know the old saying: "All work and no play makes Jack a dull boy!" That's what I keep telling George but he's such a bookworm.'

They emerged on to a long, narrow landing and Caroline stopped abruptly, causing Ruby to almost barge into her as she threw a door open. 'This is your room.'

Ruby stepped past her and looked around, very pleased with what she saw. It was a warm, cosy room with a comfortable-looking bed piled high with feather pillows and covered in a pretty patchwork quilt and a small rosewood wardrobe with a matching chest of drawers standing next to it. The windows were draped in dark-green damask curtains and a fire burnt cheerily in the small fireplace. Standing against another wall was a marble-topped washstand with a pretty china jug and bowl and in front of the window was a small table and chair where she could sit and look out at the London streets.

'It's lovely,' she told Caroline who was already striding over to the wardrobe.

She flung the door open and smiled with satisfaction. 'Ah, good. Hattie has already put your clothes away for you, and this gown is quite beautiful.'

She was stroking the green satin gown that she had been given for Christmas. 'It was a gift from Miss Wood, but I confess I have never been anywhere grand enough to wear it yet.'

'Then we *must* go to a show in that case! Anyway, I suppose I should go and get ready for dinner too else I'll have Mama scolding me.' And with that she tripped from the room leaving Ruby with a happy smile on her face. Something told her she was very much going to enjoy this trip!

# Chapter Twenty-Nine

Dinner that evening was a light-hearted affair. Ruby had changed into a smart gown in a lovely burgundy colour trimmed with a darker braid that Hermione had insisted she should have, and she felt very grand.

Caroline and George kept up a constant stream of chatter throughout the meal, which was plain but very tasty, and by the time it was over Ruby almost felt that she had always known them.

'Papa, I was saying to Ruby that we really *must* take her to a show while she's here,' Caroline said as Hattie placed their desserts, a delicious apple charlotte, in front of them. 'She's never been to London before. Or perhaps we could go to the opera or a play.'

George chuckled indulgently. 'What you mean is, *you* would like to go,' he teased.

Caroline slapped his hand and scowled. 'That isn't it at all,' she told him and he winked at Ruby causing a ripple of laughter around the table.

'I'm sure it could be arranged, my love,' her father answered indulgently.

After dinner, the men disappeared into Mr Chatsworth's study to enjoy a glass of port and a cigar while the ladies settled themselves by the fire in the drawing room with coffee and chocolates. Once again Ruby felt as if she had been transported into a different world. This was a million miles away from the life she had lived with her adoptive parents and she almost had to pinch herself to make sure that she was really there. Miss Wood, Mr Pembroke and Hermione had all been so kind to her and given her the opportunity to better herself and now she was determined not to let them down.

'So where do you live, Ruby?' Caroline asked when Miss Wood and Mrs Chatsworth began to chat.

'I live with Mr Pembroke's Aunt Hermione.'

'Oh really?' Caroline took a dainty sip of her coffee. 'Why is that? Are you an orphan?'

'Er . . . sort of.' An image of Maddie flashed in front of Ruby's eyes and seeing that she looked uncomfortable, Caroline quickly changed the subject.

'So, do you think you will make a career out of designing jewellery?'

Ruby shrugged. 'I'd like to, but I suppose it all depends if the designs sell well enough. Mr Pembroke assures me that the ones I've done up to now have.'

'Well, from what I've heard Papa say, they certainly have here in London,' Caroline told her kindly. 'You must be awfully clever. Did you design that ring you are wearing? It's quite beautiful. I've been admiring it all evening.'

Ruby stared down at the ruby ring Hermione had given her for Christmas. It was her most prized possession and she never took it off.

'No, actually Hermione designed this one and had it made for me for Christmas. She had the stone in her safe and I had admired it. It's lovely, isn't it?' She held her hand up to the light and the ruby glowed.

Caroline nodded in agreement. 'It certainly is. Now, what are you planning to do tomorrow? Would you like to go shopping?'

'I think Mr Pembroke and I are going to visit the shop in the morning,' Ruby answered.

Caroline frowned. 'Oh, what a shame. Shopping would have been so much more fun. But never mind, there will be other days.' She leant towards Ruby and lowered her voice. 'And by the way, I ought to warn you that I think my brother has a soft spot for you.' She giggled. 'Did you see the way he was gawping at you all through dinner? At one point I thought his spoon was going to miss his mouth he was so intent on watching you.'

Ruby flushed. 'Oh . . . I'm sure you're mistaken,' she muttered all of a fluster.

Caroline shook her head as she helped herself to another chocolate and offered the box to Ruby. 'I am not! I know George and I think he's smitten.'

Ruby quickly steered the conversation in another direction and the rest of the evening passed so pleasantly that before she knew it, she was stifling a yawn.

'Oh, my dear. You must be so tired after your journey,' Mrs Chatsworth said kindly. 'Please feel free to retire if you wish. I've had Hattie put a stone hot-water bottle in your bed and the fire in your room has been lit, so do go up whenever you like.'

'I think I will if you don't mind.' Ruby said her goodnights and made her way up to her room where she stood by the window and stared out at the rooftops of London.

'I wonder what you would think if you could see me now, Mam?' she whispered, thinking of the kindly woman who had brought her up. 'I hope you would be proud of me.' Then she quickly undressed and after carefully hanging her gown away she hopped into bed and within seconds of her head hitting the pillow was fast asleep.

'Morning, miss, I brought you some tea.'

As Hattie's voice reached down through the deep layers of sleep, Ruby opened her eyes and stared blearily up at her.

'Thank you,' she mumbled. 'What time is it?'

'It's after eight, miss,' Hattie informed her cheerfully as she laid the tea tray on a small table next to the bed. 'And Mrs Chatsworth says you're to join them all in the dining room as soon as you're ready.'

'*After eight!*' Ruby sat bolt upright. 'Oh, I can't believe I've overslept.'

Hattie grinned as Ruby jumped out of bed and ran about snatching up the clothes she intended to wear. 'Don't worry, miss. Mr Pembroke isn't down yet either, so there's no need to rush. While you have your tea, I'll go and get you a jug of hot water for you to have a wash.'

'Th-thank you.' Ruby felt very guilty. She had thought she would have difficulty sleeping in yet another strange bed but she had slept like a log. Hurrying over to the wardrobe she selected a gown that she thought would be suitable to wear to the shop and once Hattie had returned with the hot water she hurriedly washed and dressed and pinned up her hair. Then snatching up her folder of designs, she hastened downstairs.

Mr Pembroke had also just entered the dining room where their hosts were waiting for them but there was no sign of Miss Wood as yet, nor Caroline, although George was there, looking very handsome in a pin-striped suit and smart waistcoat.

'I'm so sorry,' Ruby said. 'I overslept.'

'Rubbish!' Mrs Chatsworth came forward and placing her arm about Ruby's slender shoulders she drew her into the room. 'You are not on the clock here, my dear. Don't forget, William is the manager of the shop so he can go in whenever he likes. Are those your designs in that folder? I know William has been looking forward to seeing them.'

Ruby nodded and shyly passed them over to Mr Chatsworth who spread them across the table and began to study them intently.

'So what do you think?' Mr Pembroke asked when William had had time to have a good look at them.

'I think they're superb.' Mr Chatsworth beamed at Ruby who blushed with pleasure. 'Nearly all of these will be suitable for platinum mounts and should be set with the expensive stones – diamonds, sapphires and rubies.' He glanced at Ruby then and explained, 'We only stock the more expensive items in the London shop because we tend to cater to a wealthier clientele here than you do in the jewellery quarter, where you have to cater to all different pockets from the working class to the richer clients. But here the sky is the limit. We've even sold to royalty, so money is no object.'

Serena breezed in at that moment looking refreshed and very pretty in a lilac gown that showed off her slim figure.

'Will was just saying how pleased he is with Ruby's designs,' Mrs Chatsworth informed her.

Serena looked almost as proud as if she had done the designs herself. 'Yes, Oscar and Hermione have both told me what flair she has,' she said with a warm smile at Ruby.

'Hm, it's just a shame that Miranda showed no interest in the business,' Esther Chatsworth replied and then almost as an afterthought she added, 'How is she, by the way?'

Serena shrugged. 'She is back at school. During the holidays she spends most of her time at her grandparents' house with her mother, although she does visit her father often. I'm not sure what she'll do when she leaves though.'

'Let's just hope that she stays with her mother,' Mrs Chatsworth said quietly to Serena. She had never had much time for Miranda, or for her mother for that matter. From what she could see they were cut from the same cloth: rude and selfish. Admittedly she had felt a little sorry for Oscar when he had told her that Lydia wanted a divorce but secretly, she thought he would be well shot of her particularly as— She stopped her thoughts from going any further. She had guessed many years ago that Serena was in love with him and wondered why he couldn't see it. But then, men tended to be very slow when it came to matters of the heart. She could only hope that eventually he would see what a wonderful, warm person she was. Her thoughts were interrupted when Caroline burst into the room looking as fresh as a daisy.

'Morning, everyone.' She smiled round at them all, noting with amusement the way George's eyes were fixed on Ruby again. 'Did everyone sleep well?'

A murmur rippled round the room in reply as the maid came in with the breakfast and they took their seats at the table.

'I thought I might come into the shop with you this morning, Papa, if you don't mind,' Caroline said as she helped herself to a slice of toast and began to spread it with butter and marmalade.

Her father's lips twitched with amusement. He could read his daughter like a book. 'Oh yes. And why would that be?'

'Well . . .' She batted her eyelashes prettily at him. 'I thought perhaps that when you were done with Ruby, she and I might find a little time to do some shopping.'

He shook his head and laughed. 'You women and your shopping. But yes, I don't see why not. There's a lot I want Ruby to see but I don't suppose it all needs to be seen today. Why don't you come to the shop at lunchtime and collect Ruby from there? You could take her for a little lunch somewhere before doing your shopping.'

Caroline quickly pecked him on the cheek and gave him a dimpled smile. 'You really are the best!'

Another ripple of laughter echoed around the table and Ruby felt herself laughing with them.

The happy atmosphere lasted for the rest of the meal with Caroline chattering like a sparrow as her brother struggled to get a word in, and despite the fact that he constantly scolded her and told her to be quiet, Ruby could see how close they were and once again she couldn't help feeling a little jealous.

When the meal was over it was time to leave so after collecting her designs together, Ruby put on her outdoor clothes and Mr Chatsworth hailed a cab to take them to the shop. The outside of it was very grand and when they entered Ruby saw that the inside was even more salubrious. Tall glass cases were spaced around the walls with lights directed on them to strategically show off the glittering jewels inside to their best effect. Along one wall was a highly polished dark-wood counter and the floor was covered in a thick, wall-to-wall carpet in a warm red colour that complemented the pale-gold damask walls.

Mr Chatsworth ushered Ruby and Mr Pembroke ahead of him to one of two doors set into the wall behind the counter, and Ruby was taken aback to find herself in an enormous workshop where a number of people were leaning over machines busily working. This, she realised, was where her designs were turned into reality and a proud lump formed in her throat. Since living with Hermione, she had closely studied all the different processes that went into making one single piece of jewellery and here in this room she could see them all taking place.

'This is my enameller, Robert,' Mr Chatsworth said proudly as he stopped at one of the machines where a man was carefully laying colourful powdered glass substances on to the precious metal and fusing it with heat. The man glanced up, nodded politely and they moved on. 'And Marianne here is doing what is known as damascening, it's a delicate process where incisions are cut into the metal and threads of gold or silver wire are introduced into the cut for embellishment. Over there is Cyril, he's working at a mandril, which is a curved metal or wooden block where, for instance, a bangle can be hammered into shape – not as easy as it looks, I assure you.' He chuckled and moved on and Ruby was so intrigued she felt she could have stayed there forever watching and learning.

Eventually, she and Mr Pembroke were led back into the shop where a very smart assistant was serving a lady who was sitting on a gilt chair examining a number of pieces laid out on a black velvet cloth on a small table in front of her. Mr Chatsworth took them through another door into his office and once they had taken off their hats and coats, they sat down at his magnificent rosewood desk to study her designs again.

'How would you feel about trying your hand at designing other things?' Mr Pembroke asked. 'For instance, salt cellars and sugar sifters are very popular amongst my clients at the moment, and the solid silver ones fetch a very good price. Also, silver cutlery?'

'I could certainly try,' Ruby said eagerly – she always liked a challenge.

For the rest of the morning they went through the designs, deciding which ones should be sent to the workshop first, and Ruby found she was enjoying herself immensely. Both Mr Pembroke and Mr Chatsworth spoke to her as an equal and it made her feel warm inside. This was all so different to the way her adoptive father used to bark orders at her and make her feel worthless.

The time seemed to pass in the blink of an eye and she was shocked when Caroline rushed in and grinned at her from ear to ear.

'So, what do you want to do first, then? Lunch or shopping?'

'Actually . . .' Ruby swallowed but found the courage to say, 'If you wouldn't mind, what I'd *really* like to do is go sightseeing. There are so many places I want to see.'

Caroline giggled. 'That's no trouble at all. Where do you want to go first?'

'Buckingham Palace,' Ruby said without hesitation as she reached for her hat and coat. She had brought her warm cloak too, for although the snow was thawing it was still bitterly cold.

'Take an omnibus if you must go gallivanting; it's very cold out there,' Mr Chatsworth advised, but he smiled at their bravery. When he was their age the cold hadn't bothered him at all either, but now when he wasn't working, he preferred the comfort of his own fireside.

'We'll be fine,' Caroline assured him cheerily and taking Ruby's arm she almost dragged her from the shop, keen to get started on their adventure.

'Oh, this is such fun,' she chirped once they were seated on an omnibus rattling through the city towards Buckingham Palace. 'I wish you could come in June when Queen Victoria is celebrating her Golden Jubilee! There are going to be so many parties being held in London around that time, and balls, I shouldn't wonder. Did you know she's supposed to have invited fifty European kings and princes from all over the world to celebrate with her? Now that really will be a party!'

Ruby smiled. Caroline's happy nature was infectious and already she felt as if she had known her forever.

'Of course, I had to tell George he wasn't allowed to come today,' Caroline prattled on with a giggle. 'It's just us girls this afternoon, I told him, so he'll probably be sulking now. He only wanted to come because of you anyway. Had I been on my own, wild horses wouldn't have dragged him away from his precious books! He can be very boring . . . Ooh, look, there's the River Thames. If it wasn't so cold, we could go on a boat ride.'

Ruby grinned as she stared from the window at the river. She didn't even attempt to get a word in. She had already discovered that when Caroline was in full flow there was no chance of stopping her. And truthfully, she wouldn't have wished her to and was enjoying every second.

# Chapter Thirty

At the house in Belgravia Miss Wood and Mrs Chats-worth were enjoying having time to themselves and were settled in the drawing room with a large pot of tea and a cheery fire. George was studying in his room and the men were still at the shop so it was a good chance for the women to have a chat.

'You're looking very well, Serena,' Esther Chatsworth commented as she helped herself to one of Cook's tasty pastries. 'I was so pleased when William told me that you would be coming. You're so much easier to talk to than Lydia. I must admit, I always found her to be very hard to get on with, although I was shocked when William informed me that she and Oscar had separated. Do you think there's any chance of a reconciliation?'

Serena looked vaguely uncomfortable as she shook her head. 'I don't think so. In fact, I'm sure that Oscar wouldn't mind me telling you that Lydia has asked for a divorce and he's agreed to it.'

'Really?' Esther Chatsworth gave her a wicked little smile. 'So just between ourselves there may be a chance for you two now?'

Serena looked shocked. 'Wh-whatever do you mean?'

'Oh, come, my dear. It's as clear as the nose on your face that you care for Oscar and I've a sneaky feeling he cares for you too.'

Serena sniffed and folded her hands primly in her lap. 'I should also point out that I am merely Oscar's housekeeper.'

'So?' Esther grinned. 'Times are changing. And don't forget that Oscar wasn't born with a silver spoon in his mouth. His father worked hard to build this business up and comes from working-class roots so Oscar doesn't have a snobbish bone in his body – although I must admit I was quite surprised to hear how he had taken Ruby under his wing. But then that was before I met her and now that I have, I can quite see why. She's a delightful young lady and she and Caroline are getting on like a house on fire. Talented too, so it's nice to see that she's been given this chance. But now, tell me about Miranda. Has her temper improved? I can admit now that I never took to the girl, she was too much like her mother.'

'Yes, she could be a little . . . difficult,' Serena agreed tactfully. 'But she seems to have calmed down now. In fact, she seems to be quite taken with Ruby lately.'

'And why is that?' Knowing Miranda as she did, something didn't sound quite right to Esther.

Serena shrugged. 'I have no idea. Perhaps she's finally growing up.'

'Hm, well I shall believe it when I see it.' Esther didn't look at all convinced but seeing that Serena was looking vaguely uncomfortable she quickly changed the subject.

'Ah here you are,' Mrs Chatsworth said cheerily as the girls returned home later that afternoon, their cheeks glowing and happy smiles on their faces.

'Oh, we've had *such* a lovely time, Mama,' Caroline said as she dropped into the seat by the fire. 'I took Ruby on a sightseeing tour and it was wonderful.'

Ruby nodded in agreement, her eyes bright. Today was a day that she would never forget; she couldn't remember a time when she had enjoyed herself more. She had seen so many of the landmarks that she had never thought she would see and she was still bubbling with excitement.

'Excellent. But now help yourselves to some tea to warm up and then you'll just have time to change before dinner,' Mrs Chatsworth said indulgently, and the girls were only too happy to oblige.

Once again, the mood was light as they all sat at the dining table that evening and Mr Chatsworth was full of praise for Ruby's designs. 'Your designs are like a breath of fresh air, my dear,' he told her and Ruby flushed with pleasure. After the morning spent at the shop, her head was already full of new ideas and she could hardly wait to get started on them.

'I've already set the goldsmiths to work on some of the ones you showed me,' Mr Chatsworth went on as he loaded his fork with tender roast beef. 'And hopefully some of them will be ready for you to see before you go home.'

'Oh, don't keep talking about work, Papa,' Caroline interrupted. 'What would you like to do tomorrow, Ruby?'

Ruby looked uncomfortable. As much as she had enjoyed her afternoon, she was very aware that she was there to work and she didn't want to take advantage of her hosts.

Seeing her discomfort Mr Chatsworth smiled at his daughter. 'I was rather hoping that Ruby would come to the shop again in the morning,' he told her. 'But I'm sure you could arrange something for the afternoon, if you wish.'

'Oh, no really . . .' Ruby looked very concerned. 'I'm quite happy to work.'

'We'll see,' Mrs Chatsworth interjected. 'But I do have a little surprise for you. For all of you as it happens. I've booked us tickets to go to the opera on Wednesday evening. Have you ever been to one, Ruby?'

Ruby shook her head as Caroline clapped her hands with delight. 'Oh, you'll be able to wear that beautiful green gown that you said you've never worn,' she told Ruby excitedly.

The thought made Ruby's heart thump with excitement.

The days seemed to fly by and Ruby was thoroughly enjoying herself. She spent most of each day at the shop with Mr Pembroke and Mr Chatsworth, and was even allowed to try some of the processes involved in the jewellery making in the workshop, where she soon discovered that they weren't as easy as the people who did them made them look. The evenings were spent in the Chatsworths' cosy sitting room playing chess and board games with George and Caroline. Then at last the day of the opera trip dawned and Mr Chatsworth told her over breakfast, 'There is no need for you to come into the shop today, my dear. I know what you young ladies are like for getting ready, so have a relaxing day in and have a bath and wash your hair or whatever it is you young things do. Oscar and I will be home in plenty of time to get you there, I promise you.'

And so that was exactly what Ruby did. After lunch, Hattie filled a bath with steaming hot water then left Ruby to have a long leisurely soak and wash her hair. When she got out, she rubbed her hair with the towel until it gleamed then sat by the fire to dry it, thinking how lovely it would be if she could live this sort of life all the time. Then she shook her head and grinned. She was happy with the life she had now and knew that she would soon grow bored of sitting about.

It had been decided that they wouldn't eat at home that evening so Mr Chatsworth had booked them a table at a restaurant for after the opera – another thing for Ruby to look forward to. She had never been to a very posh restaurant before and by five o'clock she was a bundle of nerves as she and Caroline made their way upstairs to get ready. It had been agreed that Hattie would help Caroline dress her hair and Miss Wood would help Ruby and she had scarcely got into her room when Miss Wood appeared.

'How shall we do it?' she said thoughtfully as she stared at Ruby's reflection in the dressing table mirror. Then she smiled. 'I think it would suit you piled high on top like this and then teased into little ringlets. What do you think?' She caught Ruby's hair and piled it loosely onto her crown. Ruby nodded, thinking how very grown-up it made her look.

Miss Wood had come armed with clips and slides and Ruby sat patiently while she worked her magic. And it really was magic, Ruby thought sometime later as she eyed the finished results.

'It's perfect,' she breathed, her eyes sparkling. 'Thank you so much.'

'It was a pleasure,' Miss Wood assured her. 'Now let's get you into your gown and then I really must get ready myself. I don't want to let the side down.' If truth be told she was almost as excited at the prospect of an evening out with Oscar as Ruby was, although outwardly she remained as cool as a cucumber.

Fifteen minutes later the transformation was complete and as Miss Wood turned Ruby to look in the cheval mirror, Ruby hardly recognised herself. The soft green satin complemented her complexion and she was momentarily struck dumb.

'You look absolutely stunning,' Miss Wood whispered and Ruby thought she detected a catch in her voice. But then Miss Wood turned to go, saying, 'Be sure to take your cloak, dear. It's still very cold out, and I'll see you down in the drawing room shortly.' With that she was gone, leaving Ruby to preen in the mirror as she stroked and admired the delicate guipure lace trimming her neckline.

Soon after she made her way carefully downstairs to find George and Caroline already waiting in the drawing room.

George's eyes were openly admiring as she walked in and Caroline clapped her hands together. 'Oh, Ruby, you look *just* lovely,' she declared.

'You look rather beautiful yourself,' Ruby answered, and it was the truth. Caroline was wearing a sky-blue gown that matched the colour of her eyes to perfection and her long fair hair had been pulled into the nape of her neck and tied with a matching ribbon from which ringlets cascaded down her slender back.

'You both look lovely,' George told them, bringing a dull flush to Ruby's cheeks as the men joined them.

'How about a drop of brandy before we go, Oscar?' Mr Chatsworth suggested, looking very smart in his black evening suit. 'And as it's a rather special night, I don't see why we shouldn't let these young ones have a little drop of wine. I do mean a drop though,' he warned as Caroline grinned.

Very soon the ladies joined them and Ruby noted the way Mr Pembroke's eyes rested on Miss Wood who looked really lovely. Her dress was in a pale-lilac chiffon over a satin skirt that billowed about her legs with every step she took and her hair was dressed in curls on the back of her head, making her look very sophisticated. Ruby realised with a little shock that Miss Wood was still a very attractive woman indeed – Mr Pembroke certainly seemed to think so, and the thought made her smile. Mrs Chatsworth had also made an effort and looked very regal in royal-blue velvet and pearls.

'Why, I reckon we'll be the best dressed party there tonight,' Mr Chatsworth declared as he raised his glass in a toast to them all, but then the carriage he had hired to take them to the opera was at the kerb and they rushed about putting their outside clothes on.

When they arrived, the theatre was ablaze with lights and posters advertising the opera, and smartly dressed people were making their way inside. As Ruby had whispered to Caroline, much to the girl's amusement, she was beginning to feel a little like Cinderella and just hoped that the carriage wouldn't turn into a pumpkin at midnight. The foyer was so grand that it almost took Ruby's breath away and she was so busy staring about that she even forgot to take her cloak off for a few minutes. A glittering crystal chandelier that sparkled like diamonds hung in the centre of the ceiling and a sweeping staircase on either side led up to the theatre seats. There were enormous gilt mirrors hung on the walls, and charming little gilt-legged sofas scattered about. The women seemed to be trying to outdo each other in the amount of jewels they wore, and their gowns were all the colours of the rainbow.

Once they'd left their cloaks at the ladies' cloakroom, George instantly came to Ruby's side and offered his arm. Shyly she slid her small hand through it and they began to ascend the stairs, closely followed by Miss Wood and Mr Pembroke, with Mr and Mrs Chatsworth and Caroline at the rear.

'I've booked us a box,' Mr Chatsworth informed them leading them along a corridor. 'You get a much better view of the stage from up here.' He stopped and drew aside a fringed velvet curtain and they stepped past him into the box, which did indeed look directly down on to the stage. Once again Ruby was speechless as she admired the intricately painted cherubs on the domed ceiling and the luxurious velvet seats. And the sheer size of the place! Ruby had never dreamed that such huge spaces existed.

'Oh . . . it's all so, so . . .' She struggled to find words to express how she felt. 'So *magical*, I feel as if I'm in a fairy tale,' she breathed eventually. 'I shall *never* forget this night for as long as I live!'

George took her hand and raising it he gently brushed the back of it with his lips. 'Neither shall I,' he whispered meaningfully.

Before Ruby could reply, they were ushered into their seats and she thought no more about it. She was too excited waiting for the opera to begin and she could hardly wait to see it.

It was everything and more than she could have hoped for and from the first second the curtains opened on the stage, she was utterly entranced. More than once she was moved to tears as the story unfolded, and as George watched her from the corner of his eye he smiled. He had never met a girl like Ruby before. She was so innocent and unspoilt, not to mention beautiful, and he only hoped he would get the chance to become better acquainted with her.

Halfway through there was an interval where the girls were allowed another small glass of wine and this only added to Ruby's happy state. By the time they left the theatre Ruby had stars in her eyes and couldn't stop smiling. Her happy mood was enhanced further at the restaurant where they enjoyed a wonderful meal.

'I shall never, *ever* forget this night,' she told Caroline breathlessly. She felt as if she had entered another world and was aware that it was all thanks to Miss Wood and Mr Pembroke's kindness to her. Suddenly the days and years she had spent slaving in the bakery seemed a million miles away, but still there was one thing missing. *If only I could discover who my real mother is, everything would be perfect*, she thought as George helped her down from the carriage when they arrived back at the Chatsworths', but even that seemed possible now and she refused to let anything mar the magical night.

For the rest of their stay Ruby spent much of her time at the shop with Mr Chatsworth and Mr Pembroke and all too soon it was almost time for them to go home.

'Oh, I shall miss you.' Caroline pouted the night before they were due to leave and Ruby realised with a little pang that she would miss her too. 'Promise you'll come back when you can.'

'That would all depend on your father and Mr Pembroke,' Ruby said sensibly. 'But thank you for making me so welcome. I've had a wonderful time and I've learnt so much.'

Caroline grimaced. 'I don't know how you can find all that jewellery-making interesting,' she admitted. 'All the processes involved just to produce one piece of jewellery. It's all rather gobbledegook to me, I'm afraid. I just like the finished products.'

Ruby giggled. 'I've loved trying my hand at all of them,' she admitted. 'And it's just made me realise how talented all the people who are trained to do them are.'

'Ah, but never forget that what you do is important too,' Caroline told her solemnly. 'Without the designs they wouldn't have anything to work on.'

Ruby had never thought of it like that before and felt a little thrill of pride. She supposed Caroline was right and it made her more determined than ever to succeed.

George had been quiet all evening and now he told her, 'It's going to be very quiet when you've gone with just this nuisance for company, although I shall be returning to medical school next week so I suppose I won't have to suffer her for long.'

Caroline gave his arm a playful thump and Ruby smiled knowing that she now had two new friends. It was a pleasing thought.

# Chapter Thirty-One

The carriage arrived back at Hermione's house in Bedworth late the following afternoon and Ruby realised with a little shock that she was glad to be home.

Mr Pembroke helped her inside with her luggage but politely refused Hermione's invitation to stay for dinner as he and Miss Wood had to get to the station to catch another train back to Birmingham.

'Thank you for a wonderful experience, sir,' Ruby said as he prepared to leave.

He smiled. 'It was my pleasure entirely and I think it's safe to say you made a very good impression on the Chatsworths. But I really must be off, so goodbye for now.'

Ruby stood at the door and waved until the carriage was out of sight then rushed back into the drawing room to tell Hermione about the wonderful time she had had.

Hermione listened with an indulgent smile as Ruby chattered on about Caroline and George. She told her about the opera and sightseeing and everything she had learnt in the workroom in the London shop. Suddenly she remembered that she was talking to her employer.

'I, er . . . I'm sorry to rabbit on,' she said humbly, blushing. 'Of course, most of my stay was spent working, I promise.'

'My dear girl, I'm delighted to hear you enjoyed it,' Hermione assured her. She had been surprised at how much she had missed the girl while she was away and had realised with a little jolt that she had grown fond of her. 'And your ideas for the new designs sound excellent. While you've been gone, I've had another bench installed for you in the work-room so that you don't have to make do with one end of mine.'

Ruby's face lit up, but before she could reply, Mrs B bustled in with a laden tray containing a pot of tea and some ham sandwiches. 'Just to keep you going until dinner,' she told her cheerily. 'And welcome home. We've missed you.'

'I missed you too,' Ruby told her and as she looked at their dear faces, she realised that she meant it. She had loved her stay in London but this was home now and she was happy to be back.

'I think we can safely say the trip was rather successful, don't you think?' Oscar said to Serena as they sat on the train back to Birmingham.

She nodded in agreement. 'Oh yes, I was so proud of Ruby. Nothing seemed to faze her and William seemed very taken with her designs.'

'You've grown very fond of her, haven't you?' he asked, looking at her intently.

She flushed and nodded. 'Er . . . yes, I suppose I have,' she admitted.

'Hm, I must say, I have too.' He continued to stare at her thoughtfully for a moment before saying in a quiet voice, 'I also realised during this trip that I care for you very much.'

Serena's head snapped round and her eyes were huge as she gasped, 'Oh, Oscar, don't say anything you don't mean, please. I'm happy to go on just as we are so long as I can be close to you. I'm just your housekeeper, remember!'

He took her gloved hand in his, thankful that they had the carriage to themselves. 'You stopped being just the house-keeper to me long ago,' he told her. 'But I was married to Lydia, still am – for now at least. But perhaps when my divorce comes through . . . What I'm trying to say, and very badly, is do you think you could ever care for me?'

She bowed her head as tears stung the back of her eyes. 'You must know that I love you. I've loved you for years,' she confessed in a wobbly voice.

'So, does that mean then that I can hope that perhaps one day . . . ? I mean, I wouldn't want to put you in a compromising position so I wouldn't expect anything of you until I was free again but—'

'Shush!' Her eyes met his. 'You must remember that even when you are divorced, I shall still be your housekeeper,' she reminded him gently. 'Imagine what people would say.'

'What do I care about what people say?' he scoffed. 'You are and always have been ten times the lady Lydia ever was and any man would be proud to have you on his arm. I know I certainly would.' And then without giving her a chance to say another word he leant towards her and when her lips gently met his he felt like the luckiest man in the world. When they finally broke apart, he was beaming from ear to ear and suddenly the future looked bright again.

Their happy mood continued until they eventually reached the house. Oscar quickly paid the cabbie and carried the

315

luggage inside and Betty came hurrying down the hallway to meet them.

'Welcome home,' she said, although her tone was subdued and they both sensed something was amiss. They soon found out what it was when she whispered, 'Miss Miranda is in the drawing room waiting for you, sir. She arrived this morning.'

Mr Pembroke dropped the heavy valise he was carrying with a plonk and frowned. 'Miranda! But what is she doing here? She should be in France.' He had no chance to say any more as the drawing room door opened and Miranda rushed out and threw her arms about him.

'Oh, Father, I'm so pleased you're back,' she gushed, tears pouring down her cheeks. 'I've been having such a *dreadful* time. I just *had* to come home!'

'All right, all right, give me a chance to get in,' he said somewhat shortly. 'And then you can tell me what's going on.'

She sniffed and disappeared back into the drawing room dabbing at her plump cheeks with a handkerchief as Oscar raised an eyebrow at Serena and removed his hat and coat.

'Will you excuse me? I'd better go and find out what's wrong.'

'Of course.' Serena nodded and when he disappeared off after Miranda, she sighed, the happy mood broken, for now at least.

'So, tell me what's happened,' Oscar demanded going to stand in front of the fire.

Miranda threw herself dramatically onto the sofa and sniffed. 'It was the girls at school, Father. They were bullying me. I didn't want to trouble you about it before but it got so bad that I couldn't take it anymore, so I left.'

Oscar frowned. 'You mean Madame Babineaux allowed you to travel back here all alone?'

'She didn't know I was going. I left a note and made my way to the ferry then when I got to England, I caught the train back here. I couldn't go to Mother because she's away with Lord Chumley again.'

'I see.' Oscar was aware that the amount of time Lydia was holidaying with her new beau was causing quite a scandal but he didn't care about that. He began to pace up and down the room. If what Miranda was saying was true it was appalling. The school had seemed such a happy place when he had visited it and Madame Babineaux certainly hadn't seemed the sort of woman who would allow such behaviour to go on under her roof. Eventually, he sighed. 'Very well, you can stay here until your mother returns, and in the meantime I shall have a thing or two to say about this to Madame Babineaux.'

Miranda's tears miraculously stopped, as though someone had turned off a tap, and the first niggle of doubt wriggled its way through Oscar. He knew of old that Miranda could lie through her teeth when it suited her, but she was his daughter, so for now he would just have to take her word for it.

He had hoped to dine with Serena that evening but because of Miranda's return she chose to eat in the kitchen with the staff and he and Miranda ate in the dining room.

'So how did the London trip go?' Miranda asked, loading her fork with as much food as she could cram onto it.

'Very well. I think it was very informative for Ruby.'

She looked at him with her fork halfway to her mouth. 'You took *Ruby*?' she said incredulously.

317

'Of course I did. That was the whole purpose of the trip. Her designs are proving to be very popular and I wanted her to meet William.'

'Did you stay at his house?' Miranda was scowling now.

'Yes, I always stay there when I visit the London shop.'

Miranda began to eat again with a sulky expression on her face and the rest of the meal passed in an uncomfortable silence.

Meanwhile in the kitchen Cook had a thing or two to say about the young mistress's return. 'Came in bold as brass she did,' she informed Serena. 'Not a tear in sight till she clapped eyes on her father. She can turn them on and off like a tap, that girl can, and Oscar being soft, he falls for it every time. And as for this tale about her being bullied, I don't believe a word of it. If there were any bullies at that school I wouldn't mind bettin' it would be her if her past is anythin' to go by.'

Serena was quiet. Finding Miranda here had quite taken the shine off her and Oscar revealing their feelings for each other, although they had already agreed in the cab from the station that they would keep their news to themselves until the divorce was final. But even then, she knew there would be many hurdles to overcome before they could be together.

'I'm sure Oscar will get to the bottom of it,' she told Cook calmly. 'Although whether she's lying or not, there hardly seems any point in sending her back now. She only had a few months to go until she left anyway.'

'Hm, well I just hope she don't decide she's staying here,' Cook said grumpily. 'I hate to say it, but this place has been a lot happier since she and her mother left.'

'Too true,' Betty agreed.

'And did Ruby enjoy the trip?' Bill asked then.

'Oh yes, I think she did and she loved the opera. Mr Chatsworth took us all for a treat one evening and Ruby was full of it for days after. And she got on so well with Caroline and George.'

When Bill cocked his eyebrow she explained, 'They are Mr Chatsworth's children, although they're not children really. Caroline is about the same age as Ruby and George is about nineteen or twenty, I believe, and studying medicine.'

A little spike of jealousy rushed through Bill as he asked casually, 'Nice-looking this George, is he?'

'Oh, very much so.' Serena smiled. 'And Caroline is quite beautiful. But now tell me what's been happening here while I've been away.'

The conversation moved on but Bill promised himself that he would go and see Ruby the first opportunity he got.

The next morning, to everyone's surprise, Miranda was up and dressed early.

'And what's this then?' her father teased as she joined him at breakfast.

'Oh, I just thought I'd get the early train and go and see Aunt Hermione,' she answered casually as she helped herself to a sizzling rasher of bacon.

Oscar frowned. In the past it had been all he and her mother could do to get her to see her aunt at all, and yet all of a sudden, she was going of her own accord. But he kept this thoughts to himself and merely nodded.

After Miranda had left, Serena entered the room to see if there was anything else he needed, and he grinned at her as he rose from his seat and took her in his arms.

'Only you,' he whispered into her hair.

She blushed prettily. 'Oscar, stop it,' she told him half-heartedly. 'We agreed that we wouldn't tell anyone how we felt until after your divorce but if Betty walks in on us, I think we might just give the game away, don't you?'

Oscar grinned. 'Well, there's one person I am going to tell before I leave for work and that's my father,' he told her. 'He's been dropping hints about what a wonderful person you are and what a wonderful wife you would make for long enough, so I think I need to tell him he was right and put him out of his misery.'

Serena lowered her head and said quietly, 'We don't have to wait if we were discreet. What I mean is . . . it isn't as if we've never . . . And anyway, there's something else I really must speak to you about . . .'

Oscar drew in a breath, a little shocked at her words. But his overwhelming feeling was guilt. 'If you're referring to the times we came together after Miranda's birth, I can only apologise for my behaviour. I was very unhappy, but I shouldn't have used you like that and I've felt guilty ever since. What I realise now, though, is that even then, I loved you, but at the time I just couldn't admit it to myself. Can you ever forgive me?'

She looked up at him now with a small smile on her face. 'You shouldn't feel guilty. I came to you willingly because I loved you even then. But that wasn't what I needed to tell you. You see—'

Suddenly the door began to open and they sprang apart as Betty entered the room to clear the table.

'Er . . . right.' Oscar cleared his throat. 'I'd better, er . . . nip in and have a word with my father before I leave for work.' He gave her a wicked little wink and hurried away.

Oscar found his father propped up on his pillows in bed with a breakfast tray across his lap.

The old man beamed at his son as he pulled a chair up to the side of the bed. 'So? Good trip was it?'

Oscar nodded. 'It went very well indeed. William was so impressed with Ruby's designs but . . .' He licked his lips before going on. 'What you said to me a short time ago, about Serena . . . The thing is, I've asked her if she'll be my wife when my divorce comes through and she's accepted me. Of course, we're not making it public knowledge yet – I don't want to ruin her reputation – but I felt I had to tell you.'

There was a bright twinkle in his father's eye as he clapped him on the shoulder. 'And it's about bloody time too,' he laughed. 'I thought the pair of you would never get around to admitting your feelings for each other. I'm pleased for you, lad. You've got a good 'un there.'

'I think so too,' Oscar agreed and when he left to go to work a short time later there was a spring in his step that had been absent for a very long time.

# Chapter Thirty-Two

'This is a surprise,' Hermione said when she answered the door to find her great-niece on the doorstep later that morning. 'I thought you were in France.'

'I was.' Miranda breezed past her and threw her coat across the bannister rail. 'But there were a few problems there so I decided to come home.'

'I see. And to what do we owe the pleasure of this visit so soon after the last one?' There was a trace of sarcasm in Hermione's voice but Miranda gritted her teeth and ignored it. It wouldn't do to go upsetting the old lady now.

'I just wanted to see you, that's all. And Ruby, of course,' she told her with a sickly grin.

'Then you're going to be disappointed on one score at least because Ruby is in the workshop working,' Hermione said bluntly as she snatched Miranda's coat up and hung it on the coat rack.

'Then I'll go in to her,' Miranda said brightly. 'And don't worry, I won't disturb her. I'll just watch her working.' And before Hermione could object, she was gone, leaving the older woman to shake her head.

'If that little madam isn't up to something then I'll eat my hat,' she told Mrs B as she joined her in the kitchen.

Mrs B looked up from the dough she was kneading and nodded. 'It does seem odd,' she agreed. 'She was only here at Christmas an' shouldn't she be at that posh school in France?'

'She said there had been a few problems there so she came home.'

'Huh! I've no doubt if there were any, she were the cause of 'em,' Mrs B snorted.

Miranda meanwhile had entered the workshop to find Ruby busily at work with an array of glittering gems spread out in front of her.

'Oh . . . hello, miss.'

Miranda chuckled as she lifted a rather splendid sapphire and began to examine it. 'I've told you, it's Miranda. You don't have to address me as a servant would anymore. I thought I'd call in and see you now I'm not at school.'

'Oh.' Ruby was surprised; she had thought that Miranda was going to be away till much later in the year. She was also feeling rather nervous as Miranda turned the sapphire this way and that. She and Hermione knew every single stone that was kept in the safe and they had to be counted each time they took them out and each time they put them away to ensure that none had been dropped or gone missing, for some of them were worth thousands of pounds. Thankfully Miranda put it back down after another moment and taking a seat, she cupped her chin in her hand. 'So what are you doing now?'

'I'm designing a sapphire ring for a customer of Mr Chatsworth,' she told her holding out the sketches. 'What do you think?'

Miranda gave the sketch a cursory glance but it was obvious she wasn't really interested in it.

'I don't know how you can sit there scribbling away all day every day,' she said. 'I'd be bored sick in ten minutes. It's not the most exciting of jobs, is it?'

Ignoring the comment, Ruby asked, 'And how is everyone back at your father's?'

'All well. In fact, Bill offered to drive me here today but I wouldn't let him. It's too far for the horses to come and much quicker on the train.'

Bill had actually done no such thing but Miranda wanted to let Ruby know that she was close to him, or at least she would have been if he'd allowed it. Up to now he had ignored all her advances.

'But anyway, one thing I came to tell you is that now I'm home I'm going to really concentrate on tracking down your birth mother. There are people you can hire to help, like private detectives.'

Ruby looked up at that and her heart began to beat a little faster. 'But won't that be very expensive? I don't have a lot of—'

Miranda held up her hand to block the flow of words. 'Don't you worry about that. I can afford it easily,' she boasted. 'I get an allowance off my father, and one off my mother too so it's no worry at all. But isn't it about time you stopped for lunch?'

Ruby glanced at the clock and nodded. 'Yes, but I must just put these jewels safely away first. Your aunt doesn't like them to be left lying about.' Carefully she collected them together and crossing to the safe she placed them inside and locked it before slipping the key into a cleverly hidden false drawer that was positioned beneath the workbench. Then the two girls made their way to the kitchen where they found Mrs B setting another place for lunch at the table.

Miranda left mid-afternoon with promises to come back soon and when she had gone Hermione frowned. 'I'm telling you, that girl is up to something,' she told Mrs B again. 'I just wish I knew what it was, because I have a feeling it won't be anything good.'

The following morning Miranda and her father were at breakfast when Betty came in with the mail. 'There's one with a French postmark, sir,' she told him with a glance at Miranda as she placed the letters on the end of the table and quietly left the room.

Miranda instantly looked sullen as her father lifted the envelope and slit it with a knife before quickly skimming through it, his face hardening. When he'd finished, he put the letter down and looked at his daughter. 'I think you have a little explaining to do, miss, don't you?'

'Why? What has the old witch said?' Miranda said peevishly.

'She says that she had no choice but to expel you because of your atrocious behaviour,' he told her through gritted teeth. 'And that she was going to write to me to ask me to go and fetch you but you refused to wait and walked out, putting yourself in danger.'

'Well, I got here safely, didn't I?' she said, raising her chin defiantly. Then her expression changed and she blinked as she said in a sickly voice, 'It wasn't *my* fault, Father. It was just so *awful* there; you can have no idea. I—'

'I don't want to hear any more, Miranda,' he told her, his tone dangerously low. Then he stood up so abruptly that he almost overturned his chair. 'It's never your fault, is it. I'm ashamed of you!' And with that he strode from the room leaving her to glower after him. But only for a moment. At least she was away from the hated school now and it was highly unlikely that he would try to send her to another. With a smile she helped herself to another fried egg and tucked in as if she didn't have a care in the world.

The day after Miranda's unexpected visit, Ruby was busy in the workroom when Mrs B entered to tell her that Maddie and Nell were there. She flushed with pleasure and stood up, then glanced anxiously at Hermione who was working at the other bench.

'I-I'm sorry,' she stuttered, her cheeks glowing. 'I had no idea they were coming.' She did have to work after all and she didn't want Hermione to think she was taking advantage of her good nature. 'Perhaps if I could just have an hour off to see them; I could make it up on my afternoon off? Or I could work for an hour later this evening.'

'Oh, get away with you,' Hermione told her good-naturedly. 'You work longer hours than you need to and you deserve a bit of time off.'

Ruby flashed her a grateful smile and with her heart racing she hurried to the sitting room where they were waiting for her. Perhaps today would be the day that Maddie had decided she would tell her she was her mother? She could only hope.

'Well, look at you,' Nell said when she entered the room. 'I swear you look more grown-up every time I see yer.'

'This is a nice surprise.' Ruby gave them both a kiss on the cheek. 'I wasn't expecting you.'

'We thought we'd treat usselves to a day out an' so we hopped on the train. But how are things?' Nell asked.

'Wonderful. Why don't you come through to the sitting room and I'll go and make us a pot of tea.' Ruby ushered them into the house.

'Why, this is lovely,' Maddie said, looking out of the window at the garden. 'I'd heard Hermione was a keen gardener and I can imagine this is beautiful in the summer.'

'I help her out there as well,' Ruby told them. 'And I'm getting quite good at it now. I know the names of almost all the flowers, although I must admit I was probably more of a hindrance than a help to start with and I pulled up more than a few flowers thinking they were weeds! I'm still nowhere near as good at it as Hermione is. She seems to have green fingers.'

Maddie shuddered. 'I have to admit that as much as I like to see a pretty garden, I wouldn't like to tackle one myself. It looks a bit too much like hard work to me!'

Grinning, Ruby hurried off to fetch the tea and soon returned with a tray containing not only the tea but a plate of Mrs B's hot buttered scones straight from the oven. Nell tucked into them with gusto and Ruby smiled to see her enjoying her food. She could never work out how she managed to stay so thin because she would eat anything and everything that was put in front of her.

'I know what you're thinkin' – that I'm a gannet.' Nell grinned. 'I reckon it comes from the days afore Maddie took me under her wing an' I never knew where the next meal were comin' from. I should be the size of a house by now but I reckon I must just be skinny by nature.'

'Not like me.' Maddie chuckled. 'I only have to look at anything sweet to put weight on. But I have to say, Ruby, you're looking very well and happy.' She was still feeling guilty about the things she had made Ruby do during the short time she had lived with her.

'I am very happy here,' Ruby admitted. 'I'm well looked after and I'm learning a trade that I enjoy.' Then as something suddenly occurred to her, she asked, 'But it was Mrs Petty who took me to live with Mr Pembroke . . . How did she know him?' Could it be that he was Maddie's secret gentleman caller? she wondered.

Maddie threw back her head and laughed. 'She didn't know Mr Pembroke, at least not all that well,' she told her. 'But Serena Wood and I have been friends for many years and when she knew that you were unhapp—' Her voice trailed away and she stared guiltily into her tea before confessing, 'I shouldn't have tried to draw you into my little circle of crooks, Ruby. I realise that now. Petty was against the idea from the day I took you home and when she realised how unhappy it was making you, she decided to see if Serena might find you a position in Mr Pembroke's household. Luckily, she did and had it not been for that awful Miranda you might still be there. Still, things have worked out for you so all is well that ends well, isn't it?'

Ruby gazed at her intently, willing her to go on. Surely this would be the perfect time for her to make her confession? But

328

she was disappointed when the talk went on to other things, until eventually, she gave them a little tour of the garden, although as it was February, it was nowhere near as beautiful as it would be in a few months' time.

'This is where we grow the vegetables,' she said proudly, pointing to the raised beds. 'And that there is the rose garden. You should smell it in the summer first thing in the morning – it's lovely. And those are apple and pear trees. Mrs B makes pies, jam and all manner of things with the fruit from them. And then this is the herb garden. Doesn't it smell lovely.'

Both Maddie and Nell were impressed but eventually Maddie said, 'As nice as this is, we really ought to be off now. I want to do a little shopping in the market in Nuneaton before we catch the train back to Birmingham. But take care of yourself, my dear, and do come and see us when you can.'

'I will,' Ruby promised, leading them back through the house. At the front door she stood on the step and waved them away feeling a little deflated. Once again, Maddie hadn't said the words she longed to hear. But there was still time, she consoled herself, and with a sigh she went to rejoin Hermione in the workshop.

The rest of the week passed uneventfully for Ruby but the same couldn't be said for Mr Pembroke as he had noticed a slight cooling towards him from Serena which concerned him. And so, one evening after he and Miranda had finished dinner and Miranda had gone to her room, he called her into the drawing room. 'Is everything all right, my love? You've seemed very preoccupied for the last few days.'

With her hands joined tightly at her waist Serena licked her lips as she gazed at him solemnly. 'I, er . . . I *do* have something on my mind, as it happens,' she admitted. 'And I've tried to tell you about it on a few occasions recently but we always seem to be interrupted.'

'Well there's no one here at the moment,' he pointed out, spreading his arms to encompass the empty room. 'So why don't you tell me now? It can't be that bad, surely.'

'But it is,' she said brokenly as tears began to course down her cheeks. 'And I don't know what you will think of me when I've told you.'

He stared at her, perplexed. 'I can't believe anything will ever make me think badly of you.'

Serena shook her head, trying to control her emotions. Finally, she took a deep breath and started to talk. 'It began with Maddie . . . Mrs Bamber . . .' Slowly and painfully she began to tell him the secret she had kept from him, completely unaware that outside the door, Miranda had her ear pressed to the wood and was listening to every word she said.

Soon after when she was back in her room, Miranda began to pace up and down like a caged animal as rage coursed through her.

So, her father and Miss Wood were planning to go and see Ruby at the weekend, were they? It was all happening a lot faster than she had thought it would, but all was not lost. She would make sure that she got there first. It was time to put her plan into action, but first she needed to see her mother.

# Chapter Thirty-Three

'And to what do we owe the honour of yet another visit so soon?' Hermione asked her great-niece the following morning when Miranda strolled in yet again.

'I didn't know I had to book an appointment!' Miranda said brusquely, but then immediately looked contrite as she muttered, 'Sorry, Aunt Hermione. Mama is back from her latest jaunt with Lord Chumley so I was on my way to my grandparents, but I thought I'd call in to see Ruby first as it won't be so easy to visit from there . . . And you, of course,' she added hastily as her aunt raised her eyebrow. 'But I'm not stopping for long. Father wanted Bill to take me in the carriage but as I pointed out I'm quite old enough to go alone.'

'I see. Well, Ruby is working, as you might expect,' Hermione answered.

'Then I shall go and have a look at what she's doing. She's so clever, isn't she?' Miranda hurried away leaving the elderly woman with a frown on her face. It didn't matter how charming she was being, she didn't trust the girl. She just couldn't fathom what she was up to. Sighing, she turned her attention back to the newspaper she had been reading, but her concentration was gone and she felt vaguely uneasy.

'Miranda.' Ruby looked surprised as Miranda strode purposefully into the workroom, closing the door firmly behind her. 'I didn't expect to see you today.'

'I had to come,' Miranda told her without preamble. 'I have some news for you.'

Ruby's heart began to thud with anticipation and she stood up. 'Is it good news?'

Miranda nodded, keeping an eye on the door. What she had to say was for Ruby's ears only and she didn't want them to be disturbed. She drew closer and lowering her voice began, 'You know that I told you I was going to hire someone to help us find your mother?'

Ruby nodded as the colour drained out of her face.

'Well, he got results much sooner than I'd expected and the long and the short of it is . . . I know where she is.'

Ruby's legs felt as if they had turned to jelly and she sat down on the nearest chair with a plonk.

'You *do*? Are you quite sure?'

Miranda nodded. 'There's no doubt and I'm going to take you to see her. But the thing is . . .' She hesitated. 'She's ill and I don't think you would want people to know where she is so can we keep this just between ourselves until we know more about her illness? If Hermione were to find out she might tell my father and he could prevent me from taking you to her. Could you do that?'

Ruby seemed to have temporarily lost the power of speech so she just nodded numbly.

Miranda smiled with satisfaction. 'Good. So when is your next day off?'

'Th-the day after tomorrow,' Ruby croaked.

'Right, then what I want you to do is this: just carry on as if you are popping out for a few hours to do some shopping and meet me at the train station in Nuneaton at eleven o'clock. From there we'll get a cab.'

'You mean she's in Nuneaton?' Ruby asked incredulously.

'On the outskirts, actually, but I won't tell you any more for now. I told Aunt Hermione I was only popping in and I don't want her saying that I've kept you from your work. But before I go, you couldn't get me a cold drink, could you? I'm as dry as a bone.'

'Of course.' Ruby hurried off to the kitchen, wondering how on earth she was going to keep such news to herself until Friday, but she had promised Miranda and so, somehow, she had to.

She got a glass of water from the kitchen and returned quickly to the workroom, hoping to get a bit more information from Miranda. But to her surprise, the room was empty. For a while she just stood there, not sure what to make of her disappearance. But finally, she sat down again and took up her drawing pad. Somehow, she would have to behave as normally as she could for the next few days. But it was a small price to pay for finally being able to meet her real mother.

Despite her determination to behave normally, it was very hard to concentrate for the rest of the day and she found at dinner time that she couldn't eat a thing. So as soon as she could, she pleaded a headache and took herself off for an early night, leaving Hermione with a thoughtful expression on her face. Ruby hadn't been herself since Miranda had called that morning and she wondered if the girl had upset

333

her. But then even if she had there was nothing she could do about it until Ruby confided in her, so she went back to what she had been doing and put it from her mind.

Sleep evaded Ruby as she tossed and turned throughout the night. Part of her was thrilled that at last she was going to meet the woman who had given birth to her, but the other half was full of questions. Miranda had said that she was ill. Did that mean that she might be dying and they would never have a chance to form a bond – that was assuming that her mother even wanted to? And why had she given her away in the first place? Was it because she hadn't wanted her, or because she had had no choice? So many questions were swimming around in her head that she was relieved when she saw the first streaks of dawn colouring the sky. Rising, she washed and dressed and by the time Hermione came downstairs Ruby was waiting for her in the drawing room.

'Goodness me, you're up early,' the woman commented. Peering closely at her she frowned. 'You're looking a bit peaky. Are you not feeling well?'

'Oh, I'm fine.' Ruby forced a smile. 'In fact, I've had some new ideas for designs so I think I'll get straight to work.'

'Very well.' Hermione nodded, but her mind was full of questions. The girl was as jumpy as a kitten. 'But have some breakfast first,' she advised.

Just the thought of eating at the moment made Ruby feel nauseous but she nodded. 'Of course.' And she pottered off to the kitchen to help Mrs B prepare it, although how she was going to force anything down, she didn't know. Hermione had been so kind to her and she longed to share her good news but then, she consoled herself, once the visit was over, she could tell everyone. In fact in just a few short hours she could tell the world, and the thought of it brought a lump to her throat.

The rest of the day passed interminably slowly but at last Ruby said goodnight to Hermione and Mrs B and rushed off to her room where once again she tossed and turned through the night. The next morning she was up bright and early again, although Hermione noticed she had dark circles beneath her eyes and looked worn out.

'I thought I might go out for a few hours today to do a bit of shopping,' Ruby said casually to Hermione at breakfast.

'It's your day off so you can do as you please,' Hermione pointed out as Ruby pushed the food about her plate. Once more she had barely eaten a thing and Hermione was growing concerned about her.

'Did Ruby seem herself to you?' Mrs B asked when Ruby had left shortly after breakfast.

Hermione shook her head. 'No, she didn't, and it was as if she couldn't wait to get out this morning. She was fine until Miranda called in the day before yesterday so I just wonder what that great-niece of mine has done to upset her. I know she's my flesh and blood, but between you and me I can't trust her. She's too much like her mother for my liking, which is probably why I've never taken to her.'

'I know what you mean, but you know what they say, "You can choose your friends but you can't choose your family."' Mrs B grinned and began to carry the dirty pots to the kitchen while Hermione went to start weeding her beloved garden.

A short time later Ruby stood nervously on the platform at Trent Valley railway station in Nuneaton waiting for Miranda's train to arrive, and when she saw it approaching, she breathed a sigh of relief. Once it had drawn to a halt, the porter hurried along throwing the carriage doors open and Miranda spilled out of one of them and hurried towards her.

She eyed Ruby enviously. Ruby had gone to a lot of trouble with her appearance that day and was wearing a very fetching velvet dress with a little matching jacket and a frilled blouse. Over this outfit, she wore her warm, fur-lined cloak.

'That new, is it?' Miranda asked by way of a greeting and Ruby managed a smile, although her stomach was churning with nerves. 'It's one of the outfits your aunt bought me to take to London.'

Miranda swallowed the jealousy that rose in her and forced a smile. 'It looks very nice.'

They made their way outside to where a number of cabs were waiting for fares. 'This one will do,' Miranda said shortly, opening the nearest carriage door so that Ruby could climb in. She then went round to where the driver was removing the nosebags from the horses and after telling him where they wanted to go, she climbed in beside Ruby and sat heavily back against the grubby squabs.

'So, are you going to tell me where we're going now?' Ruby asked anxiously as the carriage drew away.

'You'll see soon enough. But are you quite sure you haven't told anyone where you were going today?'

'I promise I haven't said a word to anyone.' Ruby wondered why Miranda sounded so nervous. It wasn't as if it was her mother they were going to see after all. And why did she seem to be in such a bad mood today? For months, ever since Ruby had left Miranda's home, she had been all sweetness and light each time they had met, but today she was more like the spiteful, sullen girl that Ruby remembered from when they had first met.

Her small white teeth nipped at her lower lip as she stared at all the familiar places from the carriage window. There were so many different emotions churning around in her that she barely knew if she was coming or going. Soon, she forgot all about Miranda as she tried to picture what the meeting would be like. Would her mother be pleased to see her after all these years or would she be horrified that she had been tracked down? She could have no way of knowing and suddenly she wondered if this had been such a good idea. After all, she was happy and settled with Hermione now, with a wonderful career in the jewellery trade ahead of her. Perhaps she should have been content with that and let sleeping dogs lie, as Maddie had suggested? And yet, deep down she knew that she would never be totally at peace with herself until she had found her birth mother. The need to know her was like a constant gnawing inside and she could hardly believe that at last it was really going to happen.

The carriage trundled through Abbey Green then the horses slowed slightly as they began the steep climb up Tuttle Hill. As they passed the five-sailed windmill that stood atop of it and turned towards Ansley, Ruby asked again, 'Surely you could tell me where we are going now?'

'Very well. But I don't think you're going to be too happy when you know. We're going to Hatter's Hall!'

Miranda watched as the colour drained out of Ruby's face. 'H-Hatter's Hall?' she croaked in horror. 'B-but that's a mental asylum.'

Miranda nodded. 'Quite. That's why I didn't tell you before because I knew you'd be upset. But I can assure you that's where she is.'

They were on level ground again now and the carriage swayed from side to side as the horses trotted along at a fair old pace and suddenly Ruby began to feel sick. *Hatter's Hall!* Just the mention of the place struck terror into her heart, for everyone in the town knew what a godforsaken place it was. It was shunned by the locals, particularly at night, when many people swore they could hear the screams of the poor demented patients who were incarcerated there. And now to discover that her own mother was one of them . . . it almost broke her heart.

She sat stunned as they moved on, down through Chapel End and Ansley Common, and then the horses slowed and Ruby gazed fearfully through the window at a pair of tall wrought-iron gates and the high brick wall that seemed to stretch forever on either side of them.

The horses stopped abruptly and the driver appeared at the window. 'Sorry, miss, but I ain't a goin' in there,' he told Miranda with a wary glance at the gates. 'But I'll wait 'ere for yer, if yer wish?'

'Oh, very well,' Miranda snapped as he helped her down from the carriage before turning to do the same for Ruby.

Miranda flounced towards the gates, clearly unhappy at the walk they had ahead of them. As she drew closer to the gates, an elderly man appeared from a small gatehouse. 'Miss Miranda Pembroke, I am expected,' she told him imperiously.

He nodded. 'Aye, you are,' he agreed as he fumbled in his pocket for the enormous iron key to open the padlock. 'Come on through.'

On legs that suddenly felt as if they had turned to jelly, Ruby followed Miranda's portly figure through the gates. 'Just keep goin' down the drive. Hatter's Hall is at the end of it beyond the trees,' the old man instructed as he locked the gates behind them.

They set off again, Ruby peering ahead, but as yet there was no sign of the hall. The sun was out now and the weak rays shone down through the bare branches of the trees that lined either side of the drive as they hurried along. Eventually they saw light ahead and the hall came into view. With a gasp, Ruby drew to a halt. It was enormous and looked very dark and forbidding with ivy clambering up its walls like green fingers trying to enter the windows. Instead of curtains, behind the glass of each window they saw heavy metal bars and Ruby shuddered.

'It looks more like a prison than a hospital,' she said quietly.

'It does look grim,' Miranda admitted – she couldn't truthfully have said otherwise. 'But I'm sure it will be better inside and perhaps we'll find that your mother isn't too bad after all.'

They plodded on until they stood at the bottom of three large steps that led up to a huge set of double oak doors.

Miranda climbed them and yanked on a bell pull to one side and they stood listening to the sound of the bell chime hollowly inside. Other than that, there was not a sound to be heard save for the birds in the trees and the thud of Ruby's heart, which was hammering so loudly now that she was sure Miranda must be able to hear it as well. Finally they heard echoing footsteps from behind the door, growing louder as the person came closer, and then there was the sound of a key being turned. The door swung open and they found themselves staring at a huge amazon of a woman with hands like hams who was wearing a starched nurse's uniform.

There was no welcoming smile, she merely looked from one to the other of them before asking, 'Miss Pembroke?'

'Yes.' Miranda inclined her head. 'I have an appointment with the matron.'

The nurse held the door a little wider, allowing them to pass her and instantly the sounds of people wailing and crying reached them, although the enormous hallway was empty. Another nurse appeared and the first told her, 'This is Miss Pembroke. Could you take her to Matron?' Then turning to Ruby she said, 'And you'd best come and wait with me.'

Ruby frowned, confused. 'But surely I can see the matron too? It is my mother we've come to see after all and I need to know how ill she is.'

'Of course you do, dearie,' the nurse said placatingly, but her eyes were cold. 'And so you shall, but best let Miss Pembroke speak to her first. She is the one who made the appointment after all.'

'Oh, very well,' Ruby sighed as Miranda was led away and she followed the second nurse down the corridor. But all the time she was thinking, *Very soon now I shall be meeting the woman who gave birth to me for the very first time.*

For better or worse there could be no going back now!

# Chapter Thirty-Four

Ruby was led into a clinical-looking room with nothing but two wooden chairs in it and a long window overlooking the grounds of the hall.

'Wait there,' the enormous nurse told her in a voice that brooked no argument.

She left the room and Ruby heard the sound of the key in the lock. She had been locked in. For a moment she panicked but then common sense took over. This was an asylum after all and some of the inmates could be violent so they probably had to do that to ensure the visitors' safety. Crossing to one of the chairs she folded her hands primly in her lap and sat back to wait.

She seemed to sit there for a very long time until eventually a movement outside caught her eye and glancing towards the window, she was dismayed to see Miranda walking down the steps to the drive. But why was she going without her? Or had she perhaps decided that this first special visit should be just between herself and her mother? Eventually she heard the sound of footsteps and the key being turned again, and she sighed with relief. When the door was opened, she saw the nurse who had shown her into the room with another slightly smaller nurse standing beside her.

'Why has Miss Pembroke left?' she asked before they had time to say anything. 'And may I see my mother now? We have a cab waiting at the end of the drive and I don't want to keep them waiting too long.'

'Why, of course you can,' the larger of the two said. 'And just so you know, my name is Nurse Keen. Come along of us, dearie.'

Ruby thought it quite strange that it needed two of them to direct her to her mother's room but she followed them anyway, wondering if this had been such a good idea after all as the first stirrings of unease flared to life deep in her stomach.

They led her along the hallway and up the sweeping staircase, and the higher they climbed the louder the sounds of wailing and crying became.

'I-is my mother very ill?' she asked in a faint voice.

The two nurses glanced at each other and grinned. 'Not at all,' Nurse Keen told her. 'You just come along now and you'll see for yourself soon enough.'

She found herself on a very long landing with doors either side and in each door was a small window with bars on the inside. Vacant eyes stared out at her from some of them and a large lump rose in her throat as she looked into their hopeless faces. But worse than this, the further they ventured along the landing, the worse the putrid smell of stale urine and vomit became, until Ruby had to place her hand across her mouth. But she didn't have long to think of it before Nurse Keen stopped at a door and after fiddling with the keys on a chatelaine about her ample waist, she selected one and unlocked it.

'Here we are then, in you go nice and quietly now.'

Ruby frowned thinking what a strange thing that was to say, and when she stepped inside, suddenly the door slammed shut behind her and glancing around she found herself alone. Rushing to the door she peered through the glass shouting, 'Excuse me, I think you've made a mistake. This room is empty.' But the women were already retreating along the landing as she began to rattle the doorknob, her heart thumping so hard that she was sure it would leap out of her chest and tears clogging her throat as her shouts became more frantic.

'Hello . . . Hello, can anybody hear me? *Please* . . . somebody . . . *anybody!*' But the only answer was the sobs and cries of the poor souls in the rooms on either side of her.

Panic threatened to choke her, so she took a deep breath and tried to compose herself. Miranda would get fed up of waiting for her eventually and she would come back for her. She dropped down onto the metal-framed bed and eyed the room as tears trickled down her cheeks. The walls were painted a dull, drab brown and were smeared with all manner of things that she didn't even want to think about, while the floor was rough planks, and apart from the bed and a bucket that stood in one corner which, judging by the evil smell emitting from it, served as a toilet, the room was empty. There was a tiny window but it was set so high into the wall that she doubted she would be able to see through it even if she stood on the bed, and her heart went out to the poor patients who had to live in these terrible rooms. There was not an ounce of comfort anywhere and she wondered how her mother had survived in such a place. *But she won't have to any longer*, she promised herself. *I shall get her out of this dreadful place just as soon as they realise their mistake and take me to her.*

Hermione had shown her nothing but kindness and she had no doubt that once she knew what was happening, she would let her mother stay with them so that Ruby could nurse her back to health.

Miranda clambered into the carriage waiting at the end of the drive with a smug smile on her face, and nodding to the driver she told him, 'Back to the train station, if you please.'

He frowned. 'Only the one of you, is it, miss?'

'Yes. Now drive on and mind your own business,' she told him imperiously, so with a shrug he clambered up into the driver's seat and set the horses in motion. As long as he got his fare it was no business of his after all.

It was late afternoon when Mrs B commented, 'Ruby's late, ain't she? Unless she decided to hop on the train an' go an' see Miss Wood.'

'Hm, though usually she would tell us,' Hermione answered, as she placed the carrots she had just fetched from the garden onto the table. She wasn't overly concerned as yet. After all, it was Ruby's day off to spend as she wished. But then something occurred to her. 'Did she tell you not to cook a meal for her?'

Mrs B shook her head.

'There you are then; she'll be back for dinner. Now I'd better go and get washed and changed; I think I have half the garden beneath my fingernails.' And she sailed off leaving Mrs B to prepare the meal.

As the time ticked away at Hatter's Hall, Ruby was becoming more and more distressed. Miranda had been gone for an awfully long time now and she couldn't understand why no one had yet realised their mistake in locking her in the wrong room, so once again, after pacing restlessly up and down the small space, she began to bang and hammer on the door.

'*Let me out – let me out!*' Her distress seemed to transmit itself to the people in the neighbouring rooms and when they began to add their cries to hers it became almost deafening. At last Ruby heard a sharp voice shouting in the corridor, 'Be quiet immediately else you all know what to expect!' The noise died away like magic as the face of Nurse Keen appeared at the window in the door.

'Oh, thank goodness, I thought you'd never come!' Ruby was almost sobbing with relief. 'There's been a terrible mistake. Can you please let me out and take me to my mother?'

'Yes o' course I will, dearie.' She heard the sound of the key turning in the lock and when the door opened, she was confronted with Nurse Keen and another nurse who, if it was possible, was even larger than her. They both looked like wrestlers and as she stared into their cold eyes a shiver ran down Ruby's spine.

'Come along quietly now,' Nurse Keen advised and, glad to be out of the confined space, Ruby obediently followed her as the other nurse fell into step closely behind. At the end of the corridor they ushered her into a room where a large tin bath stood full of water and she stopped abruptly.

'But I-I don't understand. Why have you brought me here and where is my mother?' she said in confusion.

Nurse Keen grinned as she advanced on her menacingly. 'Let's have no trouble, eh? Just get yourself undressed.'

'*What!*' Ruby was outraged. 'Why ever would I do that?'

The woman's face changed as she glared at her threateningly. 'You'll do it 'cause if you don't we'll 'ave to undress you.' Then turning to her colleague, she said, 'I thought we might get this. The young woman that brought her in said she could sound quite rational when she wanted to.'

Ruby's mouth gaped open in shock. 'B-but I'm here to see my mother . . . you know I am!'

'Course you are.' Reaching out, Nurse Keen grabbed her arm and before she could retaliate the second nurse grabbed the other one and they started to drag her towards the bath.

'Leave me alone!' Ruby squealed as terror ran through her veins like iced water, but the two women set about her and within minutes, she was stripped to her bare skin and sobbing.

'You're going to be sorry for this,' she whimpered as she tried to cover her breasts with her arms. 'How *dare* you treat me like this!'

'Ooh, just hark at her. She's a right little lady, ain't she.'

Nurse Keen dragged her towards the bath and before Ruby could stop her, she shoved her hard in the back and Ruby tumbled into the water with a loud splash. It was ice-cold and she came up coughing and spluttering as the nurse tossed her a bar of carbolic soap.

'Now get yerself washed wi' that or do I have to do that for yer an' all!' she ordered.

Too terrified to do any other, Ruby obeyed, although she could hardly see what she was doing for the tears that were spurting from her eyes.

'Yer wouldn't think butter would melt in her mouth to look at her, would yer?' Nurse Keen commented. 'An' yet she's a right one fer the men an' has no morals at all accordin' to the doctor's report. She's already had one baby an' God knows how long it would 'ave been before she was carryin' another. She steals an all. An' she's got the deluded idea that her mother is here!' Her eyes settled on the ring on Ruby's finger and pouncing on her she grabbed her hand and dragged it off. 'You won't be needin' that in 'ere, dearie. I'll keep it safe for yer.'

Ruby was incensed. The ring that Hermione had had specially made for her was her most prized possession and she couldn't bear to see it on Nurse Keen's little finger.

'Give that back *immediately*,' she cried.

The woman just stared at her stonily. 'I reckon it's time we let this little lady see who's in charge.' She nodded to the nurse behind her and the next instant Ruby felt strong hands force her face beneath the water. She kicked and struggled for all she was worth but her strength was no match for theirs and as the greasy, icy water filled her lungs she felt herself going light-headed.

*I'm going to die*, she thought, but suddenly she felt someone take a handful of her hair and she was yanked out of the bath and dumped on the floor. Her scalp felt as if it was on fire and she was coughing up water as the women chuckled.

'P-please tell me what's going on,' she whimpered when she was able to catch her breath again.

Nurse Keen crossed her meaty arms across her enormous chest as she stared down at her. 'You want to know, do you? Then I'll tell yer. You've been committed, dearie. Do yer know what that means?'

'I-I'm not sure!'

'It means that the person who brought you in had with her a signed paper from a doctor sayin' that you was a danger to yourself an' others. An' so you'll be havin' a little holiday 'ere with us till the doctor who committed you thinks yer safe to be let out.'

Ruby's head wagged from side to side in denial. 'But there must be some mistake? I-I came here to see my mother.'

'There yer go again, yer see?' Nurse Keen tutted. 'You ain't *got* no mother, dearie. She's a figment of yer tortured mind. An' is it a lie that yer were carryin' a child an' all?'

'Well . . . no I was, but that wasn't my fault. You see—'

Nurse Keen hauled her up from the floor while the other nurse tossed a shabby, shapeless brown gown at her.

'Put that on,' she snapped.

Rather than stand there naked, Ruby did as she was told as humiliation washed through her. But her humiliation wasn't over yet for next Nurse Keen produced a pair of sharp scissors from her pocket and nodded at the other woman. 'Hold her still while I get rid o' some o' this mop.'

Once again Ruby was seized with her arms pressed tight to her sides and seconds later, she was staring down at her red hair falling in thick ringlets to the floor. She was helpless to prevent it and prayed that she was caught in the grip of a nightmare. Surely soon she would wake up in her comfortable bed at Hermione's to find that all this had been a bad dream? When Nurse Keen finally nodded to the other nurse to release her, Ruby's hand instinctively rose to her head to feel the stubble that was all she had left there. And then suddenly what was happening hit her like a blow to the stomach and she felt sick. Miranda had tricked and betrayed her. All the time she had been pretending to be her friend was leading up to this day. But why? *What have I ever done to her to make her hate me so much?* Ruby wondered.

'So when will I be allowed to go home?' she asked in a small voice. All the fight had gone out of her for now.

Nurse Keen threw back her head and laughed. 'Did yer 'ear that, Hilda? When will she be allowed to go 'ome?' She leant in so close that Ruby could feel her fetid breath on her cheek. She could smell it too: tobacco, spirits, rotting teeth and bad breath.

'There ain't many as come in 'ere *ever* go out again 'cept in a box, so you'd better get used to the idea,' she said cruelly. Then grabbing Ruby's arm she hauled her along the corridor and flung her back into the grim little room.

Ruby crawled onto the bed and curled into a foetal position and as the horror of her situation came home to her and all hope slipped away, she sobbed as if her heart would break.

# Chapter Thirty-Five

'I might as well turn this off now, it's dry as a bone.' Mrs B sighed as the light faded from the day. She had been keeping Ruby's dinner warm over a pan of hot water on the range but it was beyond saving now.

'She'll be back when she's good and ready,' Hermione answered, pretending to concentrate on the newspaper, but she was beginning to feel a little worried too. She had never known Ruby to stay out so late before without telling them – although she was quite entitled to as she had pointed out to Mrs B earlier in the evening. It was now well after nine o'clock at night, almost her bedtime, although she knew she wouldn't sleep a wink until she knew that Ruby was safely home.

Mrs B scraped the ruined dinner into the bin and stifled a yawn.

'Why don't you go up if you're tired?' Hermione suggested. 'I can wait up for Ruby.'

Mrs B looked uncertain. 'Are you sure?'

Hermione nodded. 'Of course. Go on, there's no point in both of us sitting down here.'

Mrs B nodded and after wishing Hermione goodnight she made her way upstairs.

As soon as she was gone Hermione laid the newspaper aside and crossing to the window that looked out onto the street, she twitched the lace curtain aside and peered up and down. The road was deserted, the street lights throwing small puddles of light onto the ground. It was then with a little shock that she realised how much the girl had come to mean to her. She had never married or had children of her own but she knew that had she been fortunate enough to have a daughter, she would have wished for one just like Ruby. The girl had had a hard life up until she had arrived on her doorstep and she had felt an instant affinity with her. She wasn't sure why; she wasn't a sentimental sort of person and yet something in Ruby had appealed to her maternal instinct. Since then their closeness had grown and now the thought of anything happening to her was terrifying. She admired the girl enormously. After all, how many would have gone through what she had in her young life and not have a chip on their shoulder? But rather than let her past grind her down, Ruby had fastidiously worked at her new career and Hermione knew without doubt that if she so wished, Ruby's designs could take her a long way and her future would be secured. But where was she? She yawned and stretched. She was exhausted, but still she sat by the window waiting.

In Hatter's Hall, Ruby finally heard the key in the lock and as she peered through the gloom she saw a nurse she hadn't seen before standing in the doorway with a tray in her hand.

'Supper,' she said curtly, dropping the tray onto the bed, causing some of the contents of the dish on it to slop across the sides.

'*Please* . . . I need to see the matron,' Ruby implored, her voice hoarse from shouting and crying. She had given up eventually when she realised that no one was going to come. 'There's been a terrible mistake.'

'So they tell me,' the nurse answered with a wry grin.

'Will you take me to her then . . . please?'

The nurse shook her head, setting her double chin wobbling. 'Matron ain't here of an evening,' she said curtly. Then she smiled slyly. 'Though I could keep yer company if yer like?' She bent towards her and as her hand gently stroked Ruby's breast through the drab material of the asylum uniform they had forced her to wear, Ruby sprang away from her as if she had been stung, upsetting the tray and sending the contents crashing to the floor.

The nurse tutted. 'Now look what you've done. An' it's a long time till breakfast. Happen by then you'll be of a mind to be a bit friendlier.' And with that she left the cell, locking the door firmly behind her.

Ruby's shoulders sagged. Hermione would be worried that she hadn't returned home, she realised, and the thought perked her up a little. Hermione was sure to come looking for her, wasn't she? But the hope died almost as soon as it had sprung to life. She had merely told her that she was going out to do a little shopping, as Miranda had asked her to, and Hermione wouldn't have a clue where to start looking for her. So all she could do now was wait and pray that Miranda would have a change of heart and come back for her. Deep down, though, she feared there was little chance of that happening. Miranda had obviously planned this very carefully and Ruby had fallen for her lies and false smiles hook, line and sinker. With a little sigh she curled up on the bed again, trying to close her ears to the wails and shouts of the other souls that were trapped there, and eventually she fell into a troubled doze out of sheer exhaustion.

Early the following morning she heard movement in the corridor outside and she was instantly awake and alert. After a sleep, she felt slightly better and was determined that today she would insist on a meeting with the matron, who would surely see that she was far from insane.

The door opened and the same nurse who had brought her tray to her the night before stepped into the room, scowling at the mess of food that had now set on the floor. 'Get that cleaned up immediately,' she snapped, putting down a bucket and a mop. 'And when you've done that you can come along to the bathroom to wash yerself if you've a mind to, an' empty out your slop bucket. This ain't a hotel, yer don't get waited on 'ere. An' I'm Nurse Young by the way, so don't forget it.'

She slammed the door, and knowing that she had little choice other than to do as she was told, Ruby scraped the dry food back onto the tray and scrubbed what had now dried to a solid glutinous mess on the floor with the mop. She retrieved the slice of grey bread that had come with whatever had been in the dish from beneath the bed and dropped that onto the tray too. Her stomach was growling with hunger but she couldn't have eaten it even if she'd wanted to because it was rock hard now and she would have feared for her teeth. Eventually, when she could do no more, she sat back on the bed to wait.

Nurse Young soon reappeared and nodding towards the bucket that stood in the corner she ordered, 'Come wi' me.'

Ruby lifted the bucket, trying her utmost not to look at the contents as she carried it carefully along the corridor to the washroom she had been taken to the day before.

'Slop that lot down there.' Nurse Young pointed to a toilet. 'An' then come an' strip off an' get yerself washed over 'ere.'

The nurse settled onto a hard-backed wooden chair and once the bucket was emptied Ruby approached the sink with her cheeks burning.

'Couldn't I be given a little privacy to wash?' Ruby asked, her voice little more than a squeak at the thought of being naked in front of this abominable woman.

The nurse threw back her head and let out a throaty laugh. 'Ooh, 'ark at little Miss La-De-Da! *Privacy* indeed.' Her beady eyes narrowed as she glared at Ruby. 'Now strip off an' do as yer told or do I 'ave to do it for yer?'

Ruby tentatively pulled the scratchy gown over her head and, shivering, she crossed to the sink where she quickly used the carbolic soap and the rag that had been left there to wash herself as thoroughly as she could while the nurse watched her avidly.

'You know . . . I could make it so much nicer fer you while yer in 'ere if you decided to be nice to me,' she wheedled.

Ruby's blood ran cold at the expression on the woman's face. She had seen that look once before – on her father's face the night he had raped her.

'That's very kind of you but I'm not going to be here long,' she answered politely as she tugged the misshapen gown back over her head. 'So now may I please see the matron?'

'Yer can as it happens,' the nurse chortled as she played with the hairs that were growing out of her chin. With her thin grey hair scraped back into a straggly bun and her squinty grey eyes she really was the ugliest woman Ruby had ever seen. 'She likes to meet all the patients when they first arrive, so foller me. But no tryin' to run away, mind, else I'll have yer flat on yer back afore yer can say Jack Robinson.'

Barefoot, Ruby followed her out of the washroom to the door at the top of the long corridor where the nurse had to pause to find the right key from the many that were dangling on a chain about her waist. Eventually she found it and after ushering Ruby through it she quickly locked it again and taking Ruby's arm in a vice-like grip, she hauled her down the sweeping staircase into the hallway.

'This is the matron's office,' she said as she stopped to rap on the door.

'Come in,' a voice answered and thrusting the door open she pushed Ruby inside.

Ruby found herself in a large room comfortably furnished with an easy chair that was placed by the window and an enormous desk behind which sat an elderly woman with a stern expression on her face. She was dressed in a navy-blue uniform which was covered with a crisp white apron and a small white cap was perched precariously on her mop of thick, greying hair which was chopped off at chin length.

'Ruby Carter?' she barked.

Ruby started before remembering to nod. There was something about this woman that made her blood run cold. Her eyes reminded Ruby of the dead eyes she had seen on the fish on the marble slab in the fishmonger's; they seemed to have no life or warmth in them and Ruby's heart sank as it came to her that she would find no ally in this woman.

'I have had you brought here to make sure that you understand why you have been committed and what will happen to you,' the woman told her coldly. When Ruby remained silent she raised an eyebrow and snapped impatiently, 'Well, speak up. You have a tongue, don't you, girl?'

Ruby's mouth was so dry that she couldn't utter a single word and so snatching up a form in front of her the woman began to read aloud. 'This is the paper from Doctor Ward, who had you committed.'

Ruby shuddered as she recognised the name of the elderly doctor who used to attend Mrs Pembroke. 'He states that you have loose morals that led to you finding yourself with child. He also states that you have a tendency to cheat and lie. Finally, he states that he feels because of your loose morals you should be locked up for your own safety. Do you admit all this?'

'No, Matron, I don't.' Ruby was crying now. 'I was going to have a child, admittedly, but it was forced upon me . . . I was raped . . . and yes, I admit that I did steal a few times for the person who was caring for me at the time but—'

'That's *enough*!' The matron held her hand up and as she did the light spilling through the window caught the stone in the ring she was wearing, making it flash a rich blood red.

'Why . . . that's *my* ring you're wearing,' Ruby protested before she could stop herself.

The woman rose from her seat to glare at her. 'And this is just the sort of behaviour the doctor warned us that you are prone to,' she responded. 'So now I will tell you what is going to happen. You will remain here and receive treatment for your psychotic behaviour until the person who is paying for your stay decides otherwise. You have a lot of wickedness in you so we will begin with the leeches. Hopefully they will suck a little of the badness out of you. Take her away, nurse!'

Ruby stared at her in horror as she shuddered. 'NO! I won't let you,' she shouted as she moved forward but the nurse already had her arms pinned to her sides and as Ruby kicked and struggled she dragged her out of the room and towards the staircase where another woman ran forward to help pull her up the stairs.

When they arrived back at the little cell she had spent the night in, they shoved her forcefully through the door, causing her to land with such a thud on the floor that it knocked all the air out of her and for a moment she lay gasping for breath. But soon, as the horror of her situation hit her full force, she was back on her feet again, banging at the door and screaming for all she was worth. Once again, the other poor souls in the adjoining cells joined in and the noise became so deafening that Ruby put her hands across her ears to try to block out the sound, before throwing herself onto the hard mattress.

She had no idea how long she lay there, but eventually the door opened and yet another nurse appeared. This one was much younger and with her fair hair and blue eyes, she was nowhere near as frightening to look at.

'Hello, Ruby. I'm Nurse Downes and I was wondering if you'd like to come along to the dining room?'

Ruby shook her head, muttering sullenly, 'I'm not hungry!'

The nurse stared at her worriedly. 'But you must try to eat something or you'll make yourself ill,' she urged, then glancing across her shoulder as if to make sure they couldn't be overheard she said in a lower voice, 'And if you continue to refuse food, they'll force-feed you.'

Ruby shrugged. She was in a defiant mood now. 'They'll be sorry if they try it.'

Nurse Downes bit on her lip before trying one more time. Ruby seemed nothing like the majority of the people who were admitted here and she almost felt sorry for her. 'If I bring you a tray will you eat something in here?'

Again Ruby shook her head and turned her face away so with a sigh the nurse left, locking the door behind her. Outside, Ruby could hear the sound of shuffling footsteps and she guessed that the other patients, or at least those who were well enough, were being led to the dining room, wherever that was, for their lunch. Her stomach growled ominously and her mouth was so dry that she felt as if her tongue was swollen, but she was determined that nothing would pass her lips. Surely when they saw what lack of food was doing to her, they would be forced to release her? Turning to the wall she thought of Hermione, Miss Wood, Mrs B, Bill, Nell and Maddie, and the tears came once more.

It was late afternoon before anyone came to her again and this time when the door opened she found herself gazing at a man. Like the majority of the nurses she had seen he was a giant of a man, almost as broad as he was tall. He had a shock of ginger hair and a long beard and as he stood staring at her she felt as though a cold finger had run up her spine.

'I've been told to take yer to the dinin' room,' he told her shortly as he advanced on her.

Ruby drew her knees into her chest and pressed herself into the corner. 'I'm not hungry,' she told him defiantly with her chin in the air. She was determined not to show him how afraid she was, although her stomach felt as if it was in knots.

'In that case we'll 'ave to encourage you to eat.' His cold eyes bored into hers for a moment before he turned and left the room without so much as another word. Shortly after the key turned in the lock again and he reappeared with Nurse Keen who was carrying a tray.

'Still refusin' to eat, are yer?' she chirped cheerfully as she slapped the tray on the end of the bed. 'Then we'll 'ave to help yer, won't we? Go ahead, Bernard.'

The man advanced on her and before she knew what was happening, he had her standing with her hands clasped to her sides and her feet dangling inches above the floor. 'Carry on then, Marge,' he chuckled. 'I reckon she's just realised she wants her dinner after all.'

'I do no—' But before she could finish what she was going to say, Nurse Keen had gripped her nostrils together and Ruby's mouth automatically opened so that she could breathe. Instantly with her other hand Nurse Keen tipped a spoonful of what tasted like very unappetising watery stew into her mouth and pushed her chin up so that she either swallowed or choked. Some of the disgusting stuff splashed out of her mouth and down her drab gown but she had no time to protest and get her breath back before the process was repeated. This went on until the dish was empty and then the nurse stood back and rubbed her hands together.

'There, now that weren't so bad, were it?' she chortled as if she had told some brilliant joke. 'Now yer can either behave yerself an' join the others in the dinin' room at mealtimes or we can go through that every time. What's it to be, eh?'

Humiliated, Ruby lowered her head as the enormous man released her and she sagged back onto the bed. 'I-I'll eat in the dining room.'

The nurse nodded with satisfaction. 'Good! I thought yer would. Come on, Bernard!'

Once they had left the room, despair washed through her and Ruby rushed across to the bucket in the corner and vomited back everything they had forced down her. But then she dried her eyes and her chin came up again as her hand rose to stroke her cropped hair. Hermione or Maddie would come looking for her when she didn't come home, she was sure of it. They had to because the prospect of being left here in this godforsaken place was unthinkable.

# Chapter Thirty-Six

As Oscar helped Serena down from the cab outside his aunt's home the following morning, her heart was hammering. They had come with important news for Hermione and Ruby and she was wondering how they were both going to receive it.

Sensing her nervousness, Oscar paid the cabbie and squeezed her hand as he tucked it into his arm. 'It'll be all right, darling,' he told her reassuringly. 'I'm sure they'll both be pleased.'

It was then that he noticed Hermione at the window and by the time Mrs B had let them in she was standing waiting for them in the drawing room, her face pale. She looked tired, as if she hadn't slept well, although her back was as straight as ever and her head was high.

'Good morning, Aunt.' Oscar pecked her on the cheek. 'We've come with what I hope you will think is good news.'

'And I'm afraid I have some *not* so good news for you.'

'Oh!' Oscar was taken aback. Hermione had never been an overly demonstrative person but his welcome was usually warmer than this. 'And what would that be then?'

'It's Ruby . . . she didn't come home last night. It was her day off and she said she was going to do some shopping yesterday morning. That was the last we saw of her.' She omitted to tell him that she had been up for most of the night, hovering by the window.

Oscar and Serena were visibly shocked. 'Has she ever done this before?' Oscar asked.

'Never. But there's worse . . .' She hesitated before rushing on. 'I went to check the workroom this morning to see if perhaps there was a note or anything. There wasn't, but while I was there, I thought I may as well try to get some work done while I waited for her to come back, and when I opened the safe . . .' Clearly distressed she swallowed. 'I discovered that some very valuable jewels are missing.'

Oscar raised an eyebrow in query.

'It's the diamonds you brought recently for the design Ruby was working on. They are worth hundreds of pounds and they're all gone.'

'But *surely* you can't think that Ruby would have taken them?' Serena said in a shocked voice.

Hermione shrugged. 'I don't know what to think. If asked I would have sworn hand on heart that the girl was trustworthy, but I can't deny the evidence. She is gone and so are the jewels.'

'What about her clothes? Has she taken any of them?' Oscar asked. He and Serena had arrived with such good news but now everything had gone awry.

Mrs B entered the room carrying a tray of tea and Oscar saw that she too was upset. Her eyes were red and her usual sparkle was missing. 'I'll go up and check her room,' she offered and without another word she set off.

She was back within minutes. 'Everything is just as she left it, she ain't took a thing.' She frowned. 'But I'll tell you now I don't believe for one minute that Ruby would just up and leave. Someone is behind this, I'd stake my life on it.'

Serena nodded in agreement, her eyes filled with tears. 'I think you are right, Mrs B, there has to be some plausible explanation.'

'Perhaps she just met a friend from her past and decided to stay the night,' Oscar said hopefully.

Hermione shook her head. 'She's never mentioned a friend to me. To be honest, from the little she has said I don't think she had much of a life when she lived at the bakery. Her father was a slave-driver and her mother was under his thumb. And anyway, if that were the case, I'm sure she would have got word to us.'

'Then perhaps we should report her missing to the police,' Oscar suggested.

Again Hermione shook her head. 'Let's give her a little longer,' she said cautiously, very aware that if they went down that route they would have to tell the police that some very valuable gems had gone missing with her.

Oscar sank onto a chair as Mrs B poured the tea, but no one really wanted it and it grew cold in the cups as they racked their brains as to where the girl could be.

Ruby was lying on her bed staring into space when the cell door opened and Nurse Keen appeared with an elderly gentleman carrying a black leather doctor's bag. The man was almost as far round as he was high with thinning grey hair and a florid complexion. His suit looked as if it was good quality, although it was shiny with wear, and as he advanced on her Ruby wrinkled her nose at the smell of stale sweat, whisky and tobacco.

'So this is the new arrival, is it?' He pushed his steel-framed spectacles further up his nose and grinned, showing stained and rotting teeth.

Ruby pulled herself to a sitting position and glared at him.

'I'm Dr Pearse. And do you know what your name is?'

'Of course I do! I'm not a simpleton.' Ruby was indignant. 'My name is Ruby Carter, sir! And I am being held here against my will.'

'Of course you are, me dear.' He placed his bag on the end of the bed and after rummaging inside it Ruby shuddered with horror as she saw him produce a jar full of leeches. 'They all say that when they first arrive. But don't you worry, I'm going to make you better.'

'Not with those disgusting things you're not!' Ruby said haughtily.

He frowned as he turned to look at Nurse Keen and after giving her an almost imperceptible nod, she quickly stepped out onto the landing to summon another nurse. She then produced some thick rope from her pocket and as the two nurses advanced on her Ruby tried to push past them, guessing what they were going to do. But it was no use, within seconds they had taken an arm each and flung her onto her back on the bed, and although she kicked and fought, before she knew it, they had secured her hands to the metal bedposts.

'Please . . . *no!*' she screamed as the doctor undid the lid on the jar, but Nurse Keen ignored her as they set about tying her legs.

Soon she was trussed up like a chicken, and Nurse Keen had lifted her gown to beneath her chin. Ruby's face grew hot with humiliation as they stared down at her naked body, but worse was to come.

'Ready, doctor,' the nurse informed him with a smirk.

As Ruby felt the slimy leeches being placed upon her skin she began to buck and bounce on the bed as helpless tears began to stream down her face and her screams reverberated off the hard, cold wall.

'Ah, they're attaching nicely,' Dr Pearse said as he poked the leeches. 'Let's give them an hour to do their job, eh? That should suck some of the madness out of her and then this afternoon I recommend some cold water treatment.'

Nurse Keen nodded with satisfaction and smirked at Ruby, who was now almost hysterical, and after the doctor had snapped his bag shut they all left the room.

Ruby screamed until her throat was hoarse as she wriggled and writhed, intent on throwing the leeches off her but it was as if the vile little creatures were glued to her skin. But she was weak from lack of food and after a time, when she finally realised that no one was going to come and help her, she stopped struggling and lay still, her eyes firmly fixed on the ceiling as she tried not to think of what was happening to her.

She had no idea how long she lay there, but eventually the door was unlocked and Nurse Keen appeared with a smug grin on her face, another nurse close behind her.

'They look like they've had a nice little feast,' she chuckled to the other nurse. 'But now we'd better continue the treatment.' With a look of glee on her face she began to remove the bloated leeches and drop them back into the jar, then she and the other nurse quickly untied Ruby's hands and feet and hauled her to standing. Her wrists and ankles were chaffed and bleeding from the restraints but ignoring the wounds they dragged her out of the door and down the corridor towards the washroom where Ruby saw a large deep tin bath full of water waiting for her.

Before she could protest, they had pulled the shapeless shift up over her head and as they each took an arm and a leg, she sensed what was coming. There was no time for her to put up any sort of a fight before they lifted her effortlessly and flung her sideways into the bath. She disappeared under the water with a resounding splash that sent the water surging over the sides and onto the floor.

For a moment the ice-cold water took her breath away and she fought her way to the surface, coughing and spluttering. Almost immediately Nurse Keen put her hand on her head and forced it below the water again. Each time she fought her way up they shoved her back down again, until she began to feel light-headed. Suddenly her limbs felt heavy and the fight went out of her. She knew she was going to die, yet strangely she didn't care anymore.

And then just as she was welcoming death she was grasped viciously beneath her arms, hauled out of the bath and thrown roughly onto the cold floor. Gasping for breath, she began to heave up the vast amounts of water she had swallowed while Nurse Keen watched with her thick arms folded across her chest and a look of satisfaction on her face.

Finally the nurse threw her shift at her. 'Now get that on an' per'aps you'll know to be'ave better from now on, eh?'

For now there was no fight left in her, but somehow she managed to get to her feet and yank the shift down over her head. She was cold and shivering and had never felt so ill in her life as the nurse hauled her along the corridor.

Once back in her cell she curled up on the bed and pulled the thin grey blanket over her head and finally she slept from sheer exhaustion.

The next time the door opened Ruby opened her eyes and stared blearily at the door, relieved to see that it was Nurse Downes.

'Ruby, it's supper time. Do you feel well enough to come along to the dining room?' Her voice was soft and the kind words brought tears to Ruby's eyes again. She wanted to tell her that she wasn't hungry but then as she thought back to the way she had been forcibly fed she changed her mind and reluctantly swung her legs over the side of the bed.

'That's good.'

She made to rise, but her legs threatened to give way beneath her and the kindly nurse hurried forward and put her arm about her waist.

'Lean on me,' she urged, and as they started along the corridor she whispered, 'Just try to do as you're told and don't make a fuss and they'll leave you alone.'

'B-but I shouldn't even be here,' Ruby said with a catch in her voice. 'I truly haven't done anything wrong.'

Soon they approached a large room at the end of the corridor and through the pane of glass in the top half of it, Ruby could see rows of tables with people sitting at them, all dressed in identical drab gowns to the one she was wearing – men and women alike. Nurse Downes opened the door and ushered her in. Looking round at the faces of the other inmates, she felt as if she had been catapulted into hell. Most of their eyes were vacant and some of them were rocking backwards and forwards in their seats as if they had no idea of where they were. Others were talking to themselves and one old lady was picking at a festering wound on her arm.

She stopped abruptly, reluctant to go further, but Nurse Downes smiled at her. 'Come and sit over here by Dilys.'

Dilys turned out to be a woman who looked to be in her mid-thirties and she smiled as Ruby sat down.

Once she was seated Nurse Downes went to a long counter at the end of the room where two women were doling out the unappetising-looking food into tin bowls.

'It'll be sausage and mash tonight,' Dilys informed her. 'Although I can't promise it will taste anything like the sausage and mash you're probably used to.'

Ruby blinked with surprise. Dilys was very well spoken and she could see that, dressed properly, she would be quite attractive. She was painfully thin, admittedly, but her face was heart-shaped and when she smiled Ruby saw she had dimples in her cheeks. Her hair, although matted and tied back with a thin bit of string, was a lovely platinum blonde and her eyes were the colour of violets.

'You must be new here,' Dilys said.

Ruby nodded miserably and was surprised when the other woman squeezed her hand beneath the table. 'Just try to do as you're told and don't make a fuss,' she advised quietly, keeping her head down. 'You can't win in here – I learnt that lesson long ago – but if you behave you'll be given jobs to do.'

'What sort of jobs?' Ruby asked curiously.

'Sometimes you might be allowed to deliver meals to the patients that can't get to the dining room, or you might be allowed to work in the kitchen or the laundry. The very best job for the really well-behaved patients is the gardening. It's wonderful to get out in the fresh air. They're all hard work but it's better than being locked up in your cell all day.' She noticed at that moment that one of the nurses was watching her and she clammed up until the nurse had turned her attention elsewhere.

When another nurse placed a tin bowl full of food in front of them and handed them each a spoon, Ruby frowned. 'Where are our knives and forks?'

'You don't get them in here.' Dilys chuckled. 'Some of the poor devils would harm themselves if they were given a knife, or worse still they'd stab someone else.'

Ruby shuddered and stared down in dismay at the glutinous mess on her plate. The sausages were so shrivelled and over-cooked that she was sure she could have soled shoes with them, and the potatoes were greasy and lumpy.

'I know it's not very appetising but try to eat up,' Dilys whispered encouragingly. 'You'll only get into bother if you don't and you need to keep your strength up and your wits about you in here.'

And so Ruby forced some of the food down her throat, trying not to look at it as she lifted the spoon to her mouth and chewed. It tasted as awful as it looked but she was surprised to find that she did feel slightly better with something inside her. Some of the other patients were snatching at the food with their fingers and ramming it into their mouths making disgusting noises as they did so and Ruby tried not to look. Suddenly she found herself thinking of the lovely meals Mrs Petty and Mrs B had cooked for her and tears sprang to her eyes again. She seemed to have done little but cry since being left here and more than once she had convinced herself she had no tears left but then once again they would start. Still, at least now she had met Dilys she felt a little better and hoped that she had found at least one ally in this dreadful place.

# Chapter Thirty-Seven

'Right, Carter, look sharp, girl!'

Nurse Keen's voice roused her from an unsettled sleep early the next morning and Ruby peered towards her blearily.

'It's time to use the washroom, follow me!'

Knowing better than to disobey, Ruby reluctantly trooped along the corridor behind her. She had taken heed of what Dilys had said and had decided that she would try to be good. That was until they reached the bathroom where the nurse pushed her inside and turned the key in the lock.

'Strip off,' she ordered.

Ruby gulped. Surely she should be allowed a little privacy for washing at least? But she did as she was told, keeping her eyes averted from the nurse as colour burnt into her cheeks. Her body was covered in faint bruises from where the disgusting leeches had lain on her the day before and as she looked down at them, she had to swallow to stop herself from being sick as she remembered the slimy feel of them on her skin.

'Use that bowl there, I've put a towel an' some soap ready,' Nurse Keen barked.

Ruby began to wash when suddenly the rag she was using was snatched from her hand. Glancing up at Nurse Keen she saw there was a strange gleam in her eyes.

'Why don't yer let me help you,' she said breathily as she ran the flannel across Ruby's softly curving stomach.

Ruby stood completely still, although she wanted to scream and lash out. But then the nurse's hand rose to her breasts and the woman began to pant. Ruby stepped back and threw her arms across herself. 'Get *away* from me,' she spat. 'I'm quite capable of washing myself, thank you very much!'

A blow to the side of her head sent her sprawling onto the cold, tiled floor, but Ruby didn't care. There was no way she was going to allow this sick, perverted woman to touch her intimately, even if it meant another punishment.

'Huh! You really think yer somethin', don't yer?' the nurse ground out, making the hairs on her chin quiver. 'Well let's see how yer feel when you've had a bit o' time in solitary to think about it.' With that she strode to the door and shouted for help and within seconds the male nurse she had seen the day before appeared. Nurse Keen whispered something to him and he left again as Ruby snatched up her shift and pulled it over her head.

When the man returned, he was holding a strange-looking robe with very long sleeves with ties on them and before she could stop them, they had thrust her arms into the sleeves and then to her horror they tied them tightly about her so that she was unable to move her arms at all.

'Welcome to yer first taste of a straitjacket, me beauty,' Nurse Keen chortled gleefully.

It was then Ruby realised that this woman was probably more insane than some of the patients incarcerated there. Either that or she was pure evil. But she didn't have long to think on it for they were soon dragging her out of the washroom and along the corridor again. They stopped in front of a door that had no peephole in it and without a word they opened it and thrust her inside before slamming it resoundingly behind her.

It was pitch dark, but as Ruby's eyes became accustomed to the gloom, she saw that it was quite empty and the walls were padded. Feeling utterly helpless and frustrated she began to scream, but eventually, when she realised it was fruitless, she sat down on the floor with her back against the padded wall and made herself as comfortable as she could until at last sleep claimed her.

She had no idea how long she was left in there, nor whether it was day or night. The room was soundproofed and she had never felt so alone. But finally, the door opened and as the light streamed in, she blinked as her eyes adjusted to it.

'Come along, Ruby. Shall we get you cleaned up and back into your room?'

Shame washed through her as she realised that Nurse Downes knew that she had wet herself. There had been no choice for there was not even a bucket in the room. The nurse's kind voice brought tears to her eyes and she tried not to look at her as she crossed the room and began to undo the ties on the straitjacket. The moment she was free of it, pain coursed through her from where her arms had been kept tied so tightly to her sides and pins and needles stabbed at her fingers. Head down she followed the nurse to the washroom where a clean shift had been laid ready for her and she was grateful when Nurse Downes turned her back while she did her ablutions and quickly changed her soiled clothes.

'Oh, Ruby, if only you would stop making a fuss,' Nurse Downes said sadly. 'Life would be so much easier for you then.'

Ruby glared at her, even though she knew the nurse was giving her sound advice. She was the only one who seemed to have an ounce of kindness in her. 'So you think I should just stand there and allow that disgusting woman to paw me, do you? And I shouldn't even be here!' she told her heatedly. 'It isn't fair and I'm *not* mad, I assure you.'

'Then show the rest of the staff that,' Nurse Downes answered. 'Especially Nurse Keen. Don't give her an excuse to fetch the doctor to you or dole out punishment. Here . . . use this.'

She produced a hairbrush from the depths of her pocket and taking it from her Ruby ran it over her head. Although her hair had been almost completely cut off, there were a few tufts left, and the familiar movement and feel of the soft brush over her skin gave her some comfort.

'That's better, isn't it?' Nurse Downes smiled encouragingly before leading her into the corridor again. 'And now I'm going to take you to the dining room. You've been in the punishment cell for almost a whole day so you must be hungry. Will you at least try to eat something . . . for me?'

Ruby opened her mouth to say she didn't want anything but then, thinking better of it, she snapped it shut again. Nurse Downes was the only ally she had in the place and she didn't want to estrange her too so when she entered the dining room she took her place at Dilys's side and did her best to swallow some of the unappetising mess that was placed in front of her. It was some sort of pie but the pastry case was so hard that when she tried to break into it, it almost shot off her spoon, but still she diligently ate some of it.

'Have you been in the padded cell?' Dilys asked in a whisper after a while.

Ruby nodded.

Dilys looked at her sympathetically. 'It's horrible in there, isn't it? Just try to accept things and it will be easier for you.'

'How *can* I accept things?' Ruby retorted tearfully. 'I shouldn't even be here but the matron informs me that until the person who put me in comes back for me there's no way out. I just hope that Miranda has a conscience.'

'I used to think like that.' Dilys's voice held a wealth of sadness.

'So how long have you been in here then?' Ruby asked curiously.

Dilys shrugged. 'Some fifteen years or so now, I think. I lost track after a time.'

'And why were you put in here? Of course you don't have to tell me if you don't want to,' Ruby added hastily, fearing that she might have overstepped the mark.

'It's all right.' Dilys's eyes grew dreamy as she thought back in time. 'I was put in here because I fell in love,' she said quietly. 'The trouble was my family thought that Steven, the man I loved, was beneath me because he was working class and they did everything they could to keep us apart. And then I found out I was having a baby.' She gulped before going on. 'Steven and I thought that with a baby due they would relent and let us marry but instead they had me placed in here. I would have brought shame on their name, you see?'

Ruby was horrified. 'But didn't Steven come looking for you?'

'Oh, I'm sure he would have but they told him that I had gone to visit an aunt and that I had died in an accident.'

'But that's dreadful!' Ruby could hardly believe that anyone could be so wicked. 'And what became of your baby?'

Dilys sniffed back a tear. 'Eventually I had a beautiful baby boy. He was the image of his father and perfect in every way. But they took him away from me within hours of his birth and I never saw him again.' She glanced around to make sure they couldn't be heard by any of the staff before going on in a hushed voice, 'I've heard the nurses, the decent ones that is, saying that the matron who runs this place, Dr Pearse and Nurse Keen are as crooked as they come. It seems that the babies born here are sold to childless couples for extortionate sums of money. And that isn't the only racket they have going on, apparently. Genuine patients should not have to pay to be in here, but unfortunates like you and me are usually hidden away by people who can afford to pay to keep us locked up. There's also what I've heard referred to as the luxury wing where well-off people hide their old folk when they become an embarrassment to them, or daughters who have got themselves into trouble before they're wed. Once the babies are born the matron finds a new home for them and the girls return to their families.'

'But that's so unfair!' Ruby was incensed. 'Why hasn't anyone spoken out?'

'Because they're too afraid to. They need their jobs,' Dilys confided. 'And anyway, who could they tell? The matron runs the place and she and the doctor are hand in glove.'

When they'd finished eating, a nurse approached them to collect the dirty dishes and glancing at Dilys she told her, 'You can be on washing-up duty tonight, Beresford.' Nurse Downes had disappeared and this one seemed none too friendly, much like the majority of the nurses there who didn't seem to give a fig for the patients.

'Can Ruby help me?'

The nurse eyed Ruby up and down before shrugging. 'I suppose so. It'll save me from havin' to help. Wait there while we get the rest of the patients back to their rooms and then I'll take you both through to the kitchen.'

As she walked away Dilys grinned at Ruby. 'At least it will give you a bit longer out of your cell. Even if we are only washing dishes and cleaning.'

'I'm not afraid of hard work,' Ruby told her, thinking back to the life she had led in the bakery. 'And you're quite right; I'd scrub and clean all night if it meant not being shut up.'

Very soon they were led into a cavernous kitchen where a slovenly-looking woman who was introduced as the cook sat smoking a pipe and sipping at a glass of ale at the side of a roaring fire. The woman looked dirty and unkempt and the room was so hot that Ruby started to sweat.

Dilys began to wash the mountain of pots piled on every surface while Ruby dried them as she gazed from the window above the sink longingly. They were on the ground floor here and she wondered if it might be worth opening the window and trying to escape, but as if she could read her mind Dilys sadly shook her head.

'Don't even think about it,' she whispered, keeping a wary eye on the old cook, whose grubby cotton cap was now awry as she fought to stay awake. 'I tried that once but I never got past the gates. Old Wilf who lives in the gatehouse has got a nose on him like a bloodhound and I never even made it as far as the gates. The whipping I got was so brutal I couldn't lie on my back for a whole week.'

'But there must be *some* way we could escape.' Ruby looked so desperate that Dilys's kind heart went out to her. She could remember when she still had hope, but it seemed a long time ago now and she had resigned herself to dying in this place.

It took a considerable time to get all the pots clean and once that was done, they each took a cloth and wiped down the surfaces, which looked as if they hadn't been properly cleaned for some long time.

'What with the slop they feed us and the filthy conditions in this kitchen it's a wonder we don't all die of food poisoning,' Ruby whispered.

Dilys nodded in agreement. 'You're right, but what choice do we have? We either eat it or we starve, it's as simple as that. And please think about what I told you and try to be good. You remind me so much of myself when I was first brought here. I was always in trouble until I learnt that it was safer to just keep a low profile. All the wicked so-called treatments they dole out won't happen if you give them no reason to use them.'

Eventually the door opened and much to Ruby's relief she saw that it was Nurse Downes who had come to escort them back to their cells.

'Everywhere looks very nice. Well done, ladies,' she said approvingly as reluctantly they both allowed her to usher them upstairs again.

The following morning, after thinking on Dilys's advice, Ruby allowed herself to be meekly led along to the dining room for her breakfast without a murmur. She was discovering that what Dilys had said was true: any time out of the cell was worth behaving for, although she was still determined to figure out a way to get out of there. She simply wouldn't accept that she could be here for the foreseeable future.

Through the bars on the windows they passed, Ruby could see the sun shining in a clear blue sky and her heart ached to be out in the fresh air. Already the bloom had gone from her cheeks and she had lost weight, but her resolve to escape was still strong. She had scratched four small marks on the wall in her cell with her fingernail – one to mark each day she had been there, and she had decided she would do that every day so that she would have some idea how long she was incarcerated.

As they were sitting waiting for the lumpy porridge to be served, Ruby glanced up at the ceiling. Whoever was in the room above was screaming loudly enough to wake the dead.

Dilys noticed where she was looking and whispered, 'The really bad cases are kept up on the second floor. I've seen them occasionally when they're let out into the grounds for a breath of fresh air, although that doesn't happen very often and only when one of the kindlier nurses is on duty. Half of them don't even know night from day and they drug them with laudanum to keep them quiet.'

Ruby shuddered at the thought. 'And how often are we let out?'

Dilys shrugged. 'Again, it depends on who is on duty. Nurse Downes will usually allow us half an hour when she can, although we only get to walk around the courtyard at the back of the house. Still, that's better than nothing. At least you can feel the sun on your face and breathe clean air for a while.' Sadly, neither of them had seen Nurse Downes that day. It was probably her day off and they both knew better than to ask Nurse Keen.

But despite all her new resolutions to be a model patient, by teatime Ruby was pacing up and down her cell again. The smell from the slop bucket was already overpowering and she knew there would be no chance to rinse it out until the next morning when she was allowed to use the washroom.

*Even animals shouldn't be kept like this*, she thought as frustration rose in her like a tidal wave. And then before she could stop herself, all her good intentions were forgotten and she was banging on the door again, screaming at the top of her voice. '*Let me out! Let me out!*'

'What's all this *racket*?' Nurse Keen said sternly when she finally opened the door, Bernard, the male nurse, right behind her. By this time Ruby's eyes were red-rimmed from crying, her throat was hoarse from shouting and her fists were sore from pounding on the door, but before she could say a word, Nurse Keen nodded at Bernard and he strode forward and caught Ruby about the waist.

'What are—' Her words were blocked when a foul-smelling rag was pressed against her mouth and nose, and soon darkness rushed towards her and she knew no more.

The following morning, she woke to find Dr Pearse standing over her, once more fastening the foul leeches to her naked body. She wanted to lash out at him and stand to shake them off but her legs refused to do as she told them.

'I hear you've been very disruptive again,' he tutted. 'So I think a little more treatment is called for.'

Her head wagged weakly from side to side as a wave of hopelessness threatened to choke her and as she lay staring at the ceiling, tears slid down her face and she wished that she could die. Even death would be preferable to having to stay in this evil place.

# Chapter Thirty-Eight

Hands on hips, Mrs B glared at Hermione. 'So you've had me standin' at the stove again fer no good reason, have you?' she snapped, staring down at Hermione's untouched breakfast. It had been months now since Ruby had been gone and yet still Hermione insisted that she would come back. 'You do know that you're goin' to make yerself ill if you carry on like this, don't yer? You're hardly eatin' enough to keep a sparrow alive, an' what good is it doin'?'

When there was no reply, she gentled her voice and tried another tack. 'They're havin' a party out in the street today to celebrate the Queen's Jubilee. Why don't we get dressed up an' go an' join 'em? It'd do us both good.'

'I'm not in the mood for a party,' Hermione answered as she rose from the table. 'I think I'll go and work in the garden for a while. It's such a lovely day it's a shame to be indoors. Why don't you come and join me?'

'It's my day for scrubbin' the kitchen floor,' Mrs B responded.

Hermione laughed. 'I'm sure it wouldn't hurt to let it go just this once. It's hardly as if it gets dirty with just you and me walking on it, is it? Oh, and Oscar and Serena are coming this afternoon. I forgot to mention it.'

'Why . . . have they some news?'

Hermione shook her head sadly. 'Not as far as I know or they would have come specially to tell me.'

'Hm, in that case I'd best go and bake a cake.' With that Mrs B disappeared off to the kitchen leaving Hermione to stare out of the front window where trestle tables were being laid up and down the centre of the road ready for the celebrations later that day.

Over in the Pembroke household the mood was no lighter. Miranda had arrived the day before to spend a few days with her father and was not in the best of moods.

'I might go over to Aunt Hermione's and empty Ruby's things out of her room before I go home,' she said casually at lunch.

Oscar frowned at her. 'And why would you want to do that?' His voice was a little sharper than he had intended.

'Well, after what she's done . . . stealing the jewels, I mean, and clearing off without a word I should imagine Aunt Hermione won't want anything of her left there.' She smiled as she loaded her plate with sandwiches – because the staff were attending the street party, they were only having a light meal at lunchtime. 'I really can't understand why everyone is so shocked at what she's done,' she went on spitefully. 'I saw her for what she was from day one. She was out to make money from the family but no one else could see it. It's good riddance to bad rubbish as far as I'm concerned.'

Serena scraped her chair back from the table so quickly that it almost fell over and strode from the room with her eyes full of tears.

Furious, Oscar rounded on his daughter. 'Did you *have* to be so thoughtless?' he snapped. 'You know how fond we all were of her.'

'Huh! *That* was the trouble. She knew it and took full advantage of the fact,' she snapped back. 'From the day she arrived it was as if you didn't have time for me,' she accused with a pout.

'I've never heard such nonsense in my life.' Oscar was even more angry now. 'And in future I'll ask you to keep a civil tongue in your head in front of Serena.'

He had informed Miranda some time ago of his intention to wed Serena when his divorce from her mother was final and she hadn't taken the news well at all. In truth, he had only told her because he didn't want her to hear it from someone else, which she surely would have as they had also informed the staff of their intentions, who, unlike Miranda, were thrilled for them. Serena now joined him in the dining room for meals, much to Miranda's disgust, although she still had her own rooms.

'You are *really* going to marry a housekeeper?' Miranda had said incredulously when he had first told her. 'Why, we'll be a laughing stock!'

'Then if it offends you so much, I suggest you don't stay here anymore,' he had told her tartly and she had instantly started to cry. Like her mother, Miranda had always been able to turn the tears on at will, but they didn't cut any ice with him anymore. 'You don't seem concerned that your mother intends to marry so why should you be bothered about me doing the same?'

'But Mother is marrying a *lord*!'

'And good luck to her,' Oscar had replied. 'I hope they will be very happy. I know I will be.' And with that he had flounced from the room, leaving her in no doubt whatsoever of how much she had upset him.

For a while she had sulked, but then slowly as she thought of where Ruby was now, the sly smile had returned. None of them had any idea that she had been involved in Ruby's disappearance and it was highly unlikely that they ever would; she had planned the whole thing much too carefully. It seemed there was nothing she could do to stop her father from marrying Serena, but at least Ruby was out of the way, which was some consolation.

Now Oscar quickly left the room and found Serena standing in the drawing room gazing out of the window. 'I apologise for Miranda's behaviour back then—' he began, but she held up her hand to shush him.

'She's bound to feel a little upset.' Her voice was weary. 'She's had so many changes to contend with lately.'

Oscar shook his head. 'That is no excuse; she's not a child! What puzzles me is that she suddenly seemed to be getting on so well with Ruby and yet since she disappeared, she has seemed to relish the fact.'

When he crossed to her and took her in his arms, she laid her head gently on his chest and heaved a great sigh. 'I still can't believe that Ruby would just have gone off like that,' she said quietly. 'She had such a wonderful career ahead of her and she seemed so happy with Hermione.'

Oscar nodded in agreement. It appeared that all the people who had come to love the girl were unable to accept that she was a thief; Bill had been out searching for her every spare moment he had, and Maddie and Mrs Petty had been frequent visitors hoping for news of her. The only person who didn't seem to question it was Miranda . . .

Suddenly a feeling of unease flared to life as he thought of his daughter. Could it be that she had had anything to do with Ruby's disappearance? He rejected the idea almost immediately. Of course she couldn't have. Miranda had been at her grandparents' home with her mother on the day that Ruby had disappeared and Hermione had said that Ruby had left the house alone. Hermione had also insisted that only she and Ruby knew where the key to the safe was kept so it could only have been Ruby who had taken the diamonds. It was a mystery and all they could do now was pray that Ruby would return with some logical explanation.

'How are you feeling?' Dilys asked sympathetically one morning as she sat with Ruby at breakfast in the dining room at Hatter's Hall. Following another tantrum, Ruby had spent another day in the punishment room and her face was as pale as a piece of lint and there were dark shadows beneath her eyes. 'Why don't you do as I say and just try to accept things,' she whispered. She was growing more and more concerned for the girl.

'I do try to,' Ruby said in a shaky voice. 'But then I just get so frustrated. It's so unfair. Neither you nor I nor a number of these other people should be here,' she said bitterly.

They became aware of Nurse Keen watching them and wisely stopped talking as they ate the food that had been slapped down in front of them. Already Ruby had learnt that she only needed an excuse to dole out punishment and after the day she had just spent trussed up in a straitjacket, she wasn't keen to repeat it.

The day did take a slight turn for the better, however, when, after breakfast, the matron appeared. 'You will all be allowed half an hour's fresh air today seeing as the weather is so clement.' She pointed to a table at the other side of the room and told the nurses on duty, 'Take four patients at a time, but no more than half an hour mind.'

The first four were led away as the rest of the patients were taken back to their rooms, and at the prospect of seeing the sun and the sky Ruby felt a little brighter. It was late in the morning before Nurse Keen appeared at the door to usher her outside to a small courtyard surrounded by a high brick wall. Dilys was already there walking in circles along with two older women who merely leant against the bricks staring up at the deep blue sky.

'Half an hour!' the nurse barked, then went back into the building, locking the door behind her.

Ruby immediately began to look for a way to escape but was quickly disappointed when she found that there was no way out. The only entrance to the courtyard was the door they had just come through and the wall was far too sheer and high to climb.

Her shoulders sagged with disappointment and she glanced over to see Dilys watching her with a sad look on her face. 'I did try to tell you that there's no way out,' she said gently as Ruby started to cry tears of rage and frustration. 'And if you get yourself all worked up again it'll be back in the punishment room or the doctor will be doling out more of his so-called cures.' She took Ruby by the shoulders and forced her to look at her. 'Look, it's different for me. I know that my family will never come for me and I've had to accept it. But you told me that you have a lot of people who won't believe that you've just cleared off without a word. They'll all be worried about you and I wouldn't mind betting they'll be looking for you even as we speak. Just try to be patient and don't give up hope and it will make it so much easier for you. Will you at least try . . . for me?'

Ruby sniffed and gave her a watery smile. Without Dilys she felt she really would go mad in here but having her to talk to had helped. 'I will,' she promised as side by side they began to walk around the courtyard.

The days seemed to drift one into another but Ruby did her best to do as Dilys had advised, which at least kept her free from the leeches and the cold water baths. She lived for the times when she was let out of her cell and the moments when she could speak to Dilys, albeit briefly. She no longer knew how long she had been there, as her nails had worn down to the quick so she had not been able to mark the days on the cell wall for some time, but it felt like forever. Then one day when Nurse Downes opened the door to take her to dinner, she whispered urgently, '*Please, please* won't you help me? If you could just get word to Hermione Pembroke, the lady I was living with, about where I am, I know she would come and get me out of here.'

The young nurse glanced fearfully over her shoulder and shook her head. 'Believe me, I would if I could, Ruby,' she whispered. 'But there are things going on in here that you have no idea of. I've heard of other nurses who have tried to help patients and they've lived to regret it. It's more than I dare to do, I'm so sorry. But come along, I'm sure Dilys will be waiting for you and I tell you what I can do – I'll recommend that Dilys is moved into the room next to you. At least then you'll be able to speak to each other through the door when no one is about.'

Ruby's shoulders sagged but she nodded. Nurse Downes seemed almost as afraid of some of the nurses as the patients were, and although she was desperate to get out of there she didn't want to get her into any trouble. 'But will you at least tell me what the date is? I've lost track of time in here.'

'It's the twenty-seventh of July,' the young nurse informed her as they approached the dining room and with a nod Ruby went to take a seat at the side of Dilys.

Shortly after lunchtime Hermione bustled into her nephew's drawing room in Erdington and Oscar and Serena rose to greet her.

'Have you come with news?' Serena asked hopefully.

Hermione shook her head as she took the pin from the hat she was wearing and laid it on the back of a chair. 'No, unfortunately not . . . but I've been racking my brains as to what might have happened to Ruby, because I still don't believe for a single moment that she would have run away or stolen from me. And as I was lying in bed last night, something occurred to me . . .' She stared at Oscar for a moment, knowing that what she was about to say might offend him, but she had never been one for holding her tongue. 'The thing is, there *might* well be one other person who knew where I kept the key to the safe apart from me and Ruby.'

Serena sat forward in her chair, her eyes wide. 'And who would that be?'

Hermione straightened her back. 'As you know Miranda had taken to calling in to see Ruby. She had even promised her that she would help her try to find her mother, and on a few occasions when she called unexpectedly Ruby was busy at work in the workshop so I allowed Miranda to go in to her. Now, I know this is a long shot, but do you think it's possible that during any of those times Ruby might have unwittingly put the key away in its hiding place, thus showing Miranda where it was kept?'

Oscar looked shocked. 'But even if she had, what would this have to do with Ruby's disappearance?'

'I'm sorry to say this, Oscar, but it would have been very easy for Miranda to help herself to the jewels from the safe while Ruby was out of the room. I know for a fact that Ruby would often go to the kitchen to make them both a drink, which would have given Miranda the ideal opportunity to take the jewels and make it look like Ruby had taken them.'

Oscar began to pace up and down, clearly agitated. 'But why would she do that? Miranda isn't short of money and even if she had taken them that doesn't explain Ruby's disappearance.'

'I quite agree, but perhaps we should take this one step at a time. We could start with searching Miranda's room. Of course, I understand that if she had taken them, they could well be at her grandparents' but I think it's worth a try.'

'I could search it while she is out,' Serena offered. She was prepared to try anything.

With a deep sigh, Oscar nodded, feeling as if he was caught between the devil and the deep blue sea. 'Very well, although I am quite sure the search will prove to be fruitless. I know Miranda can be difficult but I really don't think she would be capable of doing that.'

Hermione nodded towards Serena. 'Then I suggest you give her room a thorough search at your earliest opportunity.'

Serena nodded, not daring to hope that they may be a step closer to discovering where Ruby was.

# Chapter Thirty-Nine

'Have you heard what's happened?' Dilys whispered as she and Ruby sat at supper the following evening.

Ruby shook her head, and keeping a watchful eye on the nurse who was on duty Dilys went on, 'I heard two of the nurses talking outside my door earlier this afternoon.' As yet Nurse Downes hadn't managed to get permission for them to be in adjoining rooms, so they were still at opposite ends of the corridor. 'Apparently Dr Pearse has had a massive heart attack and it doesn't look likely that we'll ever see him again. From what they were saying he was due to retire anyway. Do you realise what this will mean?'

Ruby gave her a blank look and shook her head again.

Dilys grinned and tutted. 'Dr Pearse and the matron are the ones with all the rackets going on here and now they'll have to bring another doctor in. Don't you see? This might be her comeuppance time! I can't see a good doctor going along with her schemes, can you?'

'I suppose it all depends on who he is.' Ruby didn't dare allow herself to hope just yet, although she couldn't pretend to feel sorry for Dr Pearse after the way he had treated her.

'Well, all we can do is wait and see,' Dilys said stoically. 'But for the first time in ages I'm feeling hopeful.'

It was three days later when Dilys told her, 'The new doctor is here. I heard the nurses saying earlier on. He's very young and very handsome by all accounts.'

'I wouldn't care if he had a horn and tail as long as he helped me to get out of here,' Ruby snorted. 'But how will we get to see him if we are not ill or misbehaving?'

'I suppose it's the one time I should say it's all right to play up,' Dilys admitted.

Ruby nodded thoughtfully, perhaps Dilys was right.

'Right, when I give you the nod,' Dilys whispered as she and Ruby sat together at the dining table that evening waiting for their meal.

Nurse Keen was on duty so they knew they wouldn't have to do a lot to upset her. She was always just waiting for the chance to punish them and tonight they intended to give her the opportunity. They waited until two tin dishes full of greasy-looking stew were placed in front of them then after a nod from Dilys, Ruby suddenly stood and with a roar heaved the bowl across the room. Seconds later, Dilys did the same and then all hell seemed to break loose as the rest of the inmates copied them with chortles of glee.

'*What the . . . !*' Nurse Keen glared around the room as she and the other nurses rushed forward trying to bring some sort of order. But it was no use. The patients were making the most of the break from the daily grind and were enjoying themselves enormously. Tables and chairs were sent skidding about the room and the noise was so loud that the nurses could barely make themselves heard as pandemonium reigned.

The nurses seized the older, weaker inmates first, dragging them protesting back to their cells before coming back to grapple the younger ones to the floor. And all the time Ruby and Dilys swooped about the room kicking anything in sight and screaming at the tops of their lungs until finally they were the only two left in there.

'Right, back them into a corner,' Nurse Keen growled as she and the other nurses advanced on them. Nurse Downes entered then and when she saw what was going on her hand flew to her mouth.

'Don't hurt her,' she cried as Nurse Keen grabbed Ruby and twisted her arm painfully up her back.

*'Don't hurt her!'* Nurse Keen sneered. 'Why, she'll wish she'd never been born afore I've finished wi' her, an' the other one. Get 'em into the bathrooms *now*. Happen they're both in need of a bit o' cooling down! The cold water treatment. That'll soon sort 'em out.'

'But the doctor hasn't prescribed that treatment,' Nurse Downes said feebly as the two young women were dragged past her.

But her words fell on deaf ears as Nurse Keen stamped along the corridor pushing Ruby, who was kicking and screaming, in front of her. She had cause to scream now because she knew what lay ahead of her and was genuinely terrified.

In the dining room, the young nurse stood rooted to the spot for a time, and then suddenly knowing what she must do she took to her heels and fled downstairs.

In the bathroom one nurse was filling two of the baths with ice-cold water as Nurse Keen and another nurse callously ripped the coarse gowns from Dilys and Ruby's shivering bodies. The next thing Ruby knew, she was dumped into the bath and held beneath the water. The shock of being submerged had taken her breath away and within seconds she felt as if her lungs were on fire as she fought to get her head above the surface of the water. But it was no good, Nurse Keen was as strong as an ox and slowly Ruby felt herself drifting away. Then suddenly she was yanked up by what was left of her hair, coughing and spluttering.

'I'll show you what happens to folks as try to cause a to-do on *my* shift,' Nurse Keen said threateningly. Her hands went to Ruby's shoulders and once more she was forced down under the water.

Soon Ruby gave up struggling. She knew she was no match for Nurse Keen and if truth be told death was preferable to having to spend the rest of her life in the asylum. A feeling of peace was settling over her as she thought of the people she had come to love since leaving home. Maddie was there smiling at her with Mrs Petty and Nell. And there was Mrs B and Hermione and Miss Wood and Mr Pembroke. Bill was there too and as she pictured his handsome face she began to drift away.

'Just *what the hell* do you think you are doing?' The young doctor's voice roaring from the doorway of the bathroom behind them brought the nurses jerking upright. Dilys instantly rose from beneath the water, her face chalk white as she gasped at the air, but Ruby made no attempt to surface.

'Get that girl out and onto the floor *now*!' the doctor bellowed and immediately two of the nurses hauled Ruby over the side of the bath and she dropped lifelessly to the floor.

The doctor fell to his knees, heedless of the fact that the floor was awash with water, and flipping Ruby onto her side he began to pummel her back. When this had no effect, he rolled her onto her back and began to press on her chest and finally, just as he was beginning to fear that she had gone from them, she coughed and a stream of water shot out of her mouth.

'Thank God,' he muttered, sweat standing out on his brow.

Dilys, who had grabbed a towel to wrap around herself, began to shiver and sob with relief and Nurse Downes put a comforting arm around her as Nurse Keen and the other nurses stood back, scowling at the doctor.

Now that the panic was over, the doctor was frowning as they stared down at Ruby with a concerned expression. She had not yet attempted to open her eyes, but at least she was breathing. The girl was painfully thin and someone had hacked her hair off, but for all that there was something about her that was vaguely familiar.

As he watched her carefully, Ruby opened her eyes and stared up at the doctor vacantly as she gasped for breath. But then, as his face swam into focus, a smile lit her face. 'G-George!' It was George Chatsworth, the London jeweller's son.

'Ruby!' It came to him like a bolt of lightning as he gathered her frail naked body into his arms and she began to sob with relief. 'My God! But whatever are *you* doing here?' And then seeing that she was still too weak to say much he bellowed at the nurse standing by the door. 'Get me something to wrap her in *now*! Someone's head is going to roll for this, you just mark my words! I've never before witnessed such barbaric cruelty!'

Just then, the matron, who had been informed of the ruckus going on upstairs, stormed in, her face livid with indignation. 'Just what is going on here, doctor?' she barked.

'That's *exactly* what I was going to ask you, Matron.' His voice was icy cold and even from where he was kneeling with Ruby held protectively against him, he could smell the alcoholic fumes issuing from the woman. 'Would you care to tell me why this girl is in here and who signed the committal papers.'

'I, er . . . well, it's all quite above board, I assure you,' she blustered. 'She was admitted some time ago for treatment with strict instructions that she was to stay here until further notice.'

'Hm, I see.' His voice was heavy with sarcasm. 'And would she happen to be one your *private inmates* by any chance?'

Although he had only been there for a few days he had already formed the opinion that not everything was strictly above board and he had the feeling that both the matron and the doctor who had been there before him were in on it.

She seemed incapable of answering him and after glaring at her, he wrapped Ruby in the towel that one of the nurses had given him and scooped her back into his arms saying, 'Show me where her room is and think yourself lucky that you didn't drown her or some of you might be facing a murder charge.'

Nurse Keen paled to the colour of putty and without a word led him out onto the landing to Ruby's room, while another nurse meekly took Dilys back to hers.

When he saw the state of Ruby's cell, his lip curled with contempt but he said nothing as he gently laid her on the bed. 'Have some hot tea sent in here immediately and some dry clothes for her,' he ordered the matron, who was hovering at the door.

With an indignant sniff the woman stormed from the room, although she didn't dare disobey him. Young he might be but he seemed to know what he was about and she was afraid that the little racket she had run profitably for so many years was about to blow up in her face.

Ruby lay like a rag doll until the drinks arrived and George held her head while she sipped at the hot, sweet tea, and finally her heartbeat returned to a steadier rhythm.

'Better?'

She nodded gratefully as she sat up and he turned his head while she slipped a dry coarse gown over her head.

'Good, so do you feel able to tell me what's happened and how you ended up here? We were all so worried when Oscar told us that you'd gone missing.'

And so, slowly and painfully, Ruby told him the whole sorry tale of her search for her mother and how Miranda had tricked her.

'The little bitch! I never did like her,' he snarled as he paced up and down the tiny confines of the cell, his expression grim. 'But never fear, I'm going to go down now and look at your committal notes and then somehow we'll get you out of here.'

'And will you look at Dilys's notes too?' she pleaded. She went on to tell him Dilys's story and by the time she was done, he was shaking his head in bewilderment.

'But this whole set-up is absolutely appalling!' he stormed. 'Why, I've seen animals kept in better conditions than this. But now I want you to rest – and don't worry, I'll see to it that you aren't locked in.' He patted her hand and strode from the room and for the first time since she had entered the dreadful place, Ruby felt a stirring of hope.

Once downstairs George headed straight for the matron's office, but finding no sign of her, he hailed a passing nurse. 'Do you know where Matron is?'

She shook her head. 'I'm afraid not, Dr Chatsworth. She said she had to go out urgently some minutes ago and left.'

'I'll bet she did!' he said angrily. 'Show me where she keeps all the patient files.'

The nurse hesitated, but one glance at his furious face made her rush towards the office. 'They're all in that filing cabinet there, sir.'

'Thank you, that will be all. See that I'm not disturbed.' And with that he closed the door firmly, determined to get to the bottom of things.

# Chapter Forty

The following morning, Miranda informed her father and Serena at breakfast that she had decided to return to her grandparents' for a few days and although Oscar felt guilty, he had to admit to himself that he was relieved.

After she'd left, he told Serena, 'I suppose we should take a look at her room. Not that I believe for a moment she would sink so low, but it would put our minds at rest at least.' And so, side by side, they climbed the stairs and entered Miranda's room. The maid hadn't yet had time to tidy it and there were clothes strewn everywhere.

'I don't quite know where to start,' Oscar admitted as he scratched his head and looked around at the mess.

Serena could see this was painful for him and so she laid her hand gently on his arm. 'Why don't you leave it to me? I can tidy up as I go along.'

'W-well if you're quite sure.' He had broken out in a sweat and left the room quickly, needing no further encouragement.

Serena stood with her hands on her hips as she surveyed the mess, then she began to gather the discarded clothes together and dump them on the bed before beginning her search. First, she went through all the drawers, careful to leave everything exactly as she had found it, but there was nothing. Next, she looked beneath the mattress but again with no luck. Strangely, she was not disappointed for deep down she believed that even Miranda, for all her spoilt ways, would not be capable of doing anything so appalling.

Finally, she was forced to admit defeat and with a sigh she began to hang the clothes away in the wardrobe. It was then that she noticed a number of Miranda's bags thrown into the bottom of it beneath the gowns and kneeling down she pulled them towards her and peeped inside each one, sorting through the assortment of hairpins, handkerchiefs and bits and bobs, but finding nothing unusual. She was just returning them to the wardrobe when she noticed another bag tucked away right at the back. Retrieving it, she snapped the clasp then gasped as she stared down at a small black velvet pouch. It was the same as the ones that Hermione kept her jewels in, and as she withdrew it, she found that she was shaking as she loosened the drawstring and carefully tipped the contents into the palm of her hand. They were the missing diamonds and she caught her breath as the sunlight streaming through the window made them glitter, sending rainbows of colour sparkling around the room.

On wobbly legs she slowly descended the stairs and headed for old Mr Pembroke's room where she knew she would find Oscar reading the newspaper to his father.

Both men glanced towards her when she entered and one look at Serena made the colour drain from Oscar's face.

'I ... I found them ... the diamonds!' She opened her palm, and as Oscar stared at the jewels, she saw tears start to form in his eyes.

'So, what are we going to do now?' Serena asked fearfully as she looked into Oscar's stricken face.

'We're going to get Bill to prepare the carriage and then he can take us to Miranda's grandparents' house. I think Miranda has some explaining to do.' His mouth was set in a thin, straight line and after handing the diamonds to him Serena rushed off to instruct Bill.

It was mid-afternoon before the carriage drew to a halt outside Lydia's parents' stately home and Oscar's face was grim as he helped Serena down. 'We shouldn't be too long, lad,' he told Bill as he and Serena made their way to the front door.

Bill respectfully touched his cap. 'Right you are, sir.'

A maid in a starched white apron admitted them and pointed towards the day room where she informed them Lydia and her daughter were entertaining visitors.

'But I'd best let her know you're here, sir.' She cast a curious glance at Serena. 'She won't be none too happy with me if I allow you in without introducing you.'

'Don't worry about that.' He brushed her aside and strode forward to throw the door open and the second she set eyes on him, the colour seeped out of Miranda's face.

Two very well-dressed elderly ladies were sipping tea from delicate china cups and their eyes widened at Oscar's hasty entrance, especially when they noticed Serena standing behind him.

'Why, Oscar . . . whatever—'

Completely ignoring his soon-to-be ex-wife, Oscar stabbed a shaking finger towards his daughter. 'I think you and I need to have a little talk, miss, don't you?'

'I, er . . . what about?' Miranda was squirming in her seat and looking more uncomfortable by the second.

'Oscar, *how dare* you enter the house and speak to our daughter like that!' Lydia was incensed. 'And in front of our guests, too. Have you completely forgotten your manners?' Lydia's mother had always told her that Oscar was far below her in class and his behaviour now was reinforcing it as far as she was concerned.

'Lady Chumley, please excuse us for a moment!' Beckoning to her daughter, Lydia rose and with an apologetic nod towards her future mother-in-law she ushered Miranda out of the room, her silken skirts swishing.

With Oscar and Serena following close behind, she marched towards the drawing room and once everyone was inside, she slammed the door and rounded on Oscar furiously.

'Kindly explain yourself,' she spat, glaring at Serena. 'And explain to me the need to bring your fancy woman with you!'

Serena opened her mouth to object but clamped it shut again as Oscar bore down on Miranda, making her shy away from him.

'Now, miss, would you care to explain what these diamonds were doing in your possession?' As he spilled the diamonds onto a small table, Miranda's hand flew to her mouth and she stared at her father fearfully.

'Leave her alone, you bully.' Lydia stepped forward but Oscar was not going to be silenced so easily.

'I will when she tells me what she's playing at. You must be aware that these jewels went missing at the same time as Ruby. Miranda is very aware that people thought Ruby had stolen them when all the time they were in her possession. I rather think she owes us an explanation, don't you?'

A deadly silence settled on the room as Lydia's lips worked soundlessly until finally, she sneered, 'It seems the truth is going to come out so you may as well know that it was me who was responsible for the jewels going missing. I instructed Miranda to take them.' Her back was ramrod straight and she showed no sign of remorse.

Oscar frowned. 'But why would you do that?'

'I'll tell you why!' She faced him full on, her hands clamped into fists of rage. 'I told her to do it because I know all about your *dirty* little secret.'

It was Oscar's turn to look bemused now. 'I don't know what you mean.'

'Then I'll tell you, shall I?' Lydia began to stride up and down the room, her skirts slapping about her legs. 'Some time ago our daughter happened across a diary belonging to this trollop here.' Her lip curled back from her teeth as she looked at Serena with contempt. 'And that diary confirmed the suspicions that I had had for some time – that you were having an affair with her. Do I need to go on?'

Oscar looked shamefaced. 'Serena and I did have a brief affair,' he admitted. 'It was shortly after Miranda was born when you turned me out of our room. I was hurting and she offered me comfort but I very quickly realised that I wasn't being fair to either of you and so I ended it. That doesn't pardon my behaviour, I know, but I'm telling the truth when I tell you that we didn't become close again until after you had left me.'

'Pah!' Lydia poked him in the chest.

'And anyway, that doesn't explain why Miranda, or you for that matter, would want to hurt Ruby.'

'Doesn't it? I should think it was obvious.'

Serena bowed her head as tears crept down her cheeks.

Oscar turned to Miranda again. 'So, if it was you who took the diamonds, I imagine you know where Ruby is. Just tell us and we'll leave.'

Once again, Lydia stepped in. 'You'll *never* know where the little slut went,' she ground out as she waved a trembling finger towards the door. 'And now I suggest you both get out before I have you *thrown* out!'

Oscar opened his mouth to argue but Serena hastily took his arm and almost dragged him towards the door, saying, 'Come along, Oscar. We'll learn no more here.'

'Too right you won't,' Lydia raged. 'And I hope that *trollop* rots in hell.'

Outside Oscar ran his hand across his brow as Serena hauled him towards the waiting carriage and once inside, he leant heavily back against the seats as despair washed over him.

'What do we do now?' he asked hopelessly. 'Miranda knows where Ruby is, I'm sure of it.'

'I think you're right but I truly believe she isn't going to tell us.' Serena stared dejectedly from the window as Bill set the horses into a trot and the carriage rolled forward. 'Let's just get home and think about what is best to do.'

He nodded and a silence settled between them for the rest of the journey.

As Bill reined the horses to a halt outside the house they were surprised to see another, smaller carriage already there with a driver waiting outside.

'I wonder who that can be?' Oscar groaned, he was in no mood for visitors and felt thoroughly miserable.

'There's only one way to find out.' Serena allowed him to help her down from the carriage and as Bill drove it round to the stable block, they entered the front door.

Betty hurried to meet them. 'Please, sir, there's a visitor waiting for you in the drawing room and he says he needs to see you on a matter of some urgency,' she said breathlessly.

'Oh, did he give a name?' Oscar asked as he handed her his hat.

'Yes, sir, he said it was Dr Chatsworth.'

'Young George?' Oscar was surprised. William had told him a short time ago that George had now completed his doctor's training but what could he be doing there?

With a nod at Betty he and Serena made for the drawing room.

'George, this is a surprise,' he said as he entered the room, holding his hand out to the young man. Then noting the young man's grave expression, he asked, 'Is your family all right?'

'Oh yes, sir. They're very well,' George hastened to assure him. 'My visit has nothing to do with them. But the thing is . . .'

As he began to explain why he was there, Serena wasn't sure whether to laugh or cry. She was delighted that they'd discovered where Ruby was, but horrified to think of her in such a terrible place.

'And are you *quite, quite* sure that the girl really is Ruby?' she choked.

'Oh yes, ma'am. There's no doubt about it, although I'm afraid she won't be the Ruby you remember for some time to come. She and some of the other inmates at the asylum have had a very hard time of it and I think it will be a long while before they are themselves again. I tell you, that place is like a den of vice. You wouldn't believe what I uncovered when I began to go through the files. I immediately summoned the trustees and the board of governors and they were as shocked as I was. Unfortunately, the matron, and one of the nurses who appeared to be running the racket have scarpered. The doctor who was also in on it is too ill to run anywhere but whether the women will ever be caught remains to be seen, although the police have been informed and are searching for them.'

'But why didn't you bring Ruby to us?' Serena asked.

George shook his head. 'She's refusing to go anywhere without Dilys, a friend she made at the asylum. She too was placed in there against her wishes by her family when she became pregnant some years ago, and they've paid to keep her there ever since. It seems that Mrs Pembroke was paying for Ruby to be detained but I've given both Ruby and Dilys a thorough examination and as far as I'm concerned, they are both as sane as you or I and should never have been put in there in the first place. They won't be the only ones either. You can rest assured I shall be assessing all the patients and recommending that those who shouldn't be there be discharged.'

'But in the meantime what shall we do about Ruby if she won't come out without this friend of hers?' Serena was wringing her hands.

'That's easy, we shall have her friend here as well and they can convalesce together,' Oscar said decisively. 'That's the very least we can do for her, and once she's home I'm afraid we shall have a lot of explaining to do. Would you like us to come back with you to fetch her, George?'

George shook his head. 'I think it might be better if I went alone, but I could be some time. We'll have to come by train and then I'll get a cab from the station to here when we get back into Birmingham – that is if they agree to come. Perhaps you could get some rooms prepared for them while I'm gone?'

'Of course,' Serena said hurriedly. 'And we should let Hermione know what's happened too, dear,' she suggested to Oscar. 'She's been just as worried as we have.'

'Yes, yes of course,' he agreed. 'I'll get Bill to take the train to tell her.'

And so when George left to fetch the girls, Oscar arranged for Bill to pay a visit to Hermione while Serena set about making two of the bedrooms as comfortable as she possibly could for when the two young women got back with George.

It was early evening before the carriage carrying Ruby, Dilys and George arrived and by then Serena was a bag of nerves as she thought of the explaining she was going to have to do.

Hermione and Mrs B were also there waiting after returning on the train with Bill, as were Maddie, Nell and Mrs Petty who had called in almost daily since Ruby's disappearance to see if there was any news of her.

They all stood at the window watching anxiously as George helped the two young women down from the carriage and

409

their first sight of them made tears spring to Serena's eyes. Ruby was so painfully thin and pale, with dark shadows beneath her eyes. And her wonderful hair had been chopped off and barely reached her chin, although it was still a riot of fiery curls. Suddenly Serena couldn't wait a second longer, and she ran into the hall, threw the door open and flew to meet her, wrapping her arms about her, her heart full of the love that she had held in check for so long. There were times over the last few weeks when she had feared she would never see her again, but here she was and she could hardly allow herself to believe it.

'Oh, my poor darling girl,' she sobbed as Ruby clung weakly to her. 'Come on in, Cook has kept a nice meal hot for you.' She was so thrilled to see Ruby that she barely noticed the young woman standing behind her. They were both dressed in nurses' dresses – the only outfits George had been able to find, but a distinct improvement on the coarse shifts they had been forced to wear – and they had attracted more than a few curious glances on the train journey home.

As Serena led them into the house, Hermione rushed forward to give Ruby an uncharacteristic hug and Ruby could have sworn there were tears in the woman's eyes.

She then drew herself upright and looked pointedly at Oscar and Serena. 'I think it's time for you both to have a talk to Ruby in private, don't you?'

Serena gulped and nodded. Hermione was right: it was time and it could be put off for no longer. Gently taking Ruby's arm they led her towards Oscar's study while Hermione took care of Dilys.

# Chapter Forty-One

Ruby's heart began to thud as they entered the study, wondering what on earth they needed to speak to her about. She'd seen Maddie as she'd passed the drawing room and couldn't help but feel a stab of disappointment that it wasn't her wishing to speak to her. After all, if Maddie really was her mother as Ruby had suspected all along, surely this would have been the ideal opportunity for her to admit it? It would be just too cruel if she didn't find out now after all she had gone through.

'I think it might be best if you sat down,' Oscar told her gently as he pulled a chair out for her and guided her into it. 'You see the thing is . . .' His voice trailed away as he ran his hand across his eyes.

Serena patted his arm and took over. 'I think what we're about to tell you may come as a terrible shock,' she began softly as she held Ruby's hand. 'And once you know the truth, I'm not sure that you'll ever be able to forgive us, but the thing is, Ruby . . . I am your mother and Mr Pembroke is your father.'

'*What?*' Ruby gasped, shock running through her veins like iced water.

'It's true,' Serena told her. 'And I think we owe you an explanation so I'll start at the beginning. It began a short time after Mrs Pembroke had Miranda. She and Oscar were not getting along because she was adamant that she didn't want any more children and she banned him from their room. He was lonely and eventually he turned to me for comfort.' She bowed her head and blinked back tears before going on. 'I had loved him for some time but we knew what we were doing was wrong, so we ended our relationship. But soon after I discovered that I was going to have a child and I didn't know what to do. I couldn't tell Oscar; I was so ashamed of what I had done. I loved your father but he was married and his wife had just had a baby, so there was no way we could be together. So I went to stay with my sister and my aunt for a while but I knew I couldn't stay there forever. My sister was struggling to make ends meet as it was, and I didn't think it was fair to add to her burden. I just didn't know what to do for the best. You know them well – Maddie is my sister, although she changed her surname to Bamber because she thought it sounded grander than Wood, and the person you know as Mrs Petty is actually my Aunt Ethel.'

Ruby listened in disbelief, her eyes round with shock.

'Maddie was always the rebel of the family,' Serena admitted. 'And she left the family home long before I did to go and live in Vittoria Street where Aunt Ethel joined her. It was Aunt Ethel who found a lady in Nuneaton who arranged adoptions for the babies of young women in my position through a friend of hers who was . . . let's just say "a lady of the night". When I met her, I told the woman that my name

412

was Maddie, and eventually I went to stay with her until you were born. But the minute I set eyes on you I knew that I wanted to keep you, whatever the consequences. I only got to see you briefly and I told the woman I wanted to call you Ruby because of your glorious red hair – you get that from my father, he was a redhead. Anyway, I was very ill after the birth and by all accounts I almost died, and by the time I started to recover you had already gone to a new family. I was utterly heartbroken and begged Mrs Bradley, the woman I had been staying with, to tell me where you were.

'From then on, I kept track of you from afar. Sometimes I would come and stand outside the bakery where you lived and watch you through the window. At other times Maddie or Mrs Petty would go and let me know that you were all right. And every single day since, I have had to live with the guilt. There can be no blame attached to your father,' she added as she gazed at Oscar adoringly. 'He didn't even know of your existence until you disappeared, and then I was so beside myself with worry and regret that I had to tell him . . . I'm so very sorry, my darling girl. Can you ever forgive me?'

Ruby could only stare as she tried to take it all in. 'But if Mr Pembroke didn't know about me then why would Miranda have me locked away?' she managed to ask when she found her voice.

'She found my diary and when she read about my affair with her father, she told her mother. They must have concocted the plan to get you out of the way between them. She even stole some diamonds from Hermione's to make it look as if you had run away with them, but none of us believed for a single moment that you would do that. I just thank God that George found you when he did or goodness knows how long you might have been locked away in that dreadful place. And if you wish to press charges against Miranda and Mrs Pembroke, we won't hesitate to involve the police.'

Ruby sat silently for a moment before slowly shaking her head. 'No, Miranda must have been very hurt to find out about me the way she did.' A thought suddenly occurred to her and she said incredulously, 'This means that Miranda and I are actually half-sisters, doesn't it?'

A nod from Serena confirmed it and Ruby sat back in her chair, shocked anew at this. For so long she had convinced herself that Maddie was her mother but suddenly everything was falling into place and the realisation hit her that she didn't just have a mother, but also a father, a half-sister, an aunt and a great-aunt too. It was incredible. Now she understood why Maddie had taken her in on the night she ran away, and why Mrs Petty had brought her to Miss Wood – she still could not think of her as anything else – when she disapproved of the way Maddie was treating her. But what had Maddie been doing in Nuneaton so late on the night she had run away from her adoptive father?

When she asked the question, Serena sighed. 'It was just pure chance,' she admitted. 'As you know, Maddie has her fingers in a lot of pies, not all of them legal unfortunately, although thankfully all that is about to change. While you've been gone her gentleman friend's wife has died and later this year, he has finally agreed to make an honest woman of her. Anyway, it just so happened that that evening she was, as she calls it, "doing a bit of business" with someone in the town. She was on her way to the station to catch the last train home when she came upon you, and thank goodness she did or I dread to think what might have happened to you. Before then I truly believed that you had a happy home or I promise you I would have fetched you away, even if it meant disclosing my secret.' She reached her hand out but Ruby drew away from her.

'I . . . I think I just need some time to try and take everything in,' she told them in a small voice.

Serena nodded understandingly. 'Of course you do, and while you're doing that we shall take the best possible care of you . . . and Dilys too,' she added. It hadn't been the emotional reunion she had dreamed of but then she respected that Ruby had a lot to digest and after waiting for her daughter all these years she was prepared to wait a little longer. She could hardly have expected her to fall into her arms and tell her all was forgiven, especially after everything that had happened. She was painfully aware that she had a lot of making up to do – she only hoped Ruby would allow her to do it.

'Ruby, I—' Oscar began.

Serena laid her hand gently on his arm. 'Why don't we give Ruby a few minutes alone, dear? She has a lot to take in before she sees everyone.'

'Yes, how thoughtless of me. Of course.' He was remembering now what a shock it had been when Serena had told him who Ruby really was, so he could only imagine how the poor girl must be feeling. She had clearly been through a lot in the asylum and now with this on top . . .

'I'll have some tea brought in to you,' Serena said quietly. 'And when you're ready I'll get Betty to get a nice hot bath ready, and afterwards, you must eat something.'

Outside in the hall Serena began to sob and Oscar gathered her into his arms feeling her pain.

'I don't think she will ever forgive us, or me at least,' she gasped.

'Give her time,' he replied, stroking her hair, and for a while they stood drawing comfort from each other, wondering what Ruby was thinking on the other side of the door.

Ruby sat in deep shock, staring at the window. It had certainly been a day for revelations. Suddenly she had a mother and a father, although she could never imagine calling them that. They were Mr Pembroke and Miss Wood to her and she felt a little frisson of resentment as she thought of the way her life had begun. Miss Wood had clearly decided to have her adopted even before she was born to spare her lover heartache. It didn't matter that she had admitted to wanting to keep her once she had arrived, for now Ruby was finding it hard to get past knowing that she had initially been unwanted. The door opened just then and Dilys's pale face peeped around it.

'Are you all right? Can I come in? Miss Wood said she thought you might need some company.'

'I bet she did.' There was a note of bitterness in her voice.

Dilys crossed to her and placed her arm comfortingly around Ruby's shoulders. And it was then that the tears came as the full impact of what she had been told hit her and between sobs, she began to tell Dilys what she had learnt.

Dilys's reaction wasn't at all what she had expected. 'Poor woman,' she muttered. 'Talk about being caught between the devil and the deep blue sea. She must have felt dreadful wondering what to do for the best. But she clearly loved you. Why else would she have kept track of you all these years?'

Ruby hadn't thought of it like that and she sniffed.

'And just imagine how it must have hurt her not to be able to approach you and tell you who she really was,' Dilys went on. 'Then there's Mr Pembroke. What a shock to discover that he'd had another daughter all these years without even being aware of it. He must be feeling dreadful too.'

'Yes . . . I suppose he must.' Ruby stared thoughtfully at Dilys.

'Still, in your case it seems all's well that ends well. Think of how lovely it will be from now on. They clearly want you to be properly part of the family, whereas I . . .' Her voice trailed away.

Ruby squeezed her hand. 'There must be someone we could contact who would care what had happened to you?'

'I do have an aunt I was very close to,' Dilys admitted in a small voice. 'But Matron told me that my family had put it about that I had died. It would be a terrible shock for her if she were to discover that I was actually still alive.'

'I'd say it would be a wonderful surprise,' Ruby answered. 'So when we're feeling a bit better, why don't you write to her? What harm could it do? The family can't hurt you and you can stay here for as long as you like.'

417

'I'll think about it.'

'And then there's your fiancé, what about him?'

Dilys shook her head. 'I've no doubt he'll be married to someone else by now and have a family,' she said regretfully. 'And anyway, it's highly unlikely he'd still be at the same address.'

'But if you never take the trouble to find out you'll never know, will you?'

Dilys's hand rose to her mouth. 'And what would he think of me if he could see me now?' Over the years she had suffered far worse than Ruby. At one point the doctor had even had some of her teeth pulled out as a so-called cure for badness. 'I'm so changed. I'm ugly now,' she said bitterly.

'Oh no you are not,' Ruby assured her. 'You're going to look and feel better in no time when we get you into some decent clothes and get your hair styled. But there's no need to do anything for now. I think we should both just take one day at a time until we start to feel a little better.'

'I think that's a very good idea,' Dilys agreed. 'But don't lose sight of the fact that your dearest wish was to find your birth mother. You know who she is now, and not only that, you've discovered who your father is too. I have to say from what I have seen of them that I could think of far worse people to have for your parents, my own included.'

Dilys left the room then to give Ruby time to put her thoughts into some sort of order but she had been gone only a matter of minutes when yet another tap came on the door and this time Ruby's heart did a funny little flip when Bill appeared, cap in hand.

Her hand self-consciously rose to her hair and she felt herself blush as she glanced down at the ugly dress she was wearing, but Bill appeared not to notice and she saw that his eyes were moist.

'You're back then.'

She nodded. 'Yes, I'm back, although there were times when I thought I never would be.'

'I searched for you every single day,' he confided. 'And I never for one minute believed that you'd run away. That Miranda should be horsewhipped.'

Ruby shrugged. 'What would be the point? It's over now and I just want to try and forget what's happened.'

'I can understand that but . . . I'm so pleased to see you back. I-I missed you.'

'I missed you too,' she answered shyly. And only then did she realise just how much.

'Is there anything I can get for you?'

He looked so ill at ease that she couldn't help but smile. 'No thank you, Bill. It's enough to be out of that awful place for now.' And then suddenly she was crying again and without stopping to think he crossed the room and gathered her into his arms and she realised that for the first time in a very, very long while, she suddenly felt truly safe.

'Mr Pembroke an' Miss Wood have been nearly out of their minds with worry about you,' he confided with his chin resting on her hair. 'All of us have, if it comes to that, an' I just thank God you're safe an' sound now.'

She lifted her head and glanced up at him, surprised to hear the level of emotion in his voice and before he could stop himself, he lowered his lips to hers and kissed her

419

gently. Just for a moment, it was as though all the troubles and sorrow of the past few months had disappeared. Until, suddenly he pulled away.

'I-I'm sorry about that,' he muttered.

Ruby smiled through her tears. 'Don't be. I liked it. But didn't someone say there was some dinner waiting for me?'

Bill grinned with relief at her words, and still holding tight to her hand, led her from the room.

The first few days at home were strained and sometimes Ruby wished that she had taken Hermione up on her offer of going back to stay with her, but Mr Pembroke and Miss Wood had seemed so genuinely pleased to have her back that she hadn't liked to offend them. They had proudly told everyone that Ruby was their long-lost daughter and Oscar had even informed her that he was going to see his solicitor to include her in his will, but still Ruby couldn't bring herself to address them as anything other than Miss Wood and Mr Pembroke. And though it pained them, they accepted that she needed more time to come to terms with everything.

Meanwhile Ruby finally managed to persuade Dilys to write to her aunt and they then both waited with bated breath to see if she would respond.

Four days after the letter had been posted a fine carriage drew up outside and a well-dressed elderly lady rapped on the door.

'It's someone to see you, Dilys,' Betty told her after admitting the visitor. 'Shall I bring her in?'

The colour drained from Dilys's face and she nodded numbly.

When the door finally opened, Dilys jumped from her seat and rushed across the room.

'Aunt Emily!' she cried, throwing herself in the woman's arms.

It would have been hard to say who was crying the hardest as the woman hugged her to her.

'Oh, my poor dear girl.' Eventually she held Dilys at arm's length to stare at her and she wasn't pleased with what she saw. Dilys was so thin her clothes hung off her and although she was slowly recovering from the years of abuse there were still dark circles beneath her eyes.

What she said next shocked Dilys to the core. 'If only I had known what they had done to you. It's unforgivable. I would have had you out of there like a shot. But now that you are out you must come home with me.' She smiled wryly. 'Because I'm not the only one who was delighted to hear that you were still alive.'

'Oh!' Dilys stared at her curiously.

'Surely you can guess who I am talking about?'

Dilys shook her head.

'Why, it's Steven of course! I contacted him immediately to tell him what had happened and although he was shocked and disgusted at what your parents had done to you, he was also thrilled to hear that you're still alive. He's coming to see me – and you hopefully – this evening.'

'But I was sure he would have forgotten all about me by now,' Dilys said falteringly.

'Not at all.' Aunt Emily drew her to the sofa and they sat down together.

Ruby watched the joyful reunion with a lump in her throat. It appeared there might just be a happy ending for Dilys after all and she couldn't think of anyone who deserved one more.

'He has never so much as looked at another girl since he was told that you had passed away,' Emily explained. 'And he's got his own business now, a thriving little shop with living rooms above it. He can't wait to see you . . . if you still want to see him, of course.'

'But . . .' Dilys looked worried. 'What would he think of me now? I'm hardly the girl he'd remember, am I?'

'You are still beautiful,' her aunt assured her, stroking her cheek. She turned to Ruby. 'And I believe I have reason to thank you, my dear,' she said warmly. 'Dilys explained in her letter that it was the young doctor who visited the asylum who recognised you and managed to help you both get out of that dreadful place. There's a big enquiry going on apparently and I think it's safe to say that nothing like this will ever be allowed to happen there again.'

Ruby blushed and headed for the door. 'I'm sure you two have a lot to catch up on so I'm going to give you some privacy. I'll have some tea sent in to you.' And with that she hurriedly left the room only to almost collide with Serena who was waiting in the hall.

'Isn't it wonderful? Betty told me that Dilys's aunt had arrived,' Serena said joyously.

Ruby nodded. 'Yes, it is, and better still her aunt has been in touch with the man Dilys was about to marry and he wants to see her.'

As tears sprang to Serena's eyes, Ruby felt a little fluttery feeling in her chest, and when Serena placed her arm about her, for the first time, she didn't pull away.

'I'm so happy for Dilys,' Serena said. 'But we shall miss her should she decide to leave. She feels like a part of the family already. Still, as long we still have you, I could wish for nothing more.'

The words were said with such sincerity that Ruby couldn't doubt that she meant them and tentatively she returned the embrace as Dilys's words of wisdom came back to her, '*And just imagine how it must have hurt her not to be able to approach you and tell you who she really was!*'

Two hours later, Dilys asked Serena and Ruby to join her and her aunt back in the drawing room and with tears in her eyes she told them, 'I can't thank you enough for what you've done for me and your kindness, but my aunt has invited me to go and live with her and . . .' When she blushed Ruby noted the way her eyes were shining. 'And it seems that Steven, the man I was betrothed to, wishes to see me again.'

'Oh, Dilys, I'm *so* pleased for you.' Ruby hugged her, knowing how much she was going to miss her, but she was genuinely thrilled for her. 'When will you be leaving?'

'We thought today,' Dilys told her tentatively. 'I've already imposed on your hospitality far too long.'

'Nonsense,' Serena told her. 'We've loved having you, I just wish it could have been under happier circumstances. But of course you must return with your aunt if that's what you wish. Just be sure to stay in touch. I know Ruby thinks a great deal of you, as we all do. But if you're quite sure this is what you want, I'll go and pack some clothes for you. They'll do until you can get some new ones.'

Both Dilys and Ruby had been wearing some of Ruby's clothes that Hermione had sent over for them and although they were now far too big for both young women, they had at least been better than the ones they had arrived in.

An hour later, Bill took a valise to the waiting carriage as Ruby and Dilys said goodbye. There were tears in their eyes as they embraced and promised to keep in touch.

'Look after yourself,' Dilys said in a choked voice.

Ruby nodded, her throat too thick with emotion to speak as Dilys walked out of the front door and Bill helped her into the carriage. Minutes later she was on her way, waving through the window.

Tears streamed down Ruby's cheeks and once again Serena comforted her.

'Right, young lady, you've had a big day and I want you to rest before dinner,' Serena ordered. 'And then tomorrow I have the dressmaker coming to measure you up for some new clothes.'

Ruby smiled through her tears. Finding her birth parents had been nothing like she had expected it to be, but slowly she was growing fond of them and the future was looking bright.

# Chapter Forty-Two

Over the next few days, as Serena, Oscar and Ruby really got to know each other, Ruby noticed that Bill was keeping his distance and it troubled her. He had been so happy to see her when she had first returned, but now he seemed to be avoiding her. One evening, determined to find out what was wrong, she walked across to the stables where she knew she would find him with the horses.

'Hello, Bill.'

He was busily grooming Mr Pembroke's stallion and he started. 'Oh . . . hello, Ruby.'

She instantly sensed that he was ill at ease so she asked softly, 'Have I done something to offend you? You seem to have been avoiding me.'

He shrugged. 'Not at all, miss.'

'*Miss!*' Her eyes flashed fire. 'Where did that come from? My name is Ruby.'

'Ah, but it's *Miss* Ruby now, ain't it?' He sighed as he paused in the grooming. 'Now that Mr Pembroke has recognised you as his daughter everything's changed.'

'In what way?'

'Well, I hardly think they'd want to see you walking out with a groom, do you? No doubt they'll have their sights set on a rich husband for you.'

'*What!*' Ruby was incensed. 'I never took you for a snob, Bill! I'm still exactly the same person I was when I came to live here!'

He shook his head. 'Ah, but you're not, are you? You're now the daughter of a very wealthy man while I'm hardly what you'd call rich.'

'And what difference does that make? In case you've forgotten, Mr Pembroke ... my father ...' It still felt strange to think of him as such. 'My father is going to marry his housekeeper when his divorce comes through, which proves he's far from being a snob. And anyway, you're not *only* a groom, but you're now also an apprentice goldsmith and a very good one from what I heard him saying. He has high hopes for you so don't make that an excuse for keeping your distance from me. If you don't like me, at least be big enough to tell me to my face so that I know where I stand!'

'Don't *like* you!' His eyes were flashing as he flung the grooming brush down and strode over to stand in front of her, his hands on his hips. 'Well, just so you know, miss ... No I don't *like* you – I bloody *love* you and I think I have ever since I came to live here! When Maddie first took you to live with her you were no more than a kid, but then when I came here I suddenly realised you'd turned into a young woman. So what do you think of that, eh?'

Ruby's face softened and she giggled. 'I think that's just what I wanted to hear,' she told him boldly. 'Because as it happens, I love you too.' And then suddenly she was in his arms and as his lips came down on hers finally, everything felt right with the world.

'In that case I suppose I'd better make an honest woman of you,' Bill told her when they finally came up for air. 'But first I'd better ask Mr Pemb— your father's permission, an' there's no time like the present, is there?' And so hand in hand they set off for the house with stars in their eyes.

Serena was in the hall arranging flowers in a vase when they entered and one glance at their glowing faces told her all she needed to know.

'Someone looks happy,' she teased and was amused to see Bill blush as red as a beetroot.

'I, er . . . were wondering if I might have a word with the master?'

'Then you're in luck,' she answered kindly. 'He's in his study, go on in.'

Once Bill had gone, she turned to Ruby and taking her hands she shook them gently up and down before asking softly, 'Do I detect love is in the air?'

Now it was Ruby's turn to blush as she nodded. 'Do you mind?'

'Mind!' Serena shook her head. 'All I've ever wanted was for you to be happy,' she confessed. 'And if Bill makes you happy then that's fine by me. All I would ask is that you wait until you're fully recovered before you rush off to get married. I'm selfish enough to want you to myself for just a little bit longer.'

To her delight Ruby threw herself into her arms. 'Oh, Mother, you'll *always* have me,' she whispered and Serena's heart swelled with love as she pressed her beloved girl to her.

# *Epilogue*

'Will I do, Father?'

Oscar turned to see his daughter descending the stairs in her wedding gown and the breath caught in his throat as his eyes misted with tears.

'You will do very nicely indeed, my dear,' he said throatily as she reached the bottom of the stairs, clutching her bouquet of sweet-smelling freesias. A matching garland held her gossamer-fine veil in place, and she wore a gown of ivory silk that showed off her petite but perfectly formed figure to perfection. He smiled as he thought of all the hours Ruby and her mother had spent with the dressmaker during the making of it. Serena had insisted that everything should be perfect and so far on this special day it had been. Even the sun was shining down from a cloudless blue sky.

His own wedding to Serena, which had taken place the month before after his divorce from Lydia had been finalised, had been a much more low-key affair, which was just as Serena had wanted. But for her beloved daughter she had insisted on something much grander.

Ruby had changed greatly since she had returned from the asylum and thankfully now that terrible time was a distant memory. Her hair, which today was piled into rich red curls on the top of her head, was once more waist-length and her figure had filled out. Admittedly she would never be tall and stately, but today she held herself erect and looked, Oscar thought, like royalty. Gently he offered his arm and almost bursting with pride he led her out to the carriage, which had been adorned with ivory ribbons. The new groom tipped his hat respectfully and as he helped her into the carriage, he dared to whisper, 'You look beautiful, miss.'

'Thank you, Frank.' When she smiled he blushed.

Now that Bill had completed his apprenticeship he was working in Mr Pembroke's shop in the jewellery quarter, although all that would change after today. As a wedding present, Oscar had bought them a small shop in Nuneaton with living rooms above it where they would live and work. Tradesmen were working in it even now and soon they would start their own little jewellery shop. Ruby was sure that with her designing the jewellery and Bill's skill as a goldsmith they would make a go of it.

But she wasn't thinking of that today, she was thinking of Bill, the man she loved, who was waiting at the church for her.

'Now, you are quite sure about this, aren't you, my dear?' Oscar asked as he squeezed her hand. 'It isn't too late to change your mind, you know?'

Ruby giggled. 'I've never been surer of anything in my life,' she answered, her face radiant. Then in a gentler tone she added, 'And thank you so much for all you've done to make it such a special day. I'm afraid it must have cost you an awful lot of money.'

'It doesn't matter what it cost, you're worth every penny to me and your mother. And why wouldn't I want the best for you?' There was a trace of sadness in his voice. 'You're the only daughter I'm ever going to walk down the aisle, after all.'

It had shocked them all the year before when Lydia had got in touch to tell them that Miranda had eloped with an Irish fellow who had been doing some jobs on Lord Chumley's mansion. The last they had heard of her she was living with him and his parents in Ireland. Deep down, Oscar hoped that she might make contact with him again one day – she was still his daughter after all – but he was determined that today should be Ruby and Bill's own, so he would try not to think of his sorrow over the daughter he had lost.

'I wonder if little James and baby Mathilda will behave in church?' he pondered, and they both grinned.

Maddie had finally married some two years ago, and now had a one-year-old son, James, who was the love of her life. As for Dilys, she had married Steven shortly after going to live with her aunt, and had recently given birth to Mathilda – an adorable baby on whom her parents doted.

'They can both cry all the way through the service and it won't spoil it for me,' Ruby declared happily as Frank urged the horses into a gentle trot.

Soon the church came into sight and Ruby felt a flutter of nerves. If the extensive list of invites that Serena had been busily sending out was anything to go by, the place would be packed and the thought of all those people staring at her as she walked down the aisle was a little daunting.

'Don't worry, you'll be fine.' Oscar squeezed her fingers affectionately. 'Don't forget, I shall be with you every step of the way. But before we go in, Ruby, I'd just like to say . . .' He cleared his throat self-consciously. 'I'd like to say that discovering you were my daughter was one of the best days of my life. My only regret is that I never got to see you grow up, but I want you to know I'm very proud of you and I love you very much.'

'I love you too.' Her eyes filled and Oscar gently stroked a tear from her cheek before pulling her veil down over her face.

'Right, my darling girl, I believe you and I have a wedding to go to. Are you quite ready?'

'As I'll ever be,' she answered, and taking a deep breath she allowed him to help her down from the carriage.

Just for a moment she thought of how proud Rita, her adoptive mother, would have been today and again tears trembled on her lashes. It had been many years since Rita had died, but she would always hold a special place in Ruby's heart, and she knew that the dear woman wouldn't have wanted her to be sad on such an important day. She blinked her tears away; the past was gone and she had the rest of her life to look forward to, so taking her father's arm she allowed him to lead her through the lychgate.

As she had expected, the church was filled to capacity and as the organist began to play the 'Wedding March', she felt a moment of panic. But then she looked beyond the congregation to where Bill was standing waiting for her with the sun from the stained-glass windows shining down on him. Her nerves melted away, and as she held her father's arm and walked down the aisle towards him, there might have been no one but the two of them in the church.

With Hermione and Mrs B beside her, Serena sat in her smart new pale-lilac costume and matching hat, sniffing away happy tears and feeling as if she might burst with pride as she watched her daughter float down the aisle. There had been times since Ruby's birth when she had despaired of ever being able to claim her as her own, but at last everything had come right and now she not only had a beautiful daughter but she was married to the love of her life.

In the row behind her was Mrs Petty, looking rather uncomfortable in all her new finery, and Nell – who had also turned over a new leaf and was now working in a large emporium – was there too with the young man she was walking out with, all of them smiling broadly.

It was a wedding that would be spoken about for many years and everyone there agreed that Ruby made a truly radiant bride.

Following the service, Ruby and Bill left the church in a shower of rice and rose petals and Frank drove them to the hotel where Oscar had arranged a wedding breakfast fit for a king and queen.

'Are you quite sure you will be happy living back in Nuneaton?' Oscar asked that evening as he snatched a few precious moments alone with his daughter just before she and Bill left for a few days' honeymoon in Southend. Oscar had wanted them to go abroad, as his treat, but Ruby was eager to move into the little rooms above the shop that they had been decorating and furnishing over the last few weeks in their spare time.

'The man that brought me up has been dead for some months now, if that's what you're worrying about,' she pointed out. Word had reached them that he had died of a heart attack the summer before, sadly just days after old Mr Pembroke, her grandfather, had died of the same complaint. 'And yes, I'll be happy there. But don't worry, you'll not be getting rid of me that easily. I shall be on the train regularly visiting you and Mother, and Hermione. And of course, you can visit us too. I know we'll be glad of your advice once we get the shop up and running.'

'I doubt that,' he said with a wry grin. 'I think you and Bill are going to make a real success of this business.'

Bill joined them at that moment with Serena close behind him. 'Frank is waiting to take us to the train station, love.'

They tripped outside with the guests following closely and smiled to see the tin cans and ribbons that had been tied to the back of the carriage.

'Be sure to send us a postcard,' Dilys told her as she stepped forward with little Mathilda in her arms to give her a kiss.

'And I shall want one too,' Maddie butted in.

There was a furious round of kisses and goodbyes until finally there was only Serena and Oscar standing before them.

'I'm going to miss you so much.' Serena sniffed as she mopped at her eyes with the handkerchief Oscar had handed to her. 'Make sure you take good care of her, Bill.'

'Oh, you need have no worries on that score,' Bill assured her and then after yet more kisses, he helped his wife into the carriage.

Ruby gave a little sigh of contentment as she leant back on the seat, her eyes closed.

# Acknowledgements

As always, I would love to say a massive thank you to my brilliant 'Rosie Team' at Bonnier Zaffre who all play a part in making my books as good as they can be!

Thank you to Sarah Bauer, my lovely editor, always at the end of the phone with support and encouragement, Kate Parkin for believing in me, Gillian Holmes, my amazing copy editor, Felice McKeown my marketer and Jane Howard my proofreader as well as all the rest of the team, too many to mention. You are all greatly appreciated and it's an absolute joy to work with you all.

Not forgetting my brilliant agent, Sheila Crowley without who none of this would have happened, and finally my wonderful family and all my lovely readers who make my day with their lovely comments.

Thank you all xxx

# ·MEMORY LANE·

# Welcome to the world of Rosie Goodwin!

Keep reading for more from Rosie Goodwin, to discover
a recipe that features in this novel and to find out
more about Rosie Goodwin's next book . . .

We'd also like to welcome you to Memory Lane,
a place to discuss the very best saga stories from
authors you know and love with other readers,
plus get recommendations for new books we think
you'll enjoy. Read on and join our club!

·MEMORY LANE·

**www.MemoryLane.Club**

**f /MemoryLaneClub**

Hello everyone,

I hope you are all well and looking forward to the nicer weather. Not long now and we'll all be out pottering in the gardens again and hopefully enjoying some sunshine while looking forward to our summer holidays.

It's been a very hectic few months for me as we've moved house and are busy settling in. I must admit I'd forgotten how stressful moving can be and I'm determined now never to do it again! Saying that, we do love our new home and the fur babies are very much enjoying having a bigger garden to play in.

For all those of you who have been waiting for the release of the paperback of *A Simple Wish,* here it is! I do hope you'll enjoy it and thank you so much to my lovely readers who have already read the hardback and left such glowing reviews. It really does mean a lot to us authors!

For those of you who haven't read it yet, I can tell you that in this one you'll meet Ruby, so named because of her lovely red hair. I do hope you'll come to love her as much as I did while I was writing her story. Poor girl, as always, she doesn't have an easy time of it and in this one we visit the jewellery quarter in Birmingham (one of my favourite places!) where poor Ruby is drawn into a life of crime.

Isn't the cover lovely? As soon as I saw it, it instantly became one of my favourites!

I am also pleased to say that it won't be long now until the release of *A Daughter's Destiny* and the cover for that is lovely too, so well done to my lovely team at Bonnier who have somehow managed to keep everything on track throughout the last difficult months. In this book you will meet Emerald who leads a charmed life until her family is suddenly plunged into poverty. I really loved her and can't wait for you all to read about her.

As always, I shall eagerly wait to hear what you all think of my latest offering, and I hope you all stay well. You can keep track of what myself and the other authors in The Memory Lane Club are up to on The Memory Lane website and Facebook group, do join it if you haven't already. There are always many competitions to enter and lots of lovely prizes to be won.

For now, it's back to work for me to finish the next book in the Precious Stones series!

Look forward to speaking to you all again very soon, until then take care and lots of love to you all,

*Rosie* xxx

If you enjoyed *A Simple Wish*, you'll love the next book
in the Precious Stones series . . .

## A Daughter's Destiny

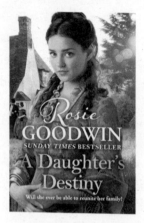

### *Warwickshire, 1875*

Emerald Pritchard has lived a privileged life with her parents and her
younger sister Abigail in the stately Astley House. But all that suddenly
changes when her father disappears leaving the family in debt. They
are forced to throw themselves on the mercy of Emerald's uncle who
begrudgingly allows them to live on his farm.

Desperate to find work, Emerald is forced to leave her family and travel
to London to become the companion of a distant aunt she's never met.

Rebellious Abigail is unwilling to lower herself to doing the menial
farm chores and instead runs away, finding work as a hostess in a club
in Soho where she soon finds herself in desperate trouble.

Will Emerald ever be able to find happiness and reunite her family again?

**Coming soon.**
**Read on for a sneak peek . . .**

## Chapter One

*March 1875*

'Is the meal not to your liking, Gerald?'

Glancing up from his untouched plate, Gerald Winter nodded. 'It's quite delicious, Dorcas, but I find I don't have much of an appetite this evening, my dear.'

'Again!' His wife sniffed her disapproval as she dabbed at her lips with a snow-white napkin while her two daughters glanced anxiously at each other. It looked like they were set for another uncomfortable evening, but they were getting used to it now. Since the month before when their father had lowered the housekeeping money, their parents seemed to be constantly squabbling and their father had become unusually quiet, often locking himself away in his office for hours.

At that moment Hetty, their maid, appeared to clear the main course pots from the table, returning a short time later with the dessert, which she lay in the centre of the crisp white cloth. It was a large apple pie with a golden crust and beside it she placed a jug of fresh whipped cream.

At sixteen, Abigail was the younger of the two girls, and she licked her lips in anticipation.

Her mother eyed it with distaste. 'I can't believe we have to resort to such *common* meals,' Dorcas said huffily. 'Was it *really* necessary to cut the housekeeping down, Gerald?'

'I wouldn't have done it if it wasn't.'

Emerald, his nineteen-year-old daughter, gave him a sympathetic smile. If asked, she would have been forced to admit that she had always been far closer to her father than her mother, who, unfortunately, was a terrible snob. It upset her to see him looking so worried and haggard but there was nothing she could do about it apart from hope things improved. He had admitted some months before that his business – a brickworks in the nearby parish of Stockingford – was struggling, and Emmy – as he affectionately called her – was not surprised. Her mother was very demanding and expected the very best of everything and more than once recently Emmy had heard her father ask her to curb her spending as it was eating up any profit they made. Yet only that afternoon she had decided that the drawing room really *must* be redecorated, even though it had only been done less than two years ago, and she had sat poring over a book of wallpaper samples that cost more per roll than most people would earn in a week.

She mentioned it now to her husband, and Emmy saw him visibly flinch, although he said not a word.

'Mrs Henderson-Ward had her room done in paper from this particular book,' she gushed. 'And it really does look quite regal. I particularly like the silk patterns, although they do tend to be a little more expensive. What do you think, dear?' Suddenly Dorcas was all smiles again but her husband merely shook his head and, rising from the table, he left the room.

'Really!' Dorcas tutted her disapproval. 'Your father's manners are quite appalling lately. He didn't even ask to be excused.'

Quite suddenly Emmy's appetite had vanished too, although Abigail more than made up for it and had second helpings. The two girls took after their father in looks with brunette hair that shone like polished conkers and deep-green eyes, but there any resemblance ended for they were like chalk and cheese in nature. Emmy, who was the tallest and the slimmest of the two, tended to be the more quiet, studious one, whilst Abigail was more like her mother: petite and quite demanding. She attended a private school in Coventry. The same one that Emmy had attended until she had reached the age of eighteen. Sometimes Emmy almost wished she was back there, for ever since she had finished school her mother had done nothing but parade what she considered to be eligible suitors for her daughter's hand in marriage under her nose, each one a little bit richer than the last.

Now, Emmy sat impatiently waiting for the meal to be over, and when it was, she immediately excused herself and went in search of her father.

'I reckon he's in his study, miss,' Hetty informed her in the hallway, and smiling her thanks, Emmy headed in that direction.

Tapping at the door, she went in and found him seated at the imposing polished mahogany desk in front of the large window that overlooked the sweeping lawns surrounding the house. His head was in his hands, but when he saw Emmy standing there he sighed with relief.

'Ah, it's you, my lovely.' He held his hand out to her. 'For a terrible moment I thought it was your mother come to tell me that she needed new furniture to go with the new wallpaper.'

'No, Papa. It's only me.' She gave his hand a gentle squeeze. 'Is there anything I can do for you?'

'Huh! I doubt there is anything *anyone* could do for me at this moment,' he said bitterly. Then instantly regretting his words he gave her an apologetic smile. 'I'm afraid I have been rather a fool, my darling . . . I should have curbed your mother's spending habits many years ago, but because she always reminded me that she had married beneath her class I always felt that I owed it to her to pander to her every whim. But whatever happens, I want you to always remember that you are one of the best things that has ever happened to me. I can remember the day you were born as if it was yesterday.' His eyes grew moist as his mind drifted back in time. 'You were *such* a beautiful baby. Even at birth your eyes had a hint of green in them, which was why I persuaded your mother to call you Emerald. She was a much gentler, less demanding person back in those days,' he said regretfully. Then with a shake of his head he pulled his thoughts back to the present to say urgently, 'Promise me you will marry for love.'

Emmy chuckled. 'Don't worry, Papa, I will. I have no intention of marrying the man of my mother's choice.'

'Good.' He rose from his seat and as his arms closed around her, much as they had when she was a little girl, she nestled contentedly into his chest. She had always run to her father for comfort as a child, because her mother had usually been too afraid of her messing up one of her expensive gowns.

They stood like that for precious moments until he gently held her away from him and stared at her as if he were trying to memorise every feature of her face, before saying softly, 'As much as I would love to spend the evening talking to you, my dear, I really must finish these accounts for the brickyard.'

'Of course, Papa.' Emmy kissed his cheek and wished him goodnight and left feeling vaguely uneasy. The feeling stayed with her for the rest of the night, and even when she retired to bed, her father's drawn face haunted her, so it was a long time before she fell asleep.

'Is Papa not joining us for breakfast?' Abigail asked the next morning as she helped herself to another slice of bacon from the covered silver salvers on the sideboard in the dining room.

'I have no idea.' Emmy glanced towards the door. It was usual for her mother to take breakfast in bed but it was very rare that her father didn't eat with them. 'Perhaps he had to be in work early?'

'Mmm.' Abigail bit into a thick juicy sausage with relish. 'Well, I intend to make a complete pig of myself until I have to go back to school after Easter. As you will remember, the food there is *so* unappetising.' She sighed dramatically. 'In fact, it's a wonder I haven't already wasted away.'

Emmy laughed and they enjoyed the rest of their break-fast in a companionable silence.

Later that morning their mother ordered the carriage and went visiting friends, leaving the two girls to their own devices.

Emmy opted to go for a long walk in the countryside that surrounded their beautiful home while Abigail chose to stay in and read a book.

When their mother returned, they all gathered in the dining room for lunch and they were just finishing it when Hetty appeared. 'Mr Pembroke is here asking to see the master, ma'am. What shall I tell him?'

Dorcas rose from the table. 'But my husband should be at the works,' she said with a frown. 'Show him into the drawing room.'

'Yes, ma'am.' Hetty bobbed her knee and rushed off to do as she was told, while Dorcas swept after her.

She found Mr Pembroke, the bookkeeper at the brick-works, standing in front of the marble fireplace she had had shipped from France, nervously rolling the brim of his hat around.

'Mr Pembroke. I'm a little confused. Hetty tells me that you wish to see my husband but I believed he was already at the works?'

He shook his head, his face grave. 'He hasn't been there at all today, ma'am,' he answered respectfully. 'And I don't know what to do. He promised me that he would give me the money to pay the suppliers this morning and I'm afraid they are not prepared to wait any longer. Without fresh supplies I shall have no choice but to shut the business down until the outstanding debts are settled.'

'*Outstanding debts*?' Dorcas looked horrified. 'What are you talking about, man? Ours is a thriving business!'

'It *was* a thriving business,' he gulped. 'But I'm afraid it hasn't been classed as such for some time now and people are baying for the money they are owed.'

Dorcas tutted with annoyance. This man clearly didn't know what he was talking about. And where was Gerald? Blast the man.

'Tell me how much you need and I shall go to the bank and get the money for you immediately,' she told him imperiously.

He withdrew a piece of paper from his pocket and handed it to her and when she saw the amount written on it her face paled, although she otherwise remained calm.

'You may go now,' she said dismissively, drawing herself up to her full height. 'And I shall bring the money to you later this afternoon.'

'Much obliged, ma'am.' He gave a little bow and scurried from the room like a frightened rabbit as Dorcas hurried away to order the carriage to be brought round to the front of the house for her.

An hour later she swept into the bank in Nuneaton in a beautiful dark-blue velvet two-piece costume with a matching hat trimmed with white feathers, and demanded to see the bank manager immediately.

Within minutes he had ushered her into his office and, after shaking her hand, he offered her a seat.

'I am so glad you've come, Mrs Winter,' he began. 'I asked your husband to call in some weeks ago.'

'*Really?* And why would you do that?'

'To discuss his, er . . . situation.'

'*What* situation?'

He swallowed, making his Adam's apple bob up and down in his throat before saying cautiously, 'About the bank loan he took out some time ago to keep his business afloat. He hasn't made any of the repayments. And so it is with deep regret that I have to inform you we now have no other option but to foreclose on the loan.'

Dorcas gasped and her hand flew to her mouth. 'B-but there must be some mistake,' she croaked.

He shook his head and took a file from his desk drawer. Opening it, he circled a large number before pushing the paper towards her. 'This is the amount outstanding.'

Her eyes popped as she stared at the staggering amount on the paper, then on legs that had suddenly turned to jelly, she rose, telling him, 'I'm sure there must be some way we can settle this matter, Mr Davidson. I shall go and see our solicitor immediately. Good day to you, sir.' She took the folder containing the unpaid bills and, cheeks burning with humiliation, sailed from the room with what dignity she could muster.

One thing was for sure, Gerald was going to have some explaining to do when she got her hands on him, but first she would seek their solicitor's advice.

## Apple Charlotte

Ruby eats apple charlotte for dessert in the Chatsworths' house. The perfect dish for a cold, winters' evening, why not try it yourself?

Serves 6

### You will need:

1.5 kg of apples, either Bramley, Cox's or a mix of both
175g of butter
75g demerara sugar, plus 2 tbsp extra to serve
30ml brandy (optional)
Grated zest of ½ a lemon
1 pinch of nutmeg
1 pinch cinnamon
1 pinch ginger
1 pinch mixed spice
8 slices of medium-thick, soft white bread, crusts cut off

### Method:

1. Peel and core the apples, cut them into thin slices.
2. Melt 75g butter in a large pan over a medium-low heat, add the apples, sugar, brandy (if using) and a tablespoon of water (you may need to add more if

you don't use brandy), then cover and cook, stirring occasionally, until the apple is soft and beginning to break down.

3. Grate in the lemon zest, taste to check the sweetness and adjust as necessary, then leave aside to cool.

4. Heat the oven to 200°C (180°C fan)/gas mark 6. Melt the remaining butter over a low heat and skim off the foam.

5. Once you see pale solids in the bottom of the pan, carefully pour off the clear liquid above into a clean, heatproof container and discard the solids. Add spices to the liquid butter.

6. Cut the crusts from the bread. Using an ovenproof mould, such as a pudding basin or a bread tin, cut the bread into rounds or strips to line it.

7. Remove the bread from the mould, dip each piece in turn into the melted butter, then use to line the dish.

8. Spoon in the apple puree, then top with the final pieces of bread, also dipped in butter. Bake for 15 minutes, then turn down the heat to 180°C (160°C fan)/gas mark 4 and bake for about another 40 minutes, or until the bread on top is golden.

9. Leave to cool in the mould for 10 minutes, then turn out, scatter with sugar and serve with cream, custard or ice-cream.

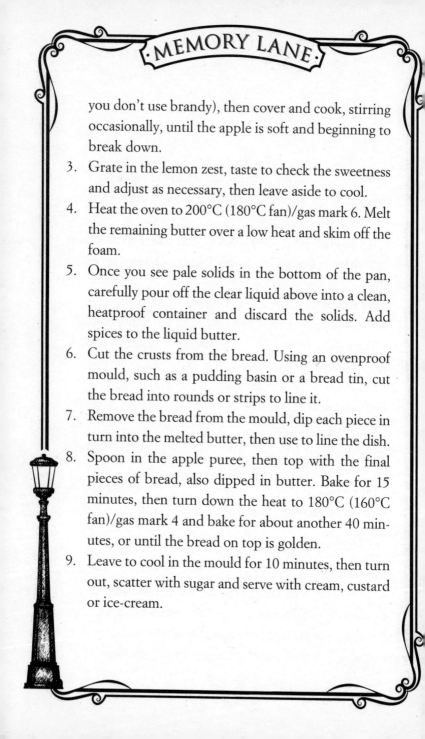

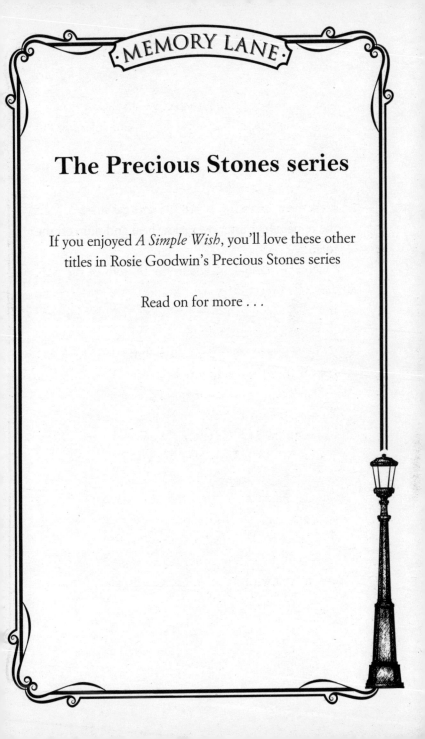

# MEMORY LANE

# The Precious Stones series

If you enjoyed *A Simple Wish*, you'll love these other
titles in Rosie Goodwin's Precious Stones series

Read on for more . . .

# The Winter Promise

## 1850.

When Opal Sharp finds herself and her younger siblings suddenly orphaned and destitute, she thinks things can get no worse. But soon three of them – including Opal – are struck down with the illness that took their father, and her brother Charlie is forced to make an impossible decision. Unable to afford a doctor, he knows the younger children will not survive. So, unbeknownst to Opal, Charlie takes their younger siblings to the workhouse. When she finds out, Opal is heartbroken.

Charlie starts taking risks to try to support what's left of the Sharp family and earn Opal's forgiveness, but he takes it too far and finds himself in trouble with the law.
Soon, he is sent on a convict ship to Australia.

**As poor Opal is forced to say goodbye to the final member of her family, she makes a promise to reunite them all one day. Will she ever see her family again?**

# An Orphan's Journey

## 1874.

Growing up in extreme poverty in London, Pearl thinks life can get no worse. But when her parents discover there's yet another baby on the way, they have to tighten the belt even further. Pearl's mother decides to send her and her younger sister Eliza to the workhouse, where they are forced into a new life of hardship and struggle.

Pearl's hopes are raised when the workhouse offers the sisters a new life in Canada and they board an orphan ship transporting unwanted children across the seas. Pearl hopes their luck has finally changed when she and Eliza are hired by the kindly Mrs Forbes to work in her grand house together. But when Pearl meets their mistress's bullying son Monty he reveals he will stop at nothing to make her life a misery.

**Will Pearl ever find the home she so craves?**

# The Days of the Week Collection

If you enjoyed *A Simple Wish*, you'll love
Rosie Goodwin's Days of the Week
collection, inspired by the Victorian
'Days of the Week' rhyme.

Turn over to find out more . . .

## Mothering Sunday

*The child born on the Sabbath Day,*
*Is bonny and blithe, and good and gay.*

1884, Nuneaton.

Fourteen-year-old Sunday has grown up in the cruelty of the Nuneaton workhouse. When she finally strikes out on her own, she is determined to return for those she left behind, and to find the long-lost mother who gave her away. But she's about to discover that the brutal world of the workhouse will not let her go without a fight.

## The Little Angel

*Monday's child is fair of face.*

1896, Nuneaton.

Left on the doorstep of Treetops Children's Home, young Kitty captures the heart of her guardian, Sunday Branning, and grows into a beguiling and favoured young girl – until she is summoned to live with her birth mother. In London, nothing is what it seems, and her old home begins to feel very far away. If Kitty is to have any chance of happiness, this little angel must protect herself from devils in disguise . . . and before it's too late.

### A Mother's Grace

*Tuesday's child is full of grace.*

1910, Nuneaton.

When her father's threatening behaviour grows worse, pious young Grace Kettle escapes her home to train to be a nun. But when she meets the dashing and devout Father Luke, her world is turned upside down. She is driven to make a scandalous choice – one she may well spend the rest of her days seeking forgiveness for.

### The Blessed Child

*Wednesday's child is full of woe.*

1864, Nuneaton.

After Nessie Carson's mother is brutally murdered and her father abandons them, Nessie knows she will do anything to keep her family safe. As her fragile young brother's health deteriorates and she attracts the attention of her lecherous landlord, soon Nessie finds herself in the darkest of times. But there is light and the promise of happiness if only she is brave enough to fight for it.

### A Maiden's Voyage

*Thursday's child has far to go.*

1912, London.

Eighteen-year-old maid Flora Butler has her life turned upside-down when her mistress's father dies in a tragic accident. Her mistress is forced to move to New York to live with her aunt until she comes of age, and begs Flora to go with her. Flora has never left the country before, and now faces a difficult decision – give up her position, or leave her family behind. Soon, Flora and her mistress head for Southampton to board the RMS *Titanic*.

### A Precious Gift

*Friday's child is loving and giving.*

1911, Nuneaton.

When Holly Farthing's overbearing grandfather tries to force her to marry a widower twice her age, she flees to London, bringing her best friend and maid, Ivy, with her. In the big smoke, Holly begins nurse training in the local hospital. There she meets the dashing Doctor Parkin, everything Holly has ever dreamt of. But soon, she discovers some shocking news that means they can never be together, and her life is suddenly thrown into turmoil. Supporting the war effort, she heads to France and throws herself into volunteering on the front line . . .

### Time to Say Goodbye

*Saturday's child works hard for their living.*

1935, Nuneaton.

Kathy has grown up at Treetops home for children, where Sunday and Tom Branning have always cared for her as one of their own. With her foster sister Livvy at her side, and a future as a nurse ahead of her, she could wish for nothing more. But when Tom dies suddenly in a riding accident, life at Treetops will never be the same again. As their financial difficulties mount, will the women of Treetops be forced to leave their home?

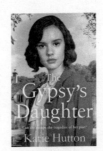

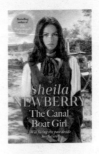

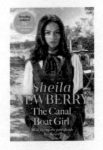

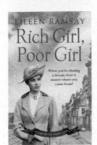

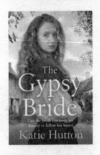